Bloody Ten

by

WILLIAM LOVE

DONALD I. FINE, INC.
New York

Library of Congress Cataloging-in-Publication Data

Love, William F.
Bloody ten / by William Love.
p.   cm.
ISBN 1-55611-275-0
I. Title.
PS3562.O848B56   1992
813'.54—dc20   91-57890
CIP

Manufactured in the United States of America

10 9 8 7 6 5 4 3 2 1

Designed by Irving Perkins Associates

To Margaret:
Mother of the Year
every year

1

IN describing my cases I always start with where *I* got involved, even if that means starting before the case began. The Bishop says that's egotistical. He should know.

Egotistically speaking, then, the Kearney case began at 2:42 P.M., Monday, July 20. I was clipping my fingernails when the phone rang— my line, not the Bishop's. I managed to get the receiver to my ear without dropping the clippers or dislodging my feet from the desk.

"Darling!" Sally Castle. "How would you like to go to a fabulous dress rehearsal Wednesday night?"

I examined a freshly clipped thumbnail. "A fabulous dress rehearsal? Sounds like a *contradictio in terminis.*" (Working for Regan has done amazing things for my vocabulary. French phrases like that just roll off my tongue.) "The last time you dragged me to something 'fabulous' was that charity affair at the Carlyle last month that nearly bored us both into early senility."

She chuckled. "Wasn't that a disaster? No, trust me, sweetheart, this is different. We're not talking rich people standing around eating fish eggs on stale crackers. This is theater, done as it should be: down in the Village at a new little place called the Lettuce Inn, poor but honest actors, audiences who care. It's *A Thousand Clowns,* the world's funniest play, it'll be fun! And my friend, Dinker Galloway—remember me telling you about her? She's playing Sandy. They open Friday and they're trying to drum up an audience for Wednesday's dress rehearsal to help them with their timing. So it's free!"

Scrunching the receiver between shoulder and ear, I put my feet on the floor and swept a few errant fingernail clippings from the desktop into the wastebasket while I considered the proposition. The price was right and it was far from being the most bizarre proposal

I'd gotten from Sally in the eight-plus years we'd dated. I sighed and pitched the clippers into my desk drawer.

"Hell, why not? Wednesday, you say? What time?"

I'd never met Dinker but Sally talked about "my friend, the actress" a lot. One of the legions of youngsters and not-so-youngsters that descend on the Big Apple every year, set on a glamorous stage career. You'll see them in every restaurant in town, waiting on or busing tables and hoping for callbacks that never come. Eventually, reality sets in and they head home to Keokuk or Kokomo or Kalamazoo to spend the rest of their lives earning a poor but honest living.

Dinker, I gathered, had been more successful than most. The previous summer she'd got the lead in Joseph Papps's *As You Like It*: the role of Rosalind, which, Sally tells me, any actress would gladly kill for.

Two nights later, I picked Sally up at 7:15 outside her co-op on East Sixty-fifth. She looked even more gorgeous than usual in a slinky little black cocktail number, black patent-leather pumps with satin bows and those pearl earrings I got her two years ago that accentuate her honey-blond hair.

We reached the Lettuce Inn, just off Bleecker, at a quarter to eight. Not a very impressive building. Dinker had told Sally it was a converted warehouse. The warehouse part I could see. But converted? All they'd done, at least to the outside, was slap a sign reading *Lettuce Inn* below the old Manhattan Steel Co. sign. Oh—and stuck a marquee over the front door:

NEW YORK'S FAVORITE COMEDY
"A THOUSAND CLOWNS"!
OVER ONE THOUSAND PERFORMANCES!
STARRING I. LEONARD ROSEN
OPENING JULY 24

You'd think a 7:45 show-up for an eight o'clock event ought to ensure you an on-time arrival. Not in New York—not if you're driving. In the Apple, finding a parking place has a way of developing into a full-time job.

But this time we got lucky. As we drove up, an ancient Mercury pulled out from a spot right in front of the marquee. Thanking whatever gods were responsible, I maneuvered the Caddy into the space. By the time I'd gotten the tires next to the curb a Yellow Cab had pulled up beside me. It was tight quarters with all the car doors opening and closing. I got out and pressed against the Seville so the cabbie's passenger could get out.

Female, tall, dark-haired, well-dressed, big hurry, loaded down with a briefcase and a sizable handbag. Good-looker, mid-twenties, great perfume. Ignored my smile, brushed by me with a low-pitched "Excuse me," dashed for the theater. Excellent legs. Before I could give them an adequate inspection, I was distracted by Sally.

"Dinker!" she screamed, scrambling out her door. The brunette skidded to a halt and swung around, shading her eyes against the sun.

"Sally?" She threw her a brief but dazzling smile. "Glad you could make it! But I'm late! See you after, okay?" She spun, pushed through the door and disappeared.

I came around the Caddy. "Dinker," Sally grinned. "Running late."

I glanced at my watch. "Sure is. She's got twelve minutes. Hope she doesn't have an early entrance."

"The way she was running, I'll bet she does."

I shrugged. "Well, it *is* only a rehearsal."

The lobby was dark after the glare outside. And, I first thought, deserted. Then I saw, through the glass of the ticket booth, a girl in an NYU sweatshirt. She looked up from a dictionary-sized book and flashed a smile. "Help you?"

Sally returned the smile. "I'm Sally Castle. I think Dinker Galloway has arranged for—"

"Oh yeah, you're all set," the coed interrupted with a grin. "Dinker just came through, doing about a hundred miles an hour. Said you were here." She glanced at a slip of paper on the counter. "Sally Castle and—" She smiled at me. "David Goldman?" I nodded. "Fine." She pointed to a door. "Right through there. Sit anywhere you like, but I'd recommend the center section. Okay?" Another smile and back to her book. My mother would have had words for her. ("What kind of a light is that to read by, young lady? Want to ruin your eyes?")

The lobby wall featured photos of the performers. Six faces, one bigger than the rest. The large one read *I. Leonard Rosen*. Handsome guy. Dinker's—it read *Diane* Galloway—was next to Rosen's. Beautiful eyes, striking cheekbones, full lips. Even the crook in her nose was appealing.

"Nice picture of Dinker," Sally commented. "Pretty, isn't she?"

"Sure is. And having already smelled her perfume up close and personal, I'm beginning to think this wasn't such a bad idea!" I ducked Sally's slap. We glanced at the other photos, one of which was of a boy who looked about twelve. Another was of Jim Kearney, though neither his name or face meant anything to me at the time.

"You'd better hurry," the ticket-booth girl called. "Curtain in two minutes."

The auditorium had very little going for it beyond the fact that it was functional. Spotlights pointing at the stage seemed to be attached to every strut and stanchion in the high ceiling. The stage, furnished as a typical New York down-at-the-heels studio apartment, was chest-high to the audience. Took up about half the room, surrounded by seats on three sides—about ten rows worth. I guessed the place would have held about two hundred with a full house. Sally's and my arrival brought that night's total attendance up to eleven.

They started exactly at eight. We'd barely had time to discover how uncomfortable the seats were when the lights went down, the sound of a TV began to swell, and the show began. Within five minutes I was glad we came, and that feeling grew. Maybe not the world's funniest play, but it was in the running. And the actors, who were excellent, weren't treating it like a rehearsal. Except for the tiny audience, it could have been a real performance.

Dinker lived up to Sally's advance billing. Her lateness didn't seem to have bothered her; she was comfortable and relaxed. And believable as the sweet, not-too-bright social worker she was playing.

But the one I really enjoyed was Lenny Rosen, the star. You say that's because he was playing a smart-ass Jew and it takes one to enjoy one? Well, you've got a right to your own opinion.

I'll admit I might have had something in common with the character. I'll confess to Jewish; and to being tall, dark and, if you insist, ruggedly handsome. But there were differences, too. Rosen's hair was all permed tight curls; he was thinner; and his features were a lot more pinched than mine. Furthermore, Murray, the character he played, was out of work, whereas I hold down *two* jobs. But all of that has nothing to do with why I liked it—the guy was funny. And the other ten people in the audience obviously agreed with me.

When it was over, we made as much noise as eleven people banging their hands together can. The actors responded in different ways. Dinker executed a perky curtsy, the men bowed and the kid actor just beamed and looked embarrassed. Rosen let the applause die down, stepped forward and raised a hand, getting immediate silence. A take-charge guy.

"Thanks for coming, folks. You've helped us more than you know. Remember, we open Friday." He grinned. "Come again—and often. Your kind of enthusiasm we can use."

The house lights came up. Dinker jumped lightly off the stage and headed our way. Her face under the makeup was even prettier than the photo in the lobby had suggested. Sally introduced us. Dinker treated my hand to a firm shake and my eyes to a dazzling smile. She turned the smile on Sally. "You guys like to go get a drink or something? Jim and I'd love you to join us."

"Jim?"

"Yeah, Jim Kearney. My temporary fiancé in the show. My boyfriend in real life. Sort of."

Sally was excited. "Love to! Okay, Davey?" I nodded.

"Great!" said Dinker. "We'll meet you there in ten minutes. Right now Lenny's going to critique us. He does everything, you know: stars, directs, cleans up after us." She grinned. "Then Jim and I'll have to ditch our makeup. Come to think of it, maybe you'd better make that twenty minutes."

"Fine," Sally said. "Meet where?"

Dinker broke out laughing. "Oh! Yeah, it'd help to know where, wouldn't it? Ivan's Down and Dirty. Go back out on the street, turn left, walk one block and you're there. Just leave your car where it is. You'll never find anything closer."

2

IVAN'S Down and Dirty was down, all right—five steps below the sidewalk—but fortunately, no dirtier than any other bar in New York. Sally and I nabbed a booth for four in the rear. Good for talking, at least when the jukebox piped down.

"Before they get here, a couple of questions," I said, after ordering a white wine for Sally and a beer for me.

She sighed. "Once a detective, always a detective. Okay, ask away."

"First, have you met this Jim? If he's anything like the character he played, I'm not sure I care to know him."

Sally grinned and shook her head. "No, he's nothing like that. I've met him a couple of times. He came from Minnesota about a year ago to be an actor. I guess his dad's a wealthy businessman, wanted Jim to come into the business. Jim tried it a few years, didn't like it, came east to try the stage. But this is the first thing I've seen him in. I was impressed."

I nodded. "If he's not a wimp, he's a good actor. He fooled me."

"Oh, he's no wimp. Dinker really likes him. They lived together for a while but then decided they'd get along better having their own places."

I grinned. "They're learning. Much as I like you, I don't think I could live with you."

Sally gave me a level look. "Uh-huh. You just like living with a bishop."

"Hey! The man's a paraplegic. He needs me."

"Yeah, Regan needs you about like I need dandruff. He's about the most self-sufficient guy I've ever met. What was your second question? I see Jim and Dinker coming in."

I glanced around, saw them and hurried my words. "Oh. Just wondered where she got her nickname. *Dinker*?"

Sally grinned. "I've known Dinks for a couple of years and it's never occurred to me to ask. Let's find out."

The two actors were in high spirits, Dinker giggling as they approached the table. She gave her escort a mock-angry push. "Settle down, sweetheart, these are my friends!" She smiled at Sally. "Sally Castle: my *ex*-friend, Jim Kearney. Jim, Sally. And this is Dave Goldman."

Without the makeup, Kearney was a tall, lanky redhead with a resonant bass voice that didn't go with his boyish face. He shook my hand, gave Sally a friendly grin, jackknifed his lanky frame into the booth and clanked his keys onto the table.

I waved for a waiter. "Before we get on anything else, Davey wants to know where you got your nickname," Sally told Dinker.

The actress tossed back her luxuriant dark hair and smiled at me. Great smile. She and Jim gave the waiter their drink orders.

"Well," Dinker said after he left, "Daddy used to call me his little stinker when I was a baby. I'd try to say it, only it came out 'Dinker.' I've been Dinker ever since." She made a face. "Now Lenny thinks Daddy had it right the first time. And just told me so in no uncertain terms."

Jim rolled his eyes. "Man! Was he ever in a bad mood!"

Sally was outraged. "You're kidding! Rosen didn't like your work tonight?"

Dinker shrugged prettily. "Hey, he was right. Come on, Sally, I wasn't exactly a ball of fire."

"I thought you were *great!*" Sally touched Dinker's hand. "I *mean* it, Dinker."

Dinker shrugged and smiled up at Jim. "Let's let an expert tell you what *he* thinks. How about it, Jim? Did I stink, or what?"

Jim grinned sympathetically and patted her arm. "Well, keep in mind, Lenny's nervous with opening night forty-eight hours away. But I guess I've seen you better. What happened? Was it because you were late? God, we were all wondering if you were even going to *make* it! And you're *never* late!"

Dinker winced and nodded. "Yeah, I really blew it." She took a sip of the Perrier the waiter had just put in front of her. Her hawklike nose, I saw, was the result of a break. I wondered where and how. It gave her a fiercely seductive look.

"See, I'd heard about this new makeup at Arden's. You know how

Lenny's been complaining that I don't look as pale as a real social worker would be. Well, I went to Arden's and tried this grayish blush, and they had some other suggestions and things just kind of got out of hand. Before I noticed the time, it was nearly seven-thirty. Geez, I totally panicked!" She looked stricken.

"So Lenny had a right to be mad. Darned unprofessional of me!" She shot Jim a sly smile. "But seems to me, after *your* sterling effort last night, you can't very well gloat."

Jim looked puzzled, then winced and nodded. He turned to Sally. "Last night I was even worse than Dinker was tonight. If you can believe *that*." Dinker dug an elbow into his ribs. "Ouch! No, really, I was awful." He flashed a grin. "We alternate being lousy."

Dinker got serious. "What *was* it with you last night, honey? You were a thousand miles away."

Jim's eyes flicked from Sally to me to the far wall. "Nick," he mumbled.

Dinker's mouth formed a silent "Oh!" She gave him a long, concerned look. "It's really got you down, hasn't it?" Jim nodded, staring at his beer.

Dinker leaned over towards Sally and me across the table. "Jim's got family troubles," she said softly. She laid a gentle hand on his arm. "Go ahead and tell them, sweetheart. It's what we're here for, right?"

Jim nodded and shifted uncomfortably. He finally met my eye. "I guess Dinker and I should apologize to you two. We had ulterior motives for inviting you tonight." I glanced at Sally. She raised her eyebrows and shrugged.

Jim bit his lip and studied the wall behind my head. "Dinker and I had a long talk Sunday night. She—"

"I told him about you, Dave," Dinker interrupted. "Sally told me you're a detective. I wanted you to hear about Jim's problem." She faced Sally. "I'm sorry, Sally. I just couldn't think of any way of telling you the truth over the phone. Please don't be mad."

Sally shrugged. "Since I don't know what you're talking about, I'm not—at least not yet. What's the big mystery?"

All eyes went to Jim. "May I tell you about it, Dave?"

I smiled at him. "You'd damn well *better* tell me about it, or I'm going to start beating it out of you with a rubber hose. What is it?"

Jim nodded. "Okay. I guess I'd better start with Nick Carney." He spelled it. "Sounds like my name, but different spelling. A groupie at the theater."

Dinker nodded. "A buddy of Lenny's," she put in. "Make that former buddy of Lenny's. They had a falling out a week or so ago. That's when Lenny told cast and crew Nick wasn't welcome around the theater any more. Wouldn't say why."

Jim nodded. "I wasn't really too surprised. I never could figure out what he and Lenny had in common anyway. Guy looks like a weasel, and the word was, he's some kind of small-time crook. But he loves the theater and he and Lenny go back a ways. So he'd hang around rehearsals sometimes. He was never really any trouble. Just come in and sit behind Lenny in the third row. Till last week." Jim took a slug of his beer.

"Anyway, him being kicked out and all, I was surprised to see him backstage Sunday night after rehearsal. He grabbed me, told me he'd figured out, through the story in the *Dispatch*, that he and I are— either of you see that story?"

Sally and I shook our heads. "Well, it was an article on off-off-Broadway theater. Last Thursday's *Dispatch*. And they did a little sidebar on me: a short bio and my picture. Nick read it and came to the theater to tell me—well, it's really kind of unbelievable. I *didn't* believe him at first. What he told me was that he and I are brothers." Kearney shook his head. "And I never even knew I *had* a brother."

I stared. "You've known this guy how long?"

"About as long as I've known Lenny. Three months. Ever since I got the part in *A Thousand Clowns*."

"And all of a sudden he figures out you and he are brothers?"

"*Half*-brothers. We have the same dad. Different moms."

I swigged beer and grinned at him. I remembered Sally'd said his dad was wealthy. "Let me take a wild guess, Jim. He wants money. Right?"

Jim's eyes widened. "How did you know?"

"A lucky guess," I said. "Look, Jim. Every time a paper does a piece on some new celebrity, grifters come out of the woodwork. Announcing they're a long-lost nephew or cousin. It's a standard scam, though brother is really taking it to the max. Hate to burst your bubble. I hope you didn't give him anything."

He shook his head. "No, I didn't give him anything and you're wrong, Davey. Oh, I felt the same way at first. But my dad admitted it. Yesterday."

I stared. Dinker jumped in. "See, Jim flew home to St. Cloud Monday. He just had to—"

"I had to confront Dad," Jim interrupted. "Nick told me he needed some money. He—"

"Several thousand, I suppose," I put in.

"Yeah, but—no, listen, Davey. Just let me talk—*then* you can shoot holes in his story." Jim took a breath. "Look. I haven't given him a thing. And I'm not going to. But you have to understand where the guy's coming from." He glanced at Dinker. "Where do I start, honey?"

She swallowed Perrier and put down her glass. "Might as well tell it from the beginning, sweetheart."

3

"OKAY," Jim said, draining his stein. (I waved at the waitress. I had the feeling this was going to be a multi-beer story.) "Dad's a West Pointer. Went to Vietnam, got decorated, came home. He was approaching thirty and planning to stay in for a full military career. Then his uncle Pete died. Pete had lived in St. Cloud all his life, never had any kids, started his own business right after World War Two. Set up a drugstore in St. Cloud, expanded into wholesaling. By the time he died, he'd sold the drugstore but had a whole network of warehouses all over Minnesota and the Dakotas. One of the biggest drug wholesalers in the upper Midwest—Kearney Pharmaceuticals, Inc. KPI, for short.

"Anyway, when he died, he left the company to my dad—provided

Dad came home and ran the company. If he didn't, the company was to be sold off and the proceeds divvied out to various charities. So Dad got out of the army and moved back to St. Cloud. He'd been stationed here in New York City at the time.

"And what nobody knew, at least nobody in St. Cloud, was that, before he went to Nam, he married a girl here in New York, and they had a baby. And the baby grew up to be Nick."

I still wasn't ready to buy it. "Oh yeah. And the guy just happened to spell his name wrong. With a *C*."

Jim didn't smile. "I know, I know, it sounds weird. But just hang on. Nick's mother's name—maiden name—was Mona Smith. She'd been a waitress here in the city. Dad met her, I guess they fell in love—well, Dad says he never really loved her, but—anyway, they got married and had a baby. Marriage lasted about as long as it took to do that; Dad split as soon as he got back from Nam. And a year or so after that, he got this inheritance and moved back home." Jim swigged beer and took a deep breath.

"Soon as he got back to St. Cloud he met Mother and they got married. And he never said word one to her about the first marriage. Or to me, after I came along. So when Nick told me that story on Sunday, I was at least as cynical as you are now."

My fingers itched for a notebook. When I'm on a case, I like to jot things down. Of course this wasn't a case. "But cynical or not, you decided to go home and confront your dad."

Jim nodded and took another sip. "Yeah, after talking it over with Dinker. I was really mixed up."

Dinker nodded, her dark eyes big. "And no wonder. It was a lot to take in, all at once."

Jim looked at me. "Funny thing is, after telling him 'no way,' I wound up doing exactly what Nick asked me to—try to get Dad to give him some money. Nick told me he's got some kind of a big debt payment coming up this weekend and no hope of getting the money anywhere else. And he said he had a justified claim against Dad, not only as his son, but because Dad cheated him and his mom on child support payments all those years. He asked me to call Dad and ask him to send him twenty thousand dollars."

"Twenty thousand dollars!" I shook my head. "That's a lot of child support."

"Yeah, but listen. According to the divorce decree—Nick says—

Dad was supposed to pay Mona a flat ten percent of his salary—at the time, $125 a month. Well, Dad's salary was into six figures well before Nick ever reached eighteen. But he went right on paying the $125 a month.

"Anyway, I told Nick nothing doing, I wasn't going to Dad. But he had so many details about Dad right, what he used to look like, his military career and everything. Not that he has any memories of him—he was just a baby when Dad walked out. But his mother told him things."

I was shaking my head. "These scam artists *always* have little touches like that. You have to understand—"

"No!" Jim almost shouted. A few people at nearby tables glanced over. Jim ducked his head and lowered his voice. "Just *listen*, Dave! Just let me tell you." I shrugged. It *was* an interesting story. Most scams are.

"*I* wasn't buying it either. But the more I talked to Dinker about it, the more I knew I had to go see Dad. I just had to know whether this guy was a liar or not. So I took off for Minnesota Monday morning to talk to Dad."

Sally grinned. "Your dad must have been shocked when you hit him with it."

Jim shook his head. "He already knew. By the time he came home from the office he'd already talked to Nick on the phone."

I stared. "How'd that happen?"

"Nick called him."

I frowned. "Nick called your dad? In St. Cloud? How'd he get the number?"

"No problem. He got KPI's number from information. The *Dispatch* had mentioned that Dad was the president."

Sally smiled briefly. "Let me guess: your dad wasn't happy."

Jim rolled his eyes. "Hah! Try livid! He got me downstairs where Mother couldn't hear. And chewed the living daylights out of me."

Dinker jumped in. "That's his dad for you! He'll never admit he's less than perfect. I've only met him once, but believe me, once is enough."

Sally's eyes stayed on Jim. "But why'd he get on *your* case? *You* didn't do anything wrong."

Jim turned up his hands. "Well, in his mind, I did. See, I came into the company out of college six years ago. And in just four years

I made vice-president." He grinned. "You tend to get promoted fast when you're the boss's son." The grin faded. "But I hated every second of it. I took drama in college and felt I was a pretty good actor. And I loved acting. So I finally figured six years was long enough doing something I hated. A year ago, I just up and quit. About killed my dad."

He took a swig, draining his stein. I waved at the waitress again. "Dad hates the whole idea of acting; more than that, he hates New York. I remember wondering at the time why he hated this town so much. *Now* I know why. It was his guilt over walking out on his wife and child." He handed the waitress his empty glass.

"Yeah, one more, please. Anyway, he said the problem with Nick was all my fault, because if it hadn't been for that story in the *Dispatch*, Nick'd never have figured the whole thing out. But as far as any feeling for Nick, forget it. His own son!"

I nodded reluctantly. "So this guy Nick *is* for real. He really *is* your half-brother."

Jim nodded. "Oh yeah. Amidst all the cursing, Dad didn't leave any doubt about it. He admitted it."

"And the cheating on the child support?"

Jim shrugged. "That he didn't admit. But I'm inclined to think so. He didn't want to talk about it. He mainly threatened me with everything from murder to total disinheritance if I dared tell Mother. Finally saw all his threats weren't doing any good and wound up *pleading* with me not to tell her. I gave him my word I'd wait till year-end. He's got to tell her by then or I'm going to."

"And," Sally added, "I don't imagine he apologized to you for keeping you in the dark all these years—about your own brother."

Dinker snorted and started to answer, but Jim beat her to it. "Oh no. My dad never apologizes. Not his nature."

I thought about it. "Didn't your mother wonder why you flew all the way to St. Cloud this week just before your show opens?"

Sally looked puzzled. "Didn't Dinker tell me they're coming for the opening this week anyway?"

Jim smiled at her. "Right. They're coming. But things that would strike other people as strange just sail right over Mom's head. See, right now she and Dad are adding on to the house and she's all flustered with that. In fact, when I walked in Monday afternoon she was having a huge fight with this dry-wall guy. She barely stopped to say hello and give me a kiss. I think that's all she ever talked about the whole time I was there—that damn addition."

Dinker grinned, her eyes twinkling. "Well, you can't blame her, Jim. That's quite a house. And I still can't believe she finally got your dad to let her redo his den!" She turned to Sally. "It's a beautiful house! Huge! But that den! A *man* wouldn't notice. Old Jim here thought it was fine." She nudged him with her elbow. "But a *steel* gun cabinet, Jim? It doesn't go with anything else in the house!"

Jim shrugged. "Well, you can rest easy. The steel's now paneled over to fit the rest of the decor. Anyway, why didn't you tell *him* that when he insisted on pulling out all those guns and showing them to us?"

Dinker, still grinning, shook her head. "I know better than to get in an argument with your dad. Which is something it wouldn't hurt *you* to learn, friend." Jim winced.

I brought the conversation back to Nick. "Well, Jim, I credit your dad for one thing: not giving Nick any money. He may be your brother, but he sounds like bad news. This demand of his is pretty close to extortion."

Jim shook his head. "I don't know. I'm sure Nick was telling the truth about the child support. It's exactly the kind of advice Jordan would give Dad."

I frowned. "Jordan? Who's Jordan?"

"Family lawyer. And a real shyster."

Sally laughed. "Aren't all lawyers?" The conversation took a lighter turn and didn't come back to Jim's family problems till much later. Sally had just made the first move toward ending the evening.

"Well, I'm sorry, but I've got to get my beauty rest," she said, pushing back her empty wine glass.

Dinker put a hand on Sally's. "Just one minute, okay?" She looked up at Jim. "Why don't you tell Dave . . . ? You know."

Jim nodded and slugged down the last of his beer. He gave me a long look. "You're a detective, right?" I nodded. "Well, here's the thing. I just wondered if you'd try to talk to Nick for me. I feel bad about this whole thing. I called him last night when I got back, asked him what he needs the money for. Told him I thought I could get Dad to help, if he'd just tell me why he needs it. He wants to get together, but I'm uncomfortable with that. I mean, I don't think I can deal with it."

Jim played with the empty beer glass. "What I wondered was, how about if you talked to him? Maybe you could find out what he owes and what he wants. If he really *needs* the money, I think I could get Dad to come around. Dad's not a monster, despite what Dinker thinks."

I frowned. "What you mean is, what would he settle for?"

"No, I—yeah, I guess that's it."

"Sure, I'll talk to him. Where can I get hold of him?"

Jim flipped a business card in front of me.

NICHOLAS K. CARNEY
BUYER AND SELLER OF FINE JEWELRY
849 West 46th Street
NEW YORK, NY 10036
(212) 459–2120

I nodded and pocketed the card. "Okay. I'll see what I can find out."

We left Ivan's around one. On the sidewalk I turned to Jim and Dinker. "Drop you somewhere?"

They looked at each other. A silent message passed between them. Jim voiced it. "Naw, that's okay. Dinker just lives a block from here."

Dinker flashed Sally and me a quick, amused look Jim didn't see and I didn't understand—yet. The amusement came through in her voice. "Got your keys, Jim?"

"Oh no!" Jim began slapping his pockets. "Dammit, don't tell me I did it again! Did you see them, Dinker?"

Sally said, "You laid them on the table when you came in. I didn't see you pick them up."

Jim was too busy going through his pockets to answer. "Better go back and get them, honey," Dinker laughed. "Before they throw them out with the trash."

Jim shook his head. "Damn! I can't believe I did it again! I'm sorry, sweetheart. I'll be right back."

Dinker put a hand on his chest. Her other hand dangled keys in his face. "Ta-da!"

Jim blushed. "She has to pick up after me," he muttered, pocketing the keys. "Someday I'll learn."

They thanked us again for the drinks, turned and walked westward on Bleecker, arm in arm. Sally and I headed the other way, for the Seville.

"So what are the odds?" I asked her as we rolled north on Bowery. "Are those two lovebirds going to wind up rich and famous with their names up in lights? Or are they doomed to reality?"

I couldn't see Sally's smile but I could hear it in her voice. "I'm a psychiatrist, darling, not a fortune teller."

It would have taken a fortune teller to have known how much she and I were going to be seeing of Jim Kearney in the next two weeks. The Kearney case had already begun and we didn't even know it.

4

WHAT I also didn't know was that I'd be back at *A Thousand Clowns* that Friday night—for the opening, believe it or not. And with the Bishop.

If that doesn't strike you as strange, you don't know me—or Regan—very well.

First me. I'd been to the theater maybe once in the previous three years, and here I was going twice in one week, and to the same show yet. And Regan? Regan never goes anywhere—theater or anywhere else.

But strange as it was for me and the Bishop to show up for opening night, it was actually all very logical—once you understand what was going on that week.

See, I have two jobs. Neither one will support me by itself. One's low-pay, the other spotty. Since you're obviously dying to hear about it . . .

First, the low-paying one. I'm special assistant to the (take a deep breath) Most Reverend Francis Xavier Regan, D.D., S.T.D., Auxiliary Bishop of the Roman Catholic Archdiocese of New York (exhale). If that sounds impressive, let me tell you, the guy's smarts are even more so. He's got over a thousand books on the shelves of various rooms in his mansion, in seven different languages—and he's read every one. A few he's written himself. Eight, to be exact, and God only knows how many articles. All on the same subject: his specialty, Scripture.

To give you an idea of the kind of stuff he writes, his last article was entitled "*Could* the Canon Be Enlarged to Include the Gospel of Thomas? And *Should* It?" When Regan saw *America* magazine sitting on my desk one day, opened to his article, he damn near smiled. He knows I never read his stuff. He asked me if I'd read it. I said, "Absolutely," so he asked if I'd enjoyed it. "Sure," I said, tapping the fourteen-word title with my fingertip, "though it was a struggle to get through. Is the *article* worth reading too?" He didn't appreciate my humor, but then, he seldom does.

Not a guy inclined to jokes, my boss. That may or may not be due to his being confined to a wheelchair for life, courtesy of a mugger who put a .38 slug in his spine. That happened outside his mansion seven years ago. It was six months after that that I went to work for him.

I give him thirty hours a week, his choice which thirty. I take dictation, type his letters and keep his files straight. Also I play general handyman around the house and chauffeur him places on those infrequent occasions he feels like going anywhere. I'm basically responsible for the whole house except the cleaning and the cooking, those being in the capable hands of Sister Ernestine Regnery, OSF—"Ernie" to me, though not to anyone else in the world. She's been Regan's chief cook and bottle washer for about fourteen years.

That's my first job. Low pay and boring as hell, but at least the board and room is free. And, thanks to Ernie, the board ain't bad.

Plus it leaves me a hundred and thirty-eight hours a week for myself. I use them carefully and selectively.

How? Lots of ways. For one, I spend time with Sally. For two, I play a little golf, and sometimes some poker, with good friends.

And finally, as Sally told Dinker and Dinker told Jim, I do some work as a private eye. My second job. Trouble with it, and the reason I hang on with the Bishop, is the long dry spells between clients.

I've never managed to build up a nice base of potential customers the way I should. And the night I met Jim Kearney, it had been more than two months since I'd had so much as a nibble.

What made it worse, the Bishop wasn't that busy either. The eight weeks from July Fourth to Labor Day are the doldrums for the archdiocesan Director of Personnel, which is what Regan's supposed to be. And we were getting on each other's nerves. I mean, even more than usual. What happened the night before I went to that dress rehearsal will show you what I mean.

I'd come back late from somewhere, saw the light under his office door at the end of the hall and gave it a tap. No real reason, just checking in.

"Come." The monosyllable should have given me fair warning, but I was in a good mood. I opened the door a crack, stuck my head in and gave him a friendly smile.

"Hi. I'm back."

Regan, at his desk, glared at me over his reading glasses. Didn't answer.

"Oops. Sorry to interrupt." What was eating him this time? "See you tomorr—"

"No. Come in. I need to talk to you."

Typical. I mean, it doesn't matter to me, but most people would have thrown in a "Have a nice time?" or something. Not Regan. Not when something's bugging him, which it usually is.

Being in a good mood, I just shrugged and widened the smile. "Fine. Talk away." Regan adjusted the purple beanie on his mop of snow-white hair. I was getting a feeling this could develop into a major brawl so I pulled the door closed behind me so as not to wake up Ernie, who sleeps downstairs. That's happened a time or two, and it doesn't make her happy.

Regan jerked his reading glasses off and waved them at what he was reading. Looked like the magazine section of the Sunday *Times*. "Have you seen this piece on capital punishment by Patrick Buchanan?"

So that was it. The previous evening, waiting for a poker quorum at Rozanski's, I'd grabbed the Sunday *Times* and noticed Buchanan's article, entitled "Liberals Weep Over Murderers, Not Victims." When I saw it dealt with capital punishment and that Buchanan's viewpoint was identical with mine, I read it carefully. The death penalty is one area—one of several—where Regan and I absolutely and irrevocably do not agree. The article gave me some excellent ammunition, and I'd even spent a moment or two pondering how I might bring it smoothly into the conversation when things needed livening up around the mansion. Never dreaming the moment would arrive so soon and be handed to me on a silver platter.

I settled back in a chair. "Sure. I read everything he writes. And generally like it." I grinned at him. "Why do I get the feeling you don't?"

Regan reapplied the reading glasses to his nose. "Then you concur, I take it, with his concluding comment: 'Far too many Americans lack the political and moral courage to enforce our Judaeo-Christian norms of morality. The correct designation for such an American is not 'liberal'; it is 'coward'!"

The Bishop glowered at me over the glasses, his green eyes shadowed in the glare of the desk lamp. "Any comment?"

"Would you repeat the question?" I joked, getting not so much as a half-smile back. "Sorry. Uh, yeah, as near as I could understand what the guy was saying, yeah, I buy it. What of it?"

"Then, I take it, I am a coward."

I'll spare you the next fifteen minutes of conversation. Suffice it to say, I stayed a gentleman a lot longer than he did. But being human, I finally blew. I know, I know, that's stupid. Seven years of living with him should have taught me something by now. Namely, that he and I can co-exist only by not getting mad at the same time. Yeah, well, easy for you to say. You ought to try putting up with what he calls his polysyllabic invective.

I finally strode from the room without extending him the courtesy of a goodnight. And, I may as well admit it, I closed the door behind me a smidge louder than was necessary.

That was Tuesday: the start of the deep freeze. We stayed away from each other on Wednesday, except right after lunch, which is when he generally dictates his letters, if any. He had a couple that day—none to the editor of the New York *Times* Magazine, thank God. Our conversation during that forced interlude of togetherness was not filled with, as he would put it, the spirit of bonhomie. Naturally, he didn't apologize. Nor did I, having nothing to apologize for.

Fortunately, that evening I had the date with Sally to get me out of the mansion. I'd had lunch in the kitchen, much to Ernestine's disgust.

"This is ridiculous, Davey," she muttered, clanging a couple of pots around the sink.

"Hey, tell me about it. You know how he is, Ernie. If he—"

She swung around, face red. A couple of gray ringlets had escaped from the kerchief she wears when she's in the kitchen. "Oh, don't tell me it's all *his* fault, Davey. You're *both* acting like little children! I'd like to give you *both* a spanking!"

"Oh yeah?" I said pugnaciously. "You and what army?"

She didn't even smile. Just turned away and banged a few more pots and pans. Women.

To give Regan credit, he responded well to my first move toward a cease-fire. It came right after lunch Thursday (I'd had mine in the kitchen again), when I was bringing in some letters he'd dictated. "David," he growled.

I looked at him, surprised at his tone. And at his using my name. He hadn't called me anything but Mr. Goldman since the fight. "Excuse me?"

"There is really no need for you to be avoiding me. I am not angry about that little contretemps the other night." His eyes looked everywhere but at me.

I also seemed to find it hard to look at him. "I'm not either," I mumbled, then thought of something. I looked him in the eye. "Umm, about the things I said that night . . . I'm sorry." He held my eye without speaking, and I got to use a line from the play I'd just seen. "'Dammit, Sandy, that was a classy apology! Don't you know that's the most you can expect out of life? A really classy apology?'"

Regan's eyes widened perceptibly. "*A Thousand Clowns*," he murmured. "I've never heard you quote from that play before, David. Or are you quoting the film?"

"Film? Hell, I didn't even know there *was* a film! Naw, I'm quoting from the play. I think I messed it up, though." I was relieved (1) to be talking to the man again; and (2) to be talking about something other than my apology. Apologies are tough.

"Yes, you misquoted, but that's unimportant. I'm interested in where you heard it. Would I be correct in concluding that you and Dr. Castle attended a performance of the play last evening?"

"Just can't get anything past you," I sneered, putting the letters on his desk. Actually, it *was* kind of sharp of him, but a little of his sharpness goes a long way.

He ignored my jeering tone, picked up the top letter, glanced at it and put it down. He peered at me over the glasses. "Curious. Today's *Times* tells of a revival of *A Thousand Clowns*, down in the Village. But it said 'Opens Friday.' What other production of the show is going on now?"

"None. Sally and I were at the one you read about. Hasn't opened yet. As a V.I.P. I get invited to dress rehearsals all the time."

"Indeed." He continued to study me. "I don't suppose you'd believe me, David, if I told you *I* played Murray in a seminary production the year before I was ordained. Back when you were in Pampers."

"Hah! Pampers? That's for rich folks, like you Boston Irish. But you playing a Jew? Nah. I'm not buying."

Regan shrugged. "I thought not. You Jews are natural cynics, as your friend Buchanan has often noted. Nonetheless, it happens to be a fact. Also a fact is my predilection for that play. I don't suppose you could use your massive influence to obtain a couple of opening night tickets for us? My treat, naturally. That is, if you're free Friday night. I am, as it happens."

"As it happens?" I guffawed. "Hell, you're free every night of the year!" Actually I didn't guffaw that. Or even say it. I just thought it.

Out loud I said, "Yeah, I'm free. About tickets, well, I don't know. Won't be easy. But when you get to my level of power and influence..." I shut up. He was back to studying his mail and had forgotten I was even in the room.

Power and influence. Yeah. Tell you the truth, I wasn't optimistic. I mean, opening night *is* opening night, even off-off. But I called Jim Kearney, figuring he owed me one with all the free detective work I was going to do for him. He said sure, no problem. Then I told him about the Bishop being a paraplegic.

"There's space for wheelchairs behind the last row on stage right— that's the left side of the auditorium as you face the stage. If you get there half an hour early, you can grab a good spot before the crush begins. Looks like a full house."

"And we can pay for the tickets when we pick them up at the box office?"

"They're on me, Davey. How can I ask you to do free detective work and then expect you to pay to see me perform?

"Oh, and speaking of that, have you had a chance to talk to Nick Carney yet?"

I assured him I was about to do that very thing. With the freebie on the tickets, what else was I going to say?

5

I C A L L E D the number on Nick Carney's business card. No answer after six rings. Well, I thought, the guy can't be all bad. At least I didn't have to listen to that "Please wait for the beep" crap. I hate answering machines.

The area west of Times Square doesn't call for a lot of dressing up, so I dressed down for the occasion: polo shirt (no alligators or other reptiles showing), lightweight khaki pants and running shoes.

I hiked up to Forty-sixth. For a July day in New York, it was downright decent: not too muggy, not too hot. I took my time getting there. The only thing I hate worse than answering machines is sweaty armpits.

Eight-forty-nine was a rehabbed three-story office building halfway between Eleventh and Twelfth that must have had a security-conscious management. Understandable in that neighborhood. A sign on the revolving door read "Closed 6:00 P.M. to 8:00 A.M. daily, and from 6:00 P.M. Friday to 8:00 A.M. Monday." Knowing they had to leave the tenants some kind of nighttime and weekend access, I looked around. Ten feet east of the revolving door was an anonymous door with bulletproof glass and a high-security lock.

But the security system didn't end there. I pushed through the revolving door into the lobby and found another locked door, also with safety glass, leading to an inner lobby with two elevators. This door required a key. For outsiders the right-hand wall provided buttons to call the office you wanted to visit.

Button 301 read "*Nicholas Carney. Fine Jewels.*" I gave it a couple of pushes. Same result as the phone call. So I pushed the next button: Fernwood Associates, Ltd. Within two seconds the lobby filled with a disembodied female voice, "Yeah, who is it?"

Looking around for something to talk into and seeing nothing, I bellowed, "Delivery!" Two seconds of silence; then the inner door gave a loud buzz. I pushed through into the inner lobby, thinking how like a chain is a security system: only as strong as its weakest link.

When they'd rehabbed the building they'd obviously scrimped on light fixtures. The third floor hall was so dark I could barely make out the *301* or the *Carney's Fine Jewelry* on the door. I tried the knob: locked. I gave it a couple of loud raps with my knuckles: nothing but silence. This obviously wasn't my day to meet Nick Carney.

To avoid the ignominy of having totally wasted my time, I walked down to 310. The sign on the door read "Please Enter." I obeyed. The noise of the typewriter increased. The rapid fingers of the plumpish, fortyish blond at the keyboard didn't miss a beat. She gave a backward jerk of her head toward the credenza. "Just drop it there."

"Sorry," I said, and waited. She finally stopped typing and looked up. "I lied," I admitted. "I don't really have a delivery. I just needed to get into the building. Do you know Nick Carney?" She studied me with cold eyes. I had a distinct feeling I wasn't going to get a lot out of this gal by coming on as a friend of Nick's.

"That way." She flipped a thumb in the general direction of Nick's office and put her fingertips back on the keyboard.

I shook my head and grinned. "Not there, lucky for him." She looked up again, her eyes a little friendlier. "He's into me for a bundle," I explained.

She studied me, a tiny smile playing on her lips. "Well, take a number, mister. And good luck."

I nodded. "Yeah, tell me about it. Why do you think I'm looking for him, anyway? Where *is* the slimeball?"

She lifted an indolent shoulder. "Who knows? Like I said, you're not the first to come looking for him. Try Paddy's Pub across the street. That's his second office."

I asked her a couple more questions but I'd gotten everything I was going to get. She was already banging away at the keyboard by the time I left. She probably had ten or fifteen words a minute on me but I had a feeling I'd take her on accuracy.

Walking into Paddy's Pub was like coming home. There can't be more than four hundred bars in New York just like it. Dark, the way drinkers want it. And filled with the fine aroma of recycled beer and yesterday's nicotine.

At the first stool, his back to the bar, with an excellent view of the street through the big front window, was the only customer in the place, a little old guy, fedora tipped back at a rakish angle, staring moodily at the sidewalk. I glanced out to see what he was scoping. Nothing. At least that I could see.

The burly bartender, a once-white apron covering his ample mid-section, gave me a vaguely hostile stare. I settled onto a stool halfway down the bar, out of earshot of the oldster, ordered a draw and got it.

I watched the bartender ring up the sale and lay the change in front of me. I left it there.

"Mets are looking good," I ventured, taking a swig.

"Yeah," he agreed, face brightening. "Swept the Cubs. Hey! Did you see Tim Burke strike out Sandburg in the tenth?" I grinned and nodded. He grinned back. "Home tonight against the Expos."

"Yeah. I'm going," I lied with enthusiasm. We were soon into the Mets' prospects for another pennant. While we talked, I pondered how to bring up the subject of one Nick Carney.

Halfway through the second brew I made my pitch. "Nick been around today?" His head swiveled to me, face impassive. "Nick Carney?" I added helpfully.

I had his attention. He looked at me, waiting for more. Didn't get it. Finally, "What do you want with Nick?"

I took another swig, considering how the name Nick had rolled off the guy's tongue. Sounded like he and Nick were friends.

I shrugged. "Buddy of mine. Owe him some money. Just up at his office but he's not there. They told me he comes in here sometimes."

The barkeep nodded, but his eyes stayed suspicious. "He comes in here sometimes, yeah. So what's your name?"

"Davey," I said. "Goldman."

He had another question for me. "If you owe the guy, how's come you're lookin' for him, 'stead of him lookin' for you?"

I took another swig. "He is. Better I find him before he finds me. Nick's not a guy I want mad at me."

That drew a grin. "You can say that again."

"Yeah. And I hear he's hurtin' lately. So he can probably use the dough."

The bartender glanced down the bar at the old guy, still sitting there studying the outside world, and leaned toward me. "Nick *has* been a little short," he muttered. "Milt Manning's after him for what he owes him. But Nick says he's coming into some dough. He's seein' a guy tomorrow night, guy owes him a bundle. And now you."

I let my face show I recognized Manning's name. Milt is one of the more important juice merchants in the city. This bartender might be Nick's friend but he had a bigger mouth than Nick should have been comfortable with. I raised my eyebrows. "So where is Nick? Any idea where I can find him?"

The bartender looked over my shoulder at the front door of the bar. "Hell, you're in luck! Here he is now!"

He raised his voice. He beamed. "Hiya, Nick. Hey! Your buddy Goldman is here looking for you." I spun around on the stool, trying for a beam of my own.

Which wasn't easy. I recognized Carney right away from Jim's description. Little guy with a pencil mustache, dark hair slicked back, walking with a limp.

He wasn't what worried me. What did was who he was with. Two guys that looked like they might have been down linemen for the New York Giants. I'd got myself into a spot I was going to have a tough time getting out of. Alive, I mean.

6

THE closer I studied the two, the more I realized they couldn't be. New York Giants, that is. They had the size and the muscle, but their eyes were too mean. None of the warmth and friendliness that L.T. and his mates are famous for. Plus, these guys were white.

Carney's small, precise features tightened as he scanned my face. He smoothed his mustache with a quick flick of his index finger, then snapped his fingers at the two gorillas.

"I don't know this clown," he said. "Wrap him up."

With no hesitation that I could see, the two monsters moved in on me, slick and smooth, their faces expressionless. I raised both hands in a gesture of peace and smiled up at them.

They stopped. Nick exploded. "Dammit, I said wrap him up! You guys listening or what?"

I sized up the situation. It was as bleak as it could get. The guy on my left went about six-four. His two hundred fifty pounds looked to be about ninety percent muscle, including his mostly bald head. The one on the right was a couple of inches shorter, about the same as me, but probably outweighed his partner by ten or fifteen pounds, with about the same ratio of muscle to body fat. His hair was sandy, brushed forward in a Caesar cut. His nose was flattened against his face and his little blue eyes looked very mean. The air began to smell of cheap cologne.

I moved my hand, very slowly, toward my hip pocket. "Come on, Nick," I wheedled. "Just hold it, gentlemen. Give me a second. I want to show you my investigator's license. All I'm looking for is a little conversation with Mr. Carney."

The two goons waited for instructions. I looked at Nick. His dark eyes flicked from me to the bartender to the two gorillas. He rubbed his finger across his mustache and shrugged.

32

"Let him take out his I.D., Jeff. If anything else comes out of his pocket, break his arm."

The taller one nodded. Cheekbones starting to ache from the smile, I pulled my wallet out—very slowly—and handed it to the short one. "Check it out," I told him. "My life's an open book."

He took it and flipped it to Nick, who caught it in one hand, flipped through it, found the P.I. license. His eyes flicked back and forth from it to my face. After a second he nodded abruptly and flipped the wallet back to me. Gave me a mean little smile.

"So you want some conversation, ace? C'mon." He limped toward the rear of the bar. I followed and so did the biggies—at first. They stopped in their tracks at a shake of Nick's head so tiny I could barely see it. Looking disappointed, they grabbed a couple of bar stools and swiveled to face us.

Carney led me all the way to the last booth and jerked his head sideways in an invitation—or perhaps an order—to sit. We sat.

He showed me his none-too-attractive teeth. "Mind if I smoke, ace?"

I decided it was no time for complete honesty. I shrugged. Carney pulled a huge cigar from the breast pocket of the expensively tailored double-breasted suit. He took his time lighting it, first rolling the end of it around in his mouth. He produced a monogrammed silver lighter from a side pocket and lit up, cigar to the side of his mouth. He exhaled and sat back.

His fingertip worried the mustache while he studied me. "Sorry about the heat, pal. Shorty and Jeff enjoy a little grabass once in a while. Not me. I'm really a gentle guy, know what I mean? But a guy my size, it makes sense to have guys around like Shorty and Jeff." He caught my eye. "You wouldn't believe it, but there's actually people out there that'd love to work me over."

Still holding my eye, he opened his mouth, gripped the two front teeth with his fingertips and pulled. Four teeth came out, held together by wires. He gave me a toothless grin, laid the bridge on the table and said, mushily, "Couple of bad-asses did that to me with a baseball bat. Last year. Worked my knee over pretty good too." His face looked misshapen and even smaller than before. But he didn't seem embarrassed. He took another puff on the cigar out of the side of his mouth.

"Gives me some problems. Only eat soft food. So maybe you can see why I'm a little cautious. Want a drink?"

He called "Rocco!" and the bartender was beside us almost before
Carney got his teeth back in place. Carney nodded at me. I shrugged
and looked up at the bartender. "Okay. Another draw, Rocco."

The big guy nodded at me and turned to Nick. "Your usual, Mr.
Carney?" and left without waiting for the answer.

Carney studied me, half-smile playing on his thin lips. "I'm half-
Irish on my daddy's side. Guess that's why I like Irish whiskey. Neat."

He sighed. "Matter of fact, I like *everything* neat. Neat and tidy.
Which is why the guys that did this to me..." He indicated his
mouth. "... ain't around no more." He grinned around the cigar.

"So I wasn't, uh, happy to find you here. But let me take a little
guess." He cocked his head, studying me. "What would you say if I
said my half-brother sent you? The one that spells his name with a *K*?"

I can normally control my face pretty well, but that one stung me.
He laughed at me.

"Gotcha!" he giggled, pointing the cigar at me.

I grinned back at him and shrugged. "Yeah. Ya got me." I waited
for him to calm down. "So let me tell you why he sent me, Nick."

Carney waved his cigar in the air. "Sure. You're an emissary of
good will and kindness, right, ace?" He sounded more genial than
sarcastic.

"Well, yeah, you could say that, Nick. Fact is, the guy thinks he
can get his—your—daddy to ante up some dough, but he wants to
know why. Why you need it, that is."

Nick gave me a long look, taking small puffs on the cigar. The
bartender arrived with our drinks. I reached for my wallet but Nick
held his hand up. "This is my party, ace."

The bartender set down our drinks and scuttled off.

Carney raised his shot glass to me, and I raised my stein. He threw
the whiskey against the back of his throat. I tilted the glass against
my lips but didn't drink.

"Jim Kearney," he mused, toying with the now-empty shot glass.
"I actually knew the guy. I couldn't believe it when he turned out
to be my brother. It took me three times through that article before
I got it." He looked up at me, eyes serious.

"See, I'd always known my old man's last name was Kearney—
with a *K*. But had no idea what hole he'd gone and jumped into. Ma
tried and tried to find him, right up to the day she died. She never
thought it was right for him to just go off and forget me. Me, I coulda
cared less." Nick gave me a grin.

"She was a good woman, my ma. I buried her two years ago. Died of emphysema." He grinned and pointed at his smoking cigar. "She told me I should quit these; said they'd get me, same as the ciggies got her. They probably will." He took a defiant puff, with a glance at me, daring me to try to stop him. I didn't.

Nick shrugged. "Well, ace, I'm gonna do you a favor. Gonna earn you a fee without you doin' a thing. You can go back and tell little brother I'm not lookin' for dough. I don't need it." I cocked my head at him and raised a suspicious eyebrow.

"You don't want the money?"

Nick waved the cigar expansively. "You got it, ace. And tell my old man the same thing. Jim don't know it, but the old man already made me an offer. But I don't want his dough." His voice tightened. "Not that he doesn't owe me." He took a deep breath. "Yeah, he owes me, but I don't need it now. So he's off the hook. You go tell him that, ace."

I was puzzled. "I hate to look a gift horse in the mouth, Nick, but why the sudden change? The way Jim talked, sounded like you were hurting bad."

Nick nodded. "Yeah. Well, I'm not anymore." He took a puff. "I've learned one thing in life, it's that the worse off you are, the better off you are. And vice versa. You read much, ace? Or go to plays?" I shook my head. "Well, you should." He gave me a long look. "I'm serious. Lotta wisdom in those old guys. I don't read much, but I go to lots of plays. I know more about Miller, Williams, O'Neill and Chekhov than most guys with a college degree. And they're good. I've learned a lot. A lot about myself. And a lot about my daddy.

"Oh, I was mad enough to kill the son of a bitch when I found out how he'd cheated me and my mother. Ten percent he owed us. Ten percent of everything he earned! And he paid us shit. But . . ." He turned his palms over with a smile. ". . . person can't stay mad forever, right, ace? Especially when blood's involved. I mean, ten percent's not worth shedding blood over, right? Plus . . ." He tilted his head toward the front of the bar. ". . . with a little help from my friends Jeff and Shorty, I now got my money problem solved."

Nick took a final puff and stubbed the cigar out in the ashtray. "So you can go back and tell little brother he can quit worryin'. Big brother's not mad any more."

I looked at him, wondering if this was a game. I decided it wasn't. There was no sarcasm in his tone. He and his two wide-bodies had pulled something off and solved his money needs. How? I decided I didn't really want to know.

Carney got to his feet, smoothed down his expensive suit, tightened the knot of his tie and flipped a twenty onto the table. Leaving the beer, I followed Nick to the front of the bar. He sauntered over to the old timer, muttered, "Hang in there, Jake," and slipped him a folded bill. Shorty and Jeff, I saw, had moved to the door and were waiting.

"Hey, thanks, Nick," the oldster chortled, immediately slapping the bill on the bar. "Hey, Rocco! I'm back in business! Another bump and a beer!"

Nick grinned at him. "Hang loose, Jake." He turned and waved to the bartender. "So long, Rocco," he called. "I'm out of here."

Out on the sidewalk, I waved at Nick. "So long, ace," I said.

He saluted back. "Overusing that 'ace' a little, aren't you?" He extended his hand and I took it. I was surprised at how small it was. "Hang loose, man," he said, turned and strode across the street, Shorty and Jeff watching both ways for cars like a couple of out-of-uniform traffic cops.

7

THE Bishop and I, friends once again, made it to the theater Friday night with time to spare. For which I take no credit. Regan insisted that Ernie serve dinner promptly at six o'clock, a good half-hour earlier than he'd normally tolerate it. Ernie complained, but that's Ernie. If you told her the Messiah was coming tomorrow, she'd say, "Can't he come next Tuesday? The house is a wreck."

Anyway, we made it in plenty of time. We were parked, in the theater and in place, by 7:36. My own seat—a folding chair next to Regan's wheelchair—was going to be even worse to sit on for two hours than what I'd sat on at the rehearsal. At three minutes to eight I'd tried every position known to man trying to get adjusted to it and had decided I was just going to have to grin and bear it, when a hand whacked my shoulder from behind.

"Hey, ace! I didn't expect to see *you* here!" I looked up, happy to see Nick Carney, if only because it gave me an excuse to stand up. I introduced him to Regan. Nick looked at the wheelchair with less embarrassment than most people. He shook the Bishop's hand. "Temporary problem, Bishop, I hope?"

Regan met his eye. "Yes, thank you. As temporary as all things human. I'll be in it only till my death."

Nick blinked, then grinned. "Oh, that temporary, huh?" He chuckled. "Not bad, Bishop. I like that." He looked around. "Looks like we're about to start. Gonna grab myself a seat. See you guys later." He limped off.

"I assume Mr. Carney is a former colleague?" Regan said dryly. I chuckled.

"Nope. He plays for the other side." Regan's eyes widened and he threw Nick a glance. He was about to say something else when the lights dimmed. We shut up and settled in for the show.

It was even better than it had been two nights before. I even forgot all about how uncomfortable my chair was. The rapport between stage and audience was like nothing I'd ever experienced and made the standing ovation at the end a pure and logical necessity.

As the applause died and the lights came up, I didn't know which to be more surprised at: the tears in the Bishop's eyes, or the fact that he wasn't trying to hide them. Maybe he was just clapping too hard to know they were there.

As the rest of the audience headed for the exits, he made no move to follow. I looked down at him. "Want to go meet Jim and thank him for the tickets?"

He put away his handkerchief and answered pleasantly—another surprise. "If you like." I'd expected his usual grumpy, "Get me home, David."

I had to give Kearney's dressing-room door an extra-loud rap to be heard over the noise coming from inside.

Making out Jim's "Yeah, come in," I held the door, then followed Regan into a closet tightly packed with people. They edged back to let us in. The Bishop in his wheelchair got the usual stares.

I said it was a closet. It was actually a dressing room the size of a closet, and certainly not intended for the number of groupies that had piled in. If a fire marshall had seen the situation, he'd have arrested all seven occupants.

Jim, sitting with his back to us, looked at me in the dressing-table mirror and waved with one hand while continuing to remove makeup with the other. Under the face cream, he was flushed and bright-eyed.

I introduced Regan to Jim, who, presiding at his dressing table, introduced the two of us to everyone else.

Jim's mother, Peggy, was a plump, round-faced lady with a couple of white streaks in her dark hair and a twinkle in her eye. Her stylish black dress and shoes were so new and so elegant I suspected they'd been liberated from someplace like Saks or Bergdorf's that very day.

As for Mike, Jim's dad, put it this way: if you had fourth and inches, and you saw him on the other side of the ball, you'd probably elect to punt. He was square in face, head and body. He'd loosened his collar and tie to accommodate his square neck.

Jerome Jordan, the lawyer, was thin and shambling. From Jim I knew he and Mike were the same age, fifty-five. He looked ten or fifteen years older. His expensive dark blue suit hung poorly on him. He had shrewd blue eyes, shielded by gold-rimmed specs, and they stayed on Regan for quite a while after the introductions.

The seventh person in the room needed no introduction. Lenny Rosen was bubbling with the triumph of opening night. His handsome face glowed as Regan poured on the praise.

"Congratulations, sir. A first-class production in every respect. Mr. Herb Gardner would be proud."

Rosen opened his mouth to answer, but Mike Kearney's raspy voice beat him to it. "Now just who the hell is Herb Gardner?"

Regan was about to answer, when Peggy jumped in. These Kearneys were no shrinking violets. "Oh, Mike! You know perfectly well who he is." Her husband glowered at her, but she wasn't intimidated. "He's the one who *wrote* the play, dear heart. It was *on* the program."

Lenny started again. "Anyway, thank you, Bish—" but Mike's raspy voice cut him off again.

"Stupidest damn show I ever saw. Bunch of tomfoolery, people not working, living off welfare. Sorry, Len, I'm not talking about you. You folks were fine. Every damn one of you. But all those weird, cockeyed ideas! Just a damn stupid show."

A moment of silence. Then, "Oh Mike!" Peggy scolded. "Why do you always have to spoil things? We came all this way to see Jim perform. And you—"

"Yeah, to see him perform. But I didn't know it'd be in a damn Commie fable. Ought to take it to Russia, you ask me." He looked around, perhaps for support. Didn't find it. "Hell with it," he shrugged. "Let's go to the hotel. A few pops'll make us all feel better." I was beginning to appreciate Jim's desire to get the hell out of St. Cloud.

"Anyway, thank you very much, Bishop," Rosen said, one eye on Mike to see if he had finally shut up for good. "It really has been a lot of fun. Sounds like you're familiar with the play."

"I wouldn't even compare my knowledge of it to yours, sir. But, yes, I've performed in it. In a highly amateurish production compared to this, I assure you. This was masterful!"

Rosen's face reddened a little more under the makeup. "Very kind of you to say, Bishop," he smiled. "I wish I—yes, Shirley?"

The pretty coed who'd been in the ticket booth Wednesday night was in the doorway.

"Sorry, Lenny," she said nervously. "Uh, Nick's here. He, uh, he told me you were supposed to have left something for him? I, uh . . ." Her voice trailed off and she backed away. I couldn't blame her. Lenny was suddenly mad as hell.

"Is he alone?" She nodded. "Okay, Shirley," Lenny sighed. "Where is he?"

"In your dressing room, Lenny. He said he'd wait for you."

Rosen nodded and turned to us. "Sorry, Bishop. Folks. Just a little something I've got to take care of."

"Anything wrong, Lenny?" Jim said, getting to his feet. He looked worried.

"Naw. Don't worry about it." Lenny tried to grin, not too successfully. "You know Nick."

Jim's return smile was puzzled. "Oh—yeah."

I was watching for reactions to the mention of Nick from Mike, Peggy and Jordan. Mike was impassive, Jordan flushed a bit, and

Peggy gave Lenny a sharp look. Something about her look struck me as interesting. Made me wonder if she was really as unaware as Jim thought.

Rosen gave the parents a little bow. "Nice to meet you, Mrs. Kearney. Uh, Mr. Kearney. See you at the hotel in a few minutes." He spun around and left.

Jim, eyes narrowed, watched him go. Then his face cleared and he smiled at me and the Bishop. "Why don't the two of you join us? Dad's got a suite at the Plaza. Everyone's invited."

"Yeah," grunted Mike. "You two join us. Mother and I'll go up there and freshen up. Come on up soon as you can. It's Suite twelve-oh-one."

In a matter of seconds the parents and Jordan swept from the room, leaving Jim, the Bishop and me. "Whew!" Jim shook his head. "Dad's *really* out of his element. Sorry about that."

"Not at all," the Bishop smiled. "I enjoyed meeting your parents—and Mr. Jordan. I do think, though, that Mr. Goldman and I would be imposing. We only came back to thank you for the tickets. We are indeed grateful. Now we'll be on our—"

"No, really!" Jim was determined. "Please come. If you can take the time."

Regan glanced up at me. "Well. If you're sure. It would be a pleasure to meet the entire cast and crew of such a marvelous show. I assume they'll all be there."

"Well, they're all invited. If you *can* come, we'd be honored to have you."

I glanced down at the Bishop. He indicated his willingness with a tiny shrug of the shoulders. "Okay," I said to Jim. "Sure."

"Good," said Jim. "I'll get changed and see you over there."

I had one more thing I needed to ask Jim. "Did you talk to Nick Carney tonight?"

"Yeah," Jim answered with a quick glance at the Bishop. "And I've got to thank you for what you did, Davey! He was as friendly as he could be. I don't know how you did it, but thanks."

"I didn't do a thing. I'll tell you about it later."

"Well, anyway, I'm glad to be on good terms with him again." Jim looked at Regan. "I'm sorry to be talking in front of you this way, Bishop. You don't know anything about any of this, do you?"

Regan shrugged. "No. But I can surmise. I take it this Mr. Carney—

that is, Nick Carney—is your half-brother, and that he and your father are estranged."

Kearney stared—first at Regan, then accusingly at me. "You told him, Dave? But I didn't want—"

I interrupted wearily. "I told him nothing, Jim. He's just showing off, don't worry about it."

"But how—?"

"It wasn't difficult, Mr. Kearney," Regan murmured. "Your tone of voice, body language and facial expression all revealed your feelings about the man. And Mr. Goldman's use of the surname. Speaking of which, I'm guessing he spells his name differently. Perhaps C-A-R-N-E-Y?"

Jim gaped. "You *must* have told him, Davey!" I shook my head. "But you *must* have! He couldn't have—!"

The Bishop intervened, his tone smug. He loves it when he guesses right. "As I said, Mr. Kearney, Mr. Goldman pronounced it as though it were a different surname. More to the point, he would have used it differently if it were simply the same as yours. No matter." Regan waved it away and continued.

"I take it, this gentleman was demanding pecuniary remuneration from your father?"

"If that means was he looking for some dough, yeah," Jim answered. "But no longer, thank God. So we can enjoy the party without worrying about that, thank God."

Right.

8

DRIVING up Sixth, I filled the Bishop in on the Nick Carney/ Mike Kearney situation, including Sally's and my long conversation with Jim and Dinker in Ivan's and my trip to Paddy's Pub that afternoon. His interest in the whole thing surprised me. Though I suppose it shouldn't have: he's always more interested in my cases than in his own work.

I found a spot in a Disabled zone near the east entrance to the Plaza, but Regan insisted on staying in the car till I'd given him the full rundown, which kept us there another half an hour. Maybe he had a premonition.

When I'd given him everything I knew, he threw his left arm over the back of the seat and used his right to tug his useless legs onto the seat to face me. "So. How intriguing. Is Miss Galloway Jewish?"

I didn't react to the implication at first. "I don't think so. Why?" I looked at him and the amused look in his eyes told me what he was driving at. I was outraged. "Would you kindly give me a break? One Jewish mother in my family is already one too many! I knew I was making a mistake the day I introduced you two!"

I'd introduced Regan to my mom about six months after I went to work for him. She'd wasted no time recruiting him—Ernie too—into what *had* been her one-woman campaign to marry me off to some nice Jewish girl. It was getting tiresome. But Regan was unfazed by my outburst.

"You have nothing, surely, at which to take umbrage, David. Your description of the young lady leads me to certain conclusions. One of which is that a future romantic involvement between the two of you is a possibility."

I shook my head. "Every time I mention meeting a pretty girl, you're thinking marriage. Well, just forget it, okay?" I glared at him and he finally shrugged. But that irritating twinkle didn't leave his eye.

He got back to business. "In your opinion, was Nick Carney telling the truth when he said his father had made him a monetary offer? His brother said nothing of any offer."

I shrugged. "Yeah, you're right. I don't know. I don't see any offer from Mike fitting into the timetable that Jim gave us. Jim saw his dad Monday night and his dad flatly refused. According to Jim. Anyway, it doesn't matter. Nick says he doesn't need—or want—his old man's money."

Regan nodded. "So your conclusion, from yesterday's meeting with Nick Carney, is that he will not pursue a monetary claim against his father?"

I shrugged. "I didn't say that. Look: at this point, you know everything I know, so your guess is as good as mine. I'd say not. But since you're about a hundred points above me on the I.Q. scale, you probably have a better idea."

"No," he muttered, thus blowing a golden opportunity to predict the confrontation that was already brewing twelve stories above us in the Kearneys' suite. If he'd done that, he'd have moved up past genius on my registry to all-seeing, all-knowing Carnak the Magnificent.

Going across the hotel lobby, I drew glares from a couple of hotel employees. Why couldn't that big, strong, able-bodied guy help that poor crippled clergyman? The one struggling across the lobby, wheelchair sinking deeper into the thick carpet with every push. The crippled clergyman's linebacker-sized shoulders and Alley Oop biceps and triceps were hidden by the clerical suit. Hate looks like that used to bother me, back when I first started with Regan. I even used to complain about it.

"Nice for you to feel so independent, Bishop. But just for my sake, couldn't you let me give you a *little* push when we're out in public every now and then? I'm sensitive. I don't enjoy having people spit at me."

"Come, come, David, it's hardly escalated to that. Furthermore, I'm certain you can easily bear all such slings and arrows. Even with your delicate sensibilities. People need to be educated about the disabled. Being pushed around would send precisely the message I'm at pains to avoid."

I'd blasted back with, "Yeah, well, if you want to send a message, use Western Union," but it got me nowhere.

Anyway, over the years my skin has thickened (and coarsened, the Bishop says) and the glares no longer bother me. I even threw a wicked smile at a pretty uniformed receptionist who was looking daggers at me, which of course made her madder yet.

Twelve-oh-one was a large living room with adjoining bedroom and it was jumping. Dinker Galloway and Peggy Kearney were over in one corner, drinks in hand, laughing and talking with a couple of men I didn't recognize at first. Then I did. One of them was Chuckles the Chipmunk—in the play. Without the makeup he looked twenty years younger. Dinker was flushed and radiant in a yellow jumpsuit. She saw me and threw me a wink and a smile. Peggy didn't recognize me till Dinker whispered something in her ear. Then she nodded and gave me a second look and a smile.

Everyone was standing around in bunches of three or four, some smoking—which didn't do much for the air quality—and all drinking. Black turtlenecks were very much in vogue. I recognized the pretty coed from the box office smiling at something Lenny Rosen was whispering in her ear.

A uniformed bartender was making drinks in the tiny kitchenette. I couldn't see Jim or Mike Kearney anywhere.

I didn't have long to wonder where they were. Before I even had time to ask the Bishop if he wanted a drink, Jim came into the mêlée through a door on the far side of the room. He looked around, brow furrowed. His mother said something to him, inaudible to me. He didn't answer or even look at her, just continued to search the room, scanning faces.

When he saw me his face relaxed and he headed my way. As he moved closer, his eyes touched on Regan.

"Hello, Bishop," he said abstractedly. "Uh, Davey, uh, could you come in the other room? Nick's here. Everything's changed. He's demanding money again and I'm afraid he and Dad are about to get into it."

He looked at the Bishop. "You, too, Bishop, if you don't mind. Maybe a Roman collar would send a message. Nick mentioned he'd met you. I, uh, I think he likes you."

Regan's face was impassive, but I could see the flicker of excitement in his eyes. He loves stuff like this.

"We'll do what we can, of course. We'll follow you."

"Well, what if *I* don't want to—" I started, but Regan was already rolling. I followed like a true gofer.

I glanced at Peggy as we went. She looked worried, her eyes following Jim. I wondered if she had any idea what was brewing in the other room. For just a second she started to come after us but decided against it. She turned back to Dinker, who hadn't seemed to notice.

I closed the door—and most of the noise—behind us. We were in a large bedroom with two king-sized beds. Jordan, the lawyer, was sitting on one of the beds, slumped against the headboard, the drink on his lap tilted at a perilous angle. He was watching Mike and Nick, something like amusement in his eyes.

Jim's prediction of a fight looked accurate. In fact it looked downright imminent. Mike's square face was red with anger as he turned away from the smaller man to face us. Nick's wasn't as red and he looked more determined than angry. Neither was holding a glass, but Nick was waving a cigar.

Mike had been barking something—I couldn't pick up the words—into his son's face when we entered. He broke off as he turned to us. He took a breath and opened his mouth but Jim, looking embarrassed, beat him to it.

"Excuse me, Dad. But why don't we calm down and see what a couple of outsiders have to say? Nick, you know the Bishop. And Dave Goldman."

Nick smiled thinly. "Yeah, I know both these guys. Welcome to St. Nick's Arena, gentlemen. Glad you're here. Hi, Bishop." He gave the Bishop a small wave and a bow and offered me a hand. I shook it, noticing again how small it was. "Maybe," Nick said, "we can now start talking some sense."

Mike didn't like that. "Your definition of sense and mine, mister, don't jibe and never will, and it's time you got that into your little head." Nick turned and grinned at him through the cigar smoke. Mike jerked away and waved at the smoke.

"Look, don't blow your damn smoke at me, I told you that before! I'm going to—"

"Please, gentlemen!" Regan's voice wasn't loud but it cut through the noise. "May I say something? I have a question."

He had everyone's eyes. Just the way he likes it. "Mr. Kearney.

What is under dispute?" His eyes were on the father but Nick answered along with him.

"This son of a—!" Mike spluttered.

"I'll tell you what—!" Nick shouted simultaneously.

"Gentlemen!" Jordan's slurred voice overrode both the others. The
lawyer struggled off the bed, put the glass on the nightstand and
joined the group, steadying himself with a hand on Mike's broad
shoulder.

"Perhaps a little legal expertise wouldn't hurt, if you don't mind.
And less noise." Mike glared at him and started to talk. Jordan put
up a hand. Mike closed his mouth.

"Thank you." Jordan looked longingly over his shoulder at his drink,
then sighed and looked down at Regan. "Let me explain what's going
on here, Bish—uh, Bishop."

Regan raised a hand. "I know about the dispute over the child-
support payments, Mr. Jordan. No need to go over old ground for
my sake. Or Mr. Goldman's."

Jordan raised his eyebrows. "Oh you do? Well, er, good." For a
second he looked disappointed. He'd been short-changed of his
chance to launch into a long legal explanation. But he recovered
nicely. "Well, let me tell you something you *don't* know. Two days
ago, Wednesday, I made this gentleman here a very generous offer,
which he not only turned down, he virtually spit it back in my face.
Now he wants to take it; but that p'tic—uh, that p'tic'lar offer is no
longer on the table."

I was interested. An offer made two days before? That confirmed
what Nick had said about his old man having made an offer. I tried
to fit a time sequence into place. Two days ago would have been
Wednesday, the day that Sally and I came to the rehearsal, the day
we met Jim, the day after Jim got back from seeing his dad in Minnesota. Jim hadn't mentioned any offer. Why not? Most likely he
hadn't known. I glanced at him and got my guess confirmed. He was
as surprised as I was. But not so the Bishop. At least he didn't look
it.

"A monetary offer, I take it," he murmured.

The question was for Jordan but Nick beat him to it, taking a step
toward Regan and putting his cigar behind his back, possibly out of
respect. "Yeah, a monetary offer," he growled. "But you ought to see
the release this son of a—excuse me, Bishop. Around a man of the

cloth I'll try to keep it clean. Though these clowns don't make it easy." He turned to Jordan and sneered, "Why don't you show him that thing, ace? If you're not too ashamed."

"Not ashamed of it at all. Okay, Mike?" Kearney nodded. Jordan pulled a number-eleven envelope from his inside coat pocket. "Okay. Here you are, Bishop. Fresh copy for you. Mr. Carney tore up the first one. And threw it in my face." He pulled a folded document from the envelope, glared at Nick and handed it to Regan. Regan unfolded the pages and I moved in behind him to read over his shoulder. It was three pages, single-spaced. Reading it, I saw why Nick'd torn it up and thrown it in Jordan's face.

It was full of *whereases* and *parties*—of the first and second parts— and it took a long time to read. A lot longer for me than for Regan, who passed me the pages as he finished reading each one. I was still struggling with the first paragraph of the second page when he'd finished the whole thing. He didn't wait for me, which made it hard both to read the thing and follow the conversation. But I managed.

The document was entitled *Release and Waiver* and was about as insulting to Nick as anything could be, if I was understanding it correctly, which I probably wasn't because of all the legalese. It had expressions like "eschew, deny and forfeit" and "renounce, waive and release." I love how lawyers never use one word if they can figure a way to work in three.

But Nick had more than just excess verbiage to be pissed at. If he signed this, he was not only giving up any future claim to any of his old man's money, he'd be actually denying his old man was his old man. It didn't specify what amount was being paid Nick in return for the release, just "certain and valuable considerations." They'd have to be very certain and pretty damned valuable for *me* to ever sign anything like it.

Trying to pay attention to the conversation while I read the legalese was a bitch. Especially when the legalese was filled with words like *asseverations* and *eschewal*.

When Regan finished reading, he didn't comment on the paper directly. Turning to Nick, he said, "I take it you rejected this cate-gorically two days ago, Mr. Carney?"

"Damn straight. See why?"

Regan gave a small nod and turned to Jordan. "And you say the offer is no longer available?"

Jordan glanced at Mike. "Well, that's up to Mike. But it was never offered on an indef—uh, indefinite basis. It's dated July twenty-second and July twenty-second's come and gone. So the offer would have to be renewed. Nick now says he needs the money. But—"

"I didn't say *need*! I said I could use it. And—"

"Please, Mr. Carney!" the Bishop said. "Let's not get bogged down in semantics. I am puzzled. You say tonight that you are willing to sign that document?" Nick nodded, reddening. "As it is?"

Reddening still more, Nick looked away and mumbled, "Yeah, sure. What do I care? When your daddy doesn't want to be your daddy, you haven't got much choice, do you?"

I couldn't believe the change in the Nick tonight from the guy I'd met just the day before. "You told me yesterday you didn't want his money, didn't you, Nick?" I asked.

He swung to me, face drawn. "A man's gotta do what a man's gotta do, ace. Blood's one thing; money's another."

I shook my head and went back to reading the document. It got worse and worse. It had Nick apologizing for ever having said he was Mike Kearney's son. While I read, Jordan began talking about the legal effects of it. I finished reading and, when Jordan took a breath, I jumped in.

"How much money are we talking about?"

Everyone looked embarrassed. Well, everyone but the Bishop, who looked as curious as I felt. Nick finally answered. "Twenty thousand bucks. Done and done." He looked miserable.

The Bishop followed up, eyes on Mike. "And this is satisfactory to you, Mr. Kearney?"

Mike frowned ferociously, glared at Jordan, who'd retrieved his drink from the nightstand and was taking a big swallow. "Yeah, I guess it's a deal."

I shook my head again and looked at the document. What had happened to Nick in the past twenty-four hours? The past *three* hours! When he'd slapped me on the shoulder before the performance, he'd been the same Nick; and now look at him.

His face was pale but relieved. He looked at Regan. "Thanks for cooling things down, man. This is really . . ." He swallowed hard. "It's really the best thing. And it'll take care of a little problem of mine. Just in time."

"Care to sign it, then?" Jordan asked. "Both copies, please. And perhaps I can ask Mr. Goldman and the good Bishop to witness your signature?"

Nick didn't hesitate. He went to the nightstand and scribbled his signature twice. Regan and I followed with ours. After we'd signed, Jordan reached for the papers but Nick beat him to it. "Hold it," he said, grinning around the cigar the way he had the day before in Paddy's. "Where's the dough?"

That started a major brawl, and it looked like the whole thing was going to come unraveled. Mike summed up the problem: "Hell, you come bouncing in here unannounced two days after you say 'Nothing doing' and expect me to have a cashier's check ready! It's *midnight*, there's no banks open! I'll mail it to you on Monday!"

"Monday's no good, don't you understand? I've got to have it to-morrow!" Nick looked on the verge of tearing the paper up all over again.

"Well, I can't get you a damned cashier's check on a Saturday morning! My money's in Minnesota and we're here in New York. You're just going to have to wait!"

Nick's voice went up nearly an octave. He was nearly out of control. "Dammit, you're just trying to—!"

"Hold it!" Jordan said. Nick looked at him, panting. His hands twitched on the folded pages of the document he'd just signed. Jordan turned to Kearney. "Mike. KPI has an account at MidCity National here for your bond-trading activity. Right?" Mike nodded. "You'd surely have enough in that. And you have power to sign on it singly." Mike nodded again. "So let me give Cliff a call first thing in the morning. You and I can cab it down there and get it done. We'll do it as a loan from KPI to you. You'll repay it on Monday—with interest, to show it's not an extraordinary dividend. This'll work."

Mike nodded abruptly. Nick looked relieved. Then he thought of something. "How are you going to get it to me?"

"The check, you mean?" Jordan asked. Nick nodded. Jordan glanced at Mike, who shrugged. "I'll bring it over to your office," Jordan finally said. "I was there just the other day so—"

"No!" Nick looked worried. "The building's not open on Saturdays. So—"

"Then come here." Nick shook his head. "Why not? What's the big deal?"

Nick's eyes shifted. "No! I've got enemies. I've got to be careful."

He looked around. "How's about Jim? What the hell, guy's my brother. How's about you bring it to me, Jim? And then I'll give you these in return." He brandished the two copies of the release.

Jim looked around. "Okay, I guess. You'll have to give me instructions."

"I'll have to give you more than that. That building of mine's a bitch to get into. Which is what I like about it. Can you come tomorrow afternoon?" Jim nodded. Nick looked around and frowned. "Okay, I'll give you the combination tomorrow morning. You be home? I'll call you. What's your phone number?" Nick pulled a small address book from his pocket and jotted down the number.

Nick put the book in his pocket, swung back to the Bishop, gave him a little bow. "You're all right, man—excuse me, Bishop. You're all right. I think this is going to work out. For everyone." He turned to his father.

"Maybe someday I'll forgive you for that ten percent you didn't pay. You're some father, you know that?" Mike reddened but didn't answer. Nick shook his head, turned on his heel and left.

9

IN our ongoing argument about the Kearney case, the Bishop's contention is that we'd have solved it a lot faster if I'd gotten involved sooner. My answer is, how can you get involved when you're out on Long Island and don't even know something has happened? Regan says if you're going to fritter away an entire weekend cavorting on Long Island with Dr. Castle, you could at least read the papers. I say, weekends on Long Island aren't for reading papers, so sue me.

Saturday morning I had to get up about two hours earlier than usual. That was in order to pick Sally up at nine, so the two of us could drive to her parents' beach house way out past Southampton. She's had me out there at least once every summer since we started dating, and it's always a kick.

The first time I went I really didn't expect it to be. I liked Sally, of course—a lot. But I'd met her parents a time or two, and had my doubts about them and how it'd be to spend an entire weekend with them. Turned out we got along, as her dad puts it, famously. Mr. and Mrs. Castle are either considerably less anti-Semitic than their neighbors or else they still haven't yet figured out that I'm Jewish. Anyway, I always have a good time, and this year was no exception.

Actually my fingers did get some newsprint on them that weekend. In fact, with a little luck, I'd have come across the story on Nick's murder Sunday morning when I skimmed the *Times* over breakfast on the veranda. But at that point I was more concerned with fresh-squeezed orange juice and Flora's blueberry waffles than with all the news that's fit to print. So when Ernie called right after breakfast to tell me Jim Kearney needed to talk to me, I didn't take it seriously. I knew what he wanted (I thought), and I'd just wait till Monday to get his report on his meeting with Nick. Nothing spoils the mood of a Long Island weekend faster than business talk.

Ernie called again late that afternoon. Sally, her parents and I were playing croquet, our last game of the weekend before Sally and I had to make that long drive back into the city.

The croquet court being about a hundred yards from the house, Flora was huffing and puffing by the time she got there. "Mr. Goldman! Sister Ernestine is on the phone again. She says she needs to talk to you right away!"

I arrived at the phone in none too good a mood. Sally and I had less than an hour left and Muffy—Sally's mom—and I were blitzing the other two. This interruption could cost us some all-important momentum.

"Yeah, Ernie," I said, trying to keep the edge out of my voice. "What is it this time?"

She sounded worried. She always sounds worried. "I'm sorry to bother you again, Davey, but did you reach Jim Kearney?"

I took a deep breath, rolled my eyes, counted to ten and used as gentle a tone as I could muster. "No I didn't, Sister. I've been busy."

Right. Well, hell, it was my weekend off, wasn't it? Is nothing sacred?

"You didn't?" She had that accusatory tone I hate.

I adopted a mocking, sing-song tone. "That's right."

"Well, he's called again, Davey. Several times. All I could tell him was I gave you the message. But he—"

I cut her off. "I'm sorry if he's been bothering you, Ernie. Look, if he calls again, just tell him I'll call him tomorrow, okay? I'll be home later this evening. Like I told you Friday."

"But Davey, he needs to talk to you! He said—"

I cut her off even more sharply, this time not bothering to hide the edge. "I really don't care what he said. I'll be back later tonight, Ernie. I'll talk to him tomorrow."

"But Davey! You don't understand! His brother is dead!"

Ernie's breathing sounded in synch with my heartbeat. I tried to take it in. "You mean *Nick*? Nick Carney's dead?"

"*Yes*, Davey! I'm sorry. I didn't know that when I called before. He was shot to death yesterday afternoon in his office. Mr. Kearney has called five or six times. The Bishop even talked to him twice. And the Bishop is angry that you didn't return Mr. Kearney's call."

In the course of a minute-and-a-half phone call my pulse rate had doubled and my mood had gone from irritated to shocked. "The Bishop is angry" was the last straw.

"Okay, Ernie. I'll call Jim. And the Bishop should mind his own business. Please tell him I said that."

"Davey—!" I hung up on her. I hated to take it out on Ernestine— I really like her, but I had a lot on my mind.

Nick Carney dead? I couldn't believe it.

I didn't feel like calling Jim but there was no way out of it. He picked up right away. "It's Dave Goldman," I said. "I just heard about Nick. I'm really sorry, man. How are you?"

He sounded glum. "Thanks for calling, Dave. I'm okay—I guess."

I cleared my throat. "Jim, I'm sorry to be so late getting back to you. Is there anything I can do?"

"Sure is. But not right now. I just got home from the theater, and I have to go back. We did a show this afternoon and have another one tonight. Lenny told me I could take off, he'd get Johnny—my understudy—to take the part tonight. But I decided I should go on. I mean, it's not like I really *knew* Nick."

"Right."

"So I don't have time to talk now—I just came home to shower between shows. But—I may be in trouble, Dave. I'm afraid the police are going to think I did it. I'd—"

I stopped him. "Did you?"

"Kill him? Hell, no! What do you think?"

"Sorry. I had to ask it. Go on."

Silence for a few seconds. Then, "Okay, Dave. I guess I can understand that." He took a breath. "Anyway, I'd like to tell you about it. Could I come by tomorrow?"

"Sure. Any time." We agreed on ten o'clock.

My three croquet companions were waiting for me. "Nothing wrong, I hope, Davey," murmured Muffy. I gave her a smile, shook my head and we resumed. Sally's worried eyes told me she wasn't buying my nonchalance. That didn't surprise me. When a gal combines woman's intuition with a psychiatrist's training, you don't put much over on her. But she let it slide till we'd said our goodbyes and were on our way in the Seville.

We hadn't hit the end of the long curving driveway before she was all over me. "Okay, sweetheart, what was the bad news? You came back looking like a ghost."

"It's Jim Kearney."

"What about him?"

"His brother—half-brother, I mean—Nick. Nick's dead."

Sally gasped. "He's—! No! My God! What happened, Davey?"

"I don't know exactly. Ernie told me he was shot." Sally gasped again. She swung her knees up on the seat to give me her full attention. I swung onto Route 27 and glanced over at her. "You brought along the *Times*, didn't you?"

She nodded. "It's on the backseat. I didn't finish the crossword."

"Never mind the crossword. Did you bring the rest of the paper?" She nodded. "Check the local news. There should be something. Apparently it happened yesterday afternoon."

It took her a couple of minutes to find it. "Here it is. I'll read it to you. Okay, Davey?" I nodded.

"Headline reads 'MOBSTER SHOT, KILLED.' Here's the story:

July 26. Nick Carney, suspected by police in a number of criminal activities but never convicted, was found by police yesterday afternoon, shot to death in his office at 849 West 46th Street,

Manhattan. Police were alerted by an anonymous phone call at 2:37 P.M. The caller reported having heard shots in the building. The police broke into Mr. Carney's office at 2:49, to find Mr. Carney's body slumped over his desk. He had been shot three times in the back of the head at point-blank range. Inspector I. M. Kessler of Manhattan Homicide, in a prepared statement, said the department has no suspects in custody and an investigation is underway. Mr. Kessler declined further comment.

"That's it, Davey." She put the paper in her lap. "I can't believe it! What could have happened?"

Sally moved closer. She shivered slightly as I put an arm around her shoulders. "It doesn't say anything about Jim," I said. "But Kessler's going to go after him."

"Why, Davey?"

"Because Jim had an appointment with Nick at precisely that time yesterday afternoon, and it was to be in Nick's office. Now Nick's been murdered—at that time and place—and Jim wants to come see me. I don't guess the police have been to see him. But they will."

Sally shook her head. "Oh God, Davey, that's awful! Poor Dinker!"

I nodded. I hadn't even thought about Dinker.

For once I didn't park and come in with Sally. I turned her over to her doorman and headed home. Arrived about nine-thirty. The Bishop was in his office, door open.

"Sister Ernestine said she gave you the news," he growled. His voice sounded unfriendly, but his eyes had that glitter they get when an exciting case is underway.

Regan loves putting his brain power to work on my cases. Seven years ago, when I first started working for him, I'd have never dreamed of bringing him a detective problem. How he ever got involved—well, that's a story in itself. It all started with him showing some interest. From there it worked up to his making "suggestions." Somehow, over the years, those "suggestions" have turned into commands, don't ask me how. By the time I got into the McClain case last year, he'd worked up to senior partner, Regan and Goldman: Detection While You Wait.

Well, not really. I mean, he doesn't help on all the cases; far from it. But when I get a tricky one it's nice to have a 220 I.Q. on my— and my client's—side.

And now it looked like he was eager to get involved in the Carney

murder. I needed to slow him down a bit. As I'd learned in Paddy's
Pub Thursday, Nick had lots of enemies in the outfit. This was undoubtedly their doing. It was just Jim's bad luck to have planned to
be in Nick's office at the exact time the murder wound up taking
place.

"I don't think this one's for me, Bishop. Or you."

Regan frowned. He didn't want to see a juicy one get away. "But
you surely haven't had time to discover what the police know about
the murder."

I shook my head. "Time *or* inclination. Look, Bishop. This isn't
our job. First of all, Jim didn't do it. Second of all, the mob did. I
have absolutely no business getting involved in this thing. And you
even less. It's got nothing to do with us."

He wasn't buying it. "But you *are* meeting with Mr. Kearney
tomorrow morning, are you not?"

That surprised me. "How'd you know that?"

"After you made your appointment this afternoon, he called here
to get directions." Regan looked smug.

I got up. "Okay, you're right. But the meeting is purely for reas-
surance. I'm going to tell him he hasn't got a thing in the world to
worry about. This was a mob hit, and the cops will solve it with
absolutely no help from you or me. And that's the end of it."

The voice of experience. So much for experience.

10

B y the time Jim came next morning at eight minutes of ten, I'd
skimmed Monday's New York *Times* and read with care the
story entitled "Police on Carney Murder: No Comment." It
didn't add much to what I already knew, beyond suggesting the cops

were getting nowhere. They *were* looking for the murder weapon—
"pistol" was as close as they came to identifying it.

"Jim." I swung open the front door of the mansion and shook his
clammy hand. I couldn't see the eyes behind the dark glasses. But
his freckles stood out like dark blotches on his drawn face.

"Sorry to bug you like this, man," he mumbled, pulling off the
shades and blinking in the dark foyer. He swallowed and tried what
he may have thought was a smile. "Can we talk, Dave?"

"Of course. Come into my office."

Kearney followed me in and plunked himself into a chair, without
giving the room the courtesy of a second glance.

Not that it deserves a second glance, the overall appearance of my
office not being at the top of my list of urgent daily concerns. Two
of Regan's Van Gogh prints are on one wall. Well, I *think* they're
Van Goghs. They're still in the same place they were when I moved
in seven years ago and Regan asked if I minded them staying. What
was to mind? I rarely look at them, but as decoration I guess they're
okay.

The office goes downhill from there. The opposite wall is all shelves,
filled with books: the Bishop's rejects. At least I assume that's what
they are. In the seven years I've used that office, the only person
that's ever touched a book on those shelves has been Ernie. Dusting.

I sat down behind my desk. "Why don't we get right to it, Jim?
What makes you think the cops are after you?"

His red-rimmed eyes met mine. He rubbed his face. "Why don't
I tell you everything that's happened since I saw you Friday night?
Then you'll know why I'm so worried."

"Good idea." I pulled a notebook out of my desk drawer. "Go
ahead. I'll just take some notes."

Jim closed his eyes hard. "Okay. Friday night I left the Plaza with
Dinker about two. We talked. I told her what had gone on with Dad
and Nick. She didn't like all the fuss. And she didn't like seeing me
getting involved. But I explained it to her and she finally saw the
point.

"But Nick changed everything. He called me at my apartment that
night. Woke me up. I—"

I raised a hand. "You're saying he called you Friday night? Instead
of waiting till Saturday morning?"

Jim squinted into space. "Right. Well, no, come to think of it, it *was* Saturday morning. About 3:00 A.M. He wanted to be sure I was coming—said it was really important. He told me a lot of things I hadn't known before." Jim rubbed his face. "God, I hope I can remember all this. So much has happened since."

I looked up from my notebook. "Take your time. Try to tell it in order. If you leave out anything, we'll go back and pick it up later."

Jim nodded and closed his eyes again. "Okay. Uh, let's see. He told me a lot of things. Said he owed money to a guy named Milt Manning. Tough customer, apparently. Nick wanted me to meet him—Manning—outside his office building. He gave me the address." Jim pulled a wrinkled piece of notepaper from his pocket and looked at it. "Eight forty-nine West Forty-sixth."

I squinted at it. "Is that what you wrote on last Friday night?"

"Uh-huh. You want it?"

"Yeah. Gimme." Jim got up and handed me the paper. His scribble was almost as illegible as Sally's and she's a doctor. "What are these other numbers, Jim?"

"Okay." Jim took a breath. Talking seemed to be helping him. "That's Milt Manning's phone number there, and below that, the combination to the outer door of Nick's office building."

I studied the paper and found each one. "Okay, go on. What else did Nick say?"

"Well, he was real cautious about giving me the combination. Told me to be sure not to let anyone else see it. And he gave me exact instructions about how to get in—how to punch the combination into the door. He told me he was coming in about noon. We talked about when would be best. He said Manning couldn't make it before one-thirty. We agreed on two o'clock. Uh, am I going too fast?"

I was scribbling furiously. "No, I'm fine," I said without looking up. "What else?"

"He said I should bring Manning into the building with me. I was supposed to call Manning ahead of time and set it up. Nick told me whatever I did, I absolutely shouldn't give Manning the combination to that door, or let Manning see me work it when we came in.

"So the deal was I'd meet Manning on the sidewalk outside the building at two, let him and me into the outer lobby, we'd buzz Nick, he'd buzz us into the inner lobby. We'd take the elevator up, I'd give Nick the check, he'd give me the signed release papers and I'd leave. He said Manning would hang around, because he and Nick had to

talk. But he did say he was going to endorse the check over to Manning."

Jim watched me write for a minute. "Okay, go on," I said, when
I'd caught up.

"Soon as I got up Saturday morning—it was about eleven—I called
Manning. He sounded nice enough, said he was expecting my call.
We agreed to meet at Nick's office building at five till two. We each
described ourselves; he said he was six-three, two-ten, sandy hair,
said he'd be wearing a sport jacket and ascot. And a beret. He had
a deep voice but sounded kind of effeminate. Kind of an affected
English accent, you know.

"Well, everything was set. And then it all fell apart. I got to the
building a little before two. I checked my watch, in fact, because
Manning wasn't there. It was 1:56. I looked around for him, but there
was nobody there—of his description or any other description. But
there was a note on the door. Taped to the inside. It said—"

I stopped him. "Don't tell me what it said. Let me have it."

Jim shook his head. "I don't have it. I guess I should have grabbed
it, but I didn't." He shrugged. "I intended to pick it up on my way
out, but I wasn't thinking too clearly at that point. Anyway, it was
from Nick. Uh, it said, 'Jim—Milt couldn't make it. Come in lobby
and buzz me. Nick.'"

I thought about it. "Typed or handwritten?"

"Handwritten. Just scribbled, really."

I made Jim go over the note again, but he remembered it the way
he'd said it the first time. I got it down exactly as he remembered
it, then told him to go ahead.

"Okay. I went in, pushed his button and he answered right away."

"You sure it was him?"

Jim nodded. "Yeah. It was him. The sound quality of that speaker
is really lousy but it was him. I knew Nick's voice and way of
speaking."

"Remember exactly what he said?"

"Yeah. Well, pretty close. He said, 'Who's there?' I said, 'Jim
Kearney.' He said, 'You alone?' I said, 'Yeah.' Then he said, 'What
was my grandmother's maiden name?'"

Jim snapped his fingers. "I guess I didn't mention that before—
we agreed on a password arrangement Friday night. He'd told me
his mother's mother's maiden name—Gagliano. I asked him if he

didn't mind Manning hearing that and he'd said, no, just be sure I didn't tell Manning ahead of time. He just didn't want Manning to have the combination to the door. Anyway, Manning wasn't there.

"I said, 'Gagliano.' He kind of chuckled—I guess at my pronunciation—and buzzed me in.

"After what's happened, I've thought about it. And that chuckle is how I know it couldn't have been anyone but him. I do lots of impersonations—I can do eight or ten foreign accents and several American dialects. I'm good at it. Not as good as Lenny, but good. Lenny's taught me a lot about accents. One of the things he says is, the hardest thing to impersonate is a chuckle or a laugh—it's so distinctive. And personal. It's really hard to do someone's chuckle. So I'm sure that was Nick."

I nodded. "Okay. So you got in—he let you in—and you took the elevator up, right?"

"Right. I got off the elevator on the third floor and the hall was dark. I could smell cordite as soon as I got off the elevator. It was faint, but I could smell it. It didn't bother me at first, but I wondered what it was."

I raised a hand and finished jotting a note. Looked at him. "You smelled cordite? How did you know that's what it was?"

Jim smiled. "Dad's always tried to teach me to shoot straight. For all the good it did. But I've had plenty of chances to smell cordite over the years. Especially down in the basement pistol-range at home.

"The smell got stronger the closer I got to the door of Nick's office. I knocked on the door but no one answered. I got down on the floor and smelled under the crack—the cordite was even stronger. I got scared and started yelling through the door. Nothing."

Jim got up to pace. Unfortunately, you can't do that in my office. It's too small. So he settled for shifting his weight from side to side, hands in pockets. "I had a lot of things going through my head, some of them totally irrational. How could he *not* be there, when I'd heard his voice just moments before, through the intercom? Was *he* shot? But how could he be? And if so, was the guy that shot him still in there? My first thought was that Manning might've come early and got in there somehow. That scared the hell out of me, I want to tell you—thinking a murderer might be right behind that door."

I frowned at Jim. His theory made sense. And if he was right, I knew, to within a few seconds, just when the killing took place: during the exact time Jim was going up on the elevator. Straight up two o'clock. I tried to nail it down. "You're sure you didn't hear a shot? I mean, when you were on the elevator?"

Jim shook his head. "No, nothing. That elevator's kind of noisy, though."

I nodded, remembering. "Yeah. Okay, go on."

"Well, I got scared. What if Manning *was* in there? Or some maniac. Was I next?" Jim shook his head. "I decided to get the hell out. When I got outside—"

"Hold it," I interrupted. "You didn't see or hear *anyone* while you were in that building?"

Jim shook his head. "Nope. No one."

I continued writing. "Okay." I looked up. "Now. Did anyone see you coming out? Of the building, I mean."

Jim nodded. "Yeah! There was a patrolman—a cop—coming up the sidewalk. He was wearing a name tag on his uniform: 'Abernathy.' I tried to tell him about it. But I sounded so stupid, even to myself, I dropped it. Seemed like he was in a hurry to get somewhere, anyway."

"What did you say to him? As exactly as you can recall."

"Oh, it was just dumb. He was looking at me, kind of irritated, you know? And I said something like, 'I was just upstairs in that building and I think there was a gunshot, you know?' He gave me a bored look and said, 'What'd it sound like?' I said, 'I didn't hear it, I smelled it.' He looked at me like I was crazy and said, 'Yeah, kid, happens all the time in this neighborhood,' and kept right on going."

I nodded. "Yeah, that's not surprising. Did you say anything else?"

Jim frowned. "No, that was it. He was obviously in a rush, and I figured I'd done my duty. Besides, I had somewhere to go myself. I'd told Dad I'd give him a complete report right after I left Nick."

"So you went from there to the Plaza? How'd you get there?"

"Walked. But I stopped at a pay phone in Times Square. First I tried Nick again. No answer. I was really getting nervous. The whole thing didn't make any sense. He'd told me over the intercom to come up, and I knew it was him. I get up there and he's gone. And I can smell gunpowder. I was scared." Jim frowned at his chair as if he'd never seen it before. Sat down.

"So I called the police. Anonymously. Just gave them the address and—"

"From the phone booth?"

"Right. I didn't tell them who I was. Just told them I thought I heard a shot. Gave them the address and Nick's name."

"When did you call?"

Jim shrugged. "I don't know. Must've been two-thirty, or a little after."

I nodded. The *Times* had said 2:37. It added up. "Okay. What did you do next?"

"Headed over to the Plaza Hotel and up to Mom and Dad's suite. Mom was still shopping, and Dad complained about that. He also complained that I woke him up. He said he'd been taking a nap. Funny thing, though: his bed hadn't been slept in. And he didn't look like he'd just woke up.

"I was surprised he wasn't madder about not bringing him that release from Nick, but he just shrugged. Said he wasn't surprised, that Nick was a flake anyway, not to worry about it. I gave him the check back. He went in the bedroom to put it away and I followed him in. That's when I saw his bed hadn't been slept in." Jim shrugged. "I don't know. Maybe he'd slept on the couch."

I shrugged. "Or maybe he'd made the bed after."

Jim snorted. "Dad doesn't make beds. Trust me."

"Okay. Was Jordan around?"

"Nope. And that kind of hacked Dad off. See, Dad had gotten three tickets to *A Chorus Line* for that night and then at the last minute, Jordan decides to go visit a friend in Jersey for the rest of the day. Dad was pissed."

"How long did you stick around the hotel?"

Jim frowned again. "Nearly an hour, I guess, waiting for Mother to get back from shopping. She never did show up. Dad was even beginning to get a little nervous. I finally had to head home to change and get to my own show.

"I was sort of worried about her, too. I called back from my apartment before leaving for the theater to be sure everything was okay, and it was, of course. Mom had got back just a couple minutes after I left, in fact."

Jim grimaced. "I want to tell you, I was *awful* Saturday night. I mean, Lenny said I was okay, but I stunk. I apologized to him after. He tried to tell me he didn't notice anything. And Dinker said I was fine. But they were just being nice.

"Dinker wanted to go out after the show, but I begged off. I was too nervous about Nick. I turned on the radio to the news station the minute I got back to my apartment. And that's when I learned that Nick was dead."

Jim rubbed his eyes again. "My God, Davey! Think about it! Nick had to have been killed right while I was going up to his office on the elevator. The more I thought about it, the scareder I got. The murderer had to have been in that office while I was pounding on the door! I didn't get much sleep that night, I'll tell you. Kept wondering if I should go to the police. Thinking." Jim shook his head. "God, poor Nick. A lousy life, and then to go out that way!"

I nodded back, still scribbling. My fingers were starting to ache. "So what did you do Sunday morning? Yesterday."

"Well, Mom and Dad had a noon flight back to Minneapolis. So I got up early—for me—and went back to the Plaza to tell them goodbye. They'd all loved *A Chorus Line*, and they were talking a lot about that."

I looked up. "You say they *all* . . . ? How many went?"

"Three," Jim said. "Jordan's plans had changed and he got back to the Plaza just in time to join Mom and Dad. Dad was pissed about *that*, can you believe it? First he was mad at Jerry for bugging out; then he was mad at him for coming back and going with them. No satisfying my Dad—as I've learned."

"Any conversation with your folks about the murder?"

"No. I don't think they'd heard. And I didn't bring it up."

I stared at him. "You didn't bring it up? Your own brother had just died and you didn't even mention it?"

Jim shrugged helplessly.

I shook my head. "Okay. What have you done since?"

"About the murder, you mean? Nothing. I had to do those two shows yesterday. Naturally I didn't say anything to any of the cast or crew. Lenny made a comment to me right after the matinee—he'd seen the story in the *Times*. Asked me if the police had been to see me."

I gave that some thought. "Why would he ask you that?"

"Oh. He knew I'd been going to see Nick. See, I ran into Lenny on the way out from the party Friday night. We got to talking, and I told him I was going to see Nick."

I nodded. "So what are you going to do now?"

Jim looked down. "I really haven't got a clue, man. We're dark Mondays and Tuesdays, so no show tonight. We're supposed to have a line reading today at two. But I'm worried. Did I do anything wrong?"

I shook my head.

"Do you think I'll be suspected of killing him?"

I scratched my head. "Well, it's complicated. On the one hand, Nick was involved in a lot of illegal activities, and he was into Milt Manning—a known mobster—for a bundle. My guess is, what happened, Milt got tired of waiting for his money, decided Nick's story about you bringing a big check was just another scam. Got there early and whacked him."

I got Jim's eye. "On the other hand, you *were* there. Right when it happened. When they're working on a murder, cops look for three things: motive, opportunity and means. God knows you had two of those. Motive: you cut a potential co-inheritor out of your dad's future will. Opportunity is obvious: you were there. So all that's lacking is the means, i.e., the weapon.

"But two out of three ain't bad. So the cops will certainly be wanting to talk to you—*if* they know you were there. Question is, will they know? Answer to that depends on a few things, mainly that note on the door. Undoubtedly the cops have it; sooner or later they're bound to figure out who 'Jim' is. Of course, there's also that patrolman you stopped outside the building, who may or may not make the connection. And even if he does, he may not report it."

"Not report it? Why wouldn't he?"

"Hey, would you? Think about it. You're a cop. A guy stops you on the street, tells you he thinks a shot's been fired. You pat him on the head, send him on his way. And less than an hour later a corpse turns up right where the guy told you. You going to turn in a report that makes you look like one of the Three Stooges?"

Jim shrugged. "I see what you mean."

I snapped my fingers. "Hey, I've got it! Let me call a buddy down at Homicide headquarters. Maybe I can find out what they've got. And what they're looking for. Hell, for all we know, they may already have the killer in custody." I didn't really believe that. We couldn't be that lucky. Jim's eyes told me he didn't think so either.

11

JOE Parker and I go back a long way. He was a raw rookie, working
in Homicide, when I left. And, as I often remind him and he just
as often denies, I taught him everything he knows. We've remained friends and I've been happy to see him move up the de-
partmental ladder. Currently he's a sergeant. Whether he'll go much
further I don't know—he's not necessarily the smoothest or the most
political guy in the world.

He and I have a working arrangement: each of us keeps the other
informed about matters of mutual interest. It's come in handy for me
on a few occasions, most notably in the McClain case, where a little
inside info from him helped me (all right, me and the Bishop) save
our client's backside. He went way out on a limb on that one, as he
constantly reminds me. In fact, I'm still trying to pay him back for
it. And he was also helpful on the Penniston case, looking the other
way while I duped a photocopy of the victim's hand. Without that
copy the Bishop never would have been able to make a crucial connection that led to the solution.

Joe's often at his desk on a Monday, writing reports, so I wasn't
surprised to catch him in.

"Yeah, Parker." He sounded like he had something in his mouth.
He has a nasty habit of chewing on erasers when he's doing paperwork.
Like most cops, he hates paperwork.

"Didn't your mother ever teach you not to talk with your mouth
full, Joe?"

He picked up on my voice right away. "Hey, Davey! What's shakin',
pal?"

"Too much, Joe, way too much. What do you know about the
Carney shooting?"

A pause. When Parker spoke again, his voice sounded guarded.

"Carney, hmm? Mind if I ask you what your interest is, Davey?"

"Hey, have we got a bad connection? I thought I was talking to Joe Parker, not Charlie Blake." Lieutenant Blake is at the top of both Joe's and my hatelists. For a whole variety of reasons that I won't bore you with right now.

Joe grunted something and I continued, "Can't I be calling just out of simple curiosity, buddy to buddy?"

Horse laugh. "Yeah, that'll be the day. You know how many times you've called me just out of simple curiosity, no client in tow? Try zilch. What's up, Davey?"

"Hey, I asked first. But I'll tell you this much, since you're so damn nosy. I've got no client—" Joe started to jump in, so I raised the volume a couple of notches.

"—but a buddy of mine would like to know what's going on. So I'm asking."

Parker sighed. I had two things going for me: our friendship and his hatred of paperwork. Talking to me might not get him promoted, but it sure beat fighting his way through all those reports. He sighed again.

"Okay, Davey, here's the skinny. I'm just doin' up a report for Kessler, so I'm current. All I need's the ballistic report and the FBI registration check on the weapon to complete it. "What we got here's a small-time crook gettin' blown away by some of his gangster buddies. You seen the *Times?*"

"Yeah."

"Then you know the basics. The *Times* reporter has the story down pretty good. For once. What's not in her story, 'cause she didn't know it, is we've got the probable weapon."

I whistled and widened my eyes at Kearney, who was watching my every move. "You're *kidding*—you've got the gun, Joe?" Jim raised his eyebrows at me.

"I'm damn near sure of it," Parker said, "though the ballistics report—hold it, I think that's what I'm gettin' right now." I heard muffled voices for a couple of seconds. Joe said, "Thanks, Sam," away from the receiver, then came back on the line.

"Yeah, got the ballistics right here, Davey. Positive I.D. All three bullets in the murdered guy's head are from the gun we found in his office."

"In his—?"

"Yeah, Davey. I'm the guy that got lucky. I wasn't on, Saturday afternoon, so I wasn't part of the rat chase that showed up there when the guy got dead. Just as well, 'cause Blake was runnin' things and you know how I like Blake."

"You know, Joe, I've never understood why you don't get along with Blake. Charlie and I practically wrote the book on homicide procedures down there. It hurts me that you don't appreciate him more."

Joe guffawed. "Yeah, Davey, you and Blake are like peas in a pod. So you'll be sorry to know that he's in a little hot water with the Inspector 'cause of doin' such a lousy job of shakin' the place down Saturday. An' I get the credit for lowerin' the boom on him."

This was sounding juicy. "Hey, I'm all ears. Not that I'd want anything bad to happen to Blake."

Parker chortled. "Right. Well, see, he didn't stick around to see the boys did a good job searching the joint. Did what Kessler's now callin' a 'superficial job.' And you know what that means."

I did. Kessler has a number of expletives he uses in his own fussy way. But "superficial job" is absolutely the worst swear word he knows. To Kessler, a superficial job is a mortal sin, beyond hope of redemption.

I chuckled again. "So Kessler's finally catching on to Blake."

"Maybe. See, Blake had a party or somethin' to go to Saturday night, so he left Cushing in charge and you know how thorough Cushing is."

I grinned. "Yeah. If the murderer'd been hiding in the closet, Cushing would have told him to clear out, he was getting in the way of a police investigation."

"Yeah, somethin' like that. Well, anyway, I had Sunday duty yesterday. I was reading Cushing's write-up. I noticed he wrote 'Murderer took weapon with him.' Now how the hell's Cushing gonna know that, I ask ya? He doesn't. He's jumpin' to freakin' conclusions again, it's just the way his stupid mind works. His and Blake's. Anyhow, I'm thinkin', I'll bet Cushing didn't give that office a real shake-down. I figured he was so convinced the murderer left with the weapon, he just gave the place a once-over and left for his *own* party."

Parker's voice was excited. He gets a kick out of his own stories. And he'd found a very willing listener.

"So I went right over there at about five in the A.M. and got the building super out of bed to let me in. Crummy neighborhood, by the way. I took two hours to Parkerize the place. And, Davey boy, just like you taught me, sometimes hunches and hard work do pay off."

"So? What the hell happened, Joe? What'd you find?" I didn't have to try to sound interested. And admiring.

"What'd I find? Just the damn murder weapon, Davey! This ballistics report clinches it!"

"So where was it?"

Parker wasn't giving up that easy. "I looked all through the place. Nothing. Went through all three desks, closets, credenzas, bureaus. Nothin'. I was ready to leave, but I still had this hunch, you know? Still eatin' at me.

"Plus, I've never forgotten the way you put it, Davey. 'After you've touched all the bases, take it around the horn one more time.' Remember?" I didn't, but wasn't going to tell Joe that. I just grunted.

"So, Davey, I went through it again, and damned if the weapon wasn't taped to the back of a bookcase in the outer office! I can't believe I didn't find it the first time. So I brought it in for ballistics and printing. 'Course, prints were all wiped off, no surpise there. When was the last time we ever got a usable off a weapon? Ever?"

He was right, but I wasn't interested. "What kind of a gun, Joe?"

"A Colt military pistol. We're doing an FBI search on the registration, but that's gonna get us nowhere. Got to be stolen. Still—it was quite a catch, findin' it."

"Hell, yes! You've got to be in good with Kessler now, right?"

"You better believe it, boy! Kessler was at my desk this morning. And, makin' things even better, he was on Blake's case big time!

"See, Blake bein' my boss, he'd tried to make the Inspector think that he ordered me to do the search. Kessler saw right through that one. He knows Blake. So he asked me—the Inspector did—where I got the idea to go look. I told him how I figured Cushing musta blown it, how he'd already made up his mind the shooter left with the weapon.

"God, then you shoulda seen Blake backin' and fillin'! Started talkin' about the need to discipline young guys like Cushing, how they're not gettin' the proper trainin' and all. Hell, Cushing's got two years on *me*. As the Inspector points out to Blake, right on the spot.

"Finally, Kessler winds up pullin' Blake off the case an' turnin' it

over to me! Says, 'Charlie, what would you think of Joe takin' this
one? Since he did such a great job of findin' the weapon that did it?'

"God, I thought Charlie was gonna have a fit! But what was he
gonna say?

"So believe it or not, Davey, I got me my first murder case. Three
detectives workin' for me, I'm reportin' direct to Kessler, full re-
sponsibility. All I gotta do is clear my desk of all this other crap and
I'm full-time on it.

"So now you understand why I need to know, who's your damn
client, Davey?"

I suddenly had an itch right in the middle of my back. I was trying
to reach it when I got a reprieve. From Joe.

"Hold it, Davey," he said into the receiver; then I heard him say,
away from the receiver, "Yeah?" Muffled conversation. Then, "Can
you hang on a minute, Davey? We're just now gettin' a fax from the
Fibbies about the gun registration. I'm gonna go check it. Want to
hang on?"

I told him I sure did. Putting a hand over the receiver I explained
to Jim that the gun had been found in the office, it was a Colt military
pistol, and the registration was just coming over the wire. Jim's reaction didn't go beyond polite interest. I'd have been watching him
a lot closer if I'd known what was then appearing on the fax at headquarters.

Holding the receiver loosely to my ear I told him, "Doesn't sound
like they're looking for you. No one saw you go in. And my buddy's
now in charge of the investigation. So we're looking good. I just—"
I raised a hand. Joe was back on the line. He was glum.

"Like I thought, Davey. Stolen gun for sure. We're gonna have to
check it out, but it's stolen." He paused, mumbling to himself as he
read. "Uh, it's a Colt, what they call the M-nineteen-eleven-A-one."
Another pause while he read on.

"Military issue," Parker finally said. "FBI was able to do a quick
check on it. This one goes back to Vietnam days, made in nineteen
sixty-seven. Latest thing we've got is, it was purchased from the army
by a guy when he got discharged. Then he added another name to
the ownership of it sixteen years ago. Doesn't show 'Stolen' but that
don't mean nothing. When we talk to the locals, that's when we'll
find out. Shit, I don't have to tell *you* that. Anyhow, it's showing
owned by that same Vietnam vet. Guy lives in St. Cloud, Minnesota,

of all places. Michael J. and James M. Kearney—they spell it with a
K."

Parker grunted and his tone changed. "Hey! Didn't hit me till I
said it out loud—it's the same name wit' a different spelling. Wonder
if that's just a coincidence—two guys with the same name, different
spelling, and one of 'em owns the gun that kills the other. Guess
we're gonna have to look into that one. What do you think, Davey?
Coincidence—or are the two guys connected somehow? Davey?"

12

A M A Z I N G how your attitude toward your fellow man can
change. Take Jim Kearney. In the space of about five seconds
my attitude toward him had gone from casual-acquaintance-
verging-on-friend to murder suspect. I began watching him a lot more
closely.

"You there, Davey?" Parker said for the third time. He was starting
to sound irritated.

"Sorry, Joe," I finally said. "Something caught in my throat. You say
the weapon hasn't been reported stolen?" Jim yawned, trying to cover
it with his hand. He seemed to be counting the threads in the carpet.

"You listening?" Parker sounded aggravated. "Like I just told you,
it's not reported stolen on this FBI sheet, but you gotta expect that.
We're contacting the St. Cloud police to see about it. But you *know*
it's stolen. Probably the idiot brought it with him to New York to
protect him and his loved ones in the big, bad city, and had it ripped
off while he was here."

"Yeah. So when are you going to be hearing from the St. Cloud
police?"

Jim's head jerked up at the words *St. Cloud.* His eyes widened as they focused on me; his face lost color. I pretended to ignore him.

"Who knows?" Parker said disgustedly. "Small town flatfeet ain't famous for providin' lotsa help to their big-city cousins, right? I marked my calendar to call the bozo Thursday if I ain't heard."

"Give you a call Thursday, then. See you."

"Hold it, Davey! You were gonna tell me your client's name! Who is it?"

I grinned. "No. *You* said I was going to tell you my client's name. *I* said I didn't have a client. Have a good day, Joe." He was sputtering as I hung up.

"Did you say St. Cloud?" Jim asked as the receiver hit the cradle. I studied him. My theory about the Carney killing being a mob hit was no longer tenable. Jim's eyes were worried—and not nearly as willing to meet mine as I'd have liked.

I stared at Jim without answering his question. Five or six seconds of that and he began to fidget. "What?" he finally demanded, now meeting my eyes squarely. "What are you staring at, man?"

He was either innocent, or way too good an actor for me. Time to bring in the heavy muscle. The Bishop.

But where was he? I glanced at my Timex: 11:05. Very unusual. The Bishop *always* comes down from his prayers promptly at eleven; and I hadn't heard the elevator or the wheelchair. Had I missed him? Was he—?

Nope. The elevator squeaked to a stop in the kitchen and the door rattled open. He was just running a little late. Maybe he'd added a prayer or two for the recently deceased Nick Carney.

Jim stared at me, frowning, as the wheelchair passed my closed office door, heading down the hall to the office. He opened his mouth but I held up a hand.

"Hold it, Jim. I've got my doubts about you." His forehead furrowed and he cocked his head. "You look—and act—innocent as hell. But you *are* an actor." Jim's frown deepened. I went on, "I need to know whether you really are innocent before I do a thing. So wait a sec, will you?"

I opened the door to Regan's office and peeked in. He glanced up from the morning's crop of mail and studied me over the reading glasses.

"Yes?" His tone was neither hostile nor inviting.

"Need your advice," I said. "On a case. Got a min?"

He shook his head. He knows I use words like "min" just to bug him. I figure if he's going to be so finicky about language, he needs somebody around who's a little *dis*respectful. But his mood wasn't feisty.

"I have a *minute*, David. Several, in fact, if you can keep your syntax within the bounds of some minimal standard of civilized discourse."

I smiled at the excitement I heard in his voice. He was delighted to have something besides today's mail to think about. He glared. He hates it that I can read him so well. I wiped off the grin, closed the door behind me and went over to him.

"I've got Jim Kearney in my office," I said quietly. "Unfortunately, I've just learned something that totally changes the read I gave you on this Carney murder last night, that it was a mob hit. Worse yet, the same information strongly suggests that Jim's it."

Regan glared at me. "Explain *it*."

"You know what I mean. That he's the murderer. That he killed Nick." I summarized the conversation with Parker and the news about the gun.

"So," I ended, "I'd like your help deciding. If he's innocent, I'd like to help him. But it doesn't look that way. He doesn't *act* guilty, but he's an actor, he's used to pulling the wool over people's eyes."

Regan's eyes narrowed. "You have had opportunity to ask Mr. Kearney to tell you of his movements Saturday afternoon?" I nodded. "Good. Tell me exactly what he told you."

Referring to my notebook, I did my best to summarize Jim's description of his busy Saturday afternoon, trying to use his own words wherever I could. Regan listened with his eyes closed and kept them shut tight a few seconds after I finished. A favorable omen. He was focusing all 220 I.Q. points on the problem at hand. When his eyes finally opened, he had a question.

"Have you told Mr. Kearney what you just learned about the weapon's provenance?"

I shook my head. "How could I? I don't even know what it means. But if you mean did I tell him what Parker said, no."

"Excellent. Get him."

Jim shook hands with the Bishop and grabbed a seat. The Bishop made sure he had his eye before beginning. "You've told Mr. Goldman about your visit to Mr. Nick Carney's office Saturday afternoon. Let me reprise. And please correct me if I err in even the tiniest detail."

He summarized my summary of what Jim had told me. Jim volunteered a couple of corrections and a few added details. Such as having to wait fifteen or twenty seconds for the elevator after being buzzed into the inner lobby by Carney. Also, his memory of Nick's instructions over the intercom had become a little more complete.

"After he'd chuckled over the way I said his mother's name, he said, 'That you this time, Jim?' I said, 'Yeah, it's me.' Then he said, 'Got a surprise for you, buddy,' and he buzzed me in."

Regan scowled. "'A surprise'? Any idea what he may have meant by that?"

Kearney frowned back. "Nope. In fact, I forgot all about it afterwards. It just came back to me now."

The Bishop got all the information about Jim's entry to and exit of Nick's office building, then got him going on what happened *after* he left. As Jim talked, the Bishop's eyes never left his face. I was glad to see Regan home in on what I considered a vital point: the note on the door.

"You say it read, 'Jim—Milt couldn't make it. Come in lobby and buzz me. Nick.'"

Jim nodded.

"Handwritten, you say." Another nod. "Any reason to think it may *not* have been written by Mr. Carney? Any reason at all?"

Jim frowned and shook his head. "No. I mean, I *was* surprised to see it. It changed the whole ball game." He grimaced. "Of course, not as much as him getting killed."

Regan stayed on the note a while but got no further. Nor was he able to get any more out of Jim about his short, unhappy stay on the third floor.

"So you came out of the building without touching the note. Was it still there, by the way, when you came down?"

Kearney shook his head. "I've thought about that. I just don't know. I didn't notice."

"All right. You came out on the sidewalk and straightway accosted that patrolman. Abernathy, you said?"

Jim nodded.

"All right. What else? What—or who—in addition to Patrolman Abernathy did you see?"

Jim seemed to be studying the intricate pattern in the Karastan rug. He scratched his head. "There *was* someone else." He looked at the Bishop. Or, rather, through him.

"Who was it?"

Jim suddenly snapped his fingers. "In the bar across the street! What's its name?" He rubbed his forehead. "I'll think of it in a second. I can almost see it.

"Anyway, there was a guy in there, looking through the window at the street. Wearing a hat—I think an old guy, but I couldn't see him very well."

I nodded. Paddy's Pub. Old Jake, Nick's buddy, with the tattered porkpie hat. Jake had been looking through the window when I'd been in there, and had the look of a guy who watched everything. I wondered whether he'd been at his post that entire afternoon. And if so, what he'd seen.

Regan reached for and rang the little silver bell to summon Ernie. It doesn't make a lot of noise, but Ernie, for all her seventy-two years, never fails to hear it. I honestly believe she could hear that bell from her convent over on Staten Island. And somehow figure out a way to be in Regan's presence ten seconds later.

This time she was there in five.

The Bishop did introductions. "Sister Ernestine Regnery: Mr. James Kearney." The two smiled at each other.

"Can we accommodate Mr. Kearney for lunch, Sister?"

Jim tried to protest but the Bishop waved him down. Ernie looked happy. Her philosophy is, the more the merrier. "Oh, surely, Bishop. We're having mulligan stew with French bread. I hope you like that, Mr. Kearney?" Jim smiled and nodded. She smiled back and left.

"Excuse me for preempting whatever luncheon plans you may have had, Mr. Kearney, but from the sound of things, you are in considerable jeopardy of being picked up by the New York Police Department." Kearney stared at him.

"So it's important," Regan went on, "if we're to take your case, that we learn as much as we can about last Saturday afternoon in the time we have. We'll continue over lunch, which will be in roughly fifteen minutes.

"Meantime, please tell us again about your visit with your parents later Saturday afternoon."

13

R EGAN didn't get much more out of Kearney about the Saturday afternoon happenings at the Plaza Hotel than I had. He probed the mysterious absence of Jordan, the shopping trip of Mom, the demeanor of Pop. This took us all the way through lunch.

I was taking notes furiously and barely touched my mulligan stew, to Ernie's considerable annoyance. She'd have had severe words for both Regan *and* me if we hadn't had a guest. As it was, she hissed "You didn't eat a thing!" at me as she swept from the room with the dirty dishes. I resolved to make it up to her later.

After lunch, back in the Bishop's office, the three of us looked at each other. Jim looked frazzled, which didn't surprise me. I've seen some expert interrogators in my day—I'm not bad at it myself—but I've never seen anyone who comes close to the Bishop in sheer ability to drag relevant—*and* irrelevant—information out of people. Including, sometimes, information they didn't even know they had.

"Well, I have no more questions," the Bishop finally allowed. "David?" I shook my head.

"All right. You've given us a great deal, Mr. Kearney. It's now time for Mr. Goldman to give *you* some information he received from the police an hour ago." Regan's eyes were intent on Jim's.

"The police," Regan said, enunciating clearly, "have found and identified the murder weapon."

Kearney's brow furrowed. "Yeah. Dave told me."

"Tell him about the weapon, David."

I got Jim's eye. "It's a Colt, Jim." Jim's frown didn't change. "Registered in the name of you and your dad."

I watched for his reaction. As did the Bishop. We got all we expected. Jim's face turned whiter than I'd ever seen it. His mouth dropped open. If he'd planned it, he was a hell of an actor. "Wha—?" he blurted.

74

I nodded sagely. "Yeah. I thought that'd wake you up. Seems your brother got it with a little Colt number—the M-nineteen-eleven-A-one. You must know all about it. Turns out the one that hit Nick is registered in your name."

Jim's bloodshot eyes were wider than ever. "The Colt—? *My* gun? But that *can't* be! I—"

I stopped him. "Why not?"

"Because I just used it last week. In St. Cloud!" I cocked an eye at him.

Jim leaned forward and got Regan's eye. "See, Bishop, I was in St. Cloud last week. While I was there, Dad asked me to shoot with him. We've got this shooting range down in the basement. He loves to go down there and shoot. I've never been very good at it, but I hate to disappoint him. He's a great shot—got all kinds of awards with sidearms while he was in the army, and has kept up with it over the years.

"Well, he's got this great gun collection. His favorite gun was his sidearm when he was in Nam. He gave it to me for my twelfth birthday. It was a big deal. Had the registration changed and everything." Jim looked at me. "I don't see how—"

"How many guns are registered in your name, Jim?" I asked him. "In Minnesota."

"That's it," he answered. "That's the only one. It's a Colt nineteen-eleven, like you said, and it's really a fine piece. But I've always hated guns, hated to shoot. I never let Dad know that, it would have killed him. He's disappointed in me enough as it is.

"So when I was home last week, he wanted us to go down to the range in the basement and do some shooting. I said fine. He pulled out my gun and a Luger for him—another trophy—and we went downstairs. I wasn't any better than ever. It—"

I stopped him, drawing a snort of annoyance from Regan. I didn't care. "Hold it just a second, Jim. Let me get this straight. You say your Dad 'pulled it out.' From that cabinet in his den you were telling me about?"

"Right. It's his gun collection. He's got, oh, fifteen or twenty there. I remember, fifteen years ago, when he gave me the Colt, he wouldn't let me keep it anywhere but in the steel cabinet. Said it wouldn't be safe. That's when he gave me the combination. Made a big deal out of it. Told me to guard it with my life."

I was thinking hard. "Okay. The gun was kept in your Dad's locked cabinet. You shot with it last week. Was that the last time you saw it?"

"Right. Dad had me put it back in the cabinet after I cleaned it. I remember he told me to be careful, putting it back, because the dry-wall guys were in the room at the time."

"Dry-wall guys—?"

"Yeah, Dave, you remember? The other night, at the Down and Dirty, I was telling you how Mom and Dad were adding on to the house. The den's always been kind of tiny—Mom wanted it bigger. So they knocked out the wall and redid it. They were just finishing up last Tuesday when Dad and I were shooting. One of the workmen even teased him about it—said something like, 'Why don't you give *me* the combination? Those are some good-looking guns.' Dad didn't think that was too funny."

I persisted. "And you specifically remember putting your gun back in the cabinet?"

Jim nodded. "Absolutely. I cleaned Dad's gun and mine and put them both back."

"Okay," I said. "Who has the combination?"

Jim frowned. "I don't know exactly. But it's not a lot of people. Mother may know it, or she may not. She's never shot a gun, as far as I know. Certainly never showed any interest in it."

"What about Jordan?"

Jim frowned at me. "You think that he could've—?"

I shrugged. "Look, Jim. This is a very bizarre thing. Unless the FBI made a mistake—and this doesn't sound like a mistake—the gun you were shooting with last Tuesday killed Nick Carney on Saturday. Somehow, during those four days, it got from that cabinet in St. Cloud to Carney's office over on Forty-sixth Street." Jim looked thoughtful.

"Now we know," I went on, "four people came from St. Cloud to New York during that time: you, your parents and Jordan."

His brow furrowed. "So you think Jordan might've—?"

Regan intervened. "I think we're getting a little ahead of ourselves." He focused on Kearney after throwing a glare my way. He hates to be interrupted.

"Mr. Goldman and I need to confer. Would you mind waiting in the other office, Mr. Kearney? After a few moments' consultation, we'll be able to tell you whether or not we'll take your case."

Jim shot me a glance. Probably thinking, "Who's the detective here, anyway?" He got up, glanced at the Bishop and headed for the door. The Bishop was already wheeling away, heading for his favorite spot at the south windows, where he could keep an eagle eye on Mrs. Mueller's garbage out back. I walked Jim to the door.

"Hang loose, Jim," I told him with a wink. "We'll figure something out." I hoped.

Back in my chair in front of the Bishopless desk, I threw a question at him, trusting he wasn't too absorbed in the solid waste out in the courtyard to hear me. "So what's this '*our* case' jazz? You're now in the detective business? I just said I wanted some *advice*."

Regan spun toward me. "If you're fearful I'll begin demanding a fee for my services—"

"Hey, I wouldn't start talking about fees, if I were you. With what you pay me, I should really—"

"—go back to starving as a private investigator, yes. But if you prefer to speak of it as *your* case, please be assured, I have no desire to take over your function."

"Naw, no big deal. In fact, I kind of like it. Especially if you think he's innocent."

Regan looked at me, began wheeling slowly in my direction. "I'm sure he is. Your concern about his being an actor is relevant but inconclusive. My judgment, based on his performance last Friday night, is that he's a good actor, but not that good. His surprise at learning that it was his own weapon that did the killing seemed genuine. I don't think any actor in the world could have been that convincing. But we have more to go on than that."

Regan, now back at his desk, frowned. "Consider, David. If Mr. Kearney is guilty, he is not only a uniquely adroit actor, but possesses an impossible combination of great cunning and incredible naiveté." He raised a finger.

"Consider. If he committed that crime, it follows that he brought the gun back from Minnesota. Nothing impossible about that, of course. He was there, and returned here. But if he did, he did it in great secrecy. Secrecy would imply premeditation and careful planning.

"But how are we to reconcile such care with the events of last Saturday afternoon?" He raised a second finger. "Consider. He obtained entrance—*ex hypothesi*—to that office, persuaded Mr. Carney to sit at his desk, maneuvered into a position behind him and shot him three times in the back of the head, killing him."

Third finger. "He then went to the bookcase and hid the gun behind it—*where it was certain to be found.*" Regan tilted his head, frowning. He looked at nothing for several seconds, turned back to me. "Have you seen anything in any of the newspaper accounts to indicate whether or not Nick Carney's keys were missing? In particular, the key to his office?" I shook my head.

"Nor have I. And that may be important, David. It's just possible that Mr. Kearney—if he is in fact guilty—may have left the gun there with the intention of returning to retrieve it later. Unlikely, but a possible explanation for actions which otherwise contain so little inner coherence as to constitute *prima facie* evidence of innocence. In that case he would have taken Nick Carney's keys. Find out if they're missing." I made a note to myself in the notebook.

Regan went back to the finger game. "Fourth, and finally, having cleverly planned the whole affair, the man goes out of the building and immediately accosts a police officer, tells him a shot was fired. Clever stratagem? Hardly—unless he's some new genus of *idiot savant*. He reinforced in that patrolman's mind his presence at the scene in a totally unnecessary way. Extremely foolish—*if* he was the murderer."

Regan sighed and spun the wheelchair ninety degrees to his left. "I am relatively certain, therefore, that Mr. Kearney is innocent— or will be if we can demonstrate that the keys of Nick Carney stayed on his person after his demise."

The Bishop frowned, eyes closed tight. "The gun is the key. We need to know more about it."

He spun back and studied me. "If we exempt Mr. James Kearney from suspicion—based on the reasoning just cited—Mr. Kearney's parents and Mr. Jordan become prime suspects. We now know—or, at least, have a reasonable presumption, based on what we've heard from Mr. Kearney—that the weapon that killed Nick Carney was in St. Cloud last Tuesday. Certainly one of those three—and no one else of whom we know—had the opportunity to bring it to New York in the following four days. Of course, Messrs. Kessler and Parker and their colleagues will conclude the same thing. In the fullness of time. Query: who transported the gun to New York?"

His eyes fixed on me. "You must look into it, David. I suggest you repair to St. Cloud as soon as possible and meet with the parents and Mr. Jordan. And obtain answers to the key questions about that gun. Is it, in fact, missing? How long has it been missing? Was it reported stolen? The answers may provide some quick and simple solu—yes, Sister?"

Ernie was in the doorway, looking at me. "Excuse me, Bishop. But Davey's office is trying to reach him. Miss Grossman says it's urgent."

14

R E G A N muttered, "We'll talk later," rolled to his desk and, with a sigh, began reading the mail he'd been about to start on when I'd interrupted him two hours before.

I hustled into my office. Jim jumped to his feet. His eyes showed both hope and fear.

I waved him back down, picked up the phone and dialed my office without looking. I gave Jim a big forced grin in lieu of conversation.

Davis Baker is my lawyer, my landlord (sort of) and one of the few people I know who's an even worse golfer than I am. I first met him in court. I was still a cop and it wasn't exactly love at first sight between us. Dave was defending a perp I'd arrested, and cross-examining me. He managed to make me feel like a combination of Blind Charlie and Attila the Hun. At the end of the day, he took me out for a beer; his way of saying no hard feelings.

When I got booted off the force, he offered me space in his law offices at Thirty-second and Broadway, which I gladly accepted. He usually gives me first shot when he needs some investigating done for a client. It's a sweet arrangement for me—he doesn't charge me any rent, lets me use any unoccupied office available when I need to work away from the mansion, and has Cheryl Grossman, his paralegal, answer my phone for me. My office phone at Regan's mansion has two lines: the Bishop's and my private one. Mine is hooked up to Cheryl's at Baker's law offices. When it rings more than three times and I don't grab it, Cheryl does and keeps my messages. I also use Cheryl's other services as needed, and she bills me at the end of each month—a bill I always pay as quick as I can for fear she'll some day realize how much she's undercharging.

Baker claims I have the best of the office arrangement, which is probably true. On the other hand, I brought him into the Delancey Street Irregulars, a bunch of golfers I pal around with, so he owes me for that.

Cheryl, as usual, let the phone ring four times before picking up. "Mr. Goldman's office."

"Me, babe," I told her. "What've you got?"

"Well!" she said teasingly. "That was quick! Your gal Ernestine is certainly close-mouthed these days. Told me she didn't know where you were. And ten seconds later you call!"

"Yeah, I was in with the Bish. Right now Ernie's scared to bug him, these being his summer doldrums. What've you got?"

Her voice became businesslike. "Sergeant Parker called. Said to tell you it was an emergency."

I frowned at Kearney as I hung up. He looked at me and opened his mouth. I stopped him with upraised hand. I was thinking ahead about how the conversation with Parker might go. If Joe happened to ask me when I last talked with Jim, I wanted to be able to say "half an hour ago" truthfully.

Parker picked up on the first ring. But all friendship was on hold if not gone forever. He started with a few expletives, of which he has a liberal supply.

"I thought we was friends, Davey!" he said after running through a partial list of his favorites. "What're you doing to me, anyhow?"

"What do you—?"

"Shut up, I'm talkin'. I tell you we got a line on that gun, and I start checkin' into it and find out the gun's owner's a good friend of yours. So I—"

"Who told you that?"

"Never effin' *mind* who told me that. Goddamn it, Davey, you're playin' fast and loose with me, and it's gonna cost you. How many times have you had your butt hanging out to dry and I pulled it in for you? How many times has Blake had you dead in his sights and I got you out of it? And then you go and pull one like this! If you—"

"Look, Joe. Just hold on, okay? What the hell you talking about?"

Parker took a deep breath and spoke a little more slowly. "Wanna know what I'm talkin' about? Okay, *friend*. I'm talkin' about Jim Kearney, the co-owner of the goddamn gun you let me believe was stolen for sure, who's a buddy of yours and who's prob'ly in your office even as we speak, that's what I'm talkin' about!"

Joe paused a moment. Then, "Any comment on that, buddy boy?"

I was thinking fast. Someone had told Parker something. Who? Parker knew, not only that Jim and I were friends, but that Jim had been heading my way. Dinker? Lenny? Did it matter? Probably not as much as keeping my friendship with Parker.

"Yeah, I've got a comment, Joe. Namely, put yourself in my shoes, man. You tell me you've got some evidence against a friend of mine. You expect me not to talk to my friend before blowing the whistle on him?"

"You talked to him, Davey?" I was opening my mouth to answer, but he hurried on. "Where is he? I got to talk to him!"

"You got a warrant out on him, Joe?"

"Hell, no! I just want to talk to him."

I grinned. Well, at least we were even. I'd lied—no, withheld some of the truth from Joe. And now he was lying to me. He said he didn't have a warrant on Jim. Well, maybe not yet. But if Jim came in to headquarters to talk, he'd be there for the duration. Or if he did leave, it would be after posting one humongous bond. Drawing up a warrant takes about ten seconds.

"Right," I said, trying not to sound sarcastic. "Well, I last talked to Jim about half an hour ago. But as to where he is right now, you'll have to check with your other informant. Who might that be, by the way? Lenny Rosen?"

That got no reaction from Joe. "I'm not givin' that out, Davey," he said after a second, "since you're not bein' forthcomin' wit' me. You're not gonna tell me where Kearney is?" I was silent. "Fine. We'll find him ourself. And you best stay outta this one, Davey.

You got no one left to pull your butt outta the fire now." He hung up.

I looked at Jim. I felt as worried as he looked.

"I've got several things to do, Jim. We're going to take your case. But before anything else, we've got to get you out of sight. Right now."

15

I DIDN'T even stop to tell the Bishop and Ernie we were going. Parker's tone bothered me. For all I knew, a squad car was already on its way to the mansion with orders to arrest and hold Jim. And maybe me.

"Come on, Jim," I snapped. His eyes widened still more. "We're getting the hell out of here. I don't want you in the slammer. At least not yet."

I headed for the door. He wasted no time following.

I didn't want to burst onto the stoop and run smack into a couple of patrolmen. I checked through the glass, saw nothing unusual. I shook my head and took a deep breath. "Here goes nothing," I said. "Follow me." Playing it safe meant running like hell. At least that was the way I was figuring it.

We hustled down the eight steps to the sidewalk, turned left and headed west for Eleventh Avenue as fast as a couple of six-foot-two-inchers can without drawing stares. Not breaking into a run took some willpower. The more I thought about it, the more convinced I was that Parker *had* called a patrol car.

Trouble is, Parker and I are a lot alike. I *know* we think alike. Which was why, the more I thought about it, the surer I got. I knew what I'd have done: send a patrolman to the mansion, tell him to wait and make sure no one came out, while I rushed over there myself to find out from one David Jacob Goldman just what the hell's going on and where the hell's my number-one suspect in my first big murder case.

And dammed if the tenth or eleventh time I looked back over my shoulder, a patrol car *didn't* come speeding around the corner from Tenth Avenue.

"Don't look back," I told Jim. "But the cops are there. If we— Hey! I said *don't* look back!"

By now, thank God, we were at the corner of Eleventh and Thirty-seventh. As we turned the corner I took a final look. Sure enough, the patrol car'd pulled up in front of the mansion. It didn't look like anyone had got out of the car—yet. What with the sun glinting off the windshield, I couldn't even tell how many cops were in the car, or whether or not they were in uniform.

Right about there, my line of thought brought me to another re-alization.

"Damn!" I muttered without thinking, drawing an anguished look from my companion. I forced a smile. "Hey, don't worry, man." I'd just seen a pay phone next to the curb, one of the more welcome sights I'd seen in a while.

"Look. Go back to the corner, will you, Jim? I've got to call the Bish. While I'm doing that, you take a peek at that patrol car in front of the mansion. Let me know what's going on."

Jim stared at me. I waved him away with my head while I searched my pocket for a quarter. He finally edged off toward the corner, looking guilty as sin. But from a hundred yards away, the cops wouldn't notice that. I hoped.

I dialed the mansion, watching Jim watch the patrolmen. He stood there looking casual, hands in pockets. Good move. Nice to have an actor for a client.

"Bishop's office." Ernie.

"Let me talk to him, will you, Ern? And quick? Please?"

Bless her, she didn't feel like arguing. Or talking. Within three seconds I had Regan.

"Me," I said. "Jim and I took a run-out. Talked to Sergeant Joe Parker and he's mad as hell. Thinks I'm shielding a murderer. I hope to hell I'm not. Uh, that *we're* not. Parker's on his way over to see me, I'm pretty sure. His advance guard is right outside, right now. A patrol car."

"The door just chimed," he muttered.

"That's okay. I'm coming right back. But it's important that you and Ernie don't tell them anything about Jim's having been there. If you—excuse me."

Jim was approaching me, eyes bigger than ever.

"Another car pulled up beside the patrol car and they're talking! They've got the street blocked off, and I think—"

What Jim was thinking had about as much interest to me right then as the price of betel nuts in Malaysia. I nodded agreeably as I cut him off. "Good work, Jim. Hang tight a second and we're out of here."

I put the receiver back to my ear. Regan was saying something, but I cut him off. I was getting good at cutting people off.

"Sorry, Bishop, no time. Jim and I gotta run. Parker's probably on his way in right now. He's parked outside. Any questions? Or instructions?"

Regan answered by hanging up. I nodded at the receiver. Effective way to answer a question. I put the phone back in place and turned to Jim, thinking hard.

"Okay . . ." I said. Only it wasn't. Parker was pissed at me, and that was bad. Furthermore, I was on the verge of committing a near-felony: hiding an accused murderer. Well, *verging* on a near-felony's no crime; not quite, anyway.

Another thing I was regretting was having to make a bunch of snap decisions, some of which would probably come back to haunt me later.

But there's worse things than being haunted, right? So I made a snap decision.

"Wait right here, Jim." I grabbed the receiver and handed it to him. "Stand here and make a call. I mean, pretend to be making a call. It's your best way to be inconspicuous. I'm going to get you a car."

I hustled the half-block to Fred's, where the Bishop keeps his Caddy. Make that, where *I* keep the Bishop's Caddy. Thank God Fred was there.

"Need a loaner, Fred," I told him, bursting into his office, much to his secretary's disgust. I wish that someday Fred would get a keeper for a secretary, so they wouldn't have to be continually getting used to me and my ways.

Fred, big workbooted feet resting on top of his scarred desk, grinned up at me. "Loaner? Shoot, Davey, the Caddy's all gassed up and ready to go."

I shook my head. "Nope. Can't use it this time. I repeat: got a loaner? And I'm in a hurry."

Fred unfolded his lanky frame from his chair and came around the desk, grinning. "What is it this time, Davey? Another emergency?"

"Right, Fred. And I was never here, okay?"

"Never here when?" He beckoned me to follow him out to the garage floor. Two minutes later I pulled out on Eleventh in a nondescript year-old gray Pontiac with sixteen thousand miles on the odometer. Turned right and beeped the horn at Jim, still on the phone. I'd have sworn he was really talking to someone. What an actor.

He jumped in and away we went. As we rolled past Thirty-seventh, I took a quick glance down the street but, outside of a vague view of a double-parked car, couldn't see a thing.

I pulled out my wallet. A few years ago a credit-card company made a mistake and sent me a credit card, inviting me to become a new customer. They had the right address but the wrong name. Sensing an opportunity, I took them up on their offer, applied for and got the card and kept it. I use it occasionally to keep them happy and always pay on time.

"Here you go," I told Jim, handing him the wallet. "Find the Visa card in there for David Holdman."

Kearney stared at the wallet, then at me.

"Don't waste time, dammit! Find that card. You're going to need it, and we don't have much time." Jim found it.

"Take it out of there and hang onto it, Jim. For the duration, you're D. J. Holdman. Normally that's *my* alter-ego, but no reason you can't use it too. At least there's no APB out on Holdman." I pulled to the curb at a bus stop just short of Thirty-ninth.

I twisted in the seat to face him. "This is goodbye for a while. Now listen up. Take the tunnel and go over to Newark Airport—know how to get there? Good. Go to the Traveler's Inn, right next to the airport. It'll be on your right as you approach the terminal. Check in. Use this card. Don't forget to sign your name 'D. J. Holdman,' just the way it reads on the card. And don't misspell it!" Jim gave me a grin. I didn't grin back.

"Not funny, Jim. Too many guys do just that. I want you to practice two things while you're driving over there. One, ask yourself your name and answer 'D. J. Holdman.' Second, practice—in your head—writing 'D. J. Holdman.' I don't want the desk clerk to think there's anything strange. You're just staying one night.

"You are *not*, repeat *not*, to use the phone in the room. Don't call *anyone*. Certainly not from your room. They'll keep a record of all your calls, and you'd better figure the cops are going to be seeing it sooner or later.

"We'll be needing to talk, but I'll call you, or if you do need to call, call me *from a pay phone*. For now don't worry about it. Any questions?"

"Yeah, a couple. First, why am I doing this?"

I nodded. "I guess you deserve to know that."

I got his eye. He looked more worried than ever. He looked awful. But he listened.

"The cops want to pick you up, Jim. They've got every reason to think you killed Nick. It was your gun, you're the last person known to have touched it. Plus, you're known to have been heading for Nick's office at the time Nick got it.

"The cops know all that. Put yourself in their shoes. What would you be doing right now if you were them?"

Jim's smile was wan. "I'd be picking up Jim Kearney for murder."

I nodded. "Damn straight, you would. And that's what they're attempting to do right now.

"So we're going to keep you out of circulation for a while. And right now I've got to get back there before a certain cop makes mincemeat out of the Bishop and Sister Ernestine. Second question?"

Jim frowned. "What about *A Thousand Clowns*? We're dark tonight and tomorrow night, thank God. But we've got a line reading scheduled for this afternoon. And Wednesday night there's a show. Shouldn't I call Lenny?"

I was in a hurry and Jim was giving me a bad case of information overload. "Hell, how should I know? Okay, call him. But no one else—till you hear from me. And make damn sure you don't tell him where you are or that you talked to me. Just tell him you're sick and you'll get back to him. And don't talk to anyone else!" I saw a look in his eye and knew exactly what it meant. "No, you *can't* call Dinker! I'll call her, Jim, first chance I get. Now don't worry. And stay put!"

Jim had no more questions. I got out and he sped away. I headed back on foot for the mansion. I wondered what it was going to feel like to be facing a friend like Parker from the other side of the law.

16

T H E patrol car had either left or gone into hiding. Anyway, it wasn't outside the mansion. I *did* see something that surprised me, parked eight or ten cars west of the mansion: Inspector Kessler's Chevy. I stopped and gave it the once-over. No question about it: police-issue plates and the department parking sticker on the windshield. So we were being honored with a visit from an Inspector. How exciting.

As I entered the house I could hear Kessler's familiar voice drifting down the hall from the Bishop's office.

I went straight into Regan's office without knocking, took in the scene and grinned.

Kessler and Regan were over by the south window, Kessler raving, Regan bored. Parker, looking as useless as a eunuch in a whorehouse, was looking on. He gave me a smile, then realized he and I weren't buddies any more and tried to turn it into a scowl. Kessler's back was to me, so he went right on ranting.

". . . can't get away with it, Bishop, and you know it! I know for a fact you were with both the victim and this guy Kearney last Friday night. That's less than twenty-four hours before the murder! For you to tell us you can't say anything without Davey present is, well, it's just—"

Kessler, groping for a word, noticed something different in the atmosphere and turned around. Seeing me got him even madder. He and I tend to rub each other the wrong way.

I took the opportunity to offer some hospitality I figured the Bishop had forgotten. "Nice to see you, Inspector, Joe. Can I get you gentlemen a drink? Coffee? Tea? Me?"

No one laughed, least of all Kessler. "Forget the humor, Davey. And forget the drinks." His salt-and-pepper beard was trembling the way it used to when it was all black. When I worked for him and one of the three thousand things that get him mad got him mad.

"What I *would* like," he said, pinning me with his eyes in the old familiar way, "is an honest answer to some questions. The Bishop's an honest man—unlike certain other individuals I could name—so he's avoiding answering by telling me you're the one I need to talk to about Jim Kearney. Well, you're here now. So talk. I need to know where Jim Kearney is. And I'd appreciate an honest answer."

I shrugged. "Jim Kearney? Sorry, Inspector. I haven't got the slightest idea where he is." You're thinking that was a bald-faced lie. Wrong. Depending on traffic, Jim could have been at the tollbooth on the Manhattan side of the tunnel, halfway through, or all the way into New Jersey. Now, if Kessler'd asked when I last *saw* the guy . . .

"So when did you see him last?" Damn.

I glanced at Regan but he was no help. He was staring out the window, probably running a fresh inventory on Sally Mueller's garbage. Nothing for it but tell the truth. Part of it, anyway. I took a breath. "Jim Kearney? About ten minutes ago."

Kessler glared at me. "Ten minutes ago." He turned his glare on the Bishop. "So you two helped a murderer escape."

Regan didn't answer. It was up to me to defend our honor. "That's a little strong, isn't it, Inspector? I mean, he hasn't been convicted. Or even indicted."

"Don't give me that, Davey! We have the gun. And we've learned a great deal about Mr. Kearney in the last twenty minutes." He smiled menacingly. "Not only does the murder weapon belong to him, he was in the building where the murder took place, at exactly the time it happened. And the victim is his half-brother, who he just learned stood to take away half his inheritance. So *you* tell *me*: are we looking for the wrong guy?"

Regan seemingly lost interest in whatever was out back and looked at Kessler. I thought he might jump in but he didn't.

"So I take it," Kessler went on, "he was just here?" I nodded. Kessler's tone turned sarcastic. "And he left just before we came, hmm? What a bad break for us." He held me with his eyes. "Well, Davey me boy, it'll be a bad break for *you* if we find out that he left on your advice. If you gave him such advice, of course, it'd be my duty to inform the state about it next time your license comes up for renewal."

He didn't let go of my eye and I didn't blink, though he wasn't making it easy. "So, Davey. Any idea where we ought to start looking for him?" His voice was dangerously soft. I was starting to sweat.

Regan finally stepped in, much to my relief. "Inspector Kessler," he snapped. "Threatening Mr. Goldman is hardly in your best interest at this point. You know Mr. Goldman as well as I do, so I needn't remind you that he relishes challenge. And danger." Kessler looked at him, impassive.

"Now," Regan continued, "you are looking for information. Neither of us has expressed any unwillingness to talk. Unfortunately, you just missed Mr. Kearney. And neither of us knows where he is at the moment. Why aren't you looking for him instead of badgering us?"

Kessler waved it away. "We *are* looking for him. We've had an APB out on him ever since we got that registration report from the FBI an hour ago."

I nodded to myself. One reason I'd sent Jim across the state line was just that. The police forces of Newark and New York cooperate with each other, but having him over there might slow the search a little. At least it would have when I was a cop.

Regan nodded. "All right. We'll be happy to answer such questions as we can."

Kessler stared at him. "You say you *will* answer questions? You just said you—"

"I said I would stand mute till Mr. Goldman returned from his errand. Now that he's here, we'll be happy to answer questions." He fingered his pectoral cross and watched Kessler without appearing to. "I suppose you want to know who wrote that note."

Kessler frowned and glanced at Parker. "Note? What note? Was there a note, Parker?" Parker, looking suspiciously at Regan, shook his head. Kessler turned back to Regan. "What note are you talking about, Bishop?"

Regan threw me a glance and went back to Kessler. "Your men found no note taped to the glass door? Then perhaps we have some valuable new information for you, Inspector. Which, naturally, we'll be happy to share." He got my eye. "Unfortunately, Mr. Goldman has an important appointment he needs to keep. Perhaps you should be on your way, David?"

"Oh yeah. Sure." What was he talking about? Regan helped me out, fingering and studying his pectoral cross as he did so.

"That letter, David, to Father Kilian. I think you should hand-deliver it."

It took me a second—then I got it. Father Kilian McDonnell, a

friend of Regan's, was a monk of St. John's Abbey. St. John's Abbey—
in St. Cloud, Minnesota. Regan was using this as his way of repeating
his earlier suggestion that I go to St. Cloud to learn more about the
murder weapon.

"Fine. Glad to, Bishop," I said. "Should I go right now?"

"By all means. I don't want the others to reach him before we do."

"Nope." I bit back a smile. "I know you don't."

Kessler—one of the "others"—was looking from Regan to me suspiciously, but had no idea what we were talking about.

"Then," Regan said, "in your absence, you have no problem with
my sharing anything we know with the Inspector?"

I glanced at Kessler, then at Parker. "Not a bit. Our life is an open
book." Kessler scowled. He knew we were up to something but not
what the something was. I turned back to Regan. "I'll call you if I
have a problem."

I dashed up to my room, wondering what had happened to that
note Nick Carney wrote—or did he? Whatever had happened to it
had happened before the cops got there Saturday afternoon. Blake's
dumb, but no one's dumb enough to miss something like that.

I stuffed some fresh underwear and a clean shirt into my small
attaché case along with a razor, toothbrush, some toothpaste and a
small stick of deodorant, turning it into a makeshift overnight bag.
Normally I don't like to travel that light, but this wasn't normal. I
didn't want the cops to know I was leaving town, and I knew for sure
Kessler had left someone outside to keep an eye on me and follow
me wherever I went.

I stood, frowning down at the attaché case. Did I need anything
else? Yes. I pulled out my address book and memorized two numbers.
Now I was ready.

17

I HUNG a left as soon as I hit the sidewalk and hoofed it westward toward Eleventh. I sighted two cops right away. It's not unusual to have loiterers in that neighborhood. But when you have two people loitering within twenty feet of each other—that's unusual. And when both strangers get the simultaneous urge to meander along in the direction you're heading the minute you come out of your house, well . . .

I took mental snapshots of both cops. He was tall and slender in sweat clothes and Nike running shoes. She was young and pretty and efficient-looking, despite the ponytail. But picking them out didn't make me overconfident. It's an old cop trick (I've pulled it plenty of times myself), to give the tailee someone obvious, let him shake the tail loose, at which point it's duck soup for the A-team who are really doing the tailing. Knowing how bad Kessler and Parker wanted Kearney, I wouldn't have been surprised if they'd had *three* teams out. But I had an airtight plan to shake the whole bunch, seen and unseen—*if* Chet Rozanski was where he was supposed to be and was willing to play ball.

I debated briefly whether I should even bother; why not lead them right to the airport? I mean, what difference did it make if Kessler knew I was going to St. Cloud? But the thought didn't last. I needed in the worst way to dig something up that would give Jim an edge. When someone had gone to so much trouble to set him up for a very big fall, it was going to take a lot of ingenuity (mine) and brainpower (Regan's) to clear him. I needed to be able to move around St. Cloud without worrying about cops getting in the way.

I rounded the corner on Eleventh and grabbed the same phone I'd called Regan from just an hour before. The ponytailed female took up a position across the street where she could observe me in the reflection of a shop window. The guy slipped into a bar. I approved of their technique.

My first call was to Mary Cowan, a good friend who also happens to be a travel agent. I had her book me on the nonstop to Minneapolis leaving LaGuardia in an hour and a quarter—just enough time to shake the tail and make the flight.

Then the crucial call: one of the two numbers I'd memorized: Chet Rozanski's new number. I wondered how hard he'd be to reach now that he was TV's Roving Police Reporter.

Just the previous month, Chet had been lured away from the Manhattan *Dispatch*, where, over a twenty-three-year span, he'd worked his way up to Crime Editor. Channel 54 had offered him more money and more perks and he'd grabbed the chance.

Chet and I go back a dozen years or so, back to my days as a cop. Since going on my own, I've often found him a useful source of background information. In return I've supplied him with several hot scoops.

One of the perks of his new job had particular interest for me at the moment: access to the Black Beauty, Channel 54's big black van, chock-full of all the latest high-tech gadgetry every TV station needs. At the moment I was less interested in the gadgetry than in where it was garaged: in the basement of Chet's building, away from the prying eyes of the police.

I hoped to catch him in his office. "WNYC," came the cheerful, feminine voice. "May I help you?"

"I hope so," I said. "Chet Rozanski, please. David Goldman calling."

"Oh," she said brightly. "Mr. Rozanski's on location right now. May I patch you through?" I told her that would be dandy.

In less than thirty seconds I had Chet. Sounding like he was talking out of the bottom of a well, but Chet. "Davey! What can I do for you, pal?"

"What can you do for me? Where's the surly guy I've always known and hated? The guy with all the deadlines. Has success spoiled Chet Rozanski?"

"Hey, I've got to justify my salary, man. Got to cultivate all the hoods, crooks and pimps I know in hopes of getting leads to stories. So give. You in jail, or what?"

"No, I'm not in jail. But I am on to a story that may put someone there. Know about the Carney shooting?"

"Hey, who do you think you're talking to? Charley Stupid? Of course I know about Carney! Mob hit, right?"

"Wrong. This afternoon's *Dispatch*, somehow recovering from the loss of its ace, will tell about how diligent police work uncovered the real murderer—the victim's long-lost half-brother from Minnesota." I went on to give Chet five minutes of background. He was agog.

"This is great, Davey! So what's *your* connection?"

"I'm working for the brother. I'm the guy that's got him stashed away somewhere secret. And—no, hold it, Chet, I'm coming to the good part. I'm also the guy that can get you an exclusive phone interview with the brother. Who just happens to be innocent, by the way. That's on no less an authority than a certain auxiliary bishop here in the archdiocese. I can get you said interview in return for a tiny little favor."

"Uh-oh, here it comes." The voice had turned surly but I knew Chet would go a long, long way to get a talk with Jim.

I laughed. "Now, settle down, it's no biggie. See, I need to get to Minnesota to dig up some stuff. But I've got company at the moment."

Chet chuckled. "Do you mean what I think you mean?"

"Yeah. Kessler's got me surrounded with tails, hoping I'll lead them to my guy. Right now I've got a half-dozen of them circling me like sharks with blood in the water. So—"

Chet was loving it. "And you want to lose them before you head off to Minnesota, right? Say no more, pal. I was afraid you'd ask me to have Commissioner Rawlins invite you to his house for dinner or something. This is a piece of cake. You sure that's all you want?"

He proceeded to give me instructions and directions. That done, he said, "Okay. Now, when do I get this phone call from your client?"

"Barring anything unusual, you'll be talking to him before I get to your place." I hung up, glanced at my watch and called the Traveler's Inn. Jim was on the line at the hotel operator's first ring, which didn't surprise me. What else did he have to do but answer my phone calls? He sounded depressed.

I tried to cheer him up by telling him where I was going and promising to give his parents his love.

He perked up a little. "Give Mom and Dad my best and tell them not to worry." He gave me directions from the Minneapolis airport to his parents' home.

"It's actually out a ways from town, on a wooded lot between

Luxemburg and St. Augusta. Sort of secluded. But with these directions, you won't have any trouble."

I asked him if he'd called anyone. "Just Lenny. He wanted to know what was going on, where I was. I did what you said, told him I was sick, I'd call him tomorrow, but to get the understudy ready. And that I didn't know when I'd be back. He wasn't very happy."

Rosen's state of mind didn't concern me. "Okay. Now I need you to make another call." I told him about Rozanski. "Don't tell him where you are, Jim. He'll try to get it out of you, but don't let him. I trust Chet, but what he doesn't know won't hurt him—or us. When he runs that interview, the cops are going to be all over him like fleas on a dog. And we'll all do better if he can just tell them he doesn't have the foggiest where you were calling from.

"Now all I want you to tell him is what happened Saturday. Just tell him the truth. Answer anything he asks, except about today. That's our secret. Okay?"

He didn't sound happy but he agreed. "What about Dinker? Lenny promised to call her, but she'll be worried anyway. Can't I call her?"

I was adamant. "*I'll* call her. I don't want you making any more phone calls than you absolutely have to."

After we hung up, I flagged a cab and gave the driver the address of Channel 54. As we screeched northward, a nondescript Chevy pulled onto Eleventh from Thirty-seventh Street, and Ponytail jumped in. I didn't see her partner. He was either driving the Chevy or had his own mode of transportation. Didn't matter.

I paid off the cabby in front of 355 East Thirtieth, a seven-story office building. Its big *Channel 54* sign looked out of place in that nondescript neighborhood. My followers were probably wondering what I was doing there. Keeping to Chet's instructions, I went in and approached the pretty receptionist.

"I think Mr. Rozanski may have left instructions."

Her expression went from bored to very friendly. "Name, please?" I told her. Her smile widened. "Could I see some identification?" She studied it, looked up at me and winked. She nodded to a door at the far end of the room.

"Right through there, Mr. Goldman. Down the hall to the very end. Go through the door marked Private, and take the stairs down to the garage. The van will be waiting. Jodi Nakamura will be your driver. Mr. Rozanski said to tell you she'll take you wherever you say."

I nodded gratefully. "And if anyone asks for me—"

She grinned. "You just asked directions to Mr. Rozanski's office."

I grinned back. "You show promise. Tell Chet to give you a raise."

"Thank you! I'll tell him," she called after me as I headed for the door. Out of the corner of my eye I saw Ponytail watching me through the door I'd come in. Their next move would be to surround the building, covering every exit. Again: good technique. But sometimes the best technique in the world won't get the job done.

The garage was tiny, barely big enough for the van to turn around. Tiny also was Jodi Nakamura, a tidy little package wrapped in a peasant blouse, miniskirt and pumps. She smiled and gave me a warm handshake, then opened the right-hand door of the black van and closed it after me. That's carrying chivalry a bit far for my taste, but I was in no position to complain. She ran around, got behind the wheel with a flash of trim, elegant legs and flicked her beautiful eyes my way. "Where to, Mr. Goldman?"

I made a quick change of plans. I'd intended to take the Black Beauty only as far as the nearest cabstand, since all I needed was to lose my pursuers. But the idea of my own chauffeur was too luxurious to give up so quickly. "LaGuardia," I commanded.

The van roared into life and, with some screeching of tires, we headed up the ramp for the streets of Manhattan. As we approached street level and open air, I slid to the floor—probably an excess of caution, what with the tinted glass all around, but it did give me an excellent view of my chauffeur's legs. Her tiny feet danced enchantingly from pedal to pedal as she negotiated some sharp turns. She accelerated eastward on Thirty-second, then screeched to a halt.

"You can get up whenever you get tired of the view," she said dryly. "No one's on our tail. And here's the tunnel."

"What do you mean, view?" I demanded, getting off the floor and back into my seat. "I'm all business, Jodi." I brushed myself off.

"Yeah, sure you are," she grinned, pitching a token into the hopper. "So now that you know my size and brand of pantyhose, my birthday's next week."

Before we reached LaGuardia, I had her address, phone number and various other pertinent data—not including her age, which remained classified, but which I estimated at twenty-four. On important stuff like that, I'm seldom far off.

18

TH E flight to Minneapolis was uneventful. The window seat Mary Cowan had got me gave me the opportunity to eyeball a lot of country I'd never seen before. We were over Canada for a minute or two, according to the pilot, so I can now say I've actually been outside the U.S., if flying over it at 37,000 feet counts.

I also got to see the Mississippi River, which we crossed thirty seconds before touchdown. From two thousand feet up it didn't look all that impressive, though I was surprised that a river that small could make it all the way to the Gulf of Mexico.

The pretty redhead at Avis who advised me about my risks in refusing the deductible impressed me. In fact, I was sizing her up for a date when I saw the wedding ring.

"Heck," I complained. "The best ones are always taken."

Her eyes widened. "Oh? Isn't the Monte Carlo all right? I could upgrade you to a—what are you doing?"

I was putting my fingertip on her wedding band. "The best ones are always taken," I repeated. She lowered her eyes and a dimple appeared. The flush on her cheeks made her blue eyes shine even more.

"Would you like me to tell you where to go?" she murmured.

"Naw, just give me directions."

I headed west on 494, fighting the late-afternoon sun. The suburbs of Minneapolis are not that different from the suburbs of New York, I guess, except a lot newer and cleaner. I prefer the ones in New York.

I hooked into 94 and continued into the sun. By the time I reached the St. Augusta exit, I'd reached a firm conclusion: all towns in Minnesota are named after either a saint, a lake or a home built by Thomas Jefferson.

For a state with ten thousand lakes, though, I didn't see many. The few I saw would've fit comfortably into Central Park.

I got lost as soon as I got off the interstate. Jim had assured me, "You can see the interstate from our backyard." Trouble was, I couldn't see their back yard from the interstate. Or from anywhere else. I tried improvising, once I saw my scribbled directions weren't working. But when I passed the same bowling alley for the third time, I had to face facts: I needed help.

Pulled into a gas station and a beefy kid in an SCSU T-shirt sauntered over.

"Fill 'er up?"

I rolled my eyes. That expression hasn't been used in New York since the nineteen-sixties. Maybe Minnesota was in a time warp.

"No thanks," I said, enunciating as distinctly as I could. "I think I'm lost. Know where St. Augusta Hills subdivision is?"

The kid ran thick fingers through his brush cut and squinted knowingly into the sun. "Sure. Know where the Persian Club is?"

Oddly enough, I did. I'd passed it three times, most recently about a minute ago. I nodded.

"Okay, hang a left at the Persian Club, go about half a mile, and watch for the sign on your right. May be hard to see with all the foliage, but keep an eye out. Says 'St. Augusta Hills.' Pull in there. Most of the homes are out of sight." He grinned. "In more ways than one! The road keeps winding around and up the hill. The homes are all on that road. Which one you looking for?"

"One-six-five-hundred," I said, reading from my notes. "The Kearneys."

"Oh, sure." The kid nodded. "They're doing some work up there. Putting on an addition. It'll be the third—no, fourth house you pass. Look for it on the left."

Not many secrets in this burg, I thought as I pulled out. Maybe I should have just asked the kid to tell me all about the gun. Save me a lot of time and effort.

His directions sure beat Jim's. Less than six minutes later I was in the Kearneys' long, curving driveway.

The Bishop's house is a mansion. In fact, technically, it's an "episcopal mansion." (Which I don't understand, by the way; it's never had any connection with the Episcopal Church.) But if the Bishop's is a mansion, the Kearneys' was a palace. Even bigger than Sally's parents' house on Long Island. It sprawled all over the top of a hill. Lots of chimneys and two-story windows, plus a four-car garage. Jim must have thought twice about walking away from a spread like that.

I got out of the car and strode to the door, checking my watch. Not quite seven-thirty. Rather, not quite six-thirty, Central Daylight Time.

I pushed the doorbell. Its ringing was followed by Mike's faint voice: "I've got it." The early odds were roughly two to one that I'd be talking to Nick's killer within the next thirty seconds.

I adjusted my face accordingly.

19

MIKE Kearney had changed since I'd last seen him three days before. He looked pale and shrunken.

It took him a second to recognize me. When he did, his eyes widened and his face came alive. "Dave Goldman!" He gave me a bone-crushing handshake and pulled me into the spacious front hall. "God, this is incredible! We were just talking about you! *Peggy!*"

The last was a bellow that echoed through the cavernous house. Sunlight filled the high-ceilinged front hallway through the twenty-foot windows to the west. The hallway went through into a sort of solarium on the other side. The solarium also had a twenty-foot ceiling and plenty of tall windows all the way around. Sort of a giant sitting room, with a three- or four-mile view. Kearney led me in there, roaring his wife's name again as we went.

"Have a seat, Dave," he said, and began to pace. "Can you tell us where Jim is? Peggy and I were just talking to Dinker on the phone and no one knows where he is. Dinker thinks you might know."

I looked around at all the chairs and couches in the room, wondering if there was any way to narrow the selection process. Before I came to a decision, I caught sight of a bar in the corner with what looked like a photo gallery behind it.

Remembering that Regan had wanted a snapshot of Jordan and the Kearneys, I strolled over to give it a look-see. There were lots of photos pinned to a large corkboard: Mike, Peggy, Jim and lots of friends.

One in particular interested me. A five-by-seven color snapshot of Mike and Peggy Kearney and Jerry Jordan, standing on a golf course, drivers in hands, leis around necks, smiling into the camera. Undoubtedly taken by one of those guys that inhabit the vacation spots of the world, standing around likely places, camera ready, looking for tourists to fleece. I was studying it when Peggy came rushing in.

Her voice was peevish at first. "For God's *sake*, what *is* it, Mike? You don't have to—oh!" I had turned to face her. "I'm sorry, I guess I didn't hear the doorbell." Suddenly her hand flew to her mouth. "Oh! You're Mr. Goldman!" Her voice became accusing. "Where's Jim?" Her dark eyes were intense and worried.

When I didn't answer immediately, she turned apologetic. "I'm sorry. Dinker says Lenny Rosen thinks you know where he is. Is he in jail? Tell me the truth."

I was ready with an answer. I should have been. I'd had four hours to think about it. But before I said anything I wanted that photo. I held it up.

"This is a great picture of the two of you and Mr. Jordan! Hawaii?"

"Maui," Mike rasped. "Jerry talked us into going. Biggest damn waste of time and money I ever—"

Peggy wasn't going to stand for that. "It was *not*, Mike! We had a perfectly wonderful time."

Mike had an answer to that but I jumped in. "Well, Jim was telling me how much he liked this picture. He asked me if I'd bring it to him. He'd like it for his living room."

They stared at me. "Jim likes it?" Peggy said. "He's never even seen it!"

"Sure he has," I lied. "Last week, when he was here. He mentioned it specifically."

Kearney shrugged. "Sure, take it to him. But could we get back to the matter of where the hell he is?"

I was ready. "He's okay. I think he wanted to get away for a day or two and get himself straight. I guess you heard, Nick Carney died."

I was watching both of them as I said it, but their reactions gave away nothing. They both nodded.

"Yes," said the mother. "Murdered. So sad. Please sit down, Mr. Goldman. What can we get you to drink?"

I sat down, slipping the photo into my jacket pocket. I looked up at Peggy. "Nothing, thank you, ma'am. Let me tell you why I came."

They perked up. Peggy moved in; Mike's eyes bored into mine.

"Jim wants me to investigate Nick's murder for him, Mr. Kearney. Maybe he told you, I'm a private investigator."

Neither parent seemed overdelighted at that piece of information. Peggy started slightly; Mike's eyes got a little colder. "So why are you here?"

I ignored his tone. "I'd just like to ask you both a few questions."

"What the hell about, Goldman? Can it help Jim?"

I shrugged. "I don't know; maybe. But that *is* the point, Mr. Kearney. To help your son."

Peggy bit her lip. Kearney said, "So you're going to help Jim." He went to the bar, grabbed a litre of Chivas and poured what looked like a triple shot into a tumbler. "Mother?" he inquired without turning.

"Nothing right now, darling," Peggy answered softly, without taking her eyes off me. Kearney came back, glass in hand.

"So. You want to ask some questions. I guess that's all right. Okay with you, Mother?" He took a sip of the scotch, made a face.

Her answer was barely audible. "Of course."

"Good!" I said heartily and thought fast. "Have you heard about the gun?"

"Did they find it?" Mike demanded.

"How did *you* know about it?" Peggy said simultaneously.

One of my worst faults is, I'll ask a question and then not listen to the answer. To this question I had *two* answers and didn't really listen to either one. "Yeah, they found it, Mr. Kearney." I held him with my eyes. "Did you know it's registered in your name?"

"Well," Kearney said, puzzled and irritated, "of *course* it's in my name! Well, mine and Jim's. I *told* them that."

I was getting confused. "Told who?"

"The Chief, when I reported it missing." He glanced at his wife. "And you haven't answered Peggy's question: how did *you* know about it?"

I shook my head, more confused than ever. "The police told me. How did *you* hear?" I raised a hand; something had just clicked. "Hold it! Did you say you reported it missing?"

Mike stared at me, started to answer and closed his mouth. He scowled. "Let's start over from scratch. Sounds like we're talking about two different things."

"Agreed. You start. You said you reported a gun missing?" He nodded. "What gun and when?"

"My Colt. Last Wednesday night. The day after Jim flew back to New York." I must have reacted, because Kearney threw me a puzzled glance. "Okay, I shouldn't really call it *my* gun, I guess. I gave it to Jim a number of years ago for one of his birthdays. But it's the sidearm I had in Vietnam, so I guess I still think of it as mine. It's registered in both our names—Jim's and mine—so maybe that gives me a right. But that was only for the law: he was a minor and I couldn't legally register any gun in his name alone."

Kearney sighed. "Anyway, somebody stole it last Wednesday." His eyes widened. "Wait a minute! You didn't even know it was missing, did you? God almighty, are you here because—? Is that the same gun that killed Nick?"

I nodded. "Yeah, sounds like it."

Kearney's eyes took on a sly look. "Well, then, Jim couldn't have done it."

I looked at him.

"Look, Goldman," Kearney said harshly. "I know what you're thinking. You're thinking Jim brought that gun back to New York with him. Well, he didn't."

"No?"

"No! Because I *saw* the gun in the cabinet Tuesday night, *after* Jim went back to New York. Saw it, hell! I had it in my hands! I cleaned the damn thing!"

20

THIS sounded good—maybe too good. "Jim's gun?" I repeated, holding his eye. "The Colt?"

Kearney met my gaze without blinking. "Damn right, the Colt! See, I told Jim to clean that gun, and mine, that morning. When I got home from work Tuesday night, I checked 'em and he'd done his usual half-assed job. So I took 'em both out and cleaned 'em." Mike raised a triumphant finger. "By which time Jim was already back in New York!"

I nodded, thinking. "Did you take him to the airport?"

"Naw, he had a car."

"A rental?"

Kearney's scowl deepened. "Naw, one of ours. And Jim screwed *that* up, too!" Kearney took a breath. "It's like this, Dave. KPI—that's my company, Kearney Pharmaceutical—we have a couple of cars for our salesmen. They go all over the country. When they leave on a flight somewhere, they leave the car at the airport and Reta—that's my secretary—Reta takes down the location where they're parked. Next guy comes back from somewhere, he calls Reta and gets the location. Picks up the car."

I frowned at him. "How do they switch keys?"

Kearney waved a hand. "They don't. We've got ten or twelve sets of keys for both cars. All the salesmen have their own. They just give Reta the mileage so we can keep track of who's using them. And who's taking joy rides around the Cities. I don't much like *that*, I can tell you." I had a strong feeling I wouldn't have wanted to be the salesman Kearney caught taking a joy ride in a company car.

"Anyway, when Jim decided to come here last week, he called Reta and arranged to use one of the cars."

I frowned. "Did Jim have his own keys?"

Kearney shook his head. "Naw, Reta told one of the salesmen to leave his keys at AirAmerica when he flew out Monday. Jim picked them up there." Kearney scowled and shook his head. "But then he went and left them in the damn car Tuesday, can you believe that?"

"Jim did? When he flew out?"

Kearney nodded wearily. "Kid hasn't got a brain in his head, I'll swear. I've got no idea how he memorizes all those lines whenever he's in a play. He can't even remember where his ass is one day to the next."

"But I take it no one stole the car?"

Kearney shrugged. "No, no one took it. Damn car was locked. Jim called me Wednesday night to tell me the keys were missing. He said he might have left them in the car. Wasn't the first time. Apologized like hell.

"So I had one of my guys drive over to the airport on Thursday. He found the car, keys in it. No problem. Just another minor aggravation."

I turned a page in the notebook. "Okay. Back to the gun. You're sure it was there Tuesday night. Right? So when did you first notice it missing?"

Kearney rolled his eyes irritably. "You listening? Wednesday night, like I said!" He shrugged and quieted down. "See, I get nervous whenever there's lots of strangers in the house. And I knew there'd been two crews of workmen in here that day. So, soon as I got home, I went straight to the gun cabinet. And Jim's Colt was missing."

I referred to my notebook. "So it must have been stolen sometime between Tuesday night and Wednesday night." I thought of something. "Could I see the gun cabinet?"

Kearney eyed me, glanced at Peggy and gave an abrupt nod. "Sure. Come on." He looked at Peggy. "Be right back, Mother. This way."

I followed him down half a flight of stairs, through another sitting room with another fireplace—all those chimneys weren't just ornamental—and down another half-flight of stairs, the smell of fresh paint growing stronger as we went. The second set of stairs led down into a room that could have been a den or a game room or a study. Whatever it was, it was a man's room.

And it was going to take quite a man to reassemble it. The walls were freshly painted and everything was out of place. Several chairs and a couch were shoved into one corner, along with some hunting trophies—a couple of moose heads, both with huge sets of antlers; a deer's head, also with antlers, not as big; a bear's head; and several kinds of stuffed birds.

"Excuse the mess," Kearney rasped. "We just finished adding on to this end of the house. The workmen only finished on Friday, and Peggy's decorator's been slow getting out here to put things back in place. This is my den."

The gun cabinet took up most of the right-hand wall. Its paneling matched the wall paneling, or would when its shiny newness wore off. Fifteen or twenty guns were displayed behind a pane of thick glass: automatics, revolvers and a few rifles. I recognized only a couple. Mike leveled a finger at the only empty spot in the display—a couple of wooden pegs. "That's where Jim's gun should be."

I studied the combination lock on the glass door. It looked solid. I gave the dial a spin. It had the tight, precise feel of expensive equipment. I felt the bolt, checked the action, found it solid. It didn't appear to have been tampered with.

"They dusted the whole cabinet for prints," Mike observed. "Chief told me later, nothing doing."

I looked at the cabinet a while, thinking. I turned to Kearney. "Any ammunition missing when the gun was taken?"

He shook his head. "Same thing the Chief asked. No. But the gun was loaded. Full clip. Seven rounds and one in the chamber."

As we headed back to the solarium, Mike said, "I still can't believe that can be the same gun that killed—"

He stopped and turned. His eyes were wide. "My God! You think *I* did it, don't you?" He had turned very pale.

"No!" I said too quickly. "I don't—"

"You've *got* to! You don't think *Jim* did. Of course he didn't. He couldn't have. But—if that's the gun that did it—it had to be him or me! Who else could have? I mean, if that's the gun that did it!" He shook his head. "God almighty! It just hit me! What am I going to do?" His face was gray and he'd suddenly aged about ten years. He looked less fearsome than I'd ever seen him. He turned away, then had a thought.

"You, uh, you know about me and Nick, don't you." It was a statement, not a question.

I looked him in the eye. "I know he was your son by your first marriage, if that's what you mean."

He met my gaze. "And you're probably wondering why I'm not even going to his funeral."

I shrugged. "None of my business." But Kearney needed to explain.

"See, Peggy doesn't know anything about it. I guess Jim told you that." I nodded. "She never knew I was married before. I always kept Mona—that's my first wife—out of my life. And I never wrote Mona directly—always through Jerry.

"I cut myself off from all that. It was part of my life before and I wasn't proud of it. I didn't want anything to do with Nick from the time Mona and I divorced. I always hoped she'd remarry so Nick could have a real father. I guess I haven't been much of a father."

Mike sighed. Then he glared at me. "But dammit, I *didn't* kill him. And now, with that gun showing up missing . . . and me being there in New York when it happened . . ."

"Hold it, Mike!" I said sharply. "I don't think you did it. And I don't think Jim did either. So let's try to figure out who did. The best way to start is for me to ask you a bunch of questions. Once I've got some answers, we can try to see where we're at."

21

WE headed back for the solarium. At Mike's call Peggy came bustling in, drying her hands on her apron. "All done?" she smiled. "I was working on dinner. I hope you can stay for—"

"Sit down, Mother," Mike interrupted. Peggy looked at him, opened her mouth and closed it. She sat down.

Mike took a breath. "Okay, look. Let's not worry about dinner. Goldman here's going to ask us some questions. We're going to try to figure this thing out, who took that gun last Wednesday."

He turned to me. "All right, Goldman. Ask ahead. Let's get to the bottom of this."

I spent the next hour asking questions and taking notes. Mike did ninety percent of the answering—though the missus wasn't shy about throwing in her two cents' worth whenever the urge moved her.

As we talked, the sun set and Peggy got up and turned on some lamps. I got plenty of information into the notebook and the atmosphere stayed reasonably pleasant.

"Like I told you, it was Wednesday night," said Mike. "I got home from the office a little before six and checked it right away—can't tell you why. I'd just cleaned the Colt and the Luger the night before, and I had the damnedest feeling that one of those two guns was going to be missing. Had a funny feeling all that day."

He took a sip of scotch.

"See, I get nervous with all the workmen. The house has been swarming with them for months. They've—"

"Not *months*, Mike!" Peggy interrupted. "They started the week before July Fourth and they finished last Friday. That's four weeks. And the house wasn't *swarming* with them! There were the carpenters, the plumbers, the—"

"Yeah, yeah," Mike cut in. "And goddamn princes, every one of 'em, I'm sure. But the thing is, Peggy, we've got some valuable stuff around here, and whenever there's outsiders running around, you worry."

"*You* worry," Peggy snorted.

Mike looked at her. "Well, that dry-waller pissed me off, whoever he was. Tall sandy-haired guy, don't know his name, he—"

"Don Soukup," Peggy sniffed. It didn't sound like Don Soukup was a favorite with *either* Kearney.

"Yeah, I guess so," Mike growled. "Anyway, he made some kind of comment—trying to be funny, I guess—about what a nice set of weapons I had, you could start a war, something like that. So I was careful not to let him see me work the combination of the cabinet whenever I got the guns out."

"So Jim left on Tuesday. And you're sure he didn't take the gun with him, because you cleaned it that night, after he'd already gone?"

Kearney nodded. "Then the gun," I went on, "must have been taken either Tuesday night or sometime during the day on Wednesday. Is that right?"

Kearney nodded again. "And no one but Peggy and me were here Tuesday night. So it had to be stolen on Wednesday. I told all this to the police when I reported it. Last Wednesday night."

I looked at him. "So who was in the house on Wednesday?"

Mike looked at Peggy. She spoke up. "Too many folks," she sighed. "That's for sure. First the dry-wall people. I was so furious with Don Soukup I was ready to spit! I'd told him they absolutely had to be finished on Tuesday, and he *promised* me they would. He *promised*! I had the whole schedule worked out like clockwork. Then Don screwed it up. And that's why last Wednesday the house was crawling with people. Coming and going. Must have been as many as a dozen in here sometimes, in and out.

"My word, between the painters and the dry-wallers, plus a couple of the plumbers coming back to fix this or that, it was like Grand Central Station."

"Yeah," Mike grumbled. "And that's the day it happened, you know. I still think one of those guys took it." He looked at me, then looked away. I sensed he was thinking the same thing I was: "But if one of the workmen took the Colt, how did it get to New York and kill Nick Carney?"

Peggy quickly pointed out the other flaw in the workmen theory. "Oh, Mike, how could one of those guys have stolen it? They didn't know the combination to the cabinet."

"I don't know." He shrugged helplessly. Then turned to me, pinning me with his fierce eyebrows. "What I *do* know, Goldman, is this: that gun was right where it was supposed to be Tuesday night. I cleaned it. No doubt about it."

He glanced at Peggy. "And next night, I check again and it's gone."

I was jotting fast. "So Wednesday's the day," I said without looking up. Kearney grunted. I went on, still writing, "So what did you do when you discovered it was missing?"

"Notified the police, of course, what do you think? The chief of the St. Cloud police is a friend of ours. Tom Henderson. I called him at home, told him what happened. He said it wasn't in his jurisdiction, strictly speaking, us being way out here in the country, but he'd look into it.

"Well, he called somebody at the sheriff's office and they told him it was no skin off their nose if he wanted to go investigate it, that he should just let them know what was happening. So he came out to the house and we told him all about it. We showed him the cabinet and the registration on the missing gun. He filled out a report, said he'd have to send a missing-gun report to the FBI and that he'd go have a talk with Soukup."

The doorbell rang. Mike frowned at Peggy. "You expecting someone, Mother?"

Peggy frowned back and shook her head. "I'll go see who it is. Excuse me, Mr. Goldman." She left.

"Out here in the country we don't get a lot of drop-in visitors," Mike told me. He cocked his head, trying to hear what was going on at the front door.

A muffled male voice came from that direction. Kearney's face lighted up. "Well, I'll be dammed! Speak of the devil! That's the Chief now!"

I swallowed hard. I wondered what the Chief of Police of St. Cloud, Minnesota, thought about big-city detectives working in his burg without first checking in with the locals.

22

HENDERSON hadn't come alone. The taller, younger man who followed him through the door, Peggy quickly informed us, was Deputy Sheriff Dale Kleinschmidt from the Stearns County Sheriff's Office. I gathered the Deputy was as much of a stranger to Peggy and Mike as he was to me.

Henderson was in his fifties, short, stout, friendly. Big, politician's smile. His wispy white hair formed an almost perfect horseshoe around his shiny dome. A stained brown-and-white tie straggled down the front of his short-sleeved white cotton shirt. A plastic pouch protected his shirt pocket from the weight of pen, pencil, ruler and air-pressure gauge. Brown slacks and Hush Puppies put the finishing touches on the total ensemble. He was obviously not making a strong run for this year's Best Dressed American Male.

Kleinschmidt was younger, taller, more athletic-looking. No tie, shirtsleeves rolled up. As serious as Henderson was jovial.

Neither looked very happy to learn who I was. Henderson's smile froze; Kleinschmidt actually asked to see my P.I. license and gave it a careful scrutiny before handing it back. His eyes were cold.

"Yeah, he's a detective all right," Mike said. "And he knows about the Colt. In fact, he may know some things about it *you* don't."

Kleinschmidt looked at Henderson. "Sorry, Chief, but I think you'd better let me handle this. The water's getting a little deep, and I think a professional approach is what we need right now."

Henderson reddened. "What do you—?"

Kleinschmidt rode over him. "I'm sorry, Tom, that came out wrong. What I mean is, this is unincorporated Stearns County, we've got a murder case to investigate, and I think I'd better handle it." Henderson didn't look happy but he didn't interfere either.

The Deputy turned back to Mike. "The Homicide department in New York City called our office just a little while ago. Your gun was apparently used to murder someone in New York City over the weekend. The New York police are flying an officer out here tomorrow to interview witnesses. And I don't think we ought to be talking to any other outsiders." His blue eyes bored in on me.

"Just what *are* you doing here, Mr. Goldman? And what do you know about the gun? What's your interest in this case?"

I frowned at him, thinking. After a second, the Deputy asked, "Questions too tough for you?"

I shook my head at him. "No, I'm just trying to think of where to start."

Kleinschmidt apparently decided to cut me a little slack. He nodded but didn't take his cold eyes off of me. I leaned back in the overstuffed chair, thinking hard. I needed to come up with some odds in a hurry.

Namely: (a) Did either of these lawmen have any information I might be able to use? (b) If they did, did I have a chance in hell of getting it out of them? And (c) What were my chances of getting pitched in the clink for interfering in police business if I stayed in this house another two minutes? A couple of seconds' consideration led me to a decision: I needed to get the hell out. I smiled at Kleinschmidt.

"Tell you the truth, sir, Mr. Kearney's a little mistaken. I'm not investigating, just looking around, trying to help a friend." I got Kearney's eye. "I was just saying goodbye to Mr. Kearney when you showed up."

I got to my feet. Looks of consternation all over the place. I especially didn't like the look on the Deputy's face. As a one-time lawman, I knew what his problem was and sympathized. Namely, how do you handle a citizen who you're pretty sure is doing something he's got no business doing, but who hasn't, as far as you can prove, broken any laws?

I moved to the door. But Kleinschmidt edged over, half-blocking my way. He held my eye. "That license gives you the right to conduct investigations in New York State, Mr. Goldman. Not Minnesota. So Chief Henderson and I won't be real happy if we run into you again. Know what I mean?"

I looked at him, then at Henderson, who was frowning uncomfortably into the middle distance.

Kleinschmidt raised his eyebrows to be sure I understood. "I mean, in the course of our investigation of this crime. Like, if you were seen talking to witnesses. We do have a thing about obstruction of justice here in Minnesota. It happens to be a crime."

I smiled at him. "But the law surely doesn't prohibit a citizen from asking friendly questions, does it, Deputy? Even in Minnesota?"

He lowered his head and glared at me under his eyebrows. " 'Course not. But there are certain courtesies we like to see observed. I mean, like, have you checked in with any of the local law-enforcement people here? That's normal practice even in New York City, isn't it? I can tell you, it sure is here. And we don't take it kindly when investigators forget."

I nodded, grinning. "Absolutely. But I got here so late in the day, you know? And you certainly wouldn't claim that talking with old friends constitutes obstruction of justice, would you?" Kleinschmidt didn't answer. Just glared.

"Well," I said, moving to edge past him, wondering if he'd let me, "I'll be sure to stop by the station in the morning to report in. You can count on it." Kleinschmidt slid to one side, giving me room to leave.

"Yeah, you do that," he said. "The Chief'll be glad to see you. Where you staying?"

I told him I had no idea, told everyone goodbye and left.

After dinner at the Persian Club—also known as A. J.'s for some reason—I drove around St. Cloud. It's a tiny place—it'd barely make a neighborhood in New York—but big enough to get lost in. Which I did.

Thing is, it's not laid out like a normal city. Both the streets and the avenues are numbered, which is confusing. And the Mississippi runs through it northwest-to-southeast, which makes everything run cockeyed. Though, I'll swear to this, I never saw the river once in the two days I was there.

Anyhow, I got lost. Fortunately, getting lost in St. Cloud doesn't put you in the same peril as getting lost in other places I could name. I mean, there *are* reasons that sane, rational people choose to live in St. Cloud, Minnesota. No roving street gangs, no potheads or winos, no panhandlers or muggers. People even oblige you with directions when asked.

Another nice thing is, no matter how lost you get, all you have to do is keep driving and you'll eventually hit Division Street, the hub of everything. I finally got tired of getting lost, and stopped at the first motel I saw, a Holiday Inn. On Division Street, where else?

Before crashing I looked up Don Soukup in the phone book. Several Soukups but only one "Don"—on 33rd Street. I dialed the number.

Got the usual answering machine. Male voice, flat Minnesota accent. "This is Don Soukup, of Soukup Construction and Rehab. We're not taking calls right now, but if you'll leave a message, I'll try to get back to you. Better yet, try back between seven and eight in the morning."

I hung up, leaving no message. I did leave a six A.M. wake-up, reminding myself that wasn't as early as it seemed, since it'd be seven A.M. New York time. I was probably asleep twenty seconds after my head hit the pillow.

23

I WAS showered, shaved and ready at five to seven, Tuesday morning. Called Soukup again. This time, the phone got picked up on the first ring. Same Minnesota voice as on the answering machine.
"Mr. Soukup?"

"You got him." Breezy and self-assured.

I paused. I'd thought out how I was going to handle it. You really louse yourself up when you start letting ordinary decency get in the way of your job. I cleared my throat authoritatively and came at him with my most official voice, letting him know by my grumpy tone that I was no one to be joshed with.

"Um. Mr. Soukup. This is Mr. Goldman. I'm investigating the theft of a firearm from the residence of one . . ." I paused. ". . . Michael James Kearney of St. Cloud. You are, I believe, aware of the crime?"

Exasperated sigh. "I've told you guys all I know about it. Which is nothing. Why do you—?"

I cut him off with enough irritation in my tone to let him know he was on thin ice. "*Mr.* Soukup. I am *not* 'you guys,' whatever you may think that means. You are saying, I take it, that you have spoken with the local police?"

"Yeah, isn't that—?"

"If you please, sir. Answering questions put you by the police is your duty as a citizen. However. I am *not* with the local police. Can I trust you, Mr. Soukup?"

Silence. Then, "Yeah, sure." The tone was questioning.

"Then I will tell you, for your ears only, the weapon stolen from Mr. Kearney has been identified as one used in a capital crime. The investigation of the theft of that weapon has broadened. I was sent here by our New York office to conduct a more thorough and intensive investigation than the local police are capable of. Because you were

112

apparently on the Kearney premises at or around the time the gun was stolen, it is very important—I would say urgent—that I hear in your own words exactly what you observed and did last Wednesday. I can assure you, if you are innocent, no criminal charges against you will eventuate. I am *not*, and I must stress this, connected with the local police."

Soukup was still hesitant. "Well, I don't know. I've got a lot of—"

I raised the intensity level another notch. "I'm afraid you don't understand, Mr. Soukup." I paused. "For the record, Mr. Soukup, you are under absolutely no obligation to talk with me. Nonetheless, I have to tell you, if you decline to be interviewed, I will have to make mention of that in my report when I return east. Frankly, I don't know how your refusal will be perceived."

I waited for the sound of a gulp. Soukup obliged. I continued.

"Now, about that interview, Mr. Soukup? I'll do my best to arrange it so that you are not inconvenienced. Or, at least, inconvenienced only minimally." (I'm not on Regan's level when it comes to tossing around three-dollar words, but I'm working on it.)

Soukup sighed again, but his tone was resigned. "Yeah, okay, I guess I could talk to you. Are you at the police station?"

This was looking up. Not that I particularly wanted to do the interview at the police station. Even as pleasant a guy as Chief Henderson might have a problem with a private eye taking over his headquarters.

"Oh, that won't be necessary, Mr. Soukup. I'll be happy to meet you at your home or your place of business. As I said, I don't care to inconvenience a citizen."

"Oh." A pause. Then, doubtfully, "Well, maybe we could meet on the job—if you'll be careful not to identify yourself. The guys, you know . . ."

"Absolutely." I had my own reasons not to identify myself. "Just give me directions."

"Fine." Soukup sounded relieved. "We're working out at St. John's today. We're doing a rehab at Benet Hall. Easiest thing would be for you to just come out to St. John's and we'll do it there. We're on the first floor of Benet."

"That's St. John's Abbey?"

"Uh, well, yeah, I guess. I think of it as a college, but, yeah, it's an abbey, too. Want directions?"

I did, and he gave them. It was the damnedest thing—the Bishop had pretended to send me to St. John's Abbey, and that's where I was headed. Soukup and I settled on eight o'clock as the time to meet.

I hung up, feeling uneasy about something, didn't know what. I looked in my notebook, counted the number of pages I'd filled since arriving in Minnesota. Fourteen. I frowned. Looked at the Timex: 7:03. In New York, 8:03. Suddenly I knew what it was. I needed advice from my guru.

But would he be available at this time of day? At eight A.M. the Bishop is usually—what am I saying, *always*—in the chapel, deep in prayer. And would be for another three hours. Could I interrupt him? Probably not, but it was worth a try.

I called the mansion collect. Got Ernie. Who wasn't thrilled at the prospect of interrupting The Man at his prayers.

"I just came downstairs, Davey. He just finished Mass. Now he's saying his thanksgiving, then he has his breviary, then meditation— *you* know, Davey. He won't want to be disturbed. *Why* do you have to talk to him? Can't it wait till eleven?"

"Sorry, Ern, I hate to lay this on you, but it's got to be now. I'm chasing around out here in Minnesota and don't know what I'm doing. Come on, he won't mind."

Ernie snorted, and with reason. She knows him even better than I do, having been his housekeeper and cook ever since he made Bishop over a dozen years ago. So she *knew* he'd mind. Still, friendship can work wonders.

"All right, Davey," she said grimly. "I'm going. But if he kills me, you've got to promise to convert to Catholicism. In memory of me."

I grinned. That'd be the day. Still, if Regan *did* kill her, I'd consider it. This was a big, big favor. I told her I'd hang on.

Two minutes went by. Suddenly Regan was on the line. "*Yes!* What *is* it?" *Very* exasperated.

"This." Courage equals grace under pressure. "Talked with the Kearneys last night. As you suggested, I concentrated on the gun— that's the key, right?" Silence. I rolled my eyes and talked faster.

"Well, I'm going out to your old stomping grounds, St. John's Abbey, in a few minutes. I'll be talking to the boss of one of the work crews that was in the Kearney house last week when the gun was stolen. So—"

"Have you eliminated the possibility that Mr. Kearney—that is, *James* Kearney—might have taken the gun?"

Normally I hate it when the Bishop cuts me off that way. Not this time, for a couple of reasons. For one, it proved he was on the line and paying attention. Second, he was not only listening, he was thinking. Which was why I'd called.

"Yeah, Jim's off the hook. Or at least it looks that way." I told him how Mike claimed to have cleaned the gun the Tuesday night after Jim had left. "And even though his son benefits, I don't think he's lying."

"Your feelings," Regan grumbled, "are generally accurate. At least, in matters other than affairs of the heart." A rare compliment. Or was it?

The Bishop was continuing. "But who *did* take it? Have you looked further into the possibility of the Kearneys *mère et père*? Or Mr. Jordan?"

I shook my head. His damn Latin. "Mare eh pair?"

He made a noise of exasperation. "The parents, David."

"Oh. Well, as regards Jordan, no. As to the Kearneys, I don't know. I didn't get around to asking if Peggy has the combination. I suspect she does. Mike blurted out something that pointed to it, I've got it somewhere in my notes."

But when I quoted Peggy—almost by chance—saying the house had been like Grand Central Station the day the gun disappeared, he got positively excited.

"By bizarre coincidence you have blundered into exactly the right course of action, David . . ." I scratched my head, wondering if I'd just been insulted. Decided I had, but kept listening anyway.

". . . going to see Soukup is exactly what I'd have recommended. Obtain from him, and from any other available sources, a complete listing of every person known to have been in the house that day. 'Grand Central Station'?

"And find out if Mr. Jordan was there that day. And whether or not he has the combination to the gun cabinet. I don't know what motive he may have had, but that can be looked into. The gun is the puzzle we must decipher if we are to solve this case. And, by the way, Inspector Kessler confirms that Nick Carney's keys were found on his body. So as far as I'm concerned, James Kearney is exonerated."

I had breakfast at the Embers. Kind of a far-out name for a family restaurant. Persian Club? The Embers? Who says St. Cloud's a stodgy town? And the cheese omelette wasn't bad either. It wasn't Ernie's, but what is?

St. John's was impressive to look at. I'd heard Regan talk about it, usually on the first day back from his retreats. I'd first confused it with the famous basketball St. John's, the one in Queens, but Regan had assured me there was no connection, beyond the fact that both were Catholic. Regan once called the church at the Minnesota place "the most perfectly designed temple for Catholic liturgy in North America," or some such.

I'm no judge of temples of Catholic liturgy, but it *was* different, I've got to give it that. Instead of a steeple, a concrete billboard with no picture. Visible from a mile or so away. As I got closer, I started seeing other buildings, also mostly concrete.

I found a parking place in the shadow of the huge billboard, which was even more imposing up close. I stifled an inclination to wander into the church to see what the inside looked like. A couple of guys in black robes were meandering around. I stopped one and asked about Benet Hall. Tall kid with dark hair.

"Benet? Right over there," he smiled, pointing. "Who you looking for?"

I mumbled, "You wouldn't know him," and headed for the building, leaving the young monk looking disappointed.

Benet Hall was brick, not concrete. It seemed like the monks had started with bricks, then either got sick of the look or else ran out of bricks, at which point they moved on to concrete. A couple of new buildings were going up—concrete. Apparently they hadn't yet got tired, or run out, of concrete.

I found the Soukup work crew—four young guys in coveralls— working just inside the front door of Benet Hall. They were in a good mood, having just finished demolishing a wall. A couple with sledge hammers were looking in satisfaction at some rusty, bent steel rods sticking up from the terrazzo floor. The rods were about all that was left of a wall that had been there. Unless you count rubble and dust. All four of them stared at me.

I looked them over. I couldn't resist. "No, no, no, no, *no!*" I yelled. Getting their complete attention. "Wrong wall! Put this wall back up! You were supposed to take out the wall at the *other* end!"

The response was all I could have asked for: three sets of horrified eyes turned to the tall, sandy-haired guy with the clipboard on his belt. His reaction was the best. He grabbed the clipboard, took a wild look at it, the demolished wall, me.

"Bullshit!" he roared. "It's perfectly clear on the plan that—!" Then he saw the look in my eyes, reddened, grinned and shook his head.

"Never mind, guys. Just a joke. Back to work, okay?"

Some grins and chuckles and a couple of admiring glances at the stranger who'd fooled them. "You're here to see me?" the foreman murmured to me, getting up close, shaking his head ruefully.

I nodded, getting serious. "I'm Goldman. Mr. Soukup?" He nodded and we shook hands. "Where can we talk?"

Soukup pointed with his head to the hall to his right. "Finish that tear-down," he instructed the crew. "Then mix some mud and follow the plan. Ollie, you're in charge." Nobody seemed to be listening, but Soukup was satisfied. Took a final look over his shoulder at the damage he and his men had wrought, squared his shoulders and led me down the hall.

24

S O U K U P and I found a dusty conference room right down the hall, the total contents of which were a big, scarred table and a few decrepit chairs. On the walls were a couple of large portraits of monks in black robes. One of them had a cross on a chain around his neck, a little like the one Regan wears.

Soukup's humorous blue eyes and the laugh lines around his mouth clearly indicated a guy who liked a joke, even when played on him.

He shook his head at me good-naturedly. "Not bad, man. You really had me going." He chuckled.

I was regretting my lapse. It didn't fit the image I was trying to create. I tried to recoup by pulling out a handkerchief and dusting off one of the chairs.

"All right, Mr. Soukup," I said, sitting down and clearing my throat to show that all levity was behind us. "Tell me everything you know about the missing gun."

"That's easy," he countered, with a slow smile. "Not a damn thing." I didn't return the smile.

"No? The gun was stolen sometime last Wednesday between the time Mr. Kearney left for work in the morning and when he returned home that evening. You *were* in the Kearneys' home all that day, were you not?"

Soukup rolled his eyes. "Don't you cops ever talk to each other? I told all this to Chief Henderson last week."

"Then let's see if what you told him agrees with what you tell me. What did you tell him?"

Soukup shook his head. He was getting mad. "You Feds think you've got all the answers, don't you?" I just stared at him. Insulted though I was to be called a Fed, I didn't correct him. Never return insult for insult.

He finally looked away. "Okay," he sighed. "I'll just tell you what I told Henderson. None of the three guys who were with me out at Kearney's last week would have done it. I gave Henderson their names. Now I suppose you want them, for all the good it'll do you. No skin off my nose."

"Why couldn't one of your men have done it?"

"I didn't say couldn't, I said wouldn't. They're not the type. For one thing, I'm the only guy on the crew with the slightest interest in guns. Mr. Kearney's got some real nice ones. I even recognized a couple of them: couple of Lugers from World War Two." His face brightened. "Oh yeah, and a Civil War piece. That one must've cost him a fortune. Which one was taken, can you tell me that?"

I shook my head. "I'm here to—"

"—ask the questions, not answer them," Don finished for me. I looked at him, unamused. "Okay, okay," he conceded. "Well, I *might* have been tempted to rip off a couple of those pieces. Only I didn't.

"And face it, whoever took it had the combination. I pointed that out to Henderson. I mean, that cabinet wasn't broken into. So whoever stole the gun must have had the combination. And how would *I* have known the combination?"

I shrugged. "You were in the house for several days. You'd seen Mr. Kearney open it. So—"

"So, nothing! You ought to see that guy when he's getting into that cabinet! I don't think God could read the combination over his shoulder. Look. Some free advice for you, Agent Goldman. Figure out who Mr. Kearney gave the combo to, and you got your criminal. At least you'll have it narrowed down some."

I turned to a blank page in the notebook. "Thanks for the suggestion. Now, about those names." Soukup looked puzzled. "Your crew. Last Wednesday."

"Oh! Same as the guys working today. Ollie Helderle, Fritz Steinman and Bernie Athman. Uh, Bernie came late, though. He was only with us in the afternoon."

"He came late?"

"Sure. You know that already. I told Henderson all about it and he told you."

"No, he didn't, as a matter of fact. Tell me about it."

Soukup snorted. "Hell he didn't. But naturally you want to see if my story changes any. Okay, here goes.

"We got there at eight in the morning, maybe a little before. Bernie wasn't feeling good, called me the night before, said he wasn't coming. Then he came after lunch, said he was feeling a little better. One of Weiskopf's crew came late, too."

I looked up from the notebook. "Weiskopf's the painting contractor?" Soukup nodded. "So you had four on your crew—counting you. How big was the paint crew?"

"Same as ours. Foreman plus three. And, like I said, one of theirs came late, too. Fred something."

I jotted notes. "Who else was on Weiskopf's crew?"

"Outside of Bill? I don't know names. Oh—one of them's Matt Betzen, I used to date his cousin. But I don't know the others." Soukup frowned, thought a minute, shook his head. "Naw. Talk to Bill. If you want, I can even tell you where he's working today. He's at a home in St. Cloud near the university." He gave me the address from memory and I wrote it down.

While writing it, I said, "See anyone else around the Kearneys' that day besides your crew and the painters?"

Soukup frowned at me. "Workmen?"

I gave him a level look. "Anyone. Anyone at all."

"Sure. Terry Madison was out—the plumber. He brought a young guy with him—must be breaking him in. I didn't get the kid's name. Might be Madison's son, I don't know."

I stopped him. "Do you have Madison's phone number?"

Soukup shrugged. "You don't need it. I just ran into him. He's fixing the men's room over at the library, just across the quad here." I asked him who else he had seen that Wednesday.

"Okay, let's see. Oh, late afternoon, another guy came—a businessman type, suit and tie and all. I happened to answer the door. He said he had to see Mrs. Kearney. I told him she was gone. He said he'd wait. Came right in, acted like he belonged there. No skin off my nose. Don't know his name. Tall, uncomfortable kind of guy. Looked like a boozer—big, red nose."

I nodded. I didn't tell Soukup, but he had a good observational eye. I couldn't have given a better short description of Jerome Jordan myself. Interesting that Jordan had been there the day the gun walked away. "How long did he stay, this businessman?" I asked.

Soukup shrugged. "No idea. I never saw him leave. For all I know, he's still there."

I was writing fast. "Anyone else?"

"Well, Miz Kearney was in and out. She'd almost had a fit the day before when I told her I couldn't finish Tuesday, meaning Weiskopf and I'd be working in there at the same time. But by Wednesday she'd calmed down." Soukup frowned. "That's about it, I guess."

25

THE big bell in the concrete billboard was tolling nine o'clock as I headed across the parking lot for the library. Sprawling, modernistic building. A plaque directed Gentlemen and Ladies to head downstairs. Gentlemen's was blocked by a makeshift Closed for Repairs sign. I ignored that, pushed open the door and went in. A grizzled, red-faced guy in coveralls, flat on his back under the sink he was applying his long-handled wrench to, threw me an angry look.

"Can't you damn kids read? This ain't in use right now!"

"I'm not here to use the facilities," I told him, flashing my investigator's license for a split second. "Though I do appreciate being called a kid. I'm Goldman, working on the Kearney gun theft. Mr. Madison?"

"Yessir." The plumber seemed satisfactorily intimidated.

"Like to ask you a few questions."

Madison laid his wrench on the floor, rolled onto his hands and knees and struggled to his feet. He wiped his hands on his coveralls. "I already been interviewed. I don't know a thing. And—"

"Just a couple more questions, sir. Then I'll let you get back to work." I opened the notebook. "You *were* on the site last Wednesday? At the Kearneys'?" He rolled his eyes and nodded wearily. "I'm interested in your work crew. How many of you were there?"

"Just me and Fred. Uh, that's Fred Glinke, my assistant."

I consulted an earlier page of my notebook. "Someone said a Fred came late. That your guy?"

"Nope." Madison shook his head decisively. "We came together."

I spent another ten minutes with him, but got no further. He was adamant that he and Glinke came alone, stayed just over two hours, finished their work and left. Nor did he notice how many others were in the house. Nor did he care. I thought briefly about applying a little more pressure, but decided not to. My overvivid imagination was busily sketching out a scenario in which Madison went to Deputy Kleinschmidt, complaining that I'd impersonated an FBI agent. My imagination ended the scenario right there, the aftermath being too gruesome to contemplate.

At nine-thirty I waved goodbye to the billboard and headed back for St. Cloud. There I got lost again. Finally found Division Street and then the address Soukup had given me: the one where Weiskopf and his crew were painting.

It was a big house on a tree-lined street, surrounded by other big houses. Quiet neighborhood. Spookily quiet.

The sign in front helped me find it: "University Painters: Educated Workmanship." Two pickup trucks in the driveway and a fifteen-year-old Chevy at the curb reinforced the idea that workers were inside. But after three pushes on the doorbell I began to wonder. I was considering going around to the rear, when the door finally opened. A little guy in coveralls holding a paint can and roller.

"I'm looking for Bill Weiskopf," I told him.

He blushed and studied the paint can. "Uh, yeah, that's me." I looked him over. Short, plump, in his twenties. Disheveled dark hair, currently speckled with white paint. Round, gold-rimmed glasses, also paint-dotted, gave him an owlish appearance.

I took a breath: "Mr. Weiskopf. I'm here from New York, investigating the gun that was stolen last week from Mr. Michael Kearney. Mind answering a few questions?"

His face got redder and he came out on the porch and put the paint and roller on the floor.

"Okay," he said nervously. "What can I do for you? Could we sit down?" He shifted his weight nervously.

I ignored his question. Holding his eye, I said, "I'm an investigator, Mr. Weiskopf. From the East Coast. What can you tell me about—"

Weiskopf interrupted. "You're an investigator." Something about the look in the dark eyes through those thick lenses made me uneasy.

"Right." But something wasn't right.

Weiskopf's brow furrowed. "Uh, could I see some I.D. or something?" He shrugged abruptly. "You know. Just in case . . ." He blushed and his voice trailed off.

I tried staring him down. Didn't work. He was just a kid and he lived in the middle of nowhere and was about as blind as a bat, but he was nobody's fool. I pulled out my wallet and flashed the P.I. license. Pulled it back.

"Uh, could I see it?"

I tried an exasperated sigh and a roll of the eyes but he just waited. I finally pulled it out again and held it up for him to read. This wasn't going well.

Weiskopf squinted at the license a couple of seconds, frowned at me and blushed more deeply. "Uh, this says *private* investigator." He returned his eyes to me, a little more confident now. I looked at him, trying to wait him out. He just returned my gaze. He was gaining confidence as fast as I was losing it. I had to get things back on track.

"Yeah," I responded briskly. "That's right. Now can we get back to the point? I'd like—"

"No, I'm sorry. It says *private*. Who're you representing, Mr. Goldman?"

"Privileged. Now, if we could—"

"Excuse me. Everything *I've* read says that private investigators aren't officers of the court. So why can't you tell me who you're representing?" I started to argue but he lifted a hand.

"Look, I don't want to get into an argument with you, Mr. Goldman. I have a job to do here, and another one waiting out at the abbey, and another one after that. So I really don't have time. If you'll excuse me?" He held out his hand for a goodbye shake.

"Oh no, you don't," I blustered. "I'm—" The look on his face stopped me. I quit blustering.

"Look," I said quietly, holding his eye. "Just let me tell you what's going on. Then *you* decide if you want to talk to me. If you don't . . ." I shrugged. ". . . well, that's your privilege."

Weiskopf glanced at his watch, shrugged.

Talking fast, I told him about Jim Kearney's troubles, the implications of the missing gun and my curiosity about the people wandering through the Kearneys' house the day the gun was stolen. Weiskopf listened without taking his eyes off me except for a couple of times when he looked down at his feet to consider a point.

When I pulled out my notebook and showed him the list of people who'd apparently been on the Kearneys' premises that day, he studied it carefully.

I was encouraged at his interest. "See, Bill, some of those names

I'm just guessing at. Have I got them right? Like your crew. How many did you have working last Wednesday?"

I handed him the notebook. Weiskopf squinted at the list through his thick glasses. "Let's see," he muttered. "You don't have my guys' names here. Matt Betzen and Maury Brand."

I took the notebook back and jotted in the names. "Okay," I said, staring at the names. "But didn't you have three?"

"Yeah, counting me."

"Nobody named Fred?"

"Nope. Madison's got a guy—"

"I know. Fred Glinke." I tried to remember something else Soukup had said. "You didn't have a guy come late that day?"

Weiskopf frowned and tried to remember. "Gee, that was way last week. No, I don't think so. But I *can* tell you, there were just three of us, counting me."

"Okay, if you're sure. Who else was there that day?"

Weiskopf rubbed his forehead and squinted. "Gee, let me think." He sat down on the top step of the porch to concentrate. Not having an official image to maintain any longer, I joined him. After a minute of thinking he said, "Okay. Terry was out. Terry Madison, the plumber, and brought a couple of guys with him."

I shook my head. People's memories. "*Two*? Know who they were?"

"Well, one of them was Fred Glinke, like you said. He works with Terry a lot. The other might've been Terry's son, I don't know who he was. Little guy."

He thought some more. "Of course, aside from the workmen, there was Mrs. Kearney. She was in and out all day. Oh—and there was a guy in a suit and tie there for a while, too. I'm not sure what Mr. Kearney looks like, but I don't think this guy was him. He didn't act like he belonged there. I didn't get his name."

I nodded and put a check next to Jordan's name in the notebook. I had a few more questions but Weiskopf didn't have answers—at least none that helped.

It was nearly eleven when I left Weiskopf and the day was growing hot. About time to head for the airport to grab my two o'clock back to New York. But before doing that, I decided it wouldn't hurt to mend some fences with the local police.

The air conditioner had barely started to cool down the car by the time I arrived at the police station in downtown St. Cloud. One of the newer buildings there. A pretty, gum-popping girl in uniform manning (womaning?) the front desk looked up at me.

I gave her a smile. "Chief Henderson around?"

She gave me back a smile a lot prettier than mine. "Sure is. But he's got someone with him. Name please? I'll tell him you're here."

She swiveled her head and looked back over her shoulder. I followed her gaze to a glass-walled office on the far side of the big room. In it sat Chief Henderson, behind his desk, chatting with a man, his back to me, in a khaki suit. I frowned and studied the back. Something about him told me I knew him. But . . .

Henderson seemed to sense he was under inspection and looked our way. His expression was blank; from that distance he couldn't recognize me. Meanwhile, the pretty desk sergeant was getting him on the phone. Still studying me, Henderson groped for the receiver.

"Chief," the Sergeant said after he picked up, "a David Goldman is here to see you. He says he can wait till you're done, if you're not going to be too long. He has a plane to catch."

Henderson nodded in our direction, turned and said something to the khaki suit, getting an immediate and violent reaction. The man jerked around in his chair, angry eyes darting my way. "I should have known," I muttered.

The deputy had told me the night before that New York was sending someone. Who more likely to come than my one-time friend and current nemesis, Sergeant Joe Parker? From a hundred feet away his expression was hard to read, especially behind the glare of the glass wall. But I knew that particular tilt of his head well enough to know he was just as surprised to see me as I was to see him. And definitely a lot unhappier.

26

SOMETHING about the way Joe was glaring at me told me I'd interrupted the two lawmen in the midst of a discussion regarding the feasibility and desirability of finding a suitable cell for one David Goldman in the Stearns County jail, just to be sure he got properly acquainted with the state of 10,000 lakes.

Henderson spoke into the phone, at the same time beckoning me with a wave.

"Chief says come on back," the pretty Sergeant informed me unnecessarily.

"It's been real," I told her. "Frankly, under the circumstances, I think I'd rather take my chances with you."

She blushed. I'd have liked to go on chatting with her but . . . might as well get it over with.

"I guess you two know each other," Henderson said as I entered the office. He came around his desk and shook my hand. He grinned at both of us.

I swung around to Parker. "Yeah," I agreed. "I guess we do. How's it shaking, Joe?"

Parker grudgingly took my hand in a brief handshake. He gave no information about how it or he was shaking. Nor did he smile. "I need a minute with you alone, Chief," he said grimly. "Excuse us, Davey."

Henderson looked surprised. "But—"

"It's okay, Chief," I said. "I don't think Joe's real happy with me right now. Anyway, I only came by to check in. I'm on my way back to New York."

Joe's eyes widened. He was outraged. "Awright, that's *it*! Chief, I want you to arrest this man for obstruction of justice!"

Henderson started to answer but Joe was yammering at me. "Dammit, Davey, I want to know who you've been talking to. If you've been tampering with witnesses, I'm going to have your damn head. You don't—"

"Hey, Joe, settle down! I've found out a little bit, yeah. And I'm perfectly willing to share it with you. In fact—"

"You damn well *better* share it with me, damn you, Davey! You had no right to—"

"Hey, I had *every* right. And you know it. I've got a client, I haven't broken any laws, and—"

"The Bishop told the Inspector he had an *errand* for you! He didn't say nothin' about you goin' to St. Cloud! I got a mind to—!"

"Joe, Joe, Joe! Listen to me. I'm willing to—no, strike that. I *want* to tell you everything I've learned from everyone here I've talked to, everything. All I want in return is, first of all, a little calm and quiet; and second of all, for you to acknowledge that Jim Kearney didn't do that murder."

Parker took a breath. The redness in his face subsided a little. His next words were quieter but still grim. "Where *is* Jim Kearney, Davey?"

I shook my head. "Joe, if I knew, I wouldn't tell you. You're trying to put the guy behind bars. And he didn't *do* it."

Joe gave me an unpleasant smirk. "He didn't, huh? Well, I think he did. And you're in deep, buddy, hiding him out. And I'm just the guy to nail you. And I'm goin' to. Now tell me where he is, right now, or you're goin' to jail."

I sat down, crossed my legs and grinned at him. "You can't make it stand up, Joe. You're outside your jurisdiction here, and the Chief's not going to arrest someone just on your say-so. He knows I could sue him and make it stick." I didn't risk a glance at Henderson, but didn't figure a gamble on his desire to stay out of harm's way was a real long shot.

I kept my eyes on Parker, who was studying me the way a poker player studies an opponent who just made a limit raise.

"But I'll tell what I will do, Joe. I'll tell you everything I've learned since I've been here. Furthermore, if I run into Jim Kearney, I'll tell him you want to talk to him."

Parker grumbled and fussed, but a couple of quick glances at Henderson confirmed for him what I'd already surmised: the Chief wasn't about to get involved in some big city dispute that didn't affect him. I was just as glad Kleinschmidt wasn't around. I had the feeling he and Parker'd have figured out a way to get me behind bars P.D.Q. and then thrown away the keys.

"Okay, Davey," he finally growled. "Tell me what you've got."

"Okay." I explained to him and Henderson what I'd learned from Mike and Peggy the night before, stressing Mike's certainty that the gun was still in the cabinet Tuesday night *after* Jim had returned to New York.

Parker was unimpressed. "Hell, Davey, the guy's his old man. Naturally he's going to alibi him." I opened my mouth but Joe went on talking. "Furthermore, even if he's telling the absolute truth as he knows it, he could still be mistaken about the time. Hell, how many times have *you* seen witnesses that were dead-sure about something or other fall to pieces on cross-examination?"

"Okay, talk to him, Joe, and make up your *own* mind. I think he's a pretty good witness, and I think the Chief here will agree. But one thing you've got to admit: if his old man's telling the truth, Jim's off the hook. He was gone before that gun disappeared."

Parker shrugged, still unconvinced. "What else did you learn?"

I summarized my conversations with Soukup, Madison and Weiskopf, and showed him my list of people who'd been in the Kearney household the previous Wednesday. "And any one of those people could have taken the gun," I ended.

Parker looked at the list, still unimpressed. "Okay, but none of them had the combination. More important, none of them were in New York last Saturday. I still think the kid took the gun. Dammit, Davey, I wanna talk to him! You produce him, or I'm gonna get you if it's the last thing I do!"

I got up. "I've got a plane to catch. Goodbye, Chief Henderson. See you back in New York, Joe."

Parker, fuming, shot me a grim smile. "Oh, I'll be seein' you, Davey. Don't you worry none about that."

27

I B R O K E my neck getting to the airport in time for the two o'clock flight, then found out it was canceled. Next thing available was the five-thirty, so I had a few hours to kill. First tried processing all the information I'd gleaned over the past thirty hours. Got nowhere with that. Wound up watching people come and go. Conclusion: Minnesotans move at about sixty-five percent of the rate of speed of New Yorkers. Not a terribly earth-shattering observation.

As soon as we were in the air, I tried to grab a nap. No soap. I was too keyed up. Mainly, I kept wondering what Regan could glean from what I'd learned. Almost certainly one of those dozen or so people who'd been in the Kearney house that day had taken the gun. I hoped the Bishop could figure out which one, because I didn't have an inkling.

I let the stew tempt me with a martini. Two, in fact. The gin didn't help the thinking much, but it did seem to make the trip go faster. Also got my mind off the murder. For some reason my mind drifted towards Dinker Galloway. Her smile, her dark hair, her crooked nose . . .

Grabbed a cab at LaGuardia and went back to thinking about all I had to tell the Bishop. The more I thought about it, the more confused I got. By the time we rounded the corner at Tenth and Thirty-seventh, I'd about settled on Jordan as the most likely suspect. I didn't notice the other cab parked in front of the mansion till I'd paid my own cabby and was heading for the steps to the stoop.

Suddenly the rear door of the parked cab opened and from it came an anxious female voice.

"Davey!"

I turned. Emerging from the cab was a very attractive set of legs, followed by the beautiful remainder of Dinker Galloway.

She ran to me. In the dim light of the street lamp, I could see her face was drawn. Breathing hard, she grabbed my hands.

"Dinker, what are—?"

"Davey! You've got to help! Do you know where Jim is?"

I frowned at her. "What's wrong, Dinker? Has something happened?"

Her eyes were wide. "The police came to see me today! They're sure Jim killed Nick! And I tried to call Jim, but I couldn't get anything but his answering machine. Lenny says you know where he is! Do you?"

I ducked the question. "What did the police want with you, Dinker?"

Her dark eyes were huge. "They think I know where he is. I only wish I *did*! A Lieutenant came to talk to me. Lieutenant Blake or something. Jim was on TV, you know."

That got me. "He was? When?" How could he—?

"Well," Dinker explained, "not really *on*. I mean, you couldn't see him or anything. It was an audiotape of a phone interview with this guy Rozanski, the crime guy at one of the TV stations." I nodded, breathing a sigh of relief.

"Anyway," she went on, "I guess this Blake was pretty upset about it. I guess someone gave him my name and told him Jim and I were friends. He was insulting. Called me a liar, and said you knew where he was and so did I. Said he was going to put *both* of us in jail if we didn't tell him where!" A sob broke through her voice.

"Davey, I don't know what to do. Do *you* know where he is?"

I put an arm around her shoulder, thinking hard. I wasn't surprised that Blake was trying to put some pressure on, though it was disappointing to find out he was back on the case. I wondered how the lines of authority ran with Joe Parker running things. Naturally Blake, like any cop, would resent people holding out on him, which is what he thought Dinker and I were doing. He was only half-right.

Meanwhile, Dinker had introduced a question that now awaited my answer: where was Jim? As his girlfriend she probably had a right to know, but I wanted to think about it. I patted her arm.

"Come on in, Dinker. Let's see what the Bishop has to say about it."

"Bishop?" she said, letting herself be guided up the steps. "Who—?"

"You saw him last Friday night, Dinker. The guy in the wheelchair. My boss. Sort of."

"But what does he have to do with it?"

"Oh, you'd be surprised. He has answers to lots of questions." I inserted a key into the front door. As I held it open for her, I studied her face in the light from the front hall. Her eyes were red-rimmed. And beautiful.

"Come on in, Dinker. Let's discuss it with a Thinker."

I closed the front door and was gratified to see a light coming through the half-open door to Regan's office at the end of the hall. "My office is here," I said, opening the door to our immediate left and turning on a light. "You wait in here while I see what The Man is up to."

Dinker couldn't get comfortable in the leather chair. She shifted from side to side, played with her purse, tossed her hair. I patted her shoulder. "Hey, relax. I'll talk to the Bishop. Maybe he's got an idea or two. He usually does."

I tapped on the connecting door and got the courtesy of a two-word invitation. Regan was hard at work, personnel files spread across his desk. He looked up at me over the reading glasses. Took them off.

"Well. Welcome back. I presume you have something to report regarding your Minnesota hegira?"

"Well, yeah, there's that. I *do* have some interesting information for you. But we'll have to put that on hold for the moment."

His eyebrows went up a notch. "Oh?"

"Yeah, oh. Dinker Galloway's here." The eyebrows stayed up. "She was laying for me out front, and—"

"Yes. Sister Ernestine reported to me that she had come not more than ten minutes ago. Looking for you, I gathered. I told Sister to tell her nothing beyond the fact that you were not on the premises. What does she want?"

"She wants to know why the cops are looking to arrest Jim Kearney. Also whether she and I are going to jail as accessories after the fact. I think she—"

"Where is she?"

"In my office."

"Bring her."

Will wonders never cease? It was now nearly ten o'clock, by which time the Bishop is normally well into the arms of Morpheus. Or at least in bed reading. I couldn't believe he really wanted to see her.

Of course, he does have a thing about pretty young women. I don't know quite how it ties in with his vows, but he does at least enjoy looking at—and talking to—them. But then why didn't he have her in when she first knocked on the door? Who knows?

Dinker was trying to take a nap in my chair. Her head was thrown back, hands in her lap, bare feet on the desk, skirt two-thirds of the way up her smooth thighs. She opened an eye as I came through the door.

I grinned at her. "Sorry to interrupt your beauty rest. My boss would have a word with you."

Her feet hit the' floor and she tugged on her pumps. "Great! Let me at him."

The Bishop gave her a courtly bow of the head, wheeling around from behind his desk. "Please, David, two chairs here." I pulled up chairs and we formed a triangle.

His green eyes went to Dinker. She met them, unblinking. He nodded at her and cleared his throat. "As an interested party, Miss Galloway, you're entitled to know what's going on. We'll begin with David telling you what transpired yesterday. Then you'll understand why the police believe that James Kearney murdered his brother. If you have any questions, we'll try to answer them, whereupon we'll ask you to excuse us. I need to have David's report of his activities today and not all of that will be of interest to you."

"That's very kind of you, Bishop. I—"

"Not at all, Miss Galloway." He turned to me. "David?"

Dinker's dark eyes distracted me at first, but I talked through the distraction. I told about Jim's calls Sunday when I was out on Long Island, his coming to see me on Monday, our discussion of the murder, Jim's denial of any involvement. Dinker's eyes got wide as I told about how he must have missed the murderer by only a couple of minutes.

"He could have been killed!" she gasped. "Suppose the murderer had come out of the office just as Jim was at the door?"

I nodded. "He was probably very lucky." I went on to tell about the discovery of the Colt and how it implicated Jim. Dinker had a hard time understanding what that meant, which wasn't surprising. I'd had the same problem at first.

"You mean, that gun in the office was Jim's? But how—?"

"I don't know either, Dinker. It looks like Jim was set up."

"Set up?" Dinker frowned. "Why would anyone want to do that?" I shrugged.

By the time I finished, twenty minutes later, Dinker either had no questions left, or she didn't want to bother me with them, or she wanted to ask me privately. Or all of the above. Anyway, she thanked the Bishop and turned to me.

"I know you and Bishop Regan have things to talk over, Davey. I just have one question before I go."

She and the Bishop exchanged goodbyes and I took her back into my office. She looked up at me as I closed the door behind us.

"Could I wait, Davey? I have some questions, but I don't feel right keeping him up." She brushed a strand of hair off of her forehead.

I thought about it. "I don't know, Dinker. We may be a while. I—"

"I'd be happy to grab a nap in here. If you don't mind." She grinned mischievously. "I promise not to listen at the door."

I shrugged, looked at the Timex. It was a quarter to eleven, and it would take at least an hour, maybe two, to fill the Bishop in. But suddenly I wasn't tired any more.

"Well, sure, if you don't mind a wait. It could be a couple of hours. We've got a lot to talk over."

Her eyes twinkled. "I don't mind, if you don't mind me using your couch." She looked longingly at the faded couch under the north window.

Over her objections, I insisted on pulling down a comforter I keep on the top shelf of my closet, and covered her with it.

"You're a dear," she assured me, her hair fanned out around her face on the cushion. I looked back at her before closing the door behind me. She was already half-asleep.

28

IT wound up taking nearly two hours to fill Regan in. He didn't
have many questions but, as usual, didn't miss a word I said. He's
the most intense listener I know; it's almost scary.

He studied the list of the people who'd been in the Kearney house
the previous Wednesday:

Mr. Kearney
Mrs. Kearney
Jerry Jordan (lawyer)
Terry Madison (plumber)
Fred Glinke (Madison's assistant)
Don Soukup (dry-wall foreman)
Ollie Helderle (on Soukup's crew)
Fritz Steinman (ditto)
Bernie Athman (also Soukup's crew—came late)
Bill Weiskopf (painting foreman)
Matt Betzen (Weiskopf's crew)
Maury Brand (ditto)

I explained the conflicting stories about the fourth man on Weiskopf's crew (or was it the third man on Madison's?).

"Someone's lying or, more likely, mistaken," Regan said. "We need
to talk further with Messrs. Weiskopf and Madison." He thought a
while. "But enough for today." He glanced up at the clock. "Or,
rather, yesterday. It's now Wednesday, I see. What are your plans
for tomorr—er, today?"

I shrugged. "Up to you."

"Good. The first person I suggest you talk to is the gentleman in
Paddy's Pub: Jake, I believe you called him. It seems possible that
he may have observed not only James Kearney but perhaps other

passersby last Saturday afternoon." He rubbed his eyes. "I suggest you start with him. Show him that photograph you brought back."

"The one of Mike, Peggy and Jordan?"

"Exactly. And do you have a picture of James Kearney? No? Pity. It would be nice to show his picture to this Jake to verify that he did indeed see him. Well. Do the best you can. I may have more suggestions after a night's sleep." He scowled. "Half a night's sleep." He wheeled grumpily toward the hallway.

I grinned at his back. He loves to pretend to be miffed at missing sleep, but he loves bizarre happenings. His eyes may have been tired, but they were also as alive as I'd seen them in a while.

I opened the interconnecting door as quietly as I could, and tiptoed in, expecting to see Dinker snoring on the couch. But she was up, stretching and yawning hugely. She looked disoriented.

"I can't sleep," she croaked, rubbing her eyes. "I'm going home. Could you call me a cab, Davey?"

"Oh, we're done. I'll give you a ride home."

Her eyes widened and started focusing. "You're done?" She cleared her throat. "But you said you'd be at least an hour! Isn't the Bishop—?"

I looked at my watch and chuckled. "It's now twenty minutes before one o'clock in the morning, dear heart. The good Bishop now knows everything I know."

Dinker stared at me and looked at her own watch. She squinted at it and shook her head. "I can't believe it! I've been sleeping nearly two hours! Davey! I've got to go!" She whirled and grabbed the comforter. "Call me a cab, would you, Davey? I'll put this away."

I went to her and took the comforter away from her. "I said I'll take you home. Get your shoes on."

She smiled at me. "Call the cab, mister, or I call a cop." She took an edge of the comforter back and helped me fold it.

I grinned at her and put the quilt back on the top shelf of the closet. "Call nine-one-one, then. Because I'm not sending a lady home in a cab at one in the morning."

She smiled at me, her eyes dancing. "The age of chivalry isn't dead after all. All right, kind sir. Let's go."

"You were going to ask me a question," I reminded her.

"Oh. It seems to have faded. I can't think of what it was right now." She smiled.

I still had to make a call, though. Fred's garage. The night guy sounded sleepy and put upon, but the car was ready when we arrived there three minutes later.

Dinker's new wide-awakeness made her chatty as we headed south on nearly-deserted Broadway.

"Can't you give me Jim's number, Davey? I promise not to bug him. And I won't give it to the police!"

I shook my head. "No can do. I just hope Lenny's made arrangements for his understudy. Jim's not going to be able to go on tomorrow—make that tonight."

She nodded. "Oh, that's all taken care of. Jim called Lenny yesterday to tell him he was hiding out." I winced. Expressions like that could come back to haunt both Jim and me.

"He told Lenny he couldn't be there," Dinker went on. "Johnny Underwood—that's Jim's understudy—will be going on instead, probably all this week. Lenny was upset about it. We had to have a run-through this evening at six o'clock, so all of us could get used to Johnny in the part and Johnny could get used to us. It was a disaster, at least, at first. Johnny was so nervous, he kept going up on his lines. Lenny finally had to stop, talk to Johnny, gave him fifteen minutes to get into the part, and start again. That helped. But he's still no Jim. Lenny's really depressed about it. The New York *Times* is going to have someone there tonight, and without Jim it won't be the same."

I nodded. "Lousy timing, whoever killed Nick."

Dinker missed the humor. "Well, the main thing is for Jim to clear himself. Everything else is—" She stopped. "Davey! I just thought of something!"

"That being?"

"Can we go by Jim's apartment? I have a key. Jim told Lenny to tell you he needs some of his things. For me to let you in there. I know what he needs. Could we go there now?"

I needed to get some sleep. But this was among the more attractive females I'd met in a fairly active life. The idea of spending a few more minutes with her outweighed the need for sleep. I made another snap decision.

"Sure. Let's do it."

We were approaching Houston. I hung a right, headed for Soho. Ten minutes later, Dinker was letting us into Jim's apartment.

She flipped on a light and I surveyed the surroundings. Though it wasn't ready for the photographers from *Home Beautiful*, it wasn't nearly as messy as I'd expected. Some Nike running shoes, high-topped, were on a chair, athletic socks slopped over them. A gray sweatshirt lay over the back of the threadworn couch. In one corner were a CD player and a large TV. Jim hadn't left *all* the comforts of home back in St. Cloud.

Dinker was obviously very much at home. She led me into the bedroom, which was in even better shape than the living room. The double bed was made, sort of. At least the coverlet was pulled up over the pillows. And I didn't see any dust balls along the walls. The only clothes in evidence were a pair of slacks and a dress shirt neatly laid across the bed.

Dinker went immediately to the closet, pulled out a battered one-suiter and opened it on the bed. As she did, I noticed some feminine things hanging in the closet. Dinker saw my look. "Jim and I don't live together any more. Officially. Unofficially, I keep stuff here. And he keeps stuff at my place." She shrugged. "For convenience's sake." She pointed at the dresser in the corner. "Underwear and socks," she told me briskly. "Two or three sets. Find some pajamas, too. I'll get his shaving kit."

She went out the door, headed for the bathroom. I smiled at her new-found energy and set about my task. I noticed a picture of Jim and Dinker on the nightstand and got an idea. I was holding it when Dinker came back, a black leather shaving kit in her hand.

"Mind if I take this along, Dinker?" I asked.

She shrugged. "Why should I mind? I mean, it's Jim's. What do you need it for?"

"I don't know. To show witnesses. I'll tell him I've got it when I talk to him next."

It took us less than five minutes to fill the suitcase. When we finished, we were standing by the bed, Dinker frowning down at the suitcase.

"Umm, I think that's all, Davey. Seems like there should be some-thing else. No telling when he'll be back . . ." Her voice trailed off and her eyes filled with tears. She leaned forward onto the suitcase and started to cry. I put a comforting arm around her and she turned to me. I took her in my arms. She fit as comfortably as if she'd been there all our lives.

"I'm sorry, Davey," she sobbed, getting my shirt damp. "I'm just so scared for Jim. I'm afraid he . . ." The rest was muffled against my shoulder. Her back shuddered under my palms. I tightened my embrace and she huddled close.

I honestly can't tell you who started the kissing. I guess it just happened. But once it did, it went on for quite a while.

But I do know who ended it. She shoved me away. "No, Davey. Thanks for the shoulder." She tried to smile and started crying again. This time I didn't touch her. With that big soft bed right there, I didn't dare.

I didn't feel right about it, nor did she. Jim's bedroom, Jim's clothes all over the place. And Jim's girl. I should have been disgusted with myself. But all I could think about was what a great kisser she was.

She took a deep, shuddering breath and turned to me, eyes steady on mine. "I'm sorry that happened, Davey. When this is over, when Jim is really out of trouble, we'll talk."

She turned and snapped the suitcase closed. I hefted it off the bed. She looked up at me. "Take me home, please, Davey."

I did. In the car she sat as far away as you can sit and still be inside. When we got to her place, she thanked me for the ride. No kiss, no offer to come in, no offer of anything. Just "Thank you very much, Davey. Goodnight."

It sounded like the end of a beautiful friendship. But heading north in the Caddy, through the empty streets, I had a feeling it was just beginning.

29

THE first order of business Wednesday morning was to get Jim an attorney. And I knew just the guy.

Davis L. Baker is probably as good at the practice of law as he's lousy at the game of golf. He's sure gotten me out of a few scrapes. And the scrape Jim was in now was easily as challenging as all of mine put together.

I called Baker at home a little after eight. "How about helping me keep a friend of mine out of jail?"

Pause. When he spoke, Baker's voice was serious. "Okay, let's have it. What've you got?"

"The Carney thing." Silence. "Come on, Dave. Surely you've been reading about it. The fence who—"

"Oh, yeah. The fence. Mob hit, right?"

"Wrong. The papers have been playing it that way, but it's not."

"Okay. How'd *you* get involved?"

"Good question. Joe Parker wants to know that, too. He's trying to bust my friend and doesn't much appreciate my trying to help. My guy's name is Jim Kearney. An actor."

"You don't say." Baker sounded interested. "They looking for the big one on him?"

"You got it. Murder One."

"Did he do it?"

"Hell, no! And I'm trying to prove he didn't."

Baker paused. "Fair enough. I assume he's in jail. Shall we meet there this morning? We can talk about—"

"Nope. He's not in jail, Davis. He's—unavailable."

Longer pause. "Unavailable? What's that supposed to mean? Is he hiding from the outfit? What's he—?"

"Davis! Get the mob out of your head, okay? This has nothing to do with the mob. Look, have you got a minute for me to give you the whole story?"

"Yeah, but first where's the suspect? Whatever his name is—Kearney."

"He's—well, he's laying low for now."

Baker sighed. "And I suppose *you* know where he is."

"Hey, why do you think the cops are looking to slap me with an accessory after the fact?"

Baker gulped. "Say what?"

I waited. Baker spoke again in a totally new tone of voice. "Davey, don't tell me you're hiding the guy out!"

"Well, I don't know as I'd put it *that* way, Davis. I'd rather say I'm advising him to remain incommunicado."

"Davey, Davey, Davey." Baker wasn't happy with me. "When the hell are you ever going to learn? One of these days, my friend, you're going to get your butt in a wringer I can't get it out of. *Then* what are you going to do?"

"I'll worry about that when it happens. Back to my original question. Do you want to hear about Kearney? And if so, when? I'd like you to represent him."

Baker sighed again. "I guess now's as good a time as any."

I took fifteen minutes filling Baker in on Nick's murder and Jim's involvement in it: the whole story, with the exception of Jim's current whereabouts. I trust Dave but I also shuffle the deck when we play poker. He hadn't said he'd take the case. Yet.

"Well," Baker said when I finished. "You and the Bishop are obviously both convinced the guy's innocent. What's your next step?"

"You going to take the case?"

"Oh, sure. But I got to tell you, I think you've mishandled it." He paused to give me a chance to complain or object. I didn't do either. "Let me tell you why, Davey. Legally, you haven't done anything wrong. Well, at least nothing I can't get you sprung from.

"But what you have done is pissed the cops off for no reason. I mean, how would *you* feel about Jim if you were still a cop and some private eye pulled what you pulled?"

That was a rhetorical question if I ever heard one, so I didn't bother to answer. Baker went on.

"Let me make a suggestion. I'll go with you to wherever Jim is and take him to the cops. I'll be right there. If they want to book him, I'll bond him out. You say his parents have dough, right? So—"

"You'll bond him out, Davis? What are the chances they'll even permit bond? They're looking for Murder One."

"I know, but—"

"No way, Davis. Jim stays right where he is. I'm not letting the cops near him till I find the guy that did it."

"Why do you want the cops pissed off, Davey? That's just dumb. Let me take him in. Kessler's not going to book him if all the stuff you've told me is true."

"You're dreaming, Davis. No way."

Baker wasn't happy. "Well, then I don't know if I'm all that interested in representing him, Davey." I didn't answer because I didn't believe him. He finally sighed. "Okay, okay, I'll represent him. Let me know when he's ready to come in. I'll draw up some kind of defense that can maybe work its way around the mess you're making of it."

I chuckled. "You're entitled to your opinion, counselor. Just so you represent my man. That entitles you to know where he is." I gave him Jim's whereabouts, including that he was now going by D. J. Holdman. I ended with, "Give him a call, Davis."

"Sure. I'll do it right now, after *you* call him to tell him who I am."

I did just that. I loved the way Jim answered.

"Holdman." Nice, confident tone.

"Great!" I said admiringly. "You're fitting into the role."

"Hi, Davey." His tone darkened. "Doing it better, but enjoying it less."

I frowned. I didn't want my man in the dumps. "Hey, cheer up, Jim! I think we're making progress. I saw your parents yesterday."

He perked up a little at that, and I told him, briefly, about my visit to St. Cloud. Then he said, "I just wish I had some clothes so I could get out of these things. I asked Lenny to—"

"Yeah, hold it right there. He did what you asked him to: passed word to Dinker, who told me. I've got a suitcase for you full of your duds." I thought a second. "Why don't I just bring them over to you right now?"

That suited Jim just fine. I gathered he was also looking forward to seeing a friendly face after forty-four hours in hiding.

"Meanwhile," I said. "While you're waiting for me you'll get a call from a lawyer friend of mine. He says he'll represent you."

"What?" Jim didn't seem to understand his need.

"No time to discuss it now. Talk to the lawyer. Davis Baker's his name, getting people out of trouble's his game. Talk to him, pay attention to what he says, and I'll be there inside of an hour."

After we hung up I left a note for the Bishop giving him my probable whereabouts for the rest of the morning and left with the suitcase. I took my time walking to the garage, thinking about how to proceed. The way I'd slipped my pursuers on the way to LaGuardia two days before, they were going to be even more careful—and tenacious— today. And this time I had a much greater need to ditch them. So I gave it some careful thought.

I could see absolutely no sign of a tail. That surprised and bothered me. They had to be on me, I knew that. That I couldn't make them was a bad sign.

At the garage, Fred came sauntering out of his office. "Bishop's Seville guy stopped by yesterday, Davey."

"What Seville guy?"

Fred frowned. "You don't know about it? Said Bishop Regan called, told him the radiator needed looking at. So he took a look. Said it seemed okay. Said he was going to talk to the Bishop about it. He was only here about ten minutes."

I asked what the guy looked like and didn't get much of a description. I didn't like it. "Can I use your phone, Fred?"

I called Joe Rivers at Joe Rivers Cadillac. If anyone is "Bishop Regan's Seville guy," it's Joe Rivers. Joe provides the Bishop—meaning me—with a new Caddy every two years. His way of getting into heaven, I guess.

Rivers was adamant. "Hell, no, Davey, I didn't send anyone over. What for? Hell, if there's any trouble with the car I always deal with you, not the Bishop, you know that. What's goin' on?"

"Nothing to worry about, Joe. Just a little mix-up. Sorry to bother you."

Fred, at his desk, had a worried look in his eye. I grinned. "Okay, Fred. We now know that was no Seville guy. That was the cops bugging the car."

I felt a lot better. Now I knew why I hadn't seen anyone tailing me. They were a couple of blocks away in a van or something, monitoring the Cadillac, just waiting for me to make a move. Then they'd follow me all the way to Jim from a safe distance. In their dreams.

I grinned. This had to be Blake's work. No one else could be that inept.

30

FRED couldn't figure it out. "But why—?"

"The cops want to follow me somewhere," I shrugged. I thought a minute. Look for the bug? A waste of time. How could I know how many bugs they'd left? Coming to that conclusion simplified my planning immensely.

"I'll see you, Fred," I said. "I won't need the car."

Jim's suitcase in hand, I headed up Eleventh, more suspicious than ever of all pedestrians. And vehicles. At Thirty-ninth a woman was getting out of a cab. I jumped into the back seat before she could close the door, earning an angry glare and a sniff from her in the process.

The black cabbie looked at me in the mirror as I closed the door. I checked the picture and the name on the medallion. *Eugene Marshall.* "You're a lot better-looking than your picture, Gene," I said.

"Thanks, man. And it's *Eu*-gene." He came down hard on the first syllable. "Where to, my man?"

"I think somebody's following me," I told him. "Lose 'em and then I'll tell you where we're going. Lose 'em good and it's a ten-buck tip."

His eyes widened and he gave a huge grin. "All *right*! Hang on, bro." He threw the Chevy in gear and roared northward with a squeal of tires. He glanced twice back over his left shoulder, bit his lip and executed a hairy, stomach-churning U-turn, and quickly had it up to fifty, screaming southward. He ran a red at Thirty-second, then hung a sliding right onto Thirty-first. I liked his style.

I watched behind us while my friend *Eu*-gene turned a few more corners. I saw no signs of anyone following—and plenty of signs that Eugene was a stock-car-circuit wannabee. We were loose. I probably had been all along. With a bug on the Caddy, my friends on the force had no reason to think they had to do anything but follow the bouncing beep all the way to Jim Kearney.

I tapped the driver's shoulder. "You're all right, Eugene. Now let's head for the Traveler's Inn at Newark Airport, okay?"

"Consider it done, bro." To my relief, Eugene promptly eliminated the racing maneuvers. We still made it in less than half an hour, the morning rush hour being in its death throes and us going against it anyway. We pulled up at the Traveler's Inn a little after 9:30.

The meter read $21.85. I slipped him fifty bucks and he dug for change. I stopped him.

"Just keep the change, Eugene. That's a deposit against the next time I need you. I've got your number off the medallion. You're a helluva driver."

"Need a ride back? I sure hate to go over to that airport and wait in line two hours."

I thought about it. "Not a bad idea. Stick around as long as you can. But if you get another fare, go ahead. I'll be about fifteen minutes or so."

"I'll be here, don't you worry."

Jim's room was decorated in standard motel kitsch: by-the-numbers landscape lithographs on three walls; big TV with remote control; two queen-sized beds; and your standard vomit-green carpet. Jim was delighted to get his suitcase and even more delighted with what was inside it. He opened it on the bed and riffled through the clothes lovingly.

"Wow! Clean underwear! And pajamas! Thanks, Davey."

I proceeded to give him a brief summary of my activities in St. Cloud. He didn't say anything or take his eyes off me for the twenty minutes it took. I ended by telling him how it now stood.

"Your dad will testify that the gun was still in the house after you left, but the cops aren't buying it. They're saying he's your dad, naturally he's going to try to get you off. So I'm suggesting you stick around here for another day or two while I continue investigating and the Bishop continues to think. Between us, maybe we can come up with something. Meanwhile, Davis Baker's working out a legal strategy in case the Bishop and I strike out. Did he call, by the way?"

"Yes. Right after I talked to you. Sounds like a guy who knows what he's doing."

"He does. You can trust Davis Baker absolutely."

Jim nodded, then frowned. "I've been thinking a lot, ever since I've been here, Davey. I haven't had much else to do. And mainly I've been thinking about that gun. If I didn't take it, who did? Whoever did must have killed Nick. Right?"

I nodded. "I can't see it any other way."

"So where does that leave Dad?" Jim frowned at me. "Do you think he did it?"

I looked at him. "One big objection to your dad being the killer is how could he have got into Nick's office. You had the combination to the outer door of the building. Did you give it to him?"

Jim shook his head. "Absolutely not."

"Or anyone else?"

"Or anyone else." His eyes were steady, his tone positive.

"So, first of all, it's hard to see how your dad could even have gotten in. But there's a second point. Aside from the way the two of you feel about each other, and aside from your dad's feelings for Nick— who was, after all, his son—it doesn't look like your dad did it. I've thought about it, too. And it looks to me like whoever killed Nick did it in a such a way as to implicate either you or your dad, by using a gun that was registered to the two of you. Well, that doesn't necessarily get your dad off the hook: he might have wanted to implicate you. But think about this: what sense does it make for your dad to go to all that trouble to implicate you, then come up with a story that gets you off? To go to all that trouble to get the gun there, then testify that the gun was still in the cabinet Tuesday night after you'd already gone back to New York? I can't see it."

Jim didn't look relieved, nor did I expect him to. I went on. "Okay. So let's talk about your mom. She's a little different. Unlike your dad, she's not alibiing you. So, from my standpoint, that makes her a more likely suspect than your dad." Jim looked pained.

I shrugged. "Sorry. But with her, there's another consideration. Motive. Did she even have one? To answer that, I need to know for sure whether she knew Nick was your half-brother. How sure are you that she didn't know about that first marriage?"

The pained look didn't leave Jim's face. "I've been thinking about that, too. I hate to say it, but I think she *did* know about Nick."

I looked at him. "But you said last week she didn't."

He nodded. "Yeah, that's what I thought at the time. But I've thought about it some since then." He shook his head. "I've been remembering some things. Little things. Like, just a couple of years ago, I happened to be home when Mom and Dad got into a fight. And she kind of screamed at him, something like, 'You can't pay Jerry Jordan to keep *this* secret!' I didn't get it at the time and I don't think Dad did either. But thinking back, I'm just wondering." He shrugged. "I just don't know."

I nodded and tucked the information away in the back of my mind. I had another thought. "What about Jordan? Do you think he knew the combination to the gun cabinet?"

Jim nodded. "I think so. He'd come over and shoot with Dad once in a while. And there were times when he'd come over and shoot by himself. I don't think I ever saw him open it, but I'll bet he knows the combination."

"And your mom?"

Jim frowned. "No. She never shoots a gun. Had no interest in it." He shrugged. "Of course, how hard would it have been for her to get it, if she ever really wanted it? With or without Dad knowing."

I got up. "Okay, Jim. I'm going to keep working. I don't know where we're going and neither does the Bishop. But we're working. You sit tight. I'll be in touch. And it shouldn't be much longer. Just tough it out. I promise you, you're in no danger of being picked up as long as you sit tight."

Famous last words.

31

E U G E N E was waiting as promised and got me back into Manhattan as quickly as he'd gotten me out of it. I had him drop me at Paddy's Pub. It was time to tilt a brew or two in a public house. Dirty work, drinking before noon, but somebody's got to do it.

I was happy to see Jake through the wide front window of the bar as I approached the door. He was sitting on the same stool he'd occupied the previous Friday. (Was he nailed to that barstool?) I thought I detected recognition in his eyes as he watched me cross the sidewalk to the front door. He was slouched over, hat pushed back on his head.

I pushed open the door and spotted Rocco the barkeep wearily swabbing down the far end of the bar. He glanced my way briefly but didn't stop swabbing. Jake, to my right, shifted his body a little but kept his eyes on the street. There was only one other stool at his end of the bar. Perhaps to keep the riffraff away, he'd draped a beat-up old sweater across the back of it. I went over, picked up the garment, folded it with care and placed it on the bar. Then plunked myself on the barstool. While I did, Jake gave me a hostile once-over. I pretended not to notice.

Imitating him, I turned my back to the bar and looked out the window. Through it I could see 849 West Forty-sixth, across the street. The view of both doors was excellent. As I watched, a young guy in a dark three-piece suit pushed through the revolving door, swung left and strode westward, out of my field of vision.

"What'll it be?" Rocco, behind my back.

"Beer for me," I called over my shoulder. "And a bump and a beer for Jake."

I turned to the beneficiary of my generosity, now openly staring at me. We studied each other. He was smaller than I'd thought, probably even shorter than Nick, making him nearly a foot shorter than me. By his sunken cheeks, covered with white bristles, I could tell he was missing more than a few teeth. His eyes were blue, watery and shrewd. Right now they were sizing me up.

"You're the guy was in here, when was it? With Nick. When was it?"

"Last Thursday."

"Yeah, Thursday. Couple days before he got it."

Rocco was back with two foaming steins and a shot glass filled with something brown. "That'll be four and a quarter," he told me, slapping the drinks on the bar, spilling some beer and some whiskey. I flipped him a ten-spot, dipped a fingertip in the spill from the shot glass and tasted it. Bourbon.

Jake picked up the shot glass. "Much obliged for the drink." He threw it back, put down the empty and picked up his beer. I did likewise.

"To your very good health, sir," I said, saluting him with my stein. We both swallowed beer.

Rocco didn't try to join our conversation, for which I was grateful. He probably saw me as bad luck, what with Nick dying the day after our first and only conversation. He may have even thought I was responsible. Whatever, he had no interest in talking.

"Another one, Jake?"

He shot me a knowing glance. "In a minute—maybe. What do you want, mister?"

"Call me Davey." He stared at me without answering. I pulled out the photo of Jim and Dinker and slid it in front of him. "Just wondered if you'd ever seen this guy."

Jake didn't take his eyes off my face. Finally he muttered, "Cops," and looked down at the picture. I expected him to give it a glance and push it away. He didn't. He studied it, even adjusted it to get better light on it, squinted at it, picked it up.

"Maybe," he sighed. "Who are they?"

"Never mind," I said. "And I'm just interested in the guy. Ever seen him?"

Jake grinned. "Like I said: maybe. Another bump'd help."

I grinned back at him and did some thinking. I liked the way this was starting out. He recognized Jim, I was sure of it. So another bump would no doubt be good value.

On the other hand: how many of these shots of bourbon could he take before he'd stop being of any use? Also, if he *had* seen Jim that Saturday afternoon, what else—or more to the point, *who* else—had he seen? I wanted the expert to hear what he had to say.

"Tell you what, Jake," I confided. "How about coming over to my place? I've got some imported beer and a better brand of bourbon. And I—"

He waved me away. "Forget that imported slop. That stuff's mouthwash. And Freddy's bourbon is just fine for me." He turned away.

I tried to recoup. "Hey, wait a minute. I've got whatever you like." (I hoped.) "Furthermore, I've got some good grub, if you want lunch. And . . ." I flipped a double sawbuck onto the bar. ". . . That's for your time."

He looked at the twenty, then at me. He shook his head. "Why can't we talk here? I can't tell you no more about him at your place than I can here."

I nodded. "I know. But I've got a friend who'd like to meet you."

Jake's eyes narrowed. "Mob captain? I thought you was fuzz."

I held his eye. "I'm neither. I'm just trying to help a friend. And the guy I want you to talk to is as far as you can get from mob. Guy's a Catholic bishop."

Jake turned away and stared into space. Scratched his head. Finally he sighed, picked up the twenty, chug-a-lugged the rest of his beer, wiped his mouth and slipped off the stool. "Okay, buddy. I'll go anywhere for twenty bucks. Well, almost anywhere."

32

M Y timing was nearly perfect. It was 11:09 when I let us into the mansion, so Regan would have been down from the chapel for eight minutes or so. Usually, when I'm not there to go through the mail for him, Ernie leaves it unopened on his desk, and he attacks it right away, leaving a mess of papers there for me to clean up later. With any luck he'd have polished the mail off, leaving him the time and energy to lend an ear to Jake. I just hoped he wouldn't be in one of his snits and refuse to talk to him, making the trip a waste of time. Not to mention twenty bucks.

I stashed Jake in my office, tapped on the Bishop's door and got the command to enter. As soon as I did, I saw he was running behind schedule, still adjusting the drapes of the south window. I'd adjusted them perfectly, just the way he likes them, at eight-fifteen, before leaving the house. Naturally, he was changing them, just to show he was still in charge around here.

"Yes, David. Anything to report?"

Good. He was on track, not in a snit. "Yeah, as a matter of fact, I do. Brought a guy for you to talk to. You'll be glad to know it's someone who can place our boy at the scene of the crime. Speaking of our boy, I just saw him. He's fine."

"Good. Now. Whom have you brought?"

"That boozer from the bar across the street from where Nick was murdered. The one Jim says he saw in the window. He recognized Jim from his picture. At least I think he did."

Regan nodded and wheeled toward his desk. "Name?"

"Jake."

The Bishop shook his head disgustedly. "Mr. Goldman. Can you imagine me addressing this man—or, on a first encounter, *anyone*—as Jake?"

I grinned. "Touché. I don't know his last name but I'll find it out. Right away. So is it okay if I go get him?"

No objections. Back in my office, Jake was trying to pace and finding it impossible, due to insufficient space.

"What the hell, buddy, a guy could die of thirst around here! If you haven't got any bourbon or good beer, I'll take the mouthwash. You're all blow and no—"

"Come on!" I grinned. "Be fair. I've already given you a twenty, right? I just had to clear the decks with the Bishop. Regan's his last name, by the way. He wants to know yours. He refuses to call anyone by their first name."

"Steiner. But what's that got to do with—?"

"Excuse me, Jake, but let me suggest something. I'll take you in there, introduce you to the man. Then I'll bring you a bump and a beer. And, to show my good faith, I'll leave the bottle of bourbon beside you, so you won't have to go thirsty again."

Jake's face lighted up and he followed me into the Bishop's office. I heard his slight intake of breath as he took in the sight of Regan in his purple robe and beanie, with the silver chain and cross around his neck.

"Bishop Francis Regan, this is Mr. Jake Steiner," I said with a slight bow in either direction. If the Bishop wanted formality, by God, he'd get formality. Regan gave Jake a nod and studied him through hooded eyes.

"Please, Mr. Steiner," he said. "Have a seat. Mr. Goldman, perhaps Mr. Steiner would like a drink."

Jake chuckled. "No perhaps about it, mister. And he knows what I want."

Regan nodded, turned to me. "And I'll have whatever Mr. Steiner is having, David."

I cocked my head at him. "But—" Regan's look shut me up. I headed for the kitchen, puzzled. Regan doesn't drink.

I ignored Ernie, grating carrots at her seat at the breakfast table, and pulled three Molsons from "my" side of the fridge. I went to the little cabinet in the corner—my bar, such as it is—and was happy to see my fifth of Jim Beam was still more than half full. I held it up to the light.

"I see you've been at this again, Ernie. It's down a good inch-and-a-half since yesterday."

She didn't even look up. "I laced the casserole with it, David. Why do you think he's in such a good mood?"

I grinned. "Not bad, Ernie!" I let out an appreciative chuckle. "Not bad at all." I got serious. "By the way, we might have an extra for lunch. Stay tuned."

"The more the merrier, David." She hadn't missed a beat with the grater when I walked out with the tray of drinks and the half-full bottle of bourbon.

Back in the office, Jake mumbled a thanks, raised his beer glass in the general direction of the Bishop, and swigged. Taking a sip of my own beer, I opened negotiations. "I showed Jake this picture, Bishop," I said, holding up the photo of Jim and Dinker. "And Jake says he recognizes the guy in it." Actually, Jake hadn't said that. But I hoped he was about to.

Jake tossed back the Jim Beam with the same speed he'd drunk the beer. Then took another sizable swig of beer. He gave me a look. "Thanks, buddy. That was worth the wait."

"Glad you think so, Mr. Steiner," the Bishop said. "You said you recognized the gentleman in the photograph?"

Jake nodded. "Saw him across the street from Freddy's last Saturday. Who is he? The guy that whacked Nick?"

"Possibly, Mr. Steiner," the Bishop said. "Though I'm inclined to think not. May we pour you some more bourbon?"

Jake shrugged. "Don't mind if I do. But I can do it myself." He reached for the bottle beside him.

"You ever met the guy before that?" I asked. "Or since?"

"Naw." He toyed with the bourbon refill but didn't drink it. "Like I said, just that once. Last Saturday."

"Then how can you be so sure it was him last Saturday?" I got up and put the picture on the table beside him. "Look at it again, will you, Jake?" He glanced down at it, shoved it away.

"I got good eyes, friend. And a good memory. I watch everything that happens out in front of Paddy's Pub, every day. Sometimes, like now, I get paid for it. So I'm sure. That's the guy I saw, you can take it to the bank."

"All right," said Regan. "You are certain. Tell us what you saw."

"Whaddaya mean? I saw *him!*"

"I realize that. I mean, what was he doing?"

Jake's eyes got crafty. "What's it worth to you, mister?"

Regan looked at me. My bailiwick. I spoke up. "Don't get greedy, Jake. I've slipped you twenty bucks, and you can have all the booze you can drink. And a good lunch." Jake opened his mouth, but I cut him off. "Tell you what. You tell us everything you saw last Saturday that had anything to do with this guy..." I pointed at Jim's photo on the table beside him. He glanced at it again. "... and everything you know about the comings and goings into and out of that building where Nick got shot—Eight Forty-nine. You do that and you get another fast twenty and a ride back to Paddy's Pub.

"But let me remind you of something else. Nick was a friend of yours and we're trying to find out who did him. So if you don't tell us, you'll just be making it harder for us to find his killer. I don't think you want to do that."

Jake pinned me with those watery eyes. They were steadier than I'd have expected after what he'd drunk. "Is that the truth? You're really looking for the guy that done Nick?" I nodded, and he then put his gaze on the Bishop. Who also nodded.

"Fine," Jake said, sipping more bourbon. He swallowed and his eyes watered. "Okay, I'll tell you everything I saw. I can use all the money I can get. But I'd also like to get the son of a bitch..." He gave Regan an apologetic nod.

"... excuse my French, mister—that did that to Nick." He drank some beer, wiped his mouth and looked at me, then the Bishop.

"We appreciate it," Regan told him. "Now. What time was it when you saw that gentleman?"

Jake frowned, looked away. "I can't tell you exactly, mister. But I *can* kind of work it out, know what I mean? He came about twenty minutes after Nick did. And I know what time it was when Nick came, 'cause he didn't come in Paddy's, and that surprised me. And that was a little after one-thirty. Maybe one-forty, I don't know. I get mixed up on exact times, know what I mean? But that's pretty close. Well, he—"

I stopped him. "You're saying Nick *always* came into the bar before he'd go into his building?"

Jake shook his head. "Not always, no, but usually. He'd come in, have a shot of Irish. Or else just slip me a fiver and go."

Jake shook his head gloomily, took a sip of beer, wiped his mouth. "It started a couple years ago, right after Valdez had his guys beat him up. Smashed in his face, broke one of his knees. I barely knew

Nick then, but I felt bad about it. He was always nice to me, know what I mean?

"Well, he went after Valdez. Him and Jeff and Shorty and couple of their buddies whipped up on Valdez somethin' fierce. And his bodyguards. There was a lot of hate goin' around right about then. Valdez swore he was gonna finish Nick." Jake took another swig.

As he did, the Bishop started to ask him a question but I waved him down. I was sure he was going to ask who Valdez was, and I already knew. Regan glanced at me sharply, then nodded and relaxed.

Jake swallowed beer and wiped his mouth. "Well sir, about a month later, I was just sittin' there in my spot in the bar. And I saw a couple guys go in Nick's building. A Wednesday mornin', it was. I'm watchin' like always, and I seen 'em go in. I didn't like it, somehow. I mean, I didn't recognize them, and they looked like hard cases.

"So I went outside and waited for Nick. When I saw him coming along the sidewalk on the other side of the street, I waved at him. He come over and I told him about the two guys I'd seen go in. Well sir, he came in the bar and called Jeff and Shorty right away, told them to get their butts over there and to bring some iron with them.

"Well sir, they come in the bar and meet Nick and then go across the street, the three of them. I guess they got the drop on the two guys waitin' inside the lobby, and then Jeff and Shorty worked 'em over a little. Maybe more'n a little. The two punks came out of there bleedin' like hell."

Jake grinned and finished his beer. I looked at the empty beer glass and raised my eyebrows. He looked at me, then at my empty. He shrugged. "Aw, what the hell, why not? Join me?"

I shrugged back. "Why not?"

Regan nodded and rang the silver bell on his desk. "Sister Ernestine can take care of it."

Jake grinned at him happily, reached for the Jim Beam and poured himself another shot. Ernie came, took orders and left. She gave a look at the untouched shot and the beer on Regan's desk but, of course, didn't say anything.

I prompted Jake. "So the two punks left. Then . . . ?"

He nodded. "So after that, Nick would always come in Paddy's first, case someone was layin' for him. We had a kind of a deal. He'd come in, ask me what I'd seen, any goons hangin' around, that kind of thing. And usually buy me a beer and a bump."

"He came in every day?"

"Naw, not every day. Sometimes he'd just throw me a wave from across the street. But he'd always at least wave. But Saturday, the second time, he didn't. He didn't come in; he didn't even look my way. Like he was in a hurry. Just went to the door, worked the combination in a hurry and went on in. I had me a bad feelin' about that. Somehow I knew things weren't going to go right when he didn't even give me a wave."

Regan frowned at him. "You say the second time?"

Jake nodded. "Nick went into that building twice last Saturday. First time, earlier, was about noon. Came in the bar for a second, just to say hello. Then went across the street."

"You're sure it was Mr. Carney?"

Jake didn't hesitate. "Oh, sure. He was right across the street. And I know him—knew him. That limp and all."

Ernie returned, carrying a tray with two bottles of beer. After she left, Regan glanced at me, then back at Jake. "He stayed in the bar only briefly?" Jake nodded. "And then how long was he in the building? The first time."

Jake shook his head. "Dunno. I musta been in the head when he left, cause I never saw him come out. But he musta,' cause he came back again at one-forty. I was surprised to see him cause I hadn't known he'd ever left. An' that was the time he didn't wave." Jake looked down. "An' that was the last time I ever saw him."

Regan thought about it. "All right, Mr. Steiner. Now, what interval of time elapsed between Mr. Carney's second entrance and the arrival of this other gentleman?" He pointed at Jim's picture, still at Jake's elbow.

Jake looked at him, deciphering the words. "Interval of time? Oh, about fifteen minutes."

"So, Mr. Carney arrived at about one-forty, and the other gentleman about one-fifty-five?"

Jake nodded. I jotted the times in my notebook. "All right," said Regan. "What made you remember the second gentleman?"

Jake shrugged. "I don't know. I just did."

"I doubt it, Mr. Steiner. There are usually reasons, if we look for them." Jake looked doubtful. "Well," said the Bishop. "Perhaps we will get it a different way. Tell us about the arrival of the second gentleman."

Jake frowned. "Like I say, he came along fifteen, twenty minutes later. He hadn't ever been there before. You could tell. First he looks around for the number on the building. Then he tries the revolving door. Sees the sign on it, sayin' it's closed weekends. Finally he gets to the side door . . . and what does he do? Just works the combo like he's done it all his life and goes on in." Jake grinned and shook his head. "You're right, mister. There *was* a reason. He stuck in my head 'cause it was funny. How'd a guy that didn't even know that was the building know what the combo was? But he knew it, and went on in. And not many people ever knew that combo, I want to tell you."

We waited while Jake took another swig of beer, wiped his mouth, gave a little belch. Regan's wince was barely perceptible, even to me. I couldn't believe how forbearing he was with this guy. When Jake didn't resume, the Bishop prompted him.

"And . . . ?"

Jake looked at him. "Sorry. Just thinkin' about Nick. A good guy. I miss him." He swallowed again.

"Okay. The redheaded guy came out of the building about ten minutes later, maybe less. I figured he must have been a delivery boy, except he didn't seem to be carryin' anything, going in or coming out. Anyway, he wasn't in that building no more'n ten minutes. Fact, I thought he musta not found whoever he was deliverin' to. 'Cause a cop was comin' along the sidewalk just as he come out of the building, and the first thing he did was stop the cop and start talkin' to him. He was pointin' at the building. The cop just shook his head at him and went on his merry way. The guy stood there lookin' after the cop, like his last friend just left town. Then he turned and looked right at me, lookin' real puzzled, and walked away. And that's the last I ever seen him."

"And what happened next?"

Jake frowned. "Somethin' was botherin' me, and I didn't know what. So I decided to go over there and see if Nick was okay. I went across the street and buzzed him. But—"

As usual, the Bishop was quicker than me. His voice came like the snap of a whip. "Excuse me, Mr. Steiner. You say you buzzed Mr. Carney. How were you able to get into the lobby in order to do that?"

Jake smiled toothlessly and shrugged. "I had the combo, a'course. Nick gave it to me a long time ago."

I shook my head disgustedly. "How many people did Nick give the combination to? Sounds like half the borough of Manhattan had it."

Jake chuckled and shook his head. "Not exactly." He sobered. "Naw, he didn't give it out much. He gave it to me, 'cause I was kind of his watchman, know what I mean? But, f'rinstance, Jeff or Shorty didn't have it. If Nick sent for 'em, they'd have to come across the street to have me open up for 'em. I don't know anyone else Nick gave it to."

"All right," the Bishop said. "Go on. You went across the street and signaled Mr. Carney. What happened?"

"Nothin'. Nobody there. I waited five minutes, so's I could buzz him again. Figured he must have gone to the head or something. Workman came through while I was waitin'. Then I—"

"Excuse me." The Bishop again. "A workman? What kind of work-man?"

"Oh, dunno. Just a janitor or workman. Wearin' overalls or some damn thing. Didn't really look at him. They're in and out of there a lot. Always workin' on something in that old building. See 'em all the time."

"In and out a lot?" Regan sounded irritated. "On a Saturday? Did you see any other workman that day?"

"Don't recollect that I did. And, yeah, that's right. They're normally not there on Saturdays. But they were that day. Least that one guy was."

"Do you recall anything else about him?"

Regan's interest was beginning to penetrate Jake. He screwed up his face. "Let's see. He might have been a little guy. Hard to tell, though, cause he was just pickin' up papers an' trash an' whatnot." He thought some more, finally shook his head. He'd told us all about the janitor he could.

"All right," Regan said. "Since you were actually in the building, did you happen to see the note taped to the inside of the glass door?"

That hadn't occurred to me. But Jake had no recollection of seeing any note, which was strange, since it had to have been there when Jake was. Regan finally shrugged it off.

He had another thought. He turned to me. "That picture that you brought back from Minnesota, if you would, David?" I nodded and headed for my office. A good idea, I thought. If Mike Kearney had gone over to that building, there was a good chance that Jake would have seen him. And if Jake saw him, he'd remember.

As I left the room Regan, was asking Jake to continue his story. Jake was talking when I returned. ". . . the cops got there a little before three."

"Very well. Now, if you would, Mr. Steiner, please examine the photograph Mr. Goldman has there. Do you recognize any of those people?"

I handed Jake the Hawaiian picture of Mike, Peggy and Jordan. He gave it a close, long look. He frowned, looked from face to face, nodded. "Uh, yeah. I think I seen this one guy. He—" Suddenly his eyes widened. "Wait a minute! Her too!" He looked at me, pointing at the photo. "I seen *two* of these people last Saturday!" I got up in a hurry, went over and stood behind him to see which faces he was pointing at.

"This guy!" he said, pointing to Jordan's ruddy face. "He came in the bar sometime that afternoon, sat in one of the booths, all by himself. Stayed quite a spell."

Jake frowned at the photo. "But the lady wasn't with him. She was on the sidewalk outside Nick's building that day! But she was there! I'm sure of it!"

Jake's shaky fingertip was touching the round, tanned face of the smiling Peggy Kearney.

The Bishop wasn't as excited as I was. At least he didn't show it. He quizzed Jake for nearly fifteen minutes, sounding a lot like Davis Baker cross-examining a hostile witness. At one point Jake blew up.

"Look, mister, if you don't want to believe me, that's just fine by me. I'm tellin' you what I saw. Now either get off my case or I'm gettin' out!"

"I beg your pardon." Regan bowed his head. "I'm merely attempting to satisfy myself that it was indeed this gentleman and this lady you saw and no one else. It *is* rather important."

Jake was mollified. A little. "Well . . ." He took a sip of beer. ". . . I expect I don't need to get on my high horse neither. You're just doin' your job, I s'pose."

Regan bowed. "Very gracious of you. And again, my apologies. Now, to recapitulate: you are completely certain that the woman whose likeness is in that photograph was 'hanging around,' as you put it, in the vicinity of Eight Forty-nine West Forty-sixth during the afternoon of Saturday last. And that the gentleman spent at least an hour, perhaps two, in the bar. Correct?"

"Correct."

"And neither of them gave any evidence of seeing the other, or being aware of the presence of the other."

"Correct again."

"And were either of them present when the police arrived a little before three?"

Jake scratched his head and screwed up his face. "The guy was. I noticed, 'cause he was sittin' down the bar from me and he was takin' almost as much interest in the goings-on as I was." Jake shut his eyes hard. "But the lady . . . I just didn't notice. Maybe she was, maybe she wasn't."

Regan waited to see if he had anything to add. Decided he didn't. "All right, Mr. Steiner. And you have never seen either of them— the woman or the man—before or since?"

"Nope."

"How long did you remain in that pub?"

"Rest of the afternoon."

"Can you recall seeing anyone else enter or leave that building before the police arrived?"

Jake shrugged. "Not that I saw. I do have to go the head every once in a while. But I didn't see anyone else come or go, up till the cop car came and they went in and found Nick dead."

"And you're certain you had never seen the man or the woman before? For instance, around that office building?"

Jake nodded. "Or since."

"And they didn't appear to know each other?"

"Hell, like I said, they didn't even *see* each other! She was only there twice, and only a minute or two each time. And she was on the sidewalk, not in the bar."

Regan looked at the floor for nearly a minute while Jake and I sat in silence. Finally Regan spun his chair around and wheeled for the west wall. And began "pacing."

As I said, my office is no good to pace in: not enough room. Well, the Bishop's is plenty big enough, and he does plenty of it, if you can call wheeling back and forth in a wheelchair pacing. He does it a lot, especially when he's thinking hard. I knew why he was doing it now. Jake's sighting of Jordan and Peggy had come at us from out

of left field. What did it mean? One thing was sure: Jim's suspicion
that Peggy had known about Nick was on the money. And what had
Jordan been doing there? He liked to drink, but he didn't just acci-
dentally pick Paddy's Pub out of the eight thousand bars in Manhattan
to go have a few early-afternoon pops. He'd been there for a reason.
But what was the reason?

Jake watched Regan for two passes, wall to wall, got tired of that
and looked at me. "Okay if I have another?"

Before I could answer, the doorbell chimed. I jumped up, told
Jake, "Help yourself," and headed for the door. Ernie was preparing
lunch, and I was hungry enough to hold her labors sacred.

It was Dinker, and I might as well admit it: my heart jumped a
little as soon as I saw her.

I swung the door open and tried to give her my Irish imperson-
ation: "And a foine marnin' it is, me girrl! Welcome to our—" but
Dinker, pale as a ghost, shouldered past me and headed down the
hall with barely a glance for the leprechaun. I was stunned. I
slammed the door and hurried after her, calling her name. Didn't
slow her a bit. She charged into the Bishop's office, followed quickly
by yours truly.

Tableau: Jake, holding his beer, nearly dropped it as he gawked at
the tall brunette. And Regan, his reverie well and truly interrupted,
glared up at her. Dinker glared back. "Do you know what you've
done?" she shrieked at him. I moved quickly to get in between them.
At the moment, Dinker looked capable of attacking him physically.
And in the mood to.

All three of us men started sentences simultaneously. I upped my
volume to get the floor. "Dinker! What the hell's the matter with
you?"

Her face scared me. It was so white I could see freckles I never
knew were there. Her lips quivered and her eyes were wild, looking
everywhere but at me. I moved in, got a firm grip on both shoulders,
waited till I had her eye and repeated my question: "What's the
matter, Dinker?"

Her eyes focused on me and filled with tears. "It's Jim!" she
said, her voice catching. She tried to clear her throat, moved side-
wards to look at Regan. "I'm sorry, Bishop," she told him in a more
normal tone. "This is awful. But I didn't know what to do, where
to go . . ."

I forced her back in front of me, got her eye again. "You said something about Jim, Dinker. What is it?"

"He just called me!" she gasped. "The police have him! They've arrested him! He's in jail, Davey!" Her voice broke on the last word. She put her head on my chest and let the tears come.

33

TH E Bishop rolled to his favorite spot next to the south window. I heard him sigh—a sigh of contentment, not exasperation. Things were happening and, by his lights at least, bad happenings are better than no happenings at all.

My own feelings were mixed. Dinker in my arms felt right. The human body has its own system of Braille: a memory of how other human bodies feel. I seemed to pick up with Dinker right where we'd left off the night before. The texture of her blouse, the ridge of her collarbone and the warmth of the skin below felt familiar; and her warm flesh made my fingertips tingle.

But my brain was distracted by something else: Jim was in jail. A brief battle over what to do about Dinker ensued: the body wanted to hang on, while the brain wanted more information.

Before mind and body could come to some agreement, Jake cleared his throat. Dinker went stiff and her head jerked sideways. She suddenly realized it wasn't just me, her and Regan in here.

I let her go and turned to Jake. "Yeah, excuse me. Miss Galloway, Mr. Steiner. Mr. Steiner, Miss Galloway."

Jake grinned at her. "Sure, I seen her before." He chuckled at my surprise. "Hey, she's the one in the picture with that other fella." His eyes narrowed at me. "Isn't she?"

I stared at him for a second; then realized he was talking about the picture of Jim I'd shown him. It had also included Dinker. "Yep. She's the one."

"I'm sorry!" Dinker's discovery of a stranger in the room seemed to bring her back to herself. And her manners. "I'm interrupting a meeting, aren't I?" She turned to me. "What picture, Davey?"

"The one I took last night," I explained. "Jake here picked Jim out from it."

Dinker's mouth formed an *oh*. She looked at Jake admiringly. "You have a good memory for faces, Mr. Steiner."

Jake grinned. "Damn good one, little lady, when a gal's as purty as you. Call me Jake."

But she'd already forgotten about him. She turned back to Regan. "I'm sorry to be so rude, Bishop. But when Jim called—from jail— after both of you promised me he'd be safe, I—"

Regan showed her a palm. "Excuse me, madame." He turned to Jake. "Mr. Steiner. I'm sorry, but I must rescind my luncheon invitation. Mr. Goldman will see to a cab for you."

Jake jumped up. "That's fine," he muttered. "I'm like a fish out of water here, anyhow." He looked up at me. "Let's go, friend. 'Bye, little lady."

He went to Dinker and shook her hand, finally getting the smile he'd been after. I couldn't blame him for that, though I did think the "little lady" took some chutzpah; she had a good two or three inches on him.

I called Jake a cab, and waited with him at the front door till it arrived. He didn't pester me with small talk or questions about Dinker. Maybe he noticed I was in no mood to listen. How in the name of God, I wondered, had the cops found Jim? I'd narrowed the possibilities some by the time the cab arrived. I let Jake out and was closing the door when the answer came—and I saw red.

Baker! It had to be! When he'd failed to get *me* to turn Jim in, he'd turned him in himself. After I'd trusted him!

I stomped back into Regan's office. He was studying Dinker and she was talking. She glanced at me but kept talking.

". . . you see, Jim really liked Nick. Oh, he thought he was a crook— like most of us in the show. But he really did like him."

Regan ignored me. "And when did you first know that they were brothers?"

Dinker looked at him. "When Jim told me a week ago Sunday. Right after Nick told him."

The Bishop nodded. He was starting a new question when Dinker glanced at me and interrupted.

"If you don't mind, Bishop. I'm too nervous to talk about it now. I've got to go see Jim. I thought maybe Davey could go with me. I don't know anything about jails." She smiled at me. Tried to, anyway. "You know about jails, don't you, Davey?"

I shrugged. I knew plenty about jails. I also knew I wanted to kill Davis Baker.

"So could you take me to see Jim?"

I shook my head. "Excuse me, Dinker. Let me see if I can figure out what's going on. I just saw Jim this morning. What happened? Did he say?"

She shook her head. "He just said he'd been arrested and I should tell you. And that you should call his lawyer."

I frowned. "Didn't he tell you how he got arrested?"

Dinker threw up her hands. "No, nothing! Do you know how to get hold of his lawyer?"

I nodded grimly. "Getting hold of him is exactly what I intend to do. Let's go call him."

Dinker got up but Regan stopped her. "Mr. Goldman doesn't need you for that, Miss Galloway. I have more questions—if you don't mind?"

Dinker looked at me. I shrugged. "Go ahead and talk. I'll be right back. I've just got a little score to settle."

Regan gave me a long, puzzled look, shrugged, turned to Dinker. She was settling back into the chair when I closed the door.

I called Baker, cutting Cheryl off when she started into her joshing routine. Probably hurt her feelings, but I was in no mood.

Baker sounded harried and rushed. "Yeah, Davey. What do you want?" His tone should have told me I was making a mistake. But I was too mad to listen for tones.

"When did you call the cops, Davis?"

"What?"

"You heard me."

"What *are* you talking about, Davey?"

"You son of a bitch, you know damn well what I'm talking about! Kearney's in jail."

"The hell you say! He's—"

"You didn't know about it?"

"*No!* Davey, what the hell! You think I'd do a thing like that, after giving you my word? What are you—?"

"Hold it." Time to use my brain. Better late than never. "Let's start over," I said in a quieter, more respectful tone. "I'm really off target, aren't I?"

"You damn well are! What the hell's the matter with you?"

I shook my head. Was I losing my grip? "Look, I'm sorry, man. I should have known better. But I couldn't think of any other explanation. I *still* can't. How did they find him? I *know* they couldn't have followed me there. There's no way!"

A new idea suddenly hit me. It was my day for brilliant ideas, all of them wrong. "How about this? Jim *told* someone! And that someone tipped the cops."

Baker wasn't buying. "Try something else, Davey. I talked to him about that very thing. He swore up and down he hadn't and wouldn't. I think he meant it."

"He told me the same thing. But there's always slip-ups."

"Not this time, and I'll tell you why. I made him name all the people he'd called since he checked into the Traveler's Inn. It totaled up to one. That was to his theater guy, the director, what the hell's his name?"

"Rosen."

"Right, Lenny Rosen. He'd called him to let him know he'd have to take him out of the show indefinitely. He says he was *very* careful not to tell Rosen where he was. Nope, Jim's not your leak."

I pounded the desk with the flat of my hand. "Damn! I wish Parker and I were still talking." I took a deep breath. "Okay, I'll just have to worry about it later. For now, how about getting over to the jail on the double and seeing if you can spring him?"

"Not going to be easy, Davey. It's the big one. Plus, as I tried to tell you this morning, Kessler's going to be pissed about him taking a run-out. So will the D.A. He's not going to want the judge to grant bail. And, depending on who the judge is, he might get his way."

"I know, I know. It's bleak. But do your best, man. And—sorry about blowing my stack."

"Don't worry about it. I'll take it out of your hide Saturday on the golf course." He probably would, at that. I walked back into Regan's office, thinking about Jim and Lenny Rosen and whether Jim had been as careful as Baker thought.

The Bishop had rolled his chair up close to his desk and set the brake. He was sitting with both elbows resting on the desktop, listening to Dinker talk about Jim. They both turned to me, eyes inquiring.

"We can take our time," I told them. "Baker's handling it. He's now on his way to headquarters, which is probably where Jim is. Dave'll call us after he's talked to him. Then I'll run you down there, Dinker. Not to worry."

She looked frail and helpless. She turned back to the Bishop, who was drumming his fingers on his desk, eyes still on her. I rolled my eyes. Normally Regan gets antsy and won't sit in one position more than five minutes. But with Dinker to look at he was perfectly content at his desk after ten all-too-short minutes. It's what I said before about the Bish and good-looking females. Not that I'm in any position to criticize.

He ignored my look. "Good. This is useful. Go ahead with what you were saying, Miss Galloway." He waved at an empty chair for me to sit down.

Dinker glanced at me. "I was just telling the Bishop that Jim flew back here from Minnesota a week ago yesterday—Tuesday afternoon. We had rehearsal that night."

"All right," said Regan. "And when did you first see him after his return? That is, when you could talk."

Dinker frowned at him. "That night after rehearsal. He came over."

Regan nodded. "And how did he seem?"

She shrugged. "What do you mean? Same as always."

"Did he mention anything about pistols? His practicing with his handgun while at home—or anything else involving guns?"

Dinker shrugged. "Nothing."

Regan nodded. "All right, let's go on to last Friday night. The party in Mr. and Mrs. Kearney's suite at the Plaza Hotel."

She nodded. "After the opening?"

"Yes. You were there—along with Mr. Goldman and me and some others. You spent some time talking with Mrs. Kearney, did you not?"

"Right." Dinker smiled.

"Did you get into any relevant topics? Such as Mr. Nick Carney.

Or the stolen gun. Or anything else that might conceivably be related to Mr. Carney's death."

Dinker frowned. "Not about the gun. As for Nick, yes, I think she did say something about him. What was it?" She rubbed her chin. "She said Mike must be in the other room with 'that poor man.' That's what she called Nick: 'that poor man.' I asked her why she called him that, but she didn't really answer. Said it was just an expression."

Regan nodded. "What about Mr. Kearney, Senior—or Mr. Jordan, the attorney? Did you have any discussion with them? Anything, that is, that might be related to Nick Carney's death?"

Dinker shook her head. "I'm sorry. No."

"All right. Now we're ready to talk about today. How did you learn of Mr. Kearney's incarceration?"

"He called me. Just half an hour ago. He said he was at police headquarters or something."

I had a question. "Did he say they were booking him?"

"Yes! *Booking!* That's the word he used."

I nodded to Regan. "Okay. That'll take them a while. And meantime, they're going to want to talk to him. They won't have taken him to jail yet." I turned to Dinker. "I spoke with the lawyer just now. He's excellent. He'll call to let us know when we can go see Jim." I turned to Regan. "Any more questions?"

He had none. "Perhaps the two of you could wait for Mr. Baker's call in your office, David?"

We were dismissed. Dinker stood and looked down at Regan. "Thank you, Bishop. Thanks for caring."

He nodded abruptly, swung his chair away, stopped and swung back. "Go with God, Miss Galloway. My prayers are with you. My best to Mr. Kearney when you see him." He headed for the south window.

34

T H E phone was ringing as Dinker and I entered my office. I hoped it was Baker. It wasn't, but it was the next best thing: Cheryl Grossman.

"Davis just called, Davey," she said, sounding hurt. "And he said to call you. I took some notes—if I can find them."

I had to make peace. "Uh, Cheryl."

"Just give me a minute, Davey." Irritated. "I said I'll find them, okay?"

"Cheryl. Listen, I just want you to know I'm sorry I was short with you before. I'm just a little harried today. Anyway, I'm sorry. Okay?"

"Sure, Davey. I understand." Still miffed, but on the mend.

It was another minute before she found her notes. "Okay, Davey. I hope you can make sense out of this. He says Parker's not back from Minnesota, they can't get hold of him, and Blake's in charge . . ." I cursed under my breath. ". . . and, uh, Harrington's requesting no bond . . ." I cursed again. ". . . and they're in the process of booking Jim Kearney. Dave says you should get right down there if you want to see the guy."

I waited. "That's it?"

"That's it, Davey."

I hung on the line another minute to finish my fence-mending with Cheryl. By the time I put down the phone we were back on decent terms. Not great but decent. I'd work on it.

"Come on, Dinker," I said, getting up. "Let's go see Jim."

Driving over, I filled her in. "You met Lieutenant Blake, right? Well, he's in temporary charge of the case. I *hope* it's only temporary."

"You know him? You didn't tell me that yesterday."

"He's not someone I care to talk about. He and I were rookies together, thirteen years ago. We disliked each other from the start and things have deteriorated since."

"Why?"

I shrugged. "He's NYU, I'm Queensboro Community College, and I guess that about says it all. He's proof positive that any idiot can get a college degree."

Dinker laughed. "Is he an idiot? He didn't strike me that way. Kind of scary, was my impression."

"Wait till you get to know him a little better. His overall dumbness sort of grows on you."

I was happy to find Molly Folsom, my favorite desk sergeant, on duty.

I pounded on the counter. "Service! Can we have some service? We common people demand to be heard!"

Molly gave me a mock glare. "Shaddup before I throw you in the slammer!" Her face relaxed. "How you doin', Davey?"

"Never better, Moll. Meet Diane Galloway. And keep a civil tongue in your head. She's a lady. You've heard of those? Diane, this is my favorite sergeant, Wholesome Folsom."

"Gladda meetcha, Diane," Molly said. Dinker smiled at her, then glanced up at me, probably wondering where the sudden "Diane" came from. So did I.

Molly turned back to me, all business now. "Davey. Mr. Baker's in Conference Room A. I told him I'd send you in as soon as you got here. Both of youse. Think you can still find it?"

"In my sleep, Molly, in my sleep. Thanks." I turned to go.

"Oh, Davey." I turned around, surprised at the change in Molly's tone. "A word to the wise, boy-o. Blake's on your case, big time." Molly's face was as serious as her tone. I winked at her and she winked back but her heart wasn't in it. I smiled at Dinker as we started toward Room A, but my heart wasn't in it either.

Baker was there as promised, feet on the battered conference table. He was writing furiously on a yellow legal pad propped up in his lap. "Ah, you're here!" He put his feet down and swung around in the chair. Saw Dinker and stood up, eyes appreciative.

"So how do we stand, Davis?" I asked after introducing them.

He tore his eyes away from Dinker. "Uh, bad. They're interrogating him right now. I've been trying to reach Parker, but I guess he's not back from Minnesota. So Blake's running the show, and you know what that means. I sure wish we had Parker."

A too-familiar voice came from behind us. "Well, you don't." Blake, in the doorway. I turned around. "And you won't. He's off the case. No more sweetheart arrangements, gentlemen. What you see is what you get. Which is—or soon will be—Assistant District Attorney Lampton. Your boy's going in the slammer."

Blake's pomaded hair, perpetual sneer and lousy disposition scented the air. He didn't offer to shake hands, which was disappointing. It would have been nice to leave him there with his hand hanging out.

Baker spoke. "Can I see my client now?"

Blake eyed him. "Which one?"

Davis rolled his eyes. "Come on, Charlie, don't go coy on me. You know damn well who I mean."

Blake grinned unpleasantly. "I thought you might've meant Davey here." He grinned at me. "Mr. Lampton's very interested in bringing charges. For obstruction of justice. You may not know it, Counselor, but this shamus advised your client—your *other* client—to go out of state and into hiding. And that's a felony."

I tried my own version of a sneer. "You can't—"

"Hold it, Davey." Baker moved in on Blake. "No way you can charge Davey, Charlie. I know exactly what he did. And I can tell you, he didn't violate a single damn law. So—"

Blake stopped him. "So sorry, Mr. Baker, but I'm a public employee. So you'll excuse me if I get *my* legal interpretations from the D.A., not you. If you don't mind?"

"You do what you damn well please, Charlie. But—"

Blake cut him off again. He loves cutting people off. "And I don't agree with your interpretation of this one, *Mister* Baker. Goldman advised Kearney to go to the Traveler's Inn in Newark and check in under an assumed name, and furnished him with the false I.D. to do it with. You know about the phony credit card?"

I couldn't hold off. "Blake, you're so dumb, you'd have to double your I.Q. to qualify as an imbecile. That's *my* credit card, I've used it for years, and there's nothing wrong with—"

Blake was getting red, which was satisfying, and about ready to start throwing punches, which was gratifying. But before I could get in another word, one that might have got things started, Baker was in my face.

"Davey," he said through his teeth. "Shut. Up." He turned to Blake and said, a little more politely but still through his teeth, "Would you excuse us, Lieutenant?"

Blake was loving it, his worst enemy quarreling with his lawyer. "Oh, absolutely. Take as long as you want, Counselor. I'll be in my office, calling the jail. Tell you what I'll do. I'll ask the boys to see if they can put him in the same cell he had the last time."

Blake strode out the door, shoulders up, step jaunty. Nice to see a guy that loves his work.

35

"DAVEY, what the hell are you doing?" Baker was livid.

"He gets on my nerves."

"Well, wake up and smell the coffee, son. Blake hasn't got anything he can make stick. But you're doing your damnedest to change that."

I did what my mother always taught me to do: took a deep breath while counting to ten. In Hebrew. By the time I got to *yod* I was feeling better. I took a deep breath. "Okay, Dave. You tell me. What're we going to do?"

He nodded. "That's better. We're going to go talk to Jim and see what he knows. Then we're going to get him out of here."

"How?"

"We'll see if the judge'll set bond. If he won't, then we'll go to work proving him innocent. If he will set bond, we'll see about posting; you said his old man's rich, didn't you?"

I nodded.

"Then we'll get him to post. Then we'll have our guy out—yes, Mike?"

Sergeant Mike Burke was at the door, burly and impassive as always. I used to work for him, back when I was in Homicide. He nodded to us briefly.

"Mr. Baker, Davey. Inspector wants to talk to you, Davey. And you can see Kearney, Mr. Baker, before we take him to jail. C'mon."

Burke spun on his heel and started down the hall, expecting us to follow. "Hold it, Mike," I called. He stopped and turned around. "May I introduce Jim Kearney's girlfriend, Miss Diane Galloway. She's—"

Burke nodded at her. "I know who she is, Davey." He turned to her. "You want to see the prisoner now, Miss Galloway, or after he's finished with his lawyer?"

Dinker looked from Baker to me, seeking guidance. Baker spoke. "She can come along now, Sergeant. My client and I have no secrets from Miss Galloway."

Burke nodded abruptly. "Fine. C'mon with me, all of youse." He took off again. We followed as instructed.

Burke strode ahead of us down the hall to Kessler's office. When he reached it he turned around. "In here, Davey."

"Thanks, Mike." I turned to Dave and Dinker. "I'll be with you in a minute. See if you can find out anything—mainly, does he have any idea how they located him?" Baker nodded. He and Dinker left, following Burke.

I tapped on the door and got invited in. The Inspector was at his desk. Across from him was a dark-haired guy about my age. I didn't know him. "Come in, Davey," Kessler said. "I don't think you know Dick Lampton. New Assistant D.A. Just came on board . . . when, Dick?"

The younger man was on his feet, unsmiling, his three piece midnight-blue pinstriped suit an armor guarding his virtue. "First of the year," he muttered, annoyed at having to give out classified information. He gave my hand a perfunctory shake and sat back down.

Kessler waited till I was down and got my eye. "You've got yourself into a jam, Davey. Some folks around here would like to throw the book at you."

"Blake," I shrugged.

"Not just Blake. But I've asked Dick to hold off for a while on any indictment to see if you can't give us some help. I know you've been scouting around on this thing. Sergeant Parker was real surprised to find you out in Minnesota digging up info about the gun. And frankly, Davey, it looks to us like you and the accused's father have worked out a little cock-and-bull story to try to show that the accused couldn't have taken the gun. Any comment?"

I shook my head. "What do you want me to say? Any answer I'd give to that would be either self-serving or incriminating. I will say for the record that, if it's a made-up story, it was made up before I ever got there. I was as surprised as anyone to hear the father tell it."

Lampton, looking both bored and officious at the same time, got to his feet. "I don't have time for this," he grumped. "If you don't need me any more, Inspector, I have work to do." He faced me. "Tell Mr. Baker he can call me if he needs any more information about the charges. Mr. Kearney is to be held in jail till a bond hearing next Monday. Before Judge McKinnick."

I nodded, which seemed sufficient response under the circumstances. Lampton stalked out.

Kessler's eyes twinkled. "Care to change your story now that he's gone, Davey?" I just shook my head. "He's new," Kessler went on. "Very full of himself."

I shrugged. "Just a guy doing his job."

Kessler's teeth showed through the beard. "Oh? Is this the new Davey Goldman? Full of peace and harmony?"

I was suddenly tired. "Do you really think my guy did it, Inspector?"

Kessler thought that one over and nodded deliberately. "Yes, I do. The circumstantial evidence against him is overwhelming. Frankly, the weakest part of our case is the motive. And it's not bad—Carney's death removed a possible claimant to his daddy's millions. Only trouble with it is, why the rush? But I'm hearing that this Nick might have been threatening to tell Kearney's mom about the daddy's first marriage, which she didn't know about."

"That's a motive for the daddy, not the son."

"Maybe. But the daddy could have made it a motive for the son. And we can't place the daddy at the scene of the crime. The son was there, we know that, right at the time the murder took place."

"Yeah," I said sarcastically. "And went straight up to Patrolman Abernathy, so Abernathy could finger him later. That sounds real logical, doesn't it?"

Kessler shrugged. "Maybe not. But I'm not about to lose any sleep over it. I know you and Bishop think that's important. Well, I can give you five or six good reasons, right off the top of my head, why a killer might have pulled that. Including, that it might fool some oversmart would-be dick into thinking he didn't do it. I'm talking about the Bishop, not you, Davey, when I say 'oversmart.' I'd never accuse you of being oversmart."

"Thanks. Nice to know I'm respected."

Kessler shrugged. "You'd be respected a lot more if you hadn't led us straight to Jim Kearney."

That got my attention. I stared at Kessler for several long seconds. He just stared back, placidly waiting. "*I* led you to Kearney?" He nodded, shrugged again. I closed my eyes and thought. Unfortunately, I'm not the Bishop and closing my eyes and thinking doesn't get the same results for me. All that came to me was a wide selection of impossible theories. My friend *Eu*-gene, the cabby: a police snitch? Impossible. A tap on our phone? Not impossible; they *could* have obtained a court order. But it had been too early to get a court order and put the tap in. Besides, knowing Kessler, if he did a tap, he wouldn't tip me to it. I had no answer. It was humiliating, but I had to ask.

"So how did I lead you to him, Inspector?"

He was loving it. Not as much as Blake would have, but enough. "You know better than to ask that, Davey. Besides, I don't really know. It was Blake's operation. And sorry to tell you this, Davey, I know how you feel about both of them, but I just jerked Parker and put Blake back in charge of the investigation. Joe just hasn't cut it. He's on his way back from Minnesota right now with zilch. Worse than zilch, because what he's got is that cockamamie story you and the dad worked out between you—no, don't bother to deny it, Davey, I know you too damn well. But Joe's starting to buy it. So he's no longer in charge. I need someone more—"

"More of a jackass."

Kessler grinned, unperturbed. "I was going to say more objective. But have it your own way, Davey, if it makes you feel any better."

He got to his feet. "I've got things to do. And you probably want to talk with your client before he gets taken to jail. I've left word it's okay for you to see him. Oh, and keep your head down, Davey. Blake's after it, and I'm going to give it to him if you pull another fast one." I got up and we shook hands. He was certainly in a good mood. Too bad good moods aren't contagious.

36

T H E visit with the prisoner—my portion of it, anyway—was short and sour. A cop guarding the door let me in and locked the door behind me. Jim looked depressed and his handshake matched: weak and listless. His face was drawn and gaunt-looking and his skin pasty. He was already feeling defeated.

Dinker looked up at me as I came in, looking nearly as frightened as Jim. And as pale. "We're about done, Davey," Baker said. "Blake wants his pound of flesh for the run-out. We don't get McKinnick till Monday. And then they want no bond. And with what they've got, they'll probably get it." He gave Jim a smile. "But not without a fight."

I felt, if possible, worse than Jim looked. "Have you talked yet about how the cops managed to find him?"

My question was for Baker but Jim answered, his low voice cracked and hoarse. "Yeah. We've talked about it but got nowhere. I *swear* I only made that one call to Lenny, and I *know* I didn't mention where I was. So it didn't come from me." I nodded, unsurprised. More confirmation of Kessler's gloat. And of my own incompetence. Dammit, how did Blake do it?

There wasn't much else to say. Davis rapped on the door and Jim and Dinker kissed, very tearfully. After the guard took Jim away,

Baker and I were left to deal with Dinker's tears. As the three of us headed for the front desk I had my arm around her shoulders, and Dave was saying things like, "This is just a temporary setback, don't you worry . . ." blah, blah, blah. But it seemed to help. A little.

Davis and I agreed to stay in touch. Then I drove Dinker to her apartment. On the way I told her how I'd screwed up by leading the cops to Jim. There's something about pretty girls that makes me tell the truth. Compulsion or something. By the time I finished, we were double-parked, motor running, in front of her building in the Village. She tried to comfort me.

"Davey, you've got nothing to be ashamed of. You did everything you could to *avoid* leading the cops to him. You didn't do anything wrong! You know what I think? I think the Inspector just said that to throw you off."

I thought about it. Out of the mouths of babes, it says somewhere, and Dinker was certainly a babe in my favorite sense of the word. So maybe she'd hit on something. I felt a little better, if no closer to solving the puzzle. She slipped out of the car without giving the driver a kiss.

"Call me, Davey," she said, leaning in the door. "Especially if anything comes up about Jim." That made me remember something we'd forgotten to talk about.

"What about Jim's mom and dad?" I said. "Who should call them?"

"Oh!" She got back in the car, leaving the door open. "Jim did ask me to call them. But I'm no good at that sort of thing. Would you mind, Davey?"

The more I thought about it, the more I liked the idea. Not that my favorite thing is telling people their son's in the clink. But it wouldn't be that big a shock, since they were already expecting it. And I wanted to test their reactions to the news. They were still two of the primary suspects as far as I was concerned. So: "No problem, Dinker. I'll call them."

She gave a sigh of relief. "Want the number, Davey? Jim just gave it to me." She reached into her purse and pulled out a notepad. "Want to take it down?"

"No need. I've already got it. Hey, don't give me that look. Isn't it . . . ?" I rattled off the ten-digit number, starting with 612.

She stared at me. "You memorized it? How do you do that?"

I shrugged. "Hey, what did you think I was, just another pretty face?" She smiled and put her notepad back in her purse. Her face got serious.

"Thanks for doing this, Davey," she said and kissed her fingertip and laid it gently against my cheek. She repeated her invitation to call. I promised I would and drove away feeling virtuous and a lot better about my own capabilities.

Back at the mansion, Regan was at his desk, a giant tome open before him. He peered up at me over his reading glasses. "News?"

"All bad," I growled. "Got time for a rundown?" He nodded, pushing the huge book to one side. I proceeded, without benefit of notebook for once, to give him the situation at headquarters. He listened carefully, adjusting and readjusting the brake on the wheelchair, but listening, mostly with eyes closed. He thought for a minute after I finished.

Finally: "So he's to be held until Monday?" I nodded. Regan must have seen me through his eyelids, because he went on, still without opening his eyes, "And the murderer remains at large."

"You know who it is?" I wouldn't have been surprised, after the stunts he's pulled in the past.

"No, David, I don't, beyond the fact that he is *not* Mr. Kearney. *James* Kearney, that is." He turned away, drumming on the arms of his wheelchair. He always does that when he's facing an unpleasant set of options.

"Hey!" I said. "You stumped? Ready to give up on it?"

He swung back to me. "Not at all. I'm simply frustrated at the difficulty—indeed, the seeming impossibility—of solving this case with only the information we already have. Or which we can expect to get here in New York."

I shrugged. "Would it help to talk about it?"

"With you? Hardly. What do you know that I don't?" He pounded the wheelchair again. "We need new *information*, David, not more talk about the information we already have. We know someone spirited that gun out of the house in St. Cloud. Who? We know that Mr. Jordan and Mrs. Kearney were in the vicinity of Nick Carney's office building last Saturday. Why? I see no way to obtain answers to either of those questions without traveling to St. Cloud."

I stared at him. "Traveling to St. Cloud? Are you nuts? I just came back from there!"

"I know, David, and your efforts were productive. Perhaps too productive. I see no way to utilize the progress you made without going there again." He scowled at me. "Both of us."

"Come on! There's got to be another way. Think!"

"Perhaps." His scowl eased off a bit and he nodded. "Two individuals here remain to be interviewed. First of all, Mr. Milt Manning. What impelled him to cancel the meeting with Mr. Carney Saturday afternoon? *Did* he in fact cancel? Perhaps you should speak with him."

I made a notation in the notebook. "No sweat. Who else?"

Regan frowned. "How well do you know Mr. Rosen?"

I stared. "Lenny Rosen?" Regan nodded. I shrugged. "No better or worse than you. Why?"

"He probably knew Nick Carney as well as anyone to whom we've spoken, with the exception of Mr. Steiner. More importantly, he was summoned by Nick Carney while we were in that dressing room last Friday night. Summoned to what purpose, I wonder?

"It's highly possible that Messrs. Manning and Rosen can tell us things about Mr. Carney which no one else can. We should learn more about their relationships. Such knowledge, we can hope, may render unnecessary what otherwise would be an arduous trip, one I'd prefer to forego. Can you arrange to meet with both Mr. Rosen and Mr. Manning? Soon?"

"Hey, consider it done." I got up and headed for my office.

I had Dinker's number, and she'd certainly know Lenny's number. As to Milt Manning, well, I'd worry about him later. I'll admit, talking to Dinker was a lot more pleasant assignment than trying to figure out how to contact a heavy like Manning.

But I couldn't call her before fulfilling the promise I'd made her— to call Jim's parents. I've have to do that first.

I punched out the Kearneys' number. Peggy answered.

"This is Davey Goldman, Mrs. Kearney. And I'm afraid I have some bad news." She made a sound. "Jim's in jail. Charged with the murder of Nick Carney. I'm sorry."

Her voice trembled, but she wasn't crying. Yet. "Should Mike and I come? I suppose we must! The poor boy!"

"May I suggest something, Mrs. Kearney? I'd like to suggest you and Mr. Kearney stay put for the time being. I'm working hard on the case, and I'm learning a few things. Jim won't be needing you right away. Why don't we see what progress I can make between now and this time tomorrow? I'll call you then, and you can decide."

Which was how we left it, though she was going to talk it over with
Mike. I had little doubt which way *his* vote would go.

Feeling virtuous, I called Dinker. Her voice was still glum.

"Me again," I said in my own witty way.

Her voice picked up. "Well! I was hoping it might be you."

My face got a little warmer. "Aw, c'mon, I bet you say that to all
the detectives. Listen, I just called Peggy and she's taking the news
quite well. I told her to stay put for now, and she's willing. Of course,
you *know* Mike's not going to worry."

She snorted. "Right. You said there was something else?"

"Oh, yeah. I need Lenny Rosen's number."

Her voice became guarded. "Oh?"

"Well, he knew Nick longer than anyone. The Bishop and I'd like
to know what he can tell us about him."

Pause. "Yeah, I see what you mean. If you're interested in that
business arrangement they had, I think the deal was, Nick put some
money into one of Lenny's shows a year or so ago. One that sort of
flopped."

"Oh? That's interesting. Anyway, I'd like to talk to him. Maybe he
could throw some light on things."

"Sure." She rattled off a phone number. Then, "Davey, it's probably none of my business, but could I make a suggestion?"

"Suggest away. I'm always open to new and bright ideas from future
Broadway stars."

"Very wise of you." Her voice got serious. "Look. Lenny's a very
private kind of a guy. And very, very sensitive. This is the third
show he's directed me in, and I feel I know him pretty well. I'm
afraid you'll offend him if you just come at him straight on. He
might clam up. He might even get mad—think you're trying to
pin it on *him*."

"*Moi?* Mr. Smoothie? Surely you jest!"

"I know, I know, but even pros sometimes slip up. Anyway, here's
my idea. Let *me* call Lenny. I could have both of you over. For dinner
or something. And you could bring up what you want to ask him in
a relaxed, friendly atmosphere. Instead of calling him out of the blue.
And, frankly, I've got another reason."

"Oh?"

"Yeah. Having two handsome men over might take my mind off of
Jim, jail, murder—all of that."

"Well, whatever I can do to help." I liked it. For several reasons.
"Okay. You got a deal. And—thanks, Dinker."

"Look, I'll talk to Lenny and call you back. What about an early
supper this afternoon, before Lenny and I go to the theater? Say five-
thirty? My place?"

I told her I'd be delighted; she said she'd call me back. And in less
than ten minutes she did.

"All set, Davey. He's anxious to talk with you. Says he didn't know
Nick all that well, but if he can help Jim, he's more than happy. Five-
thirty. And don't be late."

37

I W A S late leaving for Dinker's for two reasons: a last-minute decision to shave again and a tiff with Regan. He thought I should
have gone after Milt Manning first. I didn't agree.

"Hell, I'm going to see him first thing in the morning! What do
you want?"

"I don't see why you're getting Miss Galloway involved."

"Look. Number one, I didn't get her involved, she offered. Number
two, it's none of your business."

That didn't sit well, but you know bishops. Give 'em an inch and
they think they're a ruler.

So in my rush not to be late, I probably committed several
misdemeanors and a couple of class-B felonies driving over, but I
evaded arrest. I even overdid the haste a little and wound up
buzzing Dinker's apartment from the tiny downstairs foyer two
minutes early.

"Yes?" Her deep tones sounded tinny and far away.

"It's your friendly detective, ma'am. Thought I'd come early and see if I could shuck corn or something."

Her chuckle sounded good, even through the lousy sound system. "No corn, Davey. But you *can* entertain me while I slice some veggies."

"Great! I do a marvelous buck and wing, and—" The buzzer sounded: I'd wasted my humor on dead air. Just as well.

Dinker's apartment was as feminine as Jim's was spartan. The wallpaper was pastel, with a soothing pattern. Plants of various sizes and varieties filled the nooks and crannies. Along with some traditional artwork, I noticed a few framed photos of her and what appeared to be her family. She seemed to have three brothers, all younger.

Dinker looked about three times happier than two hours before. She was barefoot and wore a flowered apron over leggings and sweatshirt. Her luxuriant dark hair was tied back in a ponytail. Overall, she looked as scrumptious as the food smelled.

"Stroganoff," she explained in response to my sniffing. "Real easy. And I picked up some fresh asparagus at the farmers' market. I'll heat some French bread. No feast, but it'll keep body and soul together while you pump Lenny."

I followed her into the tiny kitchenette. "Let me pump *you*. Tell me about him."

She smiled. "Lenny's kind of a legend in the Village." She tossed some lettuce leaves in a big wooden bowl. "That Ibsen revival last summer may have been a financial flop but critically it made his reputation." She wrinkled her nose. "I only wish he'd try to be a little more avant garde."

I frowned. "What do you mean by avant garde?"

"Oh, you know. Do more experimental theater. He wants to stick with the tried and true: stuff like Williams, Inge, Beckett." She waved the knife in the air. "Or like A *Thousand Clowns* that we're doing now. A couple of critics—and I agree with them—have said he ought to try more, test more, get a little further out on the edge. But no one can deny his technical brilliance. I really—" The phone shrilled. Dinker made a face.

"That damn Lenny," she muttered. "If he's backing out on this . . ."

I found myself hoping she'd guessed right. If I'd known who it was, I'd have hoped even harder.

"Hello . . ." Dinker reddened and threw me a significant look. "Oh! Hi, Sally!"

I felt suddenly guilty without knowing why. Dinker continued, "Oh, I've been . . . what? Oh yes, it's—Oh!" She frowned. "Sally, wait! I guess you don't know this: Jim's in jail. Yes, in jail. . . . I know it's crazy, but they're holding him as a suspect in Nick's murder!" Dinker listened for a minute. "Oh, I know, but still—what? Yes, he's right here." Another significant look.

How did Sally know I was here? And what did she want? Then I knew—and I suddenly felt lousy. Dammit, this was Wednesday: our night to get together. The agreement is, Wednesday is "our" night— unless one of us calls to cancel, which I hadn't. The trip to St. Cloud had thrown me a day off my schedule. Okay, okay, maybe Dinker had a little to do with it too.

"No," Dinker said into the phone, eyes on me, "nothing special, I'm just whomping up some beef stroganoff. Easy fixin's. Yeah, same here, Sally. See you soon. Here's Davey." She handed me the phone, avoiding my eyes.

I took a breath. Maybe a breezy approach . . . ? "Is this *the* Sally Castle, famous lady psychiatrist?" Silence. Better try something else. What? Before I could decide, Sally spoke.

"What's with Jim?"

The tone of her voice, the abruptness of the question and her not calling me by name were all bad signs. But I proceeded gamely to tell her about Jim's arrest.

"I hope Dinker's holding up okay," Sally said, finally putting some warmth in her voice.

"Yeah, she'll be fine." I paused, trying to think of something else to say. Nothing came to me, silver-tongued devil that I am. Sally finally spoke.

"I tried to call you, Davey." Her tone was cold and businesslike again. "Sister Ernestine said you'd be at this number. I didn't even realize it was Dinker's till she answered. You two have a date or what?"

I glanced at Dinker. She was busy chopping the ends off some asparagus and trying to pretend she wasn't listening. I raised my voice. "No, it's not a *date*." Dinker winced and turned away. "Look, I'm sorry for not calling, Sally. But it *is* business."

"Oh. I see." The tone was a little frostier. "You're working on a case or something, I suppose."

"Yes, as a matter of fact, we are—I mean, *I* am."

"I see." She didn't. And didn't want to. "Well, it's not the first time your work has come between us. But why do I get the feeling there's more to it?"

"What do you mean?"

"I mean, I saw your reaction to Dinker at Ivan's last Wednesday night. And I'm *not* jealous, Davey, whatever you may think. I'm not. But you and Dinker? No way, sweetheart. This is your psychiatrist speaking."

I grinned at Dinker to hide how mad I was. Not knowing the reason, she smiled back, relieved to see me happy. Her face was flushed, making her even prettier.

"Well, Doctor," I said into the phone in as cold a tone as I could muster, "believe me, I certainly appreciate the free advice. And I'm sorry to have screwed up our Wednesday. The week kind of got away from me. But I'd recommend you save your psychiatric insight for your patients."

A buzzer sounded, probably Lenny downstairs. Dinker, who had paled during my last couple of sentences, took off like a bat, happy to be out of the line of fire.

"Well, my friend," Sally answered, her tone as frosty as mine, "I wouldn't be too sure. I've got nothing against Dinker, I like her a lot. Tell her I hope Jim's okay. But sooner or later you're going to realize that you and she are not a matched pair."

"Thank you, oh wise, all-knowing guru. And now I have to go. I'll be sure to call you next time I need your judgment." I heard the click of Sally hanging up. I felt shaky.

Dinker, now standing in the doorway, said in a near-whisper, "Lenny's coming up." I nodded and replaced the phone, wondering what the future held for Sally and me. The phone was blue. Like the wallpaper. Robin's-egg blue, I think it's called.

"Is Sally mad?" Dinker's voice was so small I could barely hear it. I shrugged and tried to smile.

"Nah. She's a psychiatrist. *I'm* mad."

"But, Davey, she's my friend. I don't want to—"

I put an arm around her and squeezed her shoulder. "Look. Dinker. You've got nothing to worry about or to apologize for. You're trying to help me help Jim, and your reward, as the Bishop says, will be great in heaven. Sally's a big girl. She'll get over it."

She tried to smile. "But will I?" Her dark eyes were moist, and I think that's what did it. Or maybe how sad she looked. One second we were looking, the next we were kissing. We kept at it till Lenny knocked. Dinker wiped lipstick off my mouth with a fingertip before she went to let him in.

38

L ENNY lightened the mood. On the chest of his T-shirt were a couple of bearded faces and the words *2 Live Jews*. Shorts and running shoes. No socks. None of which was all that funny. What made Dinker and me chuckle was the way it went—rather, *didn't* go—with the ornate yarmulke, embroidered with stars of David, pinned to the back of his mop of curly hair.

As Dinker broke from his hug, she rolled her eyes. "Geez, Lenny, you didn't have to dress up! I told you it was informal."

He shrugged lean, muscular shoulders. "Hey, you invite me, I dress up. It's the way I am." He thrust a hand at me. "Hi, Davey. Nice to see you."

Dinker departed, claiming kitchen duties and deputizing me as bartender. The worried look was back on her face. I sighed. The price you pay for having friends like Sally.

I asked Lenny what he'd have. He shrugged. "What're *you* having?"

"Nothing, yet. I just got here. Dinker's staying sober, since she's got to go on tonight and her director's a real tyrant."

Lenny snorted. "Yeah, as if she ever listened to her director!"

Dinker's voice floated in from the kitchen: "I heard that!"

Lenny laughed. "Let me have a soda, Davey. Dinker's not the only one who's going on tonight." In the kitchen I discovered Dinker had laid in a supply of Molson's—just for me, she confided.

"How'd you know that's my favorite?" I demanded, popping the top off one and pulling down a couple of Cokes.

She smiled. "Oh, you just looked like a Molson's kind of guy. You think I got where I am in life by being an insensitive clod?"

I poured beer into the glass she handed me. "Well, yeah, I sort of thought so. Obviously I was wrong."

I went back into the living room, closing the kitchen door behind me. Lenny took a sip of his Coke. "So. You want to know about me and Nick. Fine. Ask away."

He leaned back and threw one hairy leg across the other.

I pulled out my notebook. "Mind if I take some notes?"

He shrugged. "Be my guest."

"Thanks. My memory's not what it used to be. But then, it never was." I grinned at him as I opened the notebook and jotted down the date and his name. "As Dinker probably told you, I'm working for Jim Kearney. At the moment, the police think the evidence points at him. I'm trying to dig up some that points elsewhere."

Rosen smiled and raised his eyebrows. "Like at me?"

I smiled back, meeting his eye. "Hey, if the shoe fits." I shook my head. "No, not really. Just looking for anything relevant. For instance, tell me how you and Nick first met."

Rosen got serious. "Yeah, okay. It's really weird, you know, that Nick and Jim turned out to be brothers—well, half-brothers. Because I knew both of them before either one met the other. And none of us had a clue they were related. I guess if it hadn't been for that *Dispatch* article, the truth never would've come out." Lenny put his glass on the coffee table, sat back again, hands clasped behind his head.

"Funny thing is, it was also a newspaper article that originally brought Nick and *me* together. That one was in the *Times*. Couple years ago. I'd just got the idea for that Ibsen revival. My idea was, form a rep company and do all his plays over the course of one summer. I know this gal who writes for the *Times* and got her to do a story on it." He laughed. "What it really was, was a blatant appeal for funds. The article even gave my phone number, so people'd know where to call to offer help. I'm surprised she ever got it past her editors—the *Times* doesn't do things like that." He took another sip.

"That's when Nick called me. Said he was a big fan of Ibsen, wanted

to be involved. Well, I needed money, so we got together for lunch."
Rosen shook his head. "He wasn't your usual backer. I mean, I'm
from New York, but I've pretty much shucked off my New Yorkese
in eight semesters in New Haven. But this guy'd obviously never
been to New Haven or Cambridge—or even West One Hundred and
Twenty-fifth street. A dese, dem, and dose kind of guy, know what
I mean? But did he love Ibsen! And did he *know* Ibsen! First thing
out of his mouth was a line from *Hedda Gabler*, after which he went
into a penetrating analysis of why it's such a great play. I'm telling
you, he knew his theater." Rosen shook his head again and looked
away. He frowned, thinking. Threw a glance my way.

"Well." He spoke a little more slowly, not meeting my eye. "What
happened is, he wound up getting just a small piece of the action."
He glanced at me and looked away again. "I mean, by then I was
already talking to the Rockefeller Foundation, and they wound up
financing most of it, so I didn't really need Nick. But I gave him a
small equity position. The main thing is, we became friends." Lenny
took another sip of his drink. As he put it down, he glanced at me
out of the corner of his eye. His face was getting a pinkish cast.

"Well, the Ibsen thing was a fiasco from start to finish. Financially,
I mean. We were underfunded and didn't get the publicity we
needed. I've never seen so many empty seats. I lost over five grand
personally, and Nick also took a hit. Of course, the big losers were
the Rockefellers, but they can afford it." He grinned.

"What was Nick's loss?"

Lenny shrugged and looked away. "I don't know. About the same
as mine, I guess."

"And how did he react?"

Lenny looked at the ceiling. "No problem. He was a big boy and
he knew the risks. He was pretty gracious about it. Interested in
what I might do next. So when I went into rehearsal on *A Thousand
Clowns*, he wanted to be involved. Started coming to rehearsals,
meeting the cast. And that's when the . . . trouble started." He
paused.

"Trouble?"

"Uh, yeah." Lenny studied the wall behind my head. "He started,
you know, interfering in the show. Offering me advice about this and
that. Nothing major, just wanting to help out." He smiled ruefully.
His color was returning to normal. "Well, it got to be too much. Tell

you the truth, he was interfering with my direction."

Rosen put his glass down, got to his feet and began to pace, rubbing his hands. "Oh, not that he'd ever talk to the actors directly. He wasn't *that* carried away with himself. But he'd tell *me*. At first I thought it was kind of funny. Tell you the truth, it was funny, the ideas he'd get." Lenny was throwing little glances my way as he paced, but never looked me in the eye.

"Because for all his intuitive appreciation of drama, the guy had no understanding of the technical side of acting—absolutely none. And I couldn't take the time to explain to him what it was all about. So I finally had to tell him to butt out."

With the last sentence Lenny finally found himself able to look me in the eye. I nodded at him.

"So you kicked him out. When was that?"

Lenny sat down and picked up his Coke. He looked me in the eye. "Oh, just a week or two before opening." He chuckled. "I kind of missed him, tell you the truth." He sobered. "And now he's gone—murdered. God!" He shuddered, picked up his glass.

I nodded. "And now you're looking for someone else to second-guess you, hmm?" Lenny smiled. "So," I said, getting serious, "when did you find out that he and Jim were brothers?"

Lenny shook his head. "Opening night. Jim told me. I was totally flabbergasted. In fact, I refused to believe it at first. But Jim explained the whole thing."

I studied my notebook, thinking about how to put what I had to say next. Keeping Lenny in view out of the corner of an eye, I said, frowning at my notebook, "Was that what Nick wanted to talk to you about that night?" Lenny paled. I gave no indication of noticing anything, studied the notebook. And waited.

Lenny's voice was strained. "Yeah, that was it." I looked at him. He met my eye and looked away. "Yeah, he wanted to know if I knew. About him being Jim's brother."

"Did he happen to tell you anything about his money troubles?"

Lenny reddened and looked away. "Money troubles? No, he—" Lenny broke off. Jumped up, spilling some Coke on the rug. Didn't notice. "Well, I guess he had some money troubles. I guess Jim told you all about that, didn't he?"

I thought about my answer. "Yeah. He needed some money bad. Like twenty thousand. I was just wondering whether he might have asked you for help. I mean, after putting some of his money into your show, he might have expected some help back." I looked Lenny in the eye.

He met my look with a glare. "Just what the hell are you implying?"

I shrugged and raised my eyebrows. "Just what I said. I know he was looking for money. The mob was putting a lot of pressure on him to pay back a loan. He was reaching in every direction he could. It's logical he'd have come to you."

Lenny slugged down the rest of the Coke and flopped back onto the couch. He tried to smile at me. "You know, don't you, Dave?"

I didn't, but I nodded. "Why don't you tell me about it, Lenny?"

Rosen scratched a hairy leg. His voice was low. "I didn't kill him, Dave." I looked at him. He sighed. "Okay. Here's what happened." This time he met my eye.

"Nick actually put fifteen grand into the Ibsen thing. I didn't sign a note or anything, and we frankly never went into the question of whether it was a loan or an investment. After the show folded, Nick told me to forget about it, he'd had a great time, it'd been a pleasure to be involved with me in a great artistic endeavor, blah, blah.

"Then, a month ago, about halfway through rehearsals, he changed. Started getting tough. Said the fifteen had been a loan, and he wanted the money back—with vigorish. Said he was entitled to twenty-five grand but would settle for twenty."

"Must've been quite a shock to you. What'd you say?"

Lenny shook his head. "Told him he was crazy. I didn't owe him anything. And even if I did, I didn't have that kind of money! Hell, I don't have *any* kind of money! I told him that. Well, he got tougher and tougher. I finally had to tell him he wasn't welcome at rehearsals any more. But he kept calling. He sounded desperate.

"I didn't realize how desperate till last Thursday. He and a couple of goons came to my apartment." Lenny looked away and shook his head. "It was awful. I'd been up all night after rehearsals and was still sleeping—it was about two in the afternoon. I called down on the intercom, asked who it was. It was Nick. Of course he didn't tell me he had his muscle with him."

I raised a hand. "Excuse me, Lenny, let me think a minute. This was last Thursday?" Lenny nodded. Things clicked into place. That was the day I'd gone looking for Nick. That was why he hadn't been in his office: he'd gone to Lenny's, looking for money. And when he—and Jeff and Shorty—had come into Paddy's Pub, they must have just come from Lenny. "So what happened?"

Rosen winced. "I buzzed Nick up. I had a funny feeling about it. His voice had sounded a little—I don't know—tight or something, over the intercom. Not right, you know? So I kept the door of my apartment bolted. When I heard the knock, I went and looked through the peephole. I could only see Nick. I asked him if he was alone and he said, 'Hell, yes, I'm alone! Open the damn door!' So I opened it."

Lenny shook his head. "Opened it? Soon as I let go of the bolt, the two goons kicked the door open—almost took my head off. They pushed me onto the couch and Nick stood over me. He described in detail what the two guys were going to do to me if I didn't pay up by Saturday."

I shook my head. "So what did you do?"

Lenny's eyes widened. "What the hell *could* I do? I told him yes, I'd pay. I'd have told him anything to get him and those two monsters out of my face. I told him I'd beg, borrow or steal twenty grand somehow, some way. And I'd get it to him by Saturday."

I nodded. The pieces were falling into place. When Carney had come into Paddy's Pub, he'd been confident and happy. And hadn't wanted or needed his papa's money. With good reason. He and his two henchmen had just come from Rosen's. "Then came opening night," I prompted. "And you didn't have the money."

Rosen looked away and shook his head. "Right. I tried, I really did. But I struck out all over town. I even tried my dad; he just couldn't. And I couldn't tell him the trouble I was in."

"Ever think of telling the police?"

Lenny shook his head. "You kidding? I don't like to think about where parts of my anatomy would be if I even so much as thought of it." He took a breath. "And opening night! God! It was awful! I was scared to death! Especially when I heard Nick was in the audience. I don't know how I even managed to get my lines out.

"After the show I pleaded with him, told him I'd tried everything, that I just couldn't come up with the money. He was furious, but we were in the theater with people around, so he couldn't say much. And he didn't have his goons with him. He finally just sagged. Said he had something else he'd have to try. Actually shook my hand, said no hard feelings. I couldn't believe it!"

I was thinking about Nick's personality and wondering how likely that reconciliation was, when we were interrupted. "Two minutes!" Dinker called from the kitchen.

Lenny looked at me. "I didn't kill him, Davey. I'm sorry I tried to put one over on you, but you've got to believe me, I didn't kill him." I put the notebook away.

"I hear you," I said.

He scowled. "But you don't believe me?"

"I didn't say that."

He shrugged. "You didn't have to."

The mood at dinner, served in Dinker's tiny alcove, was subdued, to say the least. Lenny did a good job of hiding his mood, but the atmosphere had changed. Before we started, he looked at Dinker and me. "Mind if I lead the prayer?"

Nobody minded. And he said the blessing—in Hebrew and English. Then he ate the non-kosher dinner with gusto.

So did I. Dinker's culinary skills were definitely on a par with Ernie's, maybe a step or two ahead. The stroganoff was special, and I told her so. Lenny seemed to agree. He ate enough to please even Ernie.

I drove home thinking about Lenny Rosen. I wondered if he'd told me everything that had gone on between him and Nick. I somehow doubted that Nick would have let him off the hook as easily as he said he had.

Lenny stayed on my mind till I hit Twelfth Street. Then, unaccountably, Dinker took over. I wondered when I'd see her next. And whether she'd go back to Jim after (if?) he got out of jail. And whether . . .

39

G O T home at 7:30, in plenty of time to brief the Bishop on the state of Lenny Rosen's relationship with the late Nick Carney. It didn't seem like nearly enough to avoid a trip to Minnesota. Regan agreed. He listened with mounting impatience. My irritation grew in direct proportion to his impatience.

"All right, I blew it! Sorry I can't ask the questions a genius would ask. All I can do is my best. So fire me!"

He grimaced. "What are you talking about, David? Have I complained? Have I uttered the least syllable of criticism? Why are you so—?"

"Don't give me that! I know body language, and I can tell when you're irritated. Well, if you don't like it, get another gofer. I don't need this!"

I stomped out, leaving him shaking his head. What was going on with me?

Up in my bedroom I looked at the phone. Call Sally and apologize? For what? Furthermore, the one person I really wanted to talk to was now on stage at the Lettuce Inn.

It was Wednesday night, Sally's and my night. I had no date and nowhere to go. I called Ann Shields—I hadn't talked to her in a couple of months. She wasn't much interested in doing anything that night or any time in the foreseeable future.

Wound up turning on the TV and watching some episode of a nighttime soap. Very poor substitute for Sally's (or Dinker's or Ann's) company.

I went to bed early but didn't sleep well. Woke up in a rotten mood, as Ernie soon discovered. I was sipping coffee in the kitchen when she came down from the chapel at 8:30. She attends the Bishop's Mass every morning at 8:00. Normally I'm up before then, and she fixes my breakfast before going upstairs. My getting up this late should have tipped her off to my attitude, but she was oblivious.

"Late night, Davey?" she said, pulling on her apron and moving to the refrigerator for eggs.

I grunted, not lifting my eyes from the *Times*. Nick Carney's murder, which had slumped yesterday into a filler paragraph deep in the Metro Section, was back on page B1, thanks to Jim's arrest. Kessler was quoted: ". . . we feel we have a very strong case." The writer of the article also spent some time speculating on the part, if any, played by Rozanski's interview with the arrestee just the day before. The writer suggested that "the police may have been able to glean some clue to Mr. Kearney's whereabouts from what he said in that interview. Mr. Rozanski, when questioned about it by the *Times*, declined comment . . ."

"Aren't we talking this morning?"

I looked up. Ernie was entirely too cheery for my taste. "Talking? Yeah well, you should know plenty about talking. You might be interested in knowing that your talking blew my friendship with Dr. Castle last night. Thanks a whole bunch."

Ernie almost dropped the egg she was holding. She looked at me wide-eyed. I didn't let up. "Oh? Surprised? Well, I'll tell you, Ernie, when I leave a phone number with you, I expect you to be discreet. Not give it out to everyone who calls. I want you to know you really embarrassed me last night."

Ernie wiped her hands automatically on the apron, still staring at me. "But I—you didn't—"

"Forget it. Gals like Sally are a dime a dozen. And, as you've often reminded me, she's a *shiksa*, anyway."

That last was just a little too far below the belt for Ernie. She pulled a hankie from somewhere and dove for the door to the stairs.

I folded the *Times*, got up and headed for my office. My thoughts weren't the jolliest. Nice move, jerk. In one stroke you blew breakfast and dug yourself a hole with Ernie it'll take you a month to climb out of. If you ever get out.

I slammed the paper onto my desk and looked around savagely. Goddammit, how can a person put up with an office that's not even big enough to pace in?

I slammed into my chair and stewed. Let's see. Anyone I hadn't alienated? Nope, I'd got 'em all. I'd nailed Sally, the Bish, Ernie, the Kearneys, Joe Parker. Yep. Clean sweep. And to make it perfect, I was not a damn bit closer to the murderer of Nick Carney than when I first heard he was dead. Thinking of where I'd been when I heard reminded me of the weekend. And the fun I'd had with Sally.

I called her. "It's me." I didn't have to try to sound forlorn.

"Oh?" She didn't have to try to sound cold.

"Yeah. I just wanted to let you know I'm sorry about yesterday. It was unforgivable of me. See, I was out of town Tuesday, and I lost track of what day it—"

"Yeah, yeah. And your dog ate your homework. Just tell me something, Davey."

"Anything."

"Did you spend the night with Lady Galloway?"

I was outraged. "No, I did *not* spend the night. God, Dinker, what do you think I—" I stopped.

Sally's voice was dangerously calm. "Did I hear right? Did you just call me Dinker?"

I rolled my eyes. Davey, you got any other fancy ways to screw yourself? Or have you really and truly and finally run out? "Yeah, I guess I did." What else could I say? "Yeah, I did, Sally."

A long silence. When she broke it, she sounded more sorrowful than angry. "Davey, I think you need to sit down and figure out where you're going. We've had a—I don't know, I guess *arrangement's* as good a word as any. We've had it for eight years, and I've loved it. I really have. No ties. If you wanted to date someone else, fine. If I did, likewise. But through it all we've both tried to show a little consideration. I think that's what married people miss— that delicacy, that sensitivity to what the other person's feeling. You and I have had that. Like last year when I was sick and you spent all that time with me? That was sweet. I mean it. It really was.

"But this thing last night. And now. This isn't like you, Davey. You're going through something, I'm not sure what. And you don't seem to want help. Not mine, anyway."

"That's not true, Sally! I do! Listen, Sally, can I—"

"Davey, darling." She sounded tired. "I don't want to talk right now. Okay?" She hung up.

For the second time in twelve hours I found myself studying the color of a phone Sally had just hung up on. This one was black. Sort of greasy black.

I wanted to call Dinker but didn't. I wasn't that far gone. What to do? I looked around, suddenly realized I was hungry. That told me something. Namely, that out of the hundreds of people I'd offended, the one I most needed to apologize to was the only truly nice person who lived in this house.

But how? I couldn't go downstairs. Off limits to males. I thought of going into Regan's office and ringing his little silver bell, but she'd know it wasn't him.

Got an idea. Picked up my phone. Called the Bishop's number from my private line. The phone in the Bishop's office rang once, and she was on the line.

"Bishop's office." Voice a little trembly.

I talked fast. "This is Ebenezer Scrooge, wondering whether you could find it in your heart to forgive him for the cruel, nasty and untrue things he said about you when he was in a bad mood."

I crossed my fingers and waited.

"Oh," she finally said, her voice coy, "I might listen to Scrooge if he delivered a nice-enough apology. Say, on bended knee."

I didn't realize how long I'd held my breath till I let it out. "Well, I'm apologizing," I said in my humblest voice. "Ernie, I'm about to starve. If you'll make me that omelette, I'll eat it on my knees. Uh, while I apologize."

"That'll be worth seeing. I'll meet you in the kitchen in thirty seconds."

When I returned to my office an hour later, I felt like Scrooge reborn.

40

But Scrooge had two problems and I'd only solved one. The Spirit told Scrooge mankind's two worst enemies were Hunger and Ignorance. Well, with Ernie's help, I'd conquered Hunger but I still had a problem with Ignorance—Milt Manning's whereabouts. I put my feet up on my desk and gave it some serious thought.

Milt Manning had been a fringe player in the outfit for years. I'd never met him but had seen his picture in the papers a couple of times. I knew he'd done time for pandering. He also was reputed to be one of the top juice men in the city, with all the violence that goes with that. He'd started out as a leg breaker for Sy Lefkowitz back in the bad old days, and worked his way up to captain.

He'd always been careful to keep his nose clean. The only time he'd ever been busted and had it stick was when he'd gone outside his field and tried pimping. Once out of the joint, he'd gone back to juice and left the girls to others.

As mobsters go, he had the reputation of being scrupulously fair in living up to his end of any bargain but absolutely unforgiving of anyone who didn't live up to theirs. Word was, when you borrowed money from Milt, you got a whole schedule upfront of the penalties that went with late payment, starting with missing body parts, such as toes and fingers, and going on to facial disfigurement and the more serious organs, and finally to sleeping with the fishes. Adjustments were not up for discussion.

He was also reputed to be very bright, well educated and cultured. And gay, of course. In the outfit, that's the standard rap on anyone who's got more intelligence and good taste than a moron.

I wasted two or three minutes trying to think of how to get hold of him. Then I slapped my head: Dummy, you've already got his phone number. Jim had given it to me the previous day. That little slip of paper containing all the important numbers he'd gotten from Nick.

I pulled it out of my desk drawer and sat staring at it. After a minute I came up with an approach. I punched out the number.

"Yes." The baritone was smooth and cultured-sounding, if that's not reading too much into one syllable.

"Mr. Manning?"

"Yes. May I help you?" Even smoother and more cultured when spread over five words.

"Yes, you may. My name is David Goldman, and I represent Jim Kearney in the Nick Carney murder."

No hesitation. "Congratulations, old man. Umm, by the by, how did you obtain this number?"

"I got it from Jim Kearney, who got it from Nick Carney."

"Ah, I see. I suppose I might have deduced that myself, mightn't I? Well, I take it you're calling for a purpose."

"Yes, sir. You had a two o'clock appointment with Nick Carney last Saturday afternoon. You didn't show up for it. Why not?"

His tone remained easy and self-assured. "I'll be glad to discuss it with you, Mr.—Goldman, is it? But not over the phone. Run up here, if you like, and we can talk."

"Okay. Where do you li—" I stopped talking and hung up. A useful lesson someone once taught me is that you're not going to get much information out of a dead phone.

I thought about calling back but realized Manning had just sent me a message. He'd talk if I could find him. Now how was I going to do that?

I scratched my head. Studied Jim's scrap of paper one more time, which was a waste of energy, since I already knew there was nothing on it but the combination to Nick's office door and Manning's unlisted phone number. I went back to scratching my head. This time it helped. I got a thought: Rozanski. I called him.

The jump from underpaid reporter to overpaid TV personality hadn't taken the edge off Chet's brand of sarcasm.

"Yeah, Davey, nice to know I can count on you. Just yesterday you were going through a song-and-dance about it *not* being a mob hit; now you're looking for—who else? Milt Manning, one of our leading mobsters. Appreciate your honesty, bud."

I was patient with him. In view of the favor I needed, I couldn't afford not to be. "Come on, Chet. I didn't say Manning *did* it. I just need some information from him."

"Yeah, well, good luck." Chet's tone was skeptical. "I doubt if you're going to get much from him. A very close-mouthed guy, I hear."

"Yeah, probably. But I called him a minute ago and he told me—"

"Hold it! You just *called* him? You've got the guy's unlisted number and you don't even know where he *lives?* Hell, Davey, even *I* know that."

"Just what I wanted to hear, Chet. So how about a *quid pro quo?* Trade you the name of the last guy known to have seen Nick Carney alive for that address of Manning's. Even up, with a draft choice to be named later."

Chet was interested. "Last guy known to—? Is this for real?"

"Damn right. I can give you his name and where he hangs out." I filled him in on what I knew of Jake Steiner, whereupon Rozanski— very happily—gave me Manning's address: 211 East 78th Street.

Five minutes later I was in a cab, heading for East Seventy-eighth. The cabby apparently came from some part of India or Pakistan where they hold daily drag races. He got me there in under ten minutes. He wasn't happy about the one-buck tip, but I never asked him to scare me half to death.

Two-eleven was a twelve-story co-op. The juice racket seemed to be doing well: Manning lived in the penthouse. But the young door-man with the slicked-back hair wasn't sure about me, my business with Manning or whether he should even bother to tell Manning I was there. "Hey," I said. "He just told me on the phone he wants to see me. Not more than fifteen minutes ago."

He smoothed his hair. "Okay. I'll give it a shot. Name?" I supplied it. Keeping his eyes on me, he punched out a number on the tele-phone console.

"Gentleman to see you, Mr. Manning. A Mr. Goldman." As the doorman listened, his eyebrows went up and he gave me a more respectful look. "Yes sir, I'll send him right up."

Guys like Manning feel they'll live longer if they treat every visitor like a threat. So when the elevator doors opened on Twelve, I wasn't surprised to be greeted by a large, uniformed guard, his hand on the butt of a .45. His cold blue eyes studied me.

"Off the elevator, please, and turn around." The look in his eyes suggested the wise thing would be to do what he said without a lot of discussion. I still couldn't help muttering, "Gotta warn you, I'm ticklish."

I didn't expect an answer but he muttered, "I'll be careful," no suggestion of laughter in the tone. He frisked me quickly and efficiently. Then murmured, "Follow me, please," turned and went.

I've seen a few mobsters' hangouts in my day, so I wasn't surprised at having to walk through three anterooms (counting the one where I'd been frisked) before we got to the living room. Security.

The whole place was high class and very expensive. My feet disappeared into the heavy, deep pile carpet, different colors in each room. We went from yellow to purple to royal blue, the furnishings and decor nicely complementing the carpet in each. I caught glimpses of expensive-looking artwork on the walls, very modernistic.

When we reached the living room, the guard stood at the door, waved me in and disappeared. The room was maybe a third the size of the Kearneys' solarium, with about a tenth as many chairs. Meaning it could have easily accommodated a convention of twenty to thirty mobsters. At the moment the only mobster in it was Milt Manning.

He was bigger than I'd expected, and better-looking. His smoking jacket had set him back more than five hundred bucks. He set his book and reading glasses on the rosewood end table and rose smoothly to his feet from the long couch.

"Mr. Goldman, I presume," he said, in the smooth baritone I'd heard on the phone. His cold blue eyes and thin smile proclaimed that he was superior to me in every way that mattered. The handshake was firm but not bone-crushing.

"You presume right," I said, meeting his eye. He probably had a half-inch on me.

"Please sit down, Mr. Goldman." We sat. The view of the city through the floor-to-ceiling window was fantastic.

Manning looked me over. "Well. You certainly wasted no time getting here. How in heaven's name did you do it? Nick had my number—my *phone* number—but he never knew where I lived. I made sure of that."

"Hey, you invited me up here, remember? What was all that about if you didn't think I could find you?"

He smiled back at me with his thin, superior smile. I could get to dislike this guy in a hurry. "I just wondered how badly you wanted to see me, Mr. Goldman. And what caliber of detective you are. I thought, if you cared enough to find me and knew your business sufficiently, you'd get here. Frankly, I didn't expect to see you. Certainly not this fast." I took a deep breath, a mistake. Manning's cologne was as objectionable as his sneer.

"Well, I made it. So let's get to it."

Spreading his arms and resting them on the couch back, Manning smiled. "Fine. Let's."

I didn't smile back. "Why'd you cancel your meeting with Nick Carney last Saturday?"

"My, we are a persistent little bugger, aren't we?" Manning's smile widened for a fraction of a second, then disappeared. His eyes got colder. "What's this about? I might be inclined to help, if I knew the background."

"It's about Jim Kearney, Nick's half-brother. The cops think he killed Nick. I happen to know they're wrong. Jim says he was supposed to meet you outside Eight-forty-nine West Forty-sixth last Saturday afternoon. Two o'clock. He was on time. You never showed. Instead, he found a note from Nick on the door saying you'd canceled. So I'm wondering. Did you? Cancel, that is. And if so, why?"

The eyes turned thoughtful. "You were with the police once upon a time, weren't you, Mr. Goldman?" I didn't answer. "Oh, come, come, Mr. Goldman, that's no deep dark secret." His lips formed a tight smile.

I shrugged. "It's certainly not. I was a cop. So what?"

Manning shrugged back. "So nothing." He frowned at me and came to a decision. "All right, I'll tell you. I don't know why. Maybe because you had the brains to find me—and the guts not to be afraid of me. I like that."

He sighed. "I *didn't* cancel that appointment with Nick, Mr. Goldman. He canceled on me. In fact, I'm very perturbed with Brother Nick, dead or not. I've never been an adherent of that *De mortuis nihil nisi bona* nonsense." He waved it away.

I pulled out my notebook. "I hadn't planned to take notes," I said. "But I should get that down. What is that, Greek?"

His smile warmed up a notch. Say, to a chill factor of minus-thirty. "Put the notebook away, please. For your information, the expression was Latin. 'Say only good things about the dead.' An Oxford education has its uses." He waited while I stuffed the notebook back in my pocket, nodded and went on. "I spoke with Nick late Friday night. As you no doubt know, he owed me a substantial amount—money, incidentally, that I'll never see—and I called to remind him of his obligation. The night before he died." Manning smiled. "I'm afraid I was—a bit firm. He assured me he had arranged for the money, was having a cashier's check in the full amount of the debt delivered to him at his office the following afternoon."

The smile again. The smile that made me happy *I* wasn't in his debt. "I'll admit I had my doubts, especially when he refused to give me the combination to his outer door. I'd run into that particular problem before on a weekend, and the experience hadn't left me giddy with joy. But he assured me his very own brother would bring the check and would be able to let the two of us into the building. Jim, I believe, was the brother's name. From Minnesota, God save us.

"Frankly, it sounded a bit strange. But Saturday morning at eleven, someone purporting to be the brother, indeed, called me. As you say, we arranged to meet outside Nick's office building on Forty-sixth at two P.M. Everything seemed in order. Then, not more than twenty minutes later, Nick called. Everything was changed. He couldn't meet us at the office. He was sick."

Manning shook his head. "And he may have been, at that. He was hoarse—could barely talk. Said I should come to his apartment in Brooklyn, he'd have the money for me. Said his brother would join us there. Had the money, there would be no problem."

I was taking copious notes—all mental. "He called you and said to come to Brooklyn? Not to his office?"

Manning's cold eyes studied me for a moment. "It's what I said, isn't it?" He shut his eyes. "It was intolerable. To drive all the way to Brooklyn and then to find an empty apartment! I'm afraid I was a bit cross. I kicked in the door." Manning smiled and shrugged. "And then vented my spleen on his empty apartment. Ironical, isn't it? At the moment someone was putting three bullets into Nick's head in Manhattan, I was miles away, trashing his apartment in Brooklyn." He smiled the smile of a thug with a perfect alibi.

I met his eye. "And I imagine you had a couple of witnesses to testify that's where you were."

Manning's blue eyes drilled into mine. "Mr. Goldman. Let's not go making this into something it's not. I've already had extensive conversations with the police. I've given my statement, they've checked it out. I'm doing you a favor. Don't push it." He sighed. "Now I'm tired. So, if there are no more questions..."

There were, but he was temporarily retired from the question-answering business. I beat it. On the way home I got the conversation into my notebook as well as I could in a bouncing taxicab.

41

I G O T back in time to go through the mail before Regan came down from the chapel. I was just putting it on his desk when he came rolling into the office at eleven. He didn't look at me as he propelled himself over to the south window. "Good morning, David. Still in a snit?" He readjusted the drapes, took a peek outside and spun to face me.

I grinned at him and he nodded back. "I can see that you're not. Good. Anything further to report? I promise to do my best to control my body language."

We smiled at each other. Neither of us would have admitted it, but we were both enjoying a reversal of roles. He's the one who has snits. (Also depressions, but we don't laugh about those.) So he was delighted to have a snit of mine to throw up to me.

"Good," I said. "Do that and I promise not to get mad." I proceeded to fill him in on Manning. He wheeled around a bit while I talked.

"Interesting," he said when I finished. "How would you assess the probability that he knows more than he's telling?"

I shrugged. "Hard to say. He's not easy to read. I'm sure he's telling the truth about being in Brooklyn while Nick was getting blown away. For one thing, it jibes with what Jim told us. Of course, he still could have had one of his boys do the job. But how would they have got the gun from St. Cloud?"

"Yes," the Bishop said. "We can't seem to avoid that gun." He smiled at me. "And—don't take this the wrong way, David, but you haven't brought me the answer to that, even with your expert—*highly* expert, I should say, to forestall further snits—interviews with Messrs. Rosen and Manning. Despite your expertise, we are not spared the need to travel to St. Cloud." He started for his desk. I was apparently dismissed. But I wasn't having it.

"Whoa! Hold it." He looked up, puzzled. "Like, when? And why?"

He shook his head and took off his reading glasses. "As soon as possible. As to why, I thought I just explained it." We tried to stare each other down. I won. "All right," he grumbled, "I suppose further explanation would not be amiss." He turned to face me and took off his glasses.

"By your count, David, some eleven people were in Mr. and Mrs. Kearney's house last Wednesday. Everything we know tells us with near-certainty that someone who was in the house that day stole the weapon. We need to investigate that, and I see no other way than to question everyone in each other's presence. Only in that way, if at all, will we be able to determine who had the combination to the locked gun cabinet, who might have been alone in the room where the cabinet is. Along with that, we might see if we can find a connection one of those eleven individuals might have had with Nick Carney."

He frowned. "There is yet another question suggested by the information you brought back. To wit: was there a twelfth person in that house that day?"

I thought that one over. "A twelfth person?"

"Oh yes, indeed. It seems quite possible. Consider: Mr. Soukup was under the impression that someone named Fred was working with Mr. Weiskopf. Not so. Mr. Weiskopf thought that Mr. Madison's plumbing crew had three members, but Mr. Madison says there were two. I am visualizing a shadowy presence at the Kearneys' that day— someone floating from crew to crew, part of none, yet part of all. Perhaps interviewing everyone who was on the premises that day will reveal whether that is so, and if so, with luck, even the person's identity."

I thought about it. "You want to get all eleven together at one time in one place."

Regan nodded. "Yes. And preferably at the Kearney residence. Perhaps we could reenact the events of that day, with people situated in the locations they occupied last Wednesday."

I was suspicious. This was beginning to look like an attempt to replay our final confrontation with the murderer in the McClain case (the one a friend of mine calls the Case of the Chartreuse Clue, a description that's a bit melodramatic for my taste). That one ended with the Bishop damn near getting himself killed. His finest hour, he thinks. I was skeptical.

"Any idea how we're going to collect all those people in one place at one time? Or how we're going to get the Kearneys to let us use their house?"

The Bishop turned his palms up. "Ask them, David. Use your customary charm."

I started to object again but he'd thought of something else. "Ah!" he said. "I have an idea. One moment, David."

Without consulting his Rolodex, he punched a number into the phone. I watched and saw by the area code he was calling Minnesota.

"Father Kilian, please." A pause. "Would you please ask him to call Bishop Regan?" He gave the number of the mansion and hung up.

"St. John's Abbey," he murmured. "Father Kilian McDonnell, as you know, is the person there I know best. I want to see if they can accommodate us. Then we can decide—"

"Excuse me. Did you say us?"

"Of course. No reason for you to stay elsewhere. Once we have Father Kilian's answer, we can decide—"

"You want me to spend the night in a monastery? Forget it!"

Regan rolled his eyes. "David. Staying in a monastery is no different from living here. You'll find it quite acceptable. Now, if you'll permit me to finish my thought. Once I've spoken to Kilian, we can decide when to go. Meanwhile, it wouldn't hurt to call the Kearneys and see about arranging our confrontation with the eleven. Get Mr. or Mrs. Kearney on the line, and we can both talk."

"Okay. I'll buzz you when I've got them." I headed into my office and punched the number. Peggy answered right away.

"Davey Goldman, Mrs. Kearney. Nothing new to report on Jim. I'm doing everything I can, but—"

She cut in, her voice bright. "I talked to him last night. Mike and I are flying to New York City tomorrow to see him. The poor boy!"

I frowned. "When tomorrow?"

"Two o'clock. We'll take the Lear."

I thought fast. "Well, fine. But I wonder if you and Mr. Kearney might do something for us first. Maybe tomorrow morning? You recall meeting Bishop Regan—in the wheelchair?" I explained how Regan helped me on my cases.

She was surprised. "You mean he actually helps you solve these crimes?"

"It's often more than that. He's a brilliant man, Mrs. Kearney, and he can see connections where most people see nothing but holes. Fortunately, he's convinced Jim is innocent. He's eager to help.

"So he and I would like to come to St. Cloud and—look, let me just get him on the line." I buzzed the Bishop.

He got on and I gave him a fast rundown about the Kearneys' plan to come to New York the next afternoon. Then he took over.

"Mrs. Kearney, let me tell you what Mr. Goldman and I have in mind. Unlike the police, we are convinced your son is innocent. And unlike them, we credit your husband's account of the whereabouts of the weapon. Beginning with that supposition and with the established fact that that gun killed Nick Carney, the train of logic leads inevitably to the almost certain presence of the murderer in your house Wednesday last.

"Consequently, I have a request. I want to ask you and your husband to assemble in your home all the people who were known to be there last Wednesday. If you can do that, Mr. Goldman and I will come and attempt to uncover what happened."

Peggy's voice was as excited as I'd ever heard it. "Would you, Bishop? Mike and I'd be so glad! We'll get everyone. But—could we do it in the morning? Could you get here that fast?"

"Certainly. We, too, would prefer to do this as soon as possible. Tomorrow morning is fine."

Peggy was delighted. "Wonderful! We'll get 'em, Bishop."

"Good. Mr. Goldman and I will arrange things here. Perhaps you and he could now go over the list. We want to be certain we include everyone who was there. And now I will hang up. I look forward to seeing you tomorrow, Mrs. Kearney."

"Thank you, Bishop." She waited for him to hang up, then took the names down, making me wait after each one while she wrote.

Afterwards I went back into the Bishop's office to discuss the situation. We agreed we'd just have to stay loose and wait for Father Kilian to call. Naturally, Regan had to end things with a biblical allusion.

"We shall be like your forebears, David, at the first Passover. Loins girt, sandals on. Ready to flee at a moment's notice."

I returned to my office, shaking my head. A Jewish atheist spending the night in a Catholic monastery. This would be a first. For me, if not for the monks. Thinking about that campus—peaceful, serene— I decided it'd be a whole new experience for me. But I'd probably survive.

42

F R O M three to four that afternoon was probably the most hectic hour the Bishop and I have ever spent, and that takes in a lot of territory. If nothing else, it proved we both have strong hearts.

It came without warning. We were just sitting around, waiting for Father Kilian to call back. Regan was working on files, I was killing time in his office rearranging the file drawers, something he'd been after me to do for six months.

At 2:45 he said, "If Father Kilian doesn't call back in the next fifteen minutes, I'm going to call the Abbot."

"Don't worry about it," I said, blowing some dust off a file that probably hadn't been touched for years. "There are flights going to Minneapolis all the way up to eight o'clock."

"I'd prefer to get a decent night's sleep," he growled. "But—" The phone rang and he grabbed it. It was Father Kilian.

The conversation was short and sweet. Regan hung up and said, "He can accommodate us this evening, David. Call Miss Cowan and get us on the first available flight."

I went into my office and called. Which is where things started to get dicey. "No can do, Davey," Mary said. "Nothing to Minneapolis today. Everything's full."

"What? You've got to be kidding! Nothing?"

"Well, let me see. Umm, nope. Wait! There's two seats on a four-fifteen out of Newark. But . . . it's already after three. You'll never make that. Let's look at tomorr—"

"The hell we won't! Book it!"

"But—"

"Book it! Put it on my Visa. We'll pick the tickets up at the counter."

I dashed into Regan's office. He looked up, surprised.

"If we're going at all, it's got to be now," I told him. "The only available flight is at Newark in . . ." I checked the Timex. ". . . exactly seventy-one minutes."

The boss didn't give me a second look. He headed straight for the elevator.

I still can't believe we made that flight, and Regan deserves the credit. Though my part wasn't easy either. Try this timetable:

3:01 : Conversation with Cowan described above.

3:06 : Reached Fred at the garage, told him to bring the Seville around immediately. He grumped a bit, said he'd do his best.

3:09 : Reached Peggy Kearney in St. Cloud. Told her it was on for tomorrow, please get the people assembled. She assured me she'd start immediately.

3:14 : Tore up to my room, threw some underwear, socks, toothbrush and a razor into an overnight bag.

3:22 : Tapped on the Bishop's bedroom door, across the hall from mine on the second floor of the mansion. Heard a grumpy "Come in." Entered.

Regan, in his wheelchair, was nearly dressed, struggling with the collar button on the back of his clerical falsefront. He waved me away when I tried to help. "Just get my suitcase downstairs, David. Is the car here?"

"If it's not, it will be momentarily." I grabbed the suitcase, already packed and closed, from off his bed.

He muttered, "I'll be right down," and the collar-button struggle continued. I knew better than to get in the middle of that.

Peered through the front door; the Caddy was just pulling up. Excellent timing. Lugged the two suitcases down to the sidewalk. Jerry, Fred's number-two mechanic, jumped out from behind the wheel and grabbed them.

I told him, "Just put these in the back seat on the right-hand side. And pop the trunk for the wheelchair. I'll be right back with the Bish." I didn't have to tell Jerry to stay with the car. In our neighborhood, that goes without saying.

Back in the house, the elevator was creaking its way down. More good timing. But—oops! I hadn't told Ernie. Nor could I now. From two to four was her nap time. I dashed into my office, jotted a quick note giving her our location as St. John's Abbey and told her we'd be in touch, the house was hers for the next thirty-six hours and, for God's sake, please keep the orgies quiet.

Regan was waiting for me at the front door as I taped the message to the top of the stairs and ran to open it for him. I bumped him down the eight steps to the sidewalk. Jerry held the door and the Bishop levered himself onto the front seat. I grabbed the wheelchair, folded it quickly, stowed it in the trunk, hurled myself into the driver's seat and burned rubber, leaving Jerry to hike the block and a half back to the garage.

I gave the Bishop the plan of action on the way. "You get the tickets, I'll park the car, we'll meet at the gate."

I screeched to a halt at the Northwest gate at 4:02, popped the trunk and ran around to pull the wheelchair out, madly waving a five-spot at a gaggle of porters. One of them took a quick look at the green and hustled over. "I'll get the gentleman out," I said. "You grab the bags from the back seat." I handed him the fiver.

"The gentleman's a V.I.P.," I said as I unfolded the wheelchair and the porter hefted our bags out. "We're on the four-fifteen for Minneapolis. Get him to the ticket counter while I park." I peeled out seconds later.

I parked in a "Handicapped" spot (that tag on the license plate does come in handy sometimes) right next to the elevator on the second level, ran down the stairway all the way through the tunnel into the terminal; checked the gate number (9A) and my Timex (4:13) and kept trucking. Arrived, sweating like a maniac, at the gate one minute late to find the flight delayed fifteen minutes.

Took a deep breath and looked for Regan. Nowhere to be seen. On a hunch, I went in the nearest men's room. Still no sign of him. Till I bent down and checked under the stalls. There were the wheels and his feet, in the "Handicapped" stall. He hates that word but doesn't let it stand in his way when he's in need.

"I'll be right outside," I said. "You got the tickets?"

No answer at first. Then came his grumpy voice from behind the partition: "The flight's delayed. Wait for me outside. Of course I have the tickets."

The flight was okay, though the stews were unhappy, as they sometimes are, at getting stuck with anyone disabled. Of course they were more harried than usual with the flight so full. Regan had no trouble levering his body across to the window seat, using the chair arms.

As on Monday, I turned my Timex back an hour. We used most of the flight to map out strategy for tomorrow's get-together at the Kearneys'. It shouldn't have taken *that* long. The strategy consisted mainly of "leave it to me." I'll let your imagination supply who "me" was.

We both accepted and tried to eat the alleged "dinner." The steak turned out to be gristly hamburger, the potatoes proved that a vegetable can be heated to a thousand degrees and still be raw, and the cake was as dry as one of Regan's books. Naturally I ate it all, fearful that, compared to the monastery food I was about to be subjected to, I might look back on this as nectar of the gods. We landed right on schedule at 6:25 CDT.

The Hertz people gave us what we needed, a full-size Chevy with four doors. And thanks to an airport that considered disabled people, it wasn't impossible to get to. Of course it lacked the bars over the right-hand door the Caddy has, but Regan's strong enough to get himself from the wheelchair into about any car he wants to. I stowed the wheelchair in the trunk and we were off.

This time I knew where I was going. Regan was in a talkative mood, giving me some lessons in Minnesota history and geography. Even showed me the Mississippi when we crossed it, though the bridge blocked most of the view. He talked about the Germanic makeup of St. Cloud and St. John's.

"Very insular people, some of them, David. One of the monks told me he took his first train trip—first *train* trip, mind you, not plane trip—when he was ordained, at age twenty-eight! Till then he'd never been further than fifty miles from the farm where he was born. And this was in nineteen fifty-eight!"

He also briefed me on the monk who was acting as our host, Father Kilian McDonnell. "He happens to be the country's foremost ecumenist." Regan didn't explain what an ecumenist is, and I didn't ask, having no desire to be subjected to a fifteen-minute harangue, not a word of which I'd understand.

Exactly two hours from the moment we'd touched down in Minneapolis, the concrete billboard of St. John's came into view. It was beginning to seem like home.

We were barely out of the car when a monk, obviously on the lookout, came rushing from the main entrance, black gown billowing behind him. A smallish man with thinning, sandy hair and Coke-bottle specs. My suspicion that this was the great ecumenist was quickly confirmed as he grabbed the Bishop and greeted him in a musical tenor.

"Bishop! What a delight to have you with us!"

"I'm afraid we're imposing, Father," Regan grumbled, and introduced me.

"Nice to meet you, Mr. Goldman. Imposing? On Benedictines? *Contradictio in terminis*, Bishop! Didn't you know the *O* in OSB stands for 'ospitality?" Regan managed a smile. "So. What brings you here, Bishop?"

I looked at Regan, wondering how he'd respond. "Some personal matters in St. Cloud, Kilian," he said smoothly. "Something that came up rather suddenly. It's nice to have an 'ospitable place nearby when such emergencies occur."

The monk smiled. "When a distinguished scholar and hierarch deigns to spend the night, *we* are honored. I'm only sorry the whole community can't gather to greet you. But I understand the need for seclusion." I was beginning to feel left out and the priest seemed to sense it. "And what's your field, Mr. Goldman? Are you a Scripture scholar also?"

I choked a bit and Regan answered for me. "Mr. Goldman is my special assistant, Kilian. A highly capable man who can do all the things I can't do. And many of the things I can. Perhaps you might show us our rooms now?"

"Right this way," the priest said, swinging around and pointing toward the door from which he'd come. The Bishop pushed off with a powerful stroke. I outfought the priest for the bags and the two of us hurried after Regan.

"Father Abbot would like to say hello," Kilian said, puffing a little from catching up. "He asked me to let him know the moment you arrived. May I bring him?" He stopped at a doorway. "Here we are. Yours is the next room, Mr. Goldman. As you requested, Bishop."

"Thank you, Kilian. And yes, I'd be happy to see Father Abbot. Please give him my apologies that the visit will have to be a brief one. I'm rather tired from the trip." He looked at me. "We should talk before we retire, David. Perhaps now, while Father notifies the Abbot that we've arrived."

I nodded and the priest left. Regan surveyed the room and took a deep breath. "Very pleasant. I believe we share a bath. I trust this won't be too inconvenient, David. Perhaps you can use this phone to call Mrs. Kearney and agree on the time of our meeting tomorrow?"

The phone was in the corner. I called the Kearneys' unlisted number. Mike answered.

"Dave Goldman, Mike. I guess Peggy told you about Jim."

"Dave! Where are you? Mother and I wanted you to stay with us! Yeah, she told me what happened."

"Thanks, Mike, but the Bishop took care of it. We're staying at the Abbey. Were you able to make arrangements for that get-together?"

"It's all set, Dave. I'll let Mother tell you about it. Peggy! It's Dave Goldman. They're at the Abbey."

Peggy got on. "It's all set, Dave. I got all eleven to come—if we can do it at seven o'clock." Her voice sounded worried. "Is that too early? It was the only way I could get them all."

I informed Regan and he nodded abruptly. "That's fine, Peggy," I said. "We'll be there. And thanks."

"Thank *you*, Dave! What about Jim? Do you think . . ." Her voice trailed off.

"We'll do our best, Peggy. Keep your chin up."

I turned to Regan as I hung up and saw we were no longer alone. Father Kilian was back—with company. The monk with him was older, same sandy hair, same Coke-bottle glasses. I was beginning to wonder if nearsightedness, incipient baldness and blond hair were requirements for membership in this monastery.

Regan matched his smile. "Jerome!"

"Hello, Bishop," said the monk. They hugged as well as two people can when one of them's in a wheelchair.

"This is my assistant, David Goldman," Regan said after they got disengaged. "Abbot Jerome, David." The Abbot's smile got bigger and he gave me a bone-crunching handshake.

"Welcome to St. John's!" He turned anxiously to Regan. "Have you eaten? Can we get you anything?"

"Nothing, Jerome. Everything looks eminently satisfactory. As always."

"What about Mass? We can make whatever arrangements you like."

Regan looked at me. "We have a seven o'clock appointment at—where is it, David?"

"Near St. Augusta."

The Abbot frowned. "Then you'll want to leave before 6:45. Would you like a chapel at six o'clock?" Regan pondered that. The Abbot turned to me. "I suppose you would want to serve Mass, Mr. Goldman? Or should I—"

Regan interrupted, the ghost of a smile on his lips. "No, Mr. Goldman doesn't serve Mass, Jerome. Mr. Goldman is Jewish."

The Abbot blushed. "Oh, I'm sorry, I didn't—"

I waved it away. "Hey, I'm taken for a Catholic all the time. Don't worry about it. Embarrassing, yeah, but what the hell, it goes with the territory."

He grinned. This Abbot guy was good with the smiles, I had to give him that. With a final flurry of arrangements and felicitations, the two monks departed. With a lot of discussion of chalices and altars and stuff, the three churchmen had settled on morning arrangements. It sounded impossibly complex to me, but I wasn't involved, so I left it to them. I had my doubts that it could all work. It did, as things turned out.

My room next door, when I finally got to it, was okay. Even a TV set in the corner—and it worked! Black and white, but, hell, this *was* a monastery. I watched the news, normally a sure bet to put me to sleep. Not that night. I got almost no sleep. The place would be absolutely dead quiet for fifteen minutes, then the damn church bell would tell you the time. Loudly. I didn't want to know the time, I wanted to get some sleep. And no beer to dull my hearing. I'd be just starting to drop off, then—BONG! BONG! BONG! Eleven. Twelve. One . . . I missed three, so I guess I slept a little.

My travel alarm woke me, groggy and out of sorts, at 5:30. When I went in the bathroom, the light under the door to the Bishop's room told me he was up, which didn't surprise me. He gets up every morning at 5:00 and does half an hour of exercises on a jungle gym in his bedroom. When he's away, he has some isometrics he does. As a result, the guy's upper body is as useful as his lower is useless.

The monks had worked out different morning schedules for us. A "Brother Christian" came by for me at 6:10 to take me downstairs and see that I got properly fed. Some other Brother was to be at the Bishop's door at 5:45 to take him to some chapel where they did Mass. Apparently they had a chapel with a set-up for disabled priests—the altar has to be lower than normal. (The Bishop's chapel at the mansion has a small dining room table set up right in front of the altar.) We were to meet back in the Bishop's room at 6:30 to get going. The Bishop wouldn't get any breakfast, but he never eats breakfast anyway.

My worries about monastery fare proved unfounded. The bread, which Brother Christian bragged about at some length—some secret formula, I gathered, passed along from to monk to monk for centuries—was as good as he'd claimed, though it did require a healthy set of molars.

After breakfast Regan was waiting for me in his room. I grabbed the suitcases and we headed for the car. No goodbye committee, as per the Bishop's request.

"Well, David," the Bishop said as we drove away. "How did you find monastic life?"

"Piece of cake. But if I ever come back, I'm going to bring a cannon and blow that bell to little tiny pieces."

Regan grimaced. "Yes. The first night is always the worst. Were we staying another night, you'd find you'd sleep right through it. We may hope we can accomplish enough today that another night *won't* be necessary. What time is our return flight?"

"Five P.M. But with luck, we can move that up."

Regan sighed. "I prayed this morning for our success in exculpating Mr. Kearney. He is not guilty of this murder. But I have to confess, David, I am far from having any idea who is."

43

J U S T like the last time, I managed to get lost driving to the Kearneys.' But I blundered around, finally found my favorite landmark, the Persian Club. Regan, tense, excited and in an overall good mood, was surprisingly patient with what he called my navigational ineptitude.

We still made it by seven o'clock. We pulled into the Kearneys' long driveway to find it so full of cars and pickups I had to maneuver carefully to get near the front door.

Peggy was coming out of the house before the Bishop was off the seat and into his wheelchair. "Did you have trouble finding us?" she asked. "Coffee's on and everyone's here." Mike came striding up behind her. He looked worried.

Peggy started to tell us about it. "I think we've got a prob—"

"Let me, Mother." Mike put his arm around her and faced Regan. "Someone—I don't know who—phoned Kleinschmidt. He's a deputy sheriff here, Bishop. Davey knows him. He's the goddamnedest buttinski—sorry, Bishop—you ever want to meet, am I right, Davey?" He took a breath and faced Regan.

"Anyway, he called me last night about ten or so, I was just getting ready for bed. Told me he heard about the meeting, wouldn't tell me from who. And . . ." Kearney paused for effect. ". . . he wasn't sure if what we were doin' was legal." Mike looked into both our faces for reactions. Didn't get any. He went on.

"Well, anyhow, he said if we were gonna meet, he oughta be here, or we should just cancel. I thought I better let him come. So he's here, and everyone in there's as nervous as a cat in a room with eight rocking chairs."

Regan shrugged. "Let him stay, if you're inclined to be hospitable. We're doing nothing illegal, and he can't stop us. It may even be useful to have him. He may know something that no one else knows."

Peggy's eyes widened. "I thought you'd be mad, Bishop. I know I am. They've got Jim in jail for murder, and now they force their way into our house."

"Just remember, madame . . ." Regan was impassive. ". . . we're all after the same thing. Nick Carney's murderer. The sooner we find him, the sooner your son will be out of jail." His eyes flicked to Mike and back to Peggy. "By the way, I'd like a word with each of you, and with Mr. Jordan, after our meeting. Singly, if you don't mind."

Peggy looked startled. Mike glanced at her and rubbed his chin. "Hmm. Well, I don't know, Bishop. We're taking the Lear to New York this afternoon to go see Jim. Will it take long? I've got things I've got to take care of before we go."

"It is important," said Regan. "And I assure you, it won't take long."

Kearney scowled. "Okay, I guess. Can you tell me why?"

"Because I think each of you has information which might be useful in solving the matter, information he or she prefers not to divulge."

The couple looked at each other. Mike finally chuckled. "Well, you're honest, anyway. Yeah, okay, I guess. Okay with you, Mother?" Peggy smiled a little doubtfully and gave a small nod. "Done," Mike said, moving toward the house. "Want to come on in?"

We walked behind the Bishop as he struggled up the sloping sidewalk. I got a glance of disapproval from Peggy for not helping, which I didn't like but couldn't do anything about. One of the things you put up with when you're working for a guy who insists on being independent.

"I take it Mr. Jordan is here," Regan said, panting as he reached the top of the grade.

"Oh yes," said Peggy, pointing. "There's his car." I looked. Shiny, new Lincoln Town Car. Figured. It looked as out of place amid all the dusty pickups and muddy beaters as a chorus girl in a convent.

I bumped Regan up the three steps to the front door. As we entered, he murmured something totally insincere about what a magnificent house, blah, blah, blah. We followed the Kearneys through the front hallway into the solarium, where a bunch of people, all male, were sitting around in a circle of chairs. I recognized Dale Kleinschmidt, glowering at me in a chair over by one of the tall

windows. He looked natty in a khaki uniform. And very official. Or
was that officious?

Two seats down from him was Jerry Jordan, the lawyer, looking
even more out of place than Kleinschmidt. His pin-striped suit didn't
go any better with all the work clothes than his Lincoln went with
their pickups.

Mike handled introductions while Peggy brought coffee for Regan
and me. It looked like everyone else already had some. Except for
the deputy, who was apparently keeping his hands free. Regan nodded affably around the circle.

"I am sure Mr. and Mrs. Kearney have thanked all of you for
coming," he began. "I would like to add my thanks to theirs. As you
know, their son James—"

"Excuse me, sir. Just hold it right there." Kleinschmidt. He got
to his feet, blushing. "I got something to say, and I think I ought to
say it before you go any further." He got a little redder. Everyone
was looking at him, some with hostility. I saw Soukup, three seats to
my right, roll his eyes. Weiskopf, two seats to my left, whispered
something to the man next to him and they both snickered. Kleinschmidt swallowed and started to continue, but Regan cut him off.

"Excuse me, Mr.—Kleinschmidt, is it? You and I are here by
sufferance, sir. Mr. and Mrs. Kearney have invited Mr. Goldman
and me, along with these other gentlemen, to look into the matter
of a homicide—the murder of Nick Carney in New York City six days
ago." Some murmurs and a couple of gasps around the group.

Kleinschmidt glanced around angrily and started to jump in, but
the Bishop raised a hand and his voice. "The New York police have
arrested Mr. Kearney's son on the basis of what they undoubtedly
consider to be good and sufficient evidence. Mr. Goldman here, a
private investigator licensed by the state of New York, happens to
disagree. As do I.

"But to come to the point: Mr. Kearney—*James* Kearney—has
employed Mr. Goldman in an investigative capacity to find evidence
exculpating him. That is what Mr. Goldman is doing here this morning, with the assistance of James Kearney's parents. As to—"

Kleinschmidt was getting more and more fidgety as Regan went
on. So was I. So I wasn't too disappointed when the deputy cut in.
"So what are *you* doing here, Bishop?"

Regan took a deep breath and stared at the wall over the deputy's

head. He allowed a few seconds of silence to indicate his exasperation.
"If I may continue, Mr. Kleinschmidt. I am here because Mr. Goldman invited me to accompany him . . ." (Say what? *I* invited *him*?
When?) ". . . I occasionally offer Mr. Goldman suggestions on his
cases . . ." (*Suggestions?*) ". . . Some of which have borne fruit."
(Well, I couldn't argue with that.) "Because I have an idea or two
about the present case, he has asked me to address the people in this
room—which I am happy to do." Regan looked around. He had
everyone's attention.

"So if I may without further interruptions, I would like to ask a
few questions of these—"

"Nope." Kleinschmidt's stance hadn't changed: feet apart, hands
behind his back, head forward, eyes on Regan. "Sorry, Bishop. No
can do. A lieutenant in the New York City police department has
told me about your shenanigans. A sergeant from there was here
yesterday, and they were already unhappy about your 'associate,' this
guy Goldman, poking around. And they told me they absolutely didn't
want *you* getting involved. I only learned about this meeting late last
night, so I haven't been able to contact them about this particular
meeting. So I'm going to have to ask you to hold off till I have a
chance to talk to them."

Kleinschmidt looked at his watch. "The man in charge will be in
his office in about an hour. If you'll just hold on, I can check with
him. Maybe you can meet later on . . ." Some groans and noises of
irritation around the circle. Four men looked at their watches. One
half-raised his hand, presumably to ask permission to leave. Kleinschmidt sensed a mutiny rising, glanced around, but tried to continue.
". . . I'm telling you, you're not asking questions of *anyone* till
I've—"

"No sir." Regan raised his voice to be heard above the deputy and
the rising hubbub. He was as mad as I'd seen him in a while. He
turned to Mike. "Mr. Kearney. This is your home. I said before, Mr.
Kleinschmidt is here by sufferance. Your sufferance. As are we all.
So the present impasse can be resolved only by you." He blinked
and glanced at Peggy. "And, of course, Mrs. Kearney. My advice to
you is to ask Deputy Kleinschmidt to leave." The deputy started to
object, but Regan rode right over him.

"I had thought he could be of some assistance, but he is obstructing
what we're trying to accomplish." Kleinschmidt, reddening, started

to talk again, but Regan just upped the volume another notch. "If he refuses to leave, I suggest we adjourn this meeting to another room in the house, and prevent him—physically, if necessary—from accompanying us. But of course, it's your decision. You're the host here. Which is as it should be, since it's your son who is in jeopardy."

Regan had picked the right man to make a suggestion like that to. Kearney had been showing increasing signs of irritation during Kleinschmidt's earlier speech. Regan's suggestion of a little physical activity had him licking his chops. He turned to Kleinschmidt and smiled a mean smile.

"Sorry, Dale, you heard the man. Out."

The deputy goggled. "Aw, Mike, c'mon. You're not going to let this guy—"

"Hell I'm not. At least he's on my boy's side. And at least he's tryin' to help. All I see you doin' is obstructin'. And by God, this is still my house, and this is still the good old U.S. of A. I want you gone." Mike's nostrils flared. "And if you don't want to go, I'm just the guy that can make you." He looked like he hoped Kleinschmidt would take him up on it.

"Now you just hold on, Mike!" Kleinschmidt blustered, taking a step back. "I'm still the law in Stearns County and you can't—"

"Please, please, gentlemen!" Regan's voice cut through the yammering like a whip. "I had no intention of starting a fight." The antagonists, both breathing hard, turned to him. Regan made little pushing gestures at Kleinschmidt with his palms. And dropped his voice about three levels. "Mr. Kleinschmidt, please. You must know you have no legal standing here. You invited yourself to this meeting; Mr. and Mrs. Kearney were gracious enough to permit you to come. Why not remain peacefully—and listen? Surely they've gone far beyond what they're required to do. They—we—simply want to get at the truth and help their son along the way. If you can accept that, I'm prepared to ask Mr. Kearney to permit you to stay."

The deputy was still glowering, but for the first time he was showing signs of uncertainty. He glanced at Mike. "Okay, let's get on with it." He sat down. Now it was Mike's turn to look uncertain. He glanced at the Bishop, seeking guidance. The Bishop gave it indirectly.

Pinning the deputy with his eyes, he said, "Will you permit us to go about this undisturbed, sir?" Kleinschmidt looked away.

"I'll now ask Mr. Kearney to be seated. What time is it, Mr.

Goldman?" I checked the Timex as Kearney found a seat in the circle across from Kleinschmidt. Peggy, who'd been moving around, pouring coffee, put the silver pitcher on the coffee table in the center of the circle and found a seat.

"Seven-fourteen," I said.

Regan nodded. "And I know all of you are busy men. I apologize for the delay in starting. Can everyone stay till eight o'clock?" Nods around the circle, and a couple of sighs of relief. Apparently some had been afraid the meeting was going to last a lot longer.

"If it's not *past* eight," came a muttered comment from someone. That drew a few muttered *damn right*'s.

"Understood," Regan said crisply. "Now. We are here to discover who absconded with a Colt pistol from this house last Wednesday, nine days ago. The eleven of you were, as far as we now know, the only persons to have been on the premises that day. So—"

"This isn't everyone," said Don Soukup from his chair three down from me. "I—"

"If you will, sir," the Bishop interrupted. "That is precisely one of the things I am after. But may I ask you to hold the comment momentarily? I'll be back to you." Soukup nodded.

"Thank you. I have one question to ask before returning to your query. This: did anyone see anyone Wednesday last near the gun cabinet? Above all, did anyone at any time see the cabinet open?"

That started a lot of palaver about this or that person being in the den at one time or another, but it all added up to a big nothing. The Bishop cut off discussion after six or seven minutes, when it became clear it wasn't leading anywhere.

"All right, thank you. Please, that's enough." He finally got quiet. "A jumbled situation, but the sum of it is, no one can pinpoint an individual spending a suspicious amount of time in the vicinity of the gun cabinet." He looked around, got nothing but nods. He looked at Soukup.

"Now. Back to your comment, sir. You maintain that not all the people who were in this house last Wednesday are now present in this room."

"That's right." Soukup glanced around uneasily, his good-natured face showing signs of embarrassment at being singled out. "There was at least one other guy I saw who's not here now."

"And who is that?"

"I don't know his name." He turned to face Weiskopf, right across the circle. "Didn't you have another guy on your crew, Bill? Someone who's not here now?"

Weiskopf blinked through his thick glasses. He looked around. "Nope. Matt and Maury were the only two. And they're both here. We didn't have anyone else out here that day, did we, guys?"

The two men on either side of him, one big and burly, the other short and chunky like Weiskopf, shook their heads. "Naw," said the big one, "it's been just us three since Ted Van Allen quit, oh, when was it? Back in May sometime."

Weiskopf nodded, turned back to Soukup, who shrugged, "Okay, it wasn't you." He turned to Madison, at the far end of the circle. The plumber's ruddy face showed considerable boredom. "How about you, Terry? Didn't you have another guy working for you?" Madison disgustedly shook his head.

"Just me and Fred," he growled. The young guy next to him, previously introduced as Fred Glinke, his assistant, nodded agreement.

Soukup looked back to Regan and shrugged. "All I can say is, I saw another guy. I thought his name was also Fred." He looked around again. "Didn't anyone else see him? A little guy." Shrugs, shakes of the head. Regan cast me a quick, impenetrable glance. I gave him a slight shrug. Was he onto something?

"Yeah!" The remark startled everyone. It came from Fred Glinke. Madison next to him rolled not only his eyes, but his whole head in an "I-can't-believe-this" gesture. He was close to walking out. Glinke turned to him. "I'll bet that's the guy *we* let in. He said he was with *your* crew, Don."

Glinke was the youngest in a room full of young guys, probably just out of his teens. He reddened, glanced around. I looked at the Deputy sitting across from him. He was still glowering but also taking notes in a little notebook in his lap.

Regan stayed with Glinke. "Your name, sir?"

"Fred Glinke. I work for Terry." He flipped a thumb to his right. Madison looked like he was finally interested. Even ready to talk.

"Is that right, Mr. Madison? What were you doing here that day?"

"I'm the plumber. Fred and me had to come back out to redo the downstairs toilet. It was leaking a little. Anyhow, like Fred said, a guy was working outside or something. He was just coming around the house, eating an apple, when we showed up. So the three of us came in together. That's probably why you thought he was with us, Bill. But he said he was a dry-waller."

"You didn't get his name?" Regan asked. Madison and Glinke both shook their heads. "Can either of you tell me what he looked like?"

The two plumbers looked at each other. Madison shrugged, so Fred spoke up. "A little guy. Talked kinda funny. He was wearing a gray turtleneck shirt under his coveralls. Oh yeah—I'm not sure, but I think he had a mustache. A little black one."

Regan's eyes widened a sixteenth of an inch. Enough to alert me that he was excited. "Mr. Goldman," he said. "Have you that picture? The one you obtained from Mr. Steiner?"

I looked at him, puzzled. Then I understood. The picture of Nick that Jake had given us. Nick? Shaking my head, I pulled it out. "Show the picture to Messrs. Madison and Glinke, if you would, David." I stared at Regan, trying to get my mind around it. Nick, here in St. Cloud? Shaking my head, I got up, walked to Glinke and handed him the photo. As he took it, Regan said, "Could that be the person you saw, Mr. Glinke?"

Glinke studied it, looked at Regan, then handed it to Madison. Madison studied it and started to nod. Both men looked at Regan. Madison, for once, beat his assistant to the punch. "Yeah," he said. "Yeah, I think it is."

I shook my head and looked at Regan. He looked as smug as I'd ever seen him. And I want to tell you, that's smug.

44

Y head was whirling. Nick here? Nick—the gun thief? I
couldn't believe it. I tried to understand the implications,
but it was too much. Meanwhile, the Bishop wasn't giving
me a chance to catch my breath.

"You think so but you're not sure, gentlemen?" Glinke glanced at
Madison, shook his head.

"In a way it's him, in a way it's not." He shrugged. Madison nodded
agreement.

"And what time did you arrive?"

"Eleven o'clock," Madison said authoritatively. Glinke nodded
agreeably.

"Let everyone else see it, please. Especially this gentleman." Regan
nodded toward Soukup. The picture was passed around the circle to
Soukup. Most of the passers took a more or less long look at it. No
signs of recognition. Soukup studied it longer than Madison had. He
turned to Regan.

"Dunno. Might be, might not. I'd say not. But the guy they saw
has gotta be the guy I saw, whether this is a picture of him or not,
because the guy I saw was wearin' a turtleneck—I'd forgotten that
till now. I remember thinking, why the hell's he wearing a turtleneck
in the summertime? Shortsleeved, but still." He looked at the snapshot again and frowned. "But it's hard to tell from a photograph,
especially when I only saw the guy a short time. I can't hardly remember what he looked like. And this snapshot's not much help."

"Please, let everyone see it," Regan said. "And while you examine
it, I have more questions.

"Mrs. Kearney. You were the general contractor for the overall
house repairs and refurbishment. Any idea who this man may have
been?"

Peggy seemed a little flustered, maybe at being the only woman in the room. "No, I don't, Bishop. I don't recognize him by description. Or by that photo. And I hadn't ordered any other workers out here that day. I just don't know who it could have been."

Regan nodded at her. "Thank you." His eyes circled the group. "Now. Let me ask a question or two of those who saw the man. You're certain he had a mustache, Mr. Madison?"

We hassled on the subject of the mysterious Fred, or Nick, or whoever the guy was, for another twenty minutes. At one point I made a fool of myself by attempting to demonstrate the way Nick walked. I got in the center of the circle and tried to walk with that hitch of Nick's. To general amusement. Everyone in the group who'd met Nick—Jordan, both Kearneys and especially Regan—agreed on one thing: my demonstration was a total failure.

"A valiant effort, David," was Regan's summation, when the laughter finally died down. "It's true that Nick Carney didn't have a normal walk. But I'm afraid it was a far cry from whatever it is that you're doing."

He did make an effort to see if anyone noticed anything special about the man's walk. A couple thought they did, including Soukup, but they weren't really sure and got shouted down by the majority.

By the time we felt we had everything everyone could tell us about the mysterious workman, it was ten after eight, but their anxiety to get done with the meeting and be about their business seemed to have subsided. I took copious notes, but all the notes in the world didn't succeed in establishing whether the extra workman had been Nick Carney.

As to the mustache, the vote split down the middle: Madison certain he had one, Helderle certain he hadn't, the other two unsure. My initial shock at the possibility it might be Nick had changed to the conviction that it was. My one problem was with the group's general feeling that his walk was normal, but that seemed a minor quibble.

My mind was dying to race ahead and consider the implications of Carney's having stolen the gun, but I had to pay attention to all the commentary, take notes and watch faces to see if I could detect a glimmering of guilty knowledge on any of them. The face I mainly watched was that of Jerome Jordan, the guy most out of place.

He hadn't said a word since we'd arrived, including when Mike had made the introductions. I saw several looks thrown his way—

looks of curiosity. People wondering, probably, who's the geek in the business suit and what's he doing here? He paid close attention to everything.

The Bishop ended the proceedings at 8:15. "I thank you for coming, gentlemen. I believe you have given us some significant new information. This could be extremely helpful in the efforts to defend Mr. James Kearney. We are adjourned."

Most of the workmen took off in a hurry. Soukup sent his men on their way and got me off to the side. "Bill Weiskopf's been ribbing me about how you fooled me. I should have known right away—that gag about us knocking down the wrong wall." He laughed. "That was a good one. I should have known no narc could ever come up with anything that good."

I smiled back at him. "Sorry to lie to you, man. Glad there's no hard feelings. Bill's one of the rare ones. Not many people ask you for I.D.—and then look at it! Something you might keep in mind." He grinned sheepishly, shook my hand and took off.

Deputy Kleinschmidt was in muttered conversation with Regan while I was talking to Soukup, but by the time I got to them, he was striding toward the foyer like he was in a hurry. I looked down at Regan. "So: we going to jail for obstruction of justice?"

Regan smirked. He claims he doesn't smirk but he does. "The good deputy was just thanking me for insisting on going ahead with this morning's meeting. He acknowledged that he would never have been able to learn about this 'twelfth man,' absent from our group. He apologized for his obstructionism."

I raised my eyebrows. "I didn't know he had it in him."

Mike Kearney came back to the solarium from seeing people out. "So," he said to Regan. "You wanted to talk to Peggy and me?"

"If we could, sir. Perhaps we should begin with Mr. Jordan? Then he can be on his way."

Kearney nodded. "Yeah, fine. Now where is he?"

I'd just been asking myself the same question. And had just gotten an answer. Murmurings were coming from the direction of the kitchen. And I had a hunch. "I'll get him," I said, smiling at Mike. "I think I hear him."

Regan must have had the same hunch I had, because when Mike moved to follow me, he stopped him. "Oh, Mr. Kearney. Are you a hunter?"

Kearney spun around like Patrick Ewing with an open lane to the basket. As I went through the door into a hallway, he was saying, "Sure am. What about you?"

"I've done my share," Regan said. "Though not recently. I noticed a kennel out back. What type of dog..."

His voice faded behind me as I moved silently down the hallway. The murmuring I'd heard became voices, clearer and clearer as I approached an open door. I've learned to walk quietly, so it was easy to get close to the door without the talkers hearing me. The restricted view I had told me it was the kitchen.

"... *got* to tell Mike I know!" Peggy's voice, quiet but urgent. "He's never told me, and I never wanted to bring it up, but when Mona and Nick—"

"Peggy!" Jordan, also quiet and even more urgent. "Dammit, don't be a fool! You can't! Especially now, with all that's happened. Just leave things alone!"

"But Jerry, I can't stand it any more! Mike sneaking around for no reason. It breaks my heart to have this—misunderstanding between us. I'm sure he'd understand why you told me."

Jordan's voice was bitter. "Yeah? Because I was so drunk I couldn't keep my mouth shut?"

"Jerry, don't be so hard on yourself. You only—"

It was time to interrupt. Not that I didn't want to hear more. But as the Third Rule of Eavesdropping plainly says, Don't Get Caught. As I listened, I was facing down the hallway and saw Mike coming before he saw me.

I moved rapidly into the kitchen like I was in a hurry. Peggy spun around, hand flying to her mouth. Jordan's eyes widened. I glanced at them as I pretended to be looking for something and said, "The Bishop would like just a little more coffee and I'm afraid what we've got is getting a little cold. Do you know if—?"

They pulled themselves together. Peggy moved quickly to a big urn on the cabinet with an apologetic, "Oh, I'm so sorry!" She gave a mild titter, not meeting my eyes. "Jer—Mr. Jordan and I were just chatting. I'm neglecting my hostess duties, aren't I?"

Kearney was now in the kitchen, hands in hip pockets, obviously irritated by the delay. Following a quick glare at me, he spoke to Jordan. "Uh, Jerry, mind chatting with the Bishop a couple of minutes before you go?"

Jordan looked at Peggy quickly, then at Mike. "Oh. Sure. Sure, if it'll help Jim."

"Good. The Bishop seems to think if he can chat with all of us alone for a bit, he might be able to flush out some more information. I doubt it, but anything to help Jim, right?" He started a smile, decided it wasn't worth the effort. "Anyway, he'd like to start with you, so if you wouldn't mind? I've got to get to the office."

"Oh!" Jordan seemed to rouse himself. "Fine. Where shall we talk?"

Kearney looked at me. "Dave, why don't the three of you go down to the den and—I forgot about the stairs. That'd be tough on the Bishop, right?" I shrugged. "Uh, go ahead and talk in the solarium, why don't you? That's big enough to be private. And Peggy and I'll stay out of your hair, right, Mother? We promise not to eavesdrop." This time the smile made it through, just barely.

Peggy nodded. "Let's just go collect those coffee things. I'll bring some more coffee, Dave."

The four of us headed back for the solarium, Peggy carrying a fresh pot of coffee. Jordan said something to me, but I wasn't listening. I was trying to piece together the conversation I'd heard between him and Peggy. Regan would be interested. Very interested. I wondered if I could pass it on to him before we started with the interviews.

"Let me just have a second with the Bishop, Jerry, before we start," I said, rudely interrupting his homily on how beastly cold it gets in St. Cloud in the wintertime.

He shrugged. "Take as long as you need." He flopped on a couch about twenty feet from where the Bishop was holding out his cup to Peggy for more coffee. I went to the Bishop, gave Mike and Peggy a quick dismissive smile, and began pushing the Bishop, cup still extended, to the far end of the solarium.

"David!" he muttered fiercely. "What are you doing?" He hates, as he puts it, "being pushed around."

"Got something to tell you, so shut up!" I whispered back, just as fiercely. He clamped his lips together and listened while I murmured as exact a repetition as I could of the conversation I'd overheard in the kitchen. When I finished, his only commentary was an abrupt nod. Then, after a second: "Get Mr. Jordan."

45

I S T U D I E D Jordan, slouched back in the upholstered chair, as I flipped open my notebook. He wasn't what you'd call in tiptop shape. His cheekbones, forehead and nose were covered with tiny broken capillaries. He seemed tired, edgy.

"You had nothing to say earlier, Mr. Jordan," Regan began. "In fact, you were the only person *not* to speak. Was it that you had nothing to report, or did you simply not care to unburden yourself before those present?"

Jordan smiled sardonically. "The former."

Regan nodded appreciatively. He likes men of few words. Probably because he has so many. But his next question was a stunner. "Did you kill Nick Carney?"

Jordan handled it well. Blinked and widened his smile. "What? No Miranda warning?"

Regan didn't smile back. "No such warning is required. Mr. Goldman and I are not police officers and you're an attorney. But to remove all doubt, be assured that Mr. Goldman and I will not hesitate to use anything you say in whatever way we choose. Our sole aim is to find the murderer of Nick Carney and thus exculpate James Kearney."

Jordan got serious. "Jim's a good kid and shouldn't be in jail. And while I can't say I'm totally impressed by the way you've carried on here this morning, I appreciate what you're *trying* to do for him. No, I didn't kill Nick Carney." He raised a hand. "Nor—to answer your next question before you ask it—do I have any idea who did."

Regan nodded, with a glance at me to be sure I was getting it into my notebook. He immediately hit Jordan with another biggie. "Do you know the combination to Mr. Kearney's gun cabinet?"

Jordan stared at him, smile disappearing. "You get right to it, don't you?" His eyes narrowed. "Nicely put, too. Not, did Mike ever tell me, but do I know it?" He looked up at the ceiling, thinking; went back to Regan. "Yeah, I know the combination. I'd appreciate it if you didn't pass that on to Mike."

"How did you obtain it?"

Jordan shrugged. "Privileged."

Regan nodded. "Then you leave me no choice but to conjecture that Mrs. Kearney supplied you with it." Jordan reddened and started to speak but Regan stopped him with an upraised hand. "Let me change the question. How long have you known it?"

Jordan scowled. "Years. I've got it written down somewhere. I frankly don't remember where I got it or who gave it to me. I suppose it might have been Peggy." He gave Regan a long look. "Oh, what the hell. What have I got to lose, really?" His eyes narrowed. "In confidence?"

Regan studied him. "Unless we find it essential in our investigation or for the release of Mr. Kearney."

Jordan's eyes went to me. I nodded.

Jordan returned to Regan. "I wanted to marry her," he said after a pause. "Mike and I met her at the same time. She wanted Mike, not me. So I—" Jordan took out a handkerchief and wiped his brow. "This isn't easy."

He cleared his throat and started again. "I was in love with her, Bishop, I don't know if you can understand that. Anyway," Jordan went on, "I could see that Peggy was something special, something I wanted for myself. So I went to her and told her all about Mike. He didn't—"

Regan stopped him. "Told her exactly what?"

"Everything. About Mona, the baby, the marriage, his secrecy. I blew the whistle on him. I told her a man who kept secrets like that from her wasn't to be trusted as a husband. Well, she—"

"Weren't you violating a professional confidence of Mr. Kearney's?"

Jordan shrugged. "Maybe. But I was in love, Bishop! I was afraid I was going to lose her!" The lawyer looked away. "But it didn't work. She went ahead and married Mike anyway."

"And you subsequently married someone else?"

Jordan smiled faintly. "*Two* someone elses. Neither marriage lasted a year. No issue from either. I guess I'm just a natural bachelor." He glanced at me. I found myself resenting the probable implication: that he and I were kindred souls.

Regan thought for a minute, then changed directions. "Tell me about your initial meeting with Nick Carney last week. Was that the first time you'd met?"

Jordan nodded. "Yes, the first time. Last Tuesday night. You know all about his conversation with Jim? And Jim's trip here to St. Cloud? How about Nick's phone call to Mike?" Regan nodded again.

"Well, then you know how upset Mike was. He called me Tuesday morning, said he wanted the matter handled. Blamed it on me, said I had to handle it, said he'd go as high as fifty thousand dollars to keep it from Peggy." Jordan grinned. "Fifty thousand dollars to keep something from Peggy that she already knew. And asking *me* to take care of it. I agreed.

"I told Mike the money'd do no good unless we got a legally binding release from Nick that would stop him from ever attempting this again. So I flew to New York, got Nick on the phone and made the offer. Offered him ten thou; he came back with twenty-five, so I knew I had it made. We finally settled on twenty and agreed to get together that night in the bar across the street from his office.

"I'd drawn up a release on the plane—that paper you saw last Friday night. Made it as tight as I could, hoping that Nick needed the money so badly he'd sign whatever it took."

Jordan shook his head. "Well, he didn't, as you know. I went to that place—Paddy's Pub—and met Nick. We spoke, had a few drinks, and then I hit him with the waiver. He didn't even finish reading it before he tore it up and threw it in my face and walked out. End of meeting."

Regan nodded. "How much validity was there in Nick Carney's claim?"

Jordan frowned. "What do you mean?"

The Bishop shrugged. "Was it true that Mr. Kearney had contravened the terms of the decree of divorce? By cheating on the child-support payments?"

Jordan shifted uneasily and thought a minute before answering. "Before answering that, I should make a point. That decree was seriously flawed. That ten-percent-of-salary nonsense—strictly boilerplate. There's considerable reason to doubt it would have stood up to any sort of judicial review. Furthermore, the whole issue was moot. Past the statute of limitations."

Regan shrugged. "In other words, Mr. Kearney *was* in violation. Thank you." Jordan reddened and started to add something, changed his mind and clamped his jaw shut.

Regan went on, "I'm curious." I glanced up. Something in Regan's tone told me he was onto something. The look in his eyes confirmed it. "Let me understand," he murmured. "It was last Tuesday that you flew to New York to make that offer to Nick Carney." Jordan nodded. "And you returned to Minnesota on Wednesday." Jordan nodded again. "You were there as Mr. Kearney's agent, were you not?" Third nod.

Regan sprang the trap. "Why then, sir, did you come directly to this house on your return, rather than to Mr. Kearney's office? Did you expect to find him here?"

Jordan's face reddened as he thought about Regan's question. "I don't like what you're trying to imply," he growled.

Regan looked up at him. "And what it that, Mr. Jordan?"

Jordan, breathing hard, got to his feet and looked down at Regan. His nose looked ready to explode.

"You're suggesting I came here to see Peggy, aren't you? You think there's something going on between us. Don't you?"

"I think nothing of the sort. Is there?"

"Absolutely not! It's a damn lie, is what it is!"

"I see. That being the case, I shall avoid thinking it. Nonetheless, my question is a natural one, regardless of the implications you may think it contains. Why, returning from a trip at the behest of *Mr.* Kearney, did you come directly to *Mrs.* Kearney? Surely one might speculate whether such a course of action could have anything to do with Nick Carney's subsequent murder."

Jordan opened his mouth, closed it, looked down at his chair and came to a decision. "This interview is over," he muttered, turned and went. Regan's voice followed him.

"A final question, Mr. Jordan. What were you doing last Saturday afternoon in a bar across the street from Nick Carney's office during the time when he was being murdered?"

Jordan stopped like he'd run into a wall. He stood motionless for several seconds. Then turned, walked deliberately back to his chair and sat down. He gave Regan a long, hard look, which Regan met. "I don't suppose it'd do me any good to ask you how you know that," he muttered.

"Absolutely none," Regan said.

"I didn't think so." Jordan shook his head. "'O what a tangled web we weave, when first we practice to deceive.' Shakespeare, right?"

Regan murmured, "Not quite. Close enough."

Jordan rubbed his face with a shaky hand. "Okay. Here it is, God help me." He took a breath and looked Regan in the eye. "Peggy wanted to see Nick. Apologize to him. She told me so that morning. I made no bones about the fact that I thought it was a lousy idea, but I couldn't get through to her. I had some sort of stupid romantic notion about protecting her. So I went over there to try to head her off, but I couldn't get into the building. I didn't realize it'd be buttoned up so tight on the weekend. I went in the bar to wait for her and, frankly, forgot about her. Had a few drinks—more than a few, I guess—and finally went back to the hotel. What I want to know is how you knew—"

"And I'm not going to tell you, sir," Regan snapped. "I have no more questions for you. Nor any information."

Jordan gave him a long look. He finally got up and headed for the kitchen.

"Please tell Mr. Kearney we are at his disposal," Regan called after him. Jordan gave no sign he heard. Just continued on through the door to the hallway and the kitchen.

46

I N about thirty seconds Jordan reappeared, deep in muttered discussion with Mike. Heads bent, they continued the low-pitched
conversation in the front hallway. Giving Regan and me a chance
to go over what we'd just learned.

"For an attorney, Mr. Jordan's a rather transparent liar," Regan
murmured. "I wonder what it is he's hiding."

I raised my eyebrows. "Give you three guesses and the first two
don't count."

Regan frowned. "I'm not in a guessing mood. And if you're implying
that he's the murderer, you're jumping to an unwarranted conclusion.
I can think of at least two other motives he might have for lying."
He waved it away.

"At any rate, we can discuss it later. For now, a question before
we start with Mr. Kearney. How likely is it that he realizes his wife
knows about his first marriage?"

I frowned. "Hell, why ask me? I never claimed to be psychic."

Regan glared. He had his back to the front door, so he couldn't
see Jordan leaving and Mike approaching. He was going on, his voice
rising. "I didn't suggest you were psychic, David. All I—"

"Mr. Kearney!" I interrupted, jumping to my feet. "Have a seat."

"Can't stay long," Kearney growled. He plopped down, shooting
his sleeve back to look at his watch. "God, it's after nine! I should've
been at work a couple hours ago. Like I told you, Mother and I are
flying to New York this afternoon and I've got a ton of things to clear
away before we leave. I told the pilot we'd leave at two."

Regan nodded. "Then we'll not waste time. When did your son
first contact you?"

Kearney cocked his head at him. "My son? You mean Jim?"

"No," Regan snapped. "Your older son. Nick."

Kearney glanced over his shoulder. "Keep your voice down!" he hissed. "Peggy doesn't know about Nick. I don't want—"

"Excuse me." Regan pinned him with his eyes. "Let's talk about that. Why not?"

Kearney blinked. "Why not what?"

"Why haven't you told your wife of the earlier marriage? And about your other son?"

Kearney scowled at him. It was meant to be an intimidating scowl, but Regan didn't blink. Kearney finally looked away. "Okay, I'll tell you," he mumbled. "I wanted our marriage—Peggy's and mine—to be different. I didn't want to make the same mistake with Peggy I made with Mona."

"Mistake?"

Kearney sighed. "I was fresh out of West Point when I married Mona. I was young, she was pretty. Bang, we got married. Dumbest thing I ever did. By far." He chuckled bitterly. "It wasn't that I had to: she wasn't pregnant or anything." He shook his head and sighed.

"We had absolutely nothing in common, Bishop. She was a sweet little nothing. She'd never been anywhere, no education. We stayed together eighteen months. I can tell you, it was the longest eighteen months of my life.

"As long as it was just the two of us, it was tolerable. But then the baby came along and hell, Mona didn't have a clue how to handle a baby and neither did I. He cried all the time, night and day, and everything she did just made things worse. Every morning I'd rush out of that apartment like my pants were on fire. And come back as late I could make it. And it got worse and worse."

Kearney rubbed his chin. "I'll tell you, Bishop, getting shipped to Nam was like getting a furlough to heaven. I knew when I left I was never coming back. I mean, to Mona.

"And I didn't. I was in Nam a year. First thing I did, soon as I got shipped back stateside, was call Jerry. He was right out of law school, just passed the bar. I told him to draw up a divorce. He did all the negotiating with her. The deal was, I had to give her five thousand dollars. Doesn't seem like much today, but I'll tell you, it was more than I had then; had to borrow the money from the bank. Jerry recommended me doing that in place of alimony. A one-time payment. Plus, of course, a hundred and a quarter for child support every month till Nick turned eighteen." Kearney was going to add something but Regan had a question.

"To increase as your income increased?"

"Well..." Kearney glanced at his watch. "That was never really very clear." He cleared his throat. "I don't really know much about it, left it pretty much up to Jerry. Talk to him."

"Not clear?" Regan persisted. "But if you—"

Kearney jumped up. "Look. I've got to get to my office. Maybe you can—"

Regan interrupted, his fingertips drumming on the arm of the wheelchair. He hates looking up at people. "We're not through, Mr. Kearney. You say you left the whole issue of child-support payments to Mr. Jordan?"

Kearney shrugged. "Right. Look. *You* may not think we're through but we are. You get one more question. Then I've got to go."

Regan frowned up at him. "Only one more question? All right." He paused, holding Kearney with his eyes. "How many miles did your son James put on the company car during his visit here last week?"

I looked up, surprised. Kearney was staring, astonished, at Regan. "How many miles? What business is that of...?" He glanced at his watch again. Gave a deep, disgusted sigh, strode to a nearby table and picked up the phone there. He turned his back on us and held a muttered conversation with someone. A minute later he was back, rubbing his chin thoughtfully.

"Two hundred ninety-seven miles," he said, staring down at Regan. "Almost exactly twice what it should have been. The airport's seventy-three miles from this driveway. I've clocked it. Four times seventy-three's two hundred ninety-two. What made you ask that?"

Regan spun the chair away from him. "A certain line of reasoning, Mr. Kearney. It's not important. We can discuss it when you've more time."

"I can *take* time! Dammit, what does it mean? I want to know how you—"

Regan, his back to Kearney, shook his head. "We're done, Mr. Kearney. I'll let you go about your business." Kearney glared at him for five seconds, then switched it to me.

I stared back at him. "Hey, don't look at me. I'm in the same boat as you. Confused as hell."

Kearney reddened, turned on his heel and strode for the front door. He jerked it open, walked out and slammed it behind him. The sound reverberated through the house. Well, I guess every man's entitled to slam the front door of his own castle. Regan didn't flinch at the bang. In fact, he looked like a cat that's just polished off a canary, with a mouse for a chaser.

47

T HE slam of the door was still echoing when Peggy came bustling in, wringing her hands. She looked around. "Was that Mike? Did he leave?"

"So it appears, madame. Would you care to sit?"

"Oh. You're ready for me?" Peggy's smile didn't go with her frightened eyes and the way her hands twisted around each other. The Bishop didn't smile but his eyes and tone were friendly.

"Indeed we are. Please sit down. You'll find that neither Mr. Goldman nor I bite. Nor will we take any more of your time than we have to."

Peggy sat down in the chair Mike had just vacated, but on the edge. She looked back and forth from the Bishop to me. "I'll tell you everything I can," she said. "I'm afraid I don't know much, though."

"No? I doubt that. I suspect you know a good deal, madame. Obviously more than you care to divulge. For instance: how long have you been aware that your husband was married before? And that Nick Carney was your stepson?"

Peggy's hand flew to her mouth and she half-rose to her feet. I sensed she was about an inch away from jumping up and running.

"Wha—wha—? What marriage?"

"Come, come, madame. Sit down and relax. Good; that's better.

We know, Mrs. Kearney, that you know your husband was married once before. How long have you known?"

Peggy's dark eyes were on him. "But if you know that, why—?" She snapped her mouth shut, glanced at me, looked back at Regan. "All right. I'll tell you."

She took a deep breath. "I suspected almost from the time I met Mike. He was so big, so good-looking, so popular. And here he was, four or five years out of the Academy, all his classmates married and him not. I sort of tiptoed around the subject, dropped hints. But he just wouldn't talk about it."

She smoothed her hair. "So I got Jerry to tell me. He always had—well, a thing for me." She blushed. "And I knew it. So I—got him to tell me. It's been our secret all the years I've been married to Mike. Our little secret." Her eyes flashed. "Mike had his, so we had ours."

Regan was studying her carefully. "Then you were aware that Nick Carney was your husband's son?"

Peggy turned away. Regan let the silence grow. Finally she looked back at him. "Well," she admitted, "I suspected it." Something in Regan's look made her flush. "All right!" she exploded. "Yes! I knew about Nick."

"Thank you," Regan said dryly. "And you were aware of the child-support payments?"

The woman tossed her head. "Yes, I knew."

"But I understand the payments were made by Mr. Jordan. He told you about them?"

"Sure," she said. "He told me everything, back before Mike and I got married."

"Did you know of the divorce arrangements? Are you aware that your husband was systematically cheating his son of the agreed-upon amounts?"

Peggy nodded and closed her eyes. Her voice sounded weary. "Jerry wasn't proud of it, Bishop. It's the way Mike is: he wants other people to do his dirty work for him. Jerry's always done it. Back when Mike first started with KPI and his income was so much higher than it'd been in the army, he and Jerry had a talk. Jerry told me all about it—he was drunk at the time, of course.

"He was real worried, Jerry was. By doing what Mike wanted him to do—making the short payments—he was violating his oath as a lawyer. But Mike wouldn't hear about it. Told him what to do, wouldn't hear any argument. Jerry was desperate, Bishop. He didn't think he could survive without Mike as a client. But at the same time he was afraid it'd all come out some day and he'd be disbarred. He never felt right about it, but he could never face up to Mike."

The Bishop nodded, thought for a minute. "Let's talk about something else. Why did you go to Nick Carney's office last Saturday afternoon?"

Peggy stared at him, her eyes widening. "I didn't go to his office!" Regan's eyes pinned her. "I didn't!"

"Technically, no. The door was locked. But you tried. You were on the sidewalk outside. Why?"

Peggy shook her head. "How did you learn all this? Did Jerry tell you?"

"No. How we learned it, madame, is unimportant. Please answer my question."

Peggy shook her head. "I don't believe this. All right, since you already know. Jerry'd told me where Nick's office was. He'd also told me that Jim was taking Mike's check to Nick at two o'clock Saturday afternoon. I wanted to tell Nick I was sorry for how Mike had treated him all those years. But I didn't want Jim to know. So I waited outside, across the street, till Jim left. Then I tried to get in to talk to Nick. But I couldn't. The building was locked. I couldn't even get into the lobby."

Regan frowned at her. "You wanted to talk to him. Had you ever spoken to him before?"

"Never. And I didn't that afternoon. I couldn't get in. What are you looking at? Don't you believe me?"

Regan shrugged. "I don't know. Let's go back to your son's sudden visit home, eleven days ago. Why did he come?"

Peggy shrugged. "I think he just wanted to see the addition. I'd written him about all the work we'd done, and he was interested. He had a day off and just decided to come on the spur of the moment." I looked at her, wondering if she could be that naive. Her wide eyes and open face made it hard to tell.

Regan kept his eyes on her. "He didn't tell you anything about having met Nick Carney?" She shook her head, meeting his gaze squarely. "Nor did your husband?" Same gesture. "Nor Mr. Jordan?" Same. She was good, I thought to myself. We knew from Jordan that he'd come straight to her on his return from seeing Nick. Regan was smooth; he let it pass.

"All right. Then your son returned to New York on Tuesday. I don't suppose, by the way, that you can corroborate your husband's testimony that the gun was present in his gun cabinet Tuesday evening, thus establishing that your son could not have taken it back to New York with him."

"I could if it's necessary. In court."

Regan grimaced. "I assume you mean that as a witticism. In fact, you can't. Let's go on to Wednesday. What do you believe happened? How did the gun get out of its storage place?"

She frowned, thought a minute, nodded. "Mike and I were talking about it in the kitchen while you were talking to Jerry. We both think it was Nick in disguise. He stole the gun and took it with him back to New York."

Regan nodded. "That is a possibility. But have you considered the question of why? *Why* would he have done that? And how could he have obtained the combination to your husband's gun cabinet? Or even known of its existence? Or where you live?" Peggy shook her head and shrugged.

Regan shrugged too. "All right. Since I can't answer the questions myself, I can hardly expect you to."

He spun his chair away. "We're done, madame. You are flying to New York this afternoon?" Peggy glanced at her watch and nodded. "So are we. Perhaps we will see you over the weekend."

Regan's made a lot of prophetic statements over the years but never any truer than that.

48

REGAN and I arrived at the airport after the hour-and-a-half drive, thoroughly pissed at each other. He, because I'd talked nonstop all the way there when he wanted to think; I, because he pouted all the way when I wanted to talk. All I could get out of him were disgusted sighs. And a single complete sentence:

"Until I've had time to contemplate the entire panoply of facts we've gathered, David, any conversation about Nick Carney's murder is bootless."

Yeah, well, a good boot to his bootless would've felt pretty good to me right about then. I *had* to talk about it. I wanted to know what he thought, what conclusions he'd reached. I wanted my suspicions resolved.

And I was suspicious of everyone. What if Mike had reported the gun missing just to throw the police off, then brought it to New York and killed Nick with it? And what was with Peggy? How could that innocent face have gone on fooling her husband year after year after year? And Jordan: had *he* taken the gun? But if the murderer was one of those three (and that was looking likelier all the time, at least to me), how had he gotten into Nick's office?

And one question was developing into a full-fledged obsession. *Had* Nick come to Minnesota and stolen the gun? Aside from why he would've done such a thing, there were a ton of other questions: How had he known where the Kearneys lived? How had he known they'd have workmen in the house? Where had he learned about Mike's gun collection? Above all, where would he have got the combination to the gun cabinet?

Believe me, that's only a tiny sample of everything that was running around my brain and out of my mouth all the way to the airport. At the ticket counter I shut up long enough to get our tickets changed

to the two P.M. flight. The ticket agent was accommodating enough
to order a cart to get us to our gate on time. The driver grinned as
I explained our time bind. "Hang on, gentlemen. I'll have you there
in about one minute flat."

He proceeded to make good on his promise. I was loving it. I
especially appreciate the way people jump when they get beeped
with that air horn. We were approaching our gate when I suddenly
heard the sound of my name coming from the airport loudspeaker.
"Mr. Goldman," the nasal voice whined. "Mr. David Goldman. Please
pick up a red courtesy phone and call the operator, please. Mr. David
Goldman."

It was four minutes to two. I spotted a red phone right next to our
gate area and immediately swung around to our driver. "Hold it,
friend. I've got to get off." He screeched to a halt.

I turned to Regan and handed him his ticket. "Go ahead and board.
No telling what this could be. Only United Airlines even knows we're
here." Regan nodded. I jumped off and the cart leaped forward,
scattering people with a blast of its horn.

As I picked up the phone and identified myself, I was able to watch
the driver help Regan get into one of those narrow wheelchairs the
airlines use to get disabled people down the aisles of planes. Meanwhile, a businesslike female voice sounded in my ear. "Mr. Goldman?
Just a moment, please."

"Davey!" It took me a second to identify the new speaker. Chet
Rozanski.

I was amazed. "My God, Chet! How'd you ever track me down?"
Then, immediately. "Never mind. I don't have time to talk. Flight's
ready to take off."

Regan, in the airline wheelchair, disappeared into the walkway to
the plane. The agent at the gate glanced at his watch and grabbed
the microphone.

Meanwhile, Rozanski was saying, "Okay, I won't keep you, Davey.
But you know that Jake Steiner you put me onto?"

"Sure. What's up?" He had my attention.

Rozanski was talking fast. "Thanks to you I did a short interview
with him in my segment on the Carney murder last night. Well, after
the show he changed his story. Says he actually saw the murderer go
into the building. And says he can identify him."

I had mixed emotions. On the one hand I was riveted by what Chet was telling me. But I was torn between that and what was happening around me in the terminal. Namely, the agent's voice was bawling through the loudspeaker overhead. Something about this being the last call for our flight.

"Look, Chet," I snapped. "This is amazing. But right now I'm about to miss my flight. What is it you want?"

"Okay, okay, go." Rozanski's words tumbled over each other. "I'm wondering about putting him on tonight's segment at six. You know him. Is it a scam? Or is the guy legit?"

"Shit, I don't know! Tell you what—*Hey!*" The agent was closing the door to the walkway. I slammed down the receiver and charged for the agent, now walking away from the ominously closed door to the plane.

"*Hey! Open up!*" The surprised guy turned to me, along with about two dozen innocent bystanders. He glanced at the ticket I was waving at him and shook his head.

"Sorry, sir. You're too late. The plane's already pulling away from the gate. There's another flight going to Newark at—"

I had my wallet out and open to my investigator's license. "Well, you better get it back," I panted, thrusting the wallet two inches from his nose. "That crippled clergyman"—Regan would have my head if he ever heard me call him that—"is in my custody. He can't leave without me. You gotta bring the plane back!"

A two-second staring contest ensued. I'll win those ninety-nine times out of a hundred, and I'd already had my miss for the week with Weiskopf. The agent finally sighed. "I'll see what I can do." Shaking his head and mumbling something about New Yorkers, he headed for the gate counter.

Two minutes later, in a flurry of "Sorry, fellas, all my fault!" (me) and a chorus of "Don't let it happen again" (three reps of United Airlines), I boarded the flight. I found Regan in Row 22, where he'd comandeered three seats for the two of us.

I told him about the non-conversation with Rozanski. The Bishop's eyes narrowed. "Mr. Steiner is now saying he saw the murderer?"

"Yeah, and that's not what he told us. Maybe we didn't pay him enough. Or maybe he changes his story depending on who's asking the questions. I think—"

I shut up because we were taking off and the engines were so loud I couldn't hear myself think. When they died down, the Bish took

over the conversation. "David. You must speak with Mr. Steiner.
This evening, if possible. As you say, it may be that, motivated by
pecuniary considerations, he is simply giving full rein to his penchant
for hyperbole. If you should decide that is not the case, perhaps you
can persuade him to make a return appearance at the mansion."

I glanced at my watch. "It's two-twenty. Three-twenty, New York
time. We might get back in time to see the segment on the tube.
It'll be on the six o'clock news—if he does it."

Regan nodded. "We can hope to. Meanwhile, I need some time
to sort out all that we've learned today. Perhaps you, as well. Let us
ponder for a while. Privately." He closed his eyes and didn't open
them till we were over Ohio.

Ponder. Sure. Easy for him to say. He'd taken the window seat,
so I couldn't use the landscape for inspiration. Besides, pondering's
his thing, not mine. I checked out the magazines, but they were no
help. I finally decided to go through the notes I'd taken that morning,
hoping something would point me somewhere—anywhere.

That took half an hour. Then I inclined the seatback the full quarter-
inch allowable and tried to sleep. Got about as far with that as I had
with the pondering.

Glanced at Regan, who obviously wasn't sleeping, despite the
closed eyes. He was concentrating hard, which, believe me, is something to see. He sits perfectly still, head straight up, eyes closed tight,
mouth even tighter. His jawbone flexes every once in a while. The
captain had just announced that we were over Toledo, when Regan's
eyes popped open and turned to meet mine.

"Holy Toledo!" I told him, pointing past him out the window. He
didn't even hear me.

"I have considered the matter from every viewpoint imaginable,
David," he growled. "I refuse to think about it further till we know
what, if anything, Mr. Steiner has to add to what he told us Wednesday. I have formed a rather bizarre conjecture. If there is anything
to what Mr. Steiner apparently said to Mr. Rozanski, it may be that
he can add substance to my conjecture. I hope not. I hope I'm wrong.
But if he can—well, we shall see. In any case, further speculation is
worthless."

An announcement about being able to see Akron ("the rubber
capital of the world") on the right and Lake Erie ("the only flammable
Great Lake") on the left came over the speaker. When the pilot finally

shut up I turned to Regan. "What about Nick? Have you figured out why he might have gone all the way to Minnesota to steal the gun?"

Regan glanced at me. "He didn't."

"Didn't what?"

Regan gave a small smile. "Nick Carney didn't take the gun." I gaped at him. "I was misled, David. By the murderer, whether intentionally or not. Nick Carney could not have been the mysterious workman. If you care to, you can check your notes of this morning's meeting. What the stranger was doing when Messrs. Madison and Glinke came upon him outside the house establishes that beyond a doubt." I scratched my head and started leafing back through the notebook but Regan wasn't through.

"I was surprised and, frankly, a little disappointed when I realized that. But in life, disappointment is often the harbinger of opportunity. It was learning that Mr. Carney could not have been the interloper that led to a parallel line of thought, which in turn brought me to my present conjecture. And if Mr. Steiner can verify it—"

"So you think you know who the killer is?"

Regan gave me a disapproving look. "If I may be permitted to finish my thought. If Mr. Steiner can verify my conjecture, I think we'll have something to take to Inspector Kessler. If not . . . we'll see. In any case, I'll not discuss it further till we have spoken again with Mr. Steiner."

Regan pulled out the small, well-thumbed prayerbook he uses. "And now, if you will excuse me, David?" He perched his reading glasses on his nose and focused on the book.

While he prayed, I reread my notes quoting Madison and Glinke. I got it the third time. The guy they'd seen had been eating an apple. No way Nick Carney could ever eat an apple with that bridgework right in the middle of his mouth. I sighed.

I settled into some solid fidgeting. I glanced at Regan, still engrossed in his breviary. A sense of impending disaster was constricting my chest muscles. I tried to ignore it, figuring it was just my way of wasting time, same as the Bishop's praying was his.

49

WE landed in Newark twenty minutes late, at five minutes to six. Fortunately, they got Regan (and me) off first. There are advantages to being disabled, as I constantly remind him.

"Do we have time to view Mr. Rozanski's interview with Mr. Steiner?" he muttered as we rode down the concourse on another oversized golf cart. I was enjoying watching the New Jerseyites jump out of the way at the sound of the horn.

"Umm, yeah," I said, glancing at the Timex. "If he goes through with it. His segment always comes on in the second fifteen minutes. We're cutting it close, though."

We approached a stand-up bar, not too overcrowded with moody drinkers. I noticed the large TV was showing the Channel Two news team. I surveyed the clump of gloomy businessmen at the bar, three more standing at tables. No one was paying the slightest bit of attention to the TV.

"Hey, Calvin!" I said to our horn-happy chauffeur. "Mind if we stop and watch the news? Our bags'll probably take awhile anyway." Regan nodded.

"Hey, you got it, man." Calvin slewed the contraption into a hard right-hand turn.

"Can you make it face the TV, Calvin?" I said.

"No problem." He pulled up just outside the bar area, well within sound and sight of the set. I jumped off and aproached the bar. The bartender, a hard-faced, middle-aged guy in a tux, looked up from the glass he was polishing.

"What can I getcha?"

"I'll let you know." I jerked my head at the TV screen. "Meantime, there's a groundswell of public opinion in here demanding Channel Fifty-four. Can't you feel it?"

He shook his head. "Comedians I get. Deadbeat comedians, yet." He reached under the bar with a grunt, adjusted something, and the channel changed. Bob Parkinson, Channel 54's news anchor, face redder than on my set at home, was saying something about next month's big Central Park gala. It soon became apparent that the Mayor had just appointed a new chairman for the fest.

"Stay tuned," he said. "We'll be right back with Chet Rozanski, live from West Forty-sixth Street with a new development on a baffling mob-related murder—or is it?" A used-car dealer flashed onto the screen.

I strolled over to Regan, who, eyes on the set, appeared lost in thought. "Maybe Chet got Jake to remember some things you couldn't get him to," I remarked.

Regan sniffed. "Let's await the event, shall we?"

Parkinson was soon back. So was his co-anchor, Elvira Madsen. "And now, over to West Forty-sixth, where Chet Rozanski's standing by with a key witness in a murder investigation. What've you got, Chet?"

Rozanski's tanned face gleamed in the late afternoon sun. He squinted into the camera. "Plenty, Elvira," he said. "As we've been reporting the past two days, last Saturday Nick Carney was brutally murdered in his office in the building you see immediately behind me. The police have arrested the victim's half-brother, Jim Kearney, of St. Cloud, Minnesota, an actor currently appearing in an off-off-Broadway production of *A Thousand Clowns*. And, as reported last night, Channel Fifty-four, through a reliable informant, has learned that the two half-brothers met for the first time this summer."

As Chet paused, the camera backed away, enlarging the view to include Jake, now revealed standing at Chet's side. Jake blinked into the camera and looked uncomfortable.

Rozanski went on. "A number of developments have come out of last night's story. Here with us again, at the murder scene, is Jake Steiner, a friend of the victim." Chet glanced down at Jake. "We were too pressed for time last night to get all of Mr. Steiner's story. He has something very dramatic to add." He turned to Jake. "Can you tell us what you saw last Saturday afternoon, during the time the murder was being committed? You were in a position to see everyone who went in or came out that door, weren't you?"

"That's right, sonny." Jake looked from Chet to the camera, back to Chet.

"And you were right across the street—situated just about where we're standing?" Jake nodded. "So tell our viewers what you saw."

Jake frowned. "Well, I saw that fella, Jim Kearney, I guess his name is, I saw him go into the building. Uh, through that door you were talkin' about, right over there." Jake swung his arm in the direction of the glass door across the street. The camera moved in to a close-up of the door. Jake paused, then his voice continued, now off-camera. "So I seen him go in. And I also seen the murderer." The camera shifted back to Jake, came in for a close-up. Beads of sweat could be seen on his forehead and through the stubble on his cheeks. Jake scowled up at the now-invisible Chet. "Only I ain't sayin' no more till I get *paid* somethin'!"

The camera jerked a little, then pulled back to include both men. "Well, Mr. Steiner," Chet said rapidly, "we'll certainly see what can be done. No reward has as yet been offered but I'm sure—"

"I ain't talkin' 'bout no reward, sonny. I'm talkin' 'bout what you promised. First you say you're—"

Jake's voice faded as Chet pulled the mike away. Holding it close to his own mouth and speaking even more rapidly, he said, "Well, Elvira, a little misunderstanding here. Perhaps we can straighten this out for 'Live at Ten.' If we can—"

Jake's faint voice could be heard off-camera. "Wanna give my love to the little lady. You promised—"

Rozanski tried to smile. "Yes, Elvira, we did promise Mr. Steiner a word to his wife . . ." Jake's voice, fainter and indistinguishable, could be heard again, but Chet rode over it: "So, back to you in the studio, Elvira and Bob."

Chet, now in close-up, smiled into the camera. His face stayed on the screen long enough for his eyes to flick two or three times to the side, probably wondering when the hell the camera would get off him. Jake's voice was still audible off-camera. After several seconds of that embarrassment, Parkinson and Madsen were back. Neither seemed to know what to say. Finally Parkinson came through with, "Yes. Well . . . thanks, Chet." He smiled at his co-anchor. "You just never know what Chet's going to come up with, do you, Elvira?"

"No," said the woman. "And sometimes, perhaps, neither does Chet." The two tittered, Parkinson glanced off-camera, nodded and looked back into the camera.

"Well. In other news today, Mayor David Dinkins announced the formation of . . ."

But I was already back on my seat on the contraption. "Roll it, Calvin."

"You got it." He grinned and we were off with the honk of the wild goose.

I guess Regan was as puzzled as I was about Jake's performance— or non-performance. His first comment on it came a half-hour later, in the Caddy, while we were inching through the tunnel. "Mr. Steiner is obviously convinced he's found a mother lode in the murder of his erstwhile friend. And when Mr. Rozanski balked at paying his price— whatever that may have been—he refused to talk. The question is, does he really know anything? Or is he merely attempting to parlay his friendship with Nick into his fortune?"

"I doubt if he knows anything," I said. "That is, anything beyond what he's already told us. I think you got everything he knew on Wednesday in your office."

"I thought so too." Regan's voice was puzzled. "But his tone is different now. Something's happened; he may have come across some further information. Either that or his reflection on his experience has resulted in some memory floating to the surface of his consciousness. I think you should talk to him, David. As soon as feasible."

So as soon as I had the Bishop safely back up the steps and into his office, and the Caddy back in Fred's tender loving care, I called Paddy's Pub and asked for Jake Steiner. I didn't recognize the voice on the phone—it wasn't Rocco, I was sure of that. Whoever it was knew Jake—though it did take him a minute to absorb the "Steiner." Apparently no one in Paddy's thought Jake even *had* a last name.

"Yeah!" Jake sounded angry. Or scared.

"Jake, it's Davey." Silence. "You know, the Bishop's buddy. I talked to you two days ago—about Nick."

"Oh yeah." The tone was guarded. "Suppose you saw me on the TV. Well, I gotta tell ya, I don't appreciate you siccin' that guy on me—Rose-a-whatski, or whatever his damn name is. Guy's a four-flusher."

"No, he's not, Jake. Listen—"

"No, *you* listen! He promised me five hunnert bucks for telling him who the killer was. Then, right before we start, he tells me he can't do it. Says 'against studio policy' or some sorta horseshit like that. 'Well,' I tells him. 'If it's agin' company policy, I ain't talkin'.'"

"You told him that? Ahead of time? It looked to me like you surprised him pretty good, Jake."

"Yeah, well, maybe. I mean, we talked a little and maybe I said I'd talk. But standin' there waitin', I got madder an' madder. So when we went on, I clammed up." Jake chuckled. "Did you see me?"

"Yeah, I saw." No wonder Chet had looked so surprised. And so mad. "Look, Jake. We need to talk."

"How much?"

"How—? You still looking to make some dough off the death of your friend?"

A pause. When Jake spoke again his voice was quieter and angrier. "Look, buddy. You had me goin' purty damn good the other day. You and your buddy, Bishop Muck-a-tee-muck, whatever his name is. But now I've had some time to think about it. One thing Nick always told me was, 'Get it while you can.' So don't gimme none of that 'friend' business. And no double sawbucks neither. You wanna play, you're gonna pay. Got it?"

I shook my head. Did the guy think I was made out of money? I decided Jake and I needed a sit-down.

"Look, Jake, stay right there, okay? I'm sure we can do some business. I'll be right over."

"Hell," he chuckled. "I ain't goin' nowhere."

Regan was upstairs, probably still struggling from his clerical suit into his robe. I buzzed him on the house phone and told him what was up.

"Good," he said tersely. "If he can be persuaded to come back here, all the better."

I told Regan I'd try to bring him but shook my head while saying it. He was grasping at straws if he thought Jake knew anything. As far as I was concerned, Jake had figured out how to turn a friend's murder into a lucrative source of funding.

I gave a couple of seconds' consideration to calling Rozanski. A little briefing wouldn't have hurt. But something made me antsy; I didn't want to wait. My chest was more constricted than ever. Felt like a belt pulled tight around it. I flagged a cab instead of walking.

The ride took three minutes: just long enough to work out a strategy. I'd go as high as a hundred; if Jake wanted more, to hell with him. I slipped the cabbie a fiver, asked him for a single back and got it along with a snort and a disgusted shake of the head. That started a new train of thought, leading to a new strategy: why not let the Bish do the negotiating? *And* the paying. My job, I decided, was getting Jake over to the mansion. Regan could take it from there.

Paddy's was different in a way I couldn't identify: ominously different. It wasn't just all the people, the noise, the loud music. Though I was surprised at how the place had filled up with wall-to-wall yuppies. Behind the bar three bartenders were running around like mad, none of them Rocco. I looked to my right between two attractive brunettes and realized what was wrong: no Jake. On his stool was some broker-type trying to make time with a blond. The blond was perched on the stool that should have held Jake's sweater. Feeling strangely panicky, I elbowed up to the bar. Getting the eye of the bartender nearest me, a young, tough-looking kid with a brush cut, I said, "Where the hell's Jake?"

The bartender looked me over, blinked, swiveled his head and yelled, "Hey, Joe! That guy, Jake? Guy here's lookin' for him!"

The short, stocky bartender down the bar filling a stein looked up and caught my eye. "You Goldman?" I nodded, surprised. How'd he know my name? He topped off the head on the beer, slid it across the bar, rang up the sale. Ignoring several shouted drink orders, he moved to me.

He ignored a couple of frantic wavers to my right and gave me his eye. "You here to see Jake?" I nodded. "He can't make it. He got a better offer."

I stared at him. "Better offer? From who?"

"Don't know. You're the guy that called, right? Well, right after you called, someone else called. And whoever it was sure made Jake awful happy. Said he hit the big kahuna. Said he hadda run meet someone, he was in the bucks big time, and went tearin' out. A second later he sticks his head back in and yells, 'If Goldman comes, tell 'im to blow it out the other end!'" The bartender grinned. "Sorry, man. I'm just tellin' you what he said. Like a beer?"

I stared at him for a minute, then shook my head. "Nah, that's okay. You sure that's all he said?"

"Sorry, man, that's it." He looked anxious to get back to his customers. The belt around my chest tightened another notch. Somewhere in the back of my mind a thought began to form: *If I was the killer, and I'd seen Jake on TV, what would I do?* I didn't like the answer.

I had one more question, not the most brilliant of my career. "Did he say where he was headed?" The bartender shook his head. I gave him a strained smile. "Okay. Thanks, man."

Joe gave me a thumbs-up and turned to the crowd. "Hey, the kid is back! Who's next, folks?" He laughingly recoiled at the near-riot that followed.

Out on the street, I began walking to clear my thoughts, heading west towards civilization—some more traffic and neon, anyway. At Eighth Avenue I turned south, gradually becoming aware of a siren. An ambulance, getting closer. It never ceases to amaze me how few people can tell the difference between the various kinds of sirens: police car, ambulance and fire equipment. People just don't pay attention to the different sounds they make. Cops can. And ex-cops. The siren got closer and closer till the ambulance screamed up Eighth and stopped at Forty-first, cutting the siren as it did. It pulled up in front of the Port Authority entrance down the block. Two paramedics carrying equipment and a stretcher jumped out and ran down the stairs to the subway and disappeared. I watched them go, stood for a second, then started running after them. Something inside told me things had taken a drastic turn for the worse.

50

I W A S panting by the time I hit the subway entrance. That was ridiculous: I'd only run forty yards. But the belt was beginning to hurt. It was hard to breathe. As I ran down the stairs, I saw two businessmen coming up, suit jackets over their arms, and caught a snatch of their muttered conversation. The words ". . . poor damn wino . . ." stopped me cold. I moved in front of them.

"Excuse me," I said, getting their eye. "Was there an accident down there?"

They both took me in. Their expressions went from irritation to curiosity to something as close to excitement as two yuppie businessmen will ever permit their faces to show. "Yeah!" said Blue Suit, shifting his jacket from one arm to the other. "Some wino got mangled."

"Fell off the platform or something," added the other helpfully.

"It was our train that hit him." Blue Suit again. "God! We were bouncing all over the place! The driver tried like hell to stop. I've never heard the brakes scream like that. Shit, I *hope* it was the brakes."

Gray Suit was about to add something else but I cut him off. "Did either of you see the guy that got mangled?"

"God, no!" said Blue Suit. "We just heard people talking about it. If you—"

I cut him off again. "Were you headed uptown or downtown?"

"Uptown."

"Thanks." I shouldered past them, wishing to hell I had better sources about what was going on. I took the stairs two at a time.

At the bottom a clump of people were milling around the turnstyle. From the other side a large black woman in a Transit Authority uniform was yelling at them. ". . . can't come through here! We're closed!" She took a breath and, having got a little quiet from the crowd, added in a more normal voice, "You'll have to go over to Seventh Avenue for a train!"

As the crowd started to disperse, I caught her eye, flashed my license, and vaulted over the railing. She looked disapproving but let it go at that. It sometimes helps to have the look of a cop.

I made my way through a horde of people heading for the exit. Others were waiting around like vultures to see what was happening. I ran toward the stairway to the northbound platform. I was too late— in every sense of the word. Twenty feet before I reached the down stairway, the paramedics appeared at the top of the stairs, carting a stretcher. On the stretcher was a motionless lump, the approximate size and shape of a human being, covered with a sheet. Helping them force their way through the people was a uniformed cop. Arm out, he looked and talked people off, repeating "Stand back, please, comin' through . . . stand back, please, comin' through. Excuse me, ma'am, you'll have to stand back . . ." The paramedics, both tall, good-looking and very grim, kept their eyes down.

My mind was like a puppy, running off in three or four different directions at the same time.

Was the body on the stretcher Jake? I didn't know, but I did. I also didn't know, but knew, that the guy on the stretcher hadn't fallen, he'd been pushed. And that the guy that pushed him was the same guy who'd shot Nick. And that the pusher couldn't be far away.

So what was my best plan? Follow the paramedics upstairs and try to catch a look at the body? Or engage the cop or paramedics in conversation, find out the victim's name? What were the chances they'd even know it?

So I let the medical team go and headed down to where the "accident" had happened. I knew there'd be people down on the platform, including at least one more cop taking names of witnesses and working up a report.

A male voice blared over the loudspeaker before I hit the bottom of the stairs. The words were almost impossible to make out, since the T.A.'s main goal is to keep all messages unintelligible. But it had something to do with the station being temporarily closed and please go to Times Square for a train.

Meanwhile, I had too many questions and the list was growing. Where were Mike and Peggy Kearney and Jerry Jordan right at this moment? And where had they been when that newscast was on? (Mike's words echoed in my head: "I told the pilot we need to leave St. Cloud by two o'clock." If they had, they'd have been on the ground at LaGuardia by five, and to the Waldorf by six, in time for Rozanski's interview with Jake.)

What about Joe the bartender? Had he taken that second call? Would he remember the voice?

How should I handle the cops? Tell them everything I knew? Or hold back? How best to get them to share their information with me?

To get all the answers I had to have right away, I would need to be about five places at once. So I had to set priorities.

The subway platform had been partially cordoned off with yellow NYPD tape. Three subway policemen were there. Make that a policeman and two policewomen. Two were chatting with bystanders while one—a tall middle-aged woman in horn-rims—took a witness's statement, jotting the information onto her clipboard. She was also getting it on a tape recorder. The agitated black woman she was talking to was illustrating her words with plenty of hand gestures.

The patrolwoman outside the tape looked familiar. I edged close enough to read the name on her uniform: *Blackman*. It rang a bell. I studied her face and, after a few seconds, dredged a first name out of my memory bank: Enid. I hoped.

Enid Blackman had started on the force the year I got the boot. Her group of rookies had come through Homicide as part of their training. I'd been assigned to give her and three of her classmates some pointers. She'd been older than the others—maybe even older than me—and was the toughest rookie—physically and mentally— I'd ever met. I'd liked her. I hoped she'd liked me too. And would remember me.

"Hi, Enid," I said, sidling up to her and flashing my P.I. license. "Davey Goldman. Remember?" She tilted her dark face up at me, eyes suspicious. She glanced at the license. "Yeah, yeah. Whaddaya want?"

"Aw, come on, Enid, don't give me that whaddaya want crap. You know damn well you'd never have made sergeant if I hadn't taught you everything there is to know about identifying a corpse."

She gave me a closer look. Her face changed. "Hey! Davey! Davey Goldman! Sorry, my man, got a lot on my mind."

I breathed a little easier. "Well, that's more like it. I was beginning to feel like the ugly American."

She smiled indulgently. "Oh, I don't know about ugly." She nodded at my license. "But what's this shit? You gone private?"

I nodded.

"So how's it hangin'?"

"Just scraping by, Enid, just scraping by."

Her eyes became businesslike. "So. I repeat, Davey: whaddaya want?"

"Well, I'm curious. I take it some guy just got hit by a train?"

"Yeah."

"He dead?"

"Deader'n dead. Goddamn wheel ran over his head. Ever dropped an egg on the sidewalk from the second floor?"

I winced.

"So what was the victim's name?"

She gave me a disapproving look. "We're reserving that till we notify next of—" I stopped her by sawing away at an imaginary violin. She grinned. "All right, all right. One for old time's sake, Davey. *If* I can trust you not to blow the whistle on me." I nodded.

"Okay." She glanced quickly over her shoulder and then down at her clipboard. "'Jacob T. Steiner.'" She gave me a quick glance. "Hey! Don't tell me you knew him?"

I rubbed my mouth. My face had given me away. Now I was at

risk of getting hung up with an interview, having to go I.D. the body, etc. I shrugged. "Yeah, maybe. What happened to him?"

"Guy either fell or was pushed." She glanced around at the cop talking to the witness. "You really oughtta talk to the Lieutenant there if you knew him. Right now we don't know shit. Guy's wallet's all we got."

"You say he might have been pushed?"

"Hard to say. Couple witnesses say he got shoved from behind. The gangs'll sometimes do that. Assholes. Only thing is, no one we've talked to yet saw any gang activity. But they're always around. Assholes. You know what I'd like to do to them? Next time they . . ."

My mind was starting to race again. I was feeling bad about Jake, but had no time to think about it. Now that I knew he was dead—murdered, I was sure—I needed all the more to find out where the Kearneys were. And Jordan. If they were all together, and had been for the previous half hour, that was one thing. If not . . .

I cut into Enid's diatribe on gangs. "Listen, Enid, thanks a bunch. Gotta run."

"But if you knew the victim, you need to—"

"Didn't really know him all that well." I handed her my business card. "That's where you can get me if you need me. Hey, and I'd appreciate a call if you turn up anything." I turned and took off, waving an apologetic hand at her protests.

I hustled up the stairs and suddenly thought of Rozanski. *Another* guy I had to talk to. He'd be *very* appreciative of this information. Maybe he could give me some behind-the-scenes stuff about Jake's last interview.

I reached the sidewalk and stopped to think. I had some information. What was the fastest way to go about collecting more? Priorities, priorities. I pulled out a handful of change, found a phone and made two calls, neither of which got me anywhere. Rozanski hadn't got back to the studio. And no one at the Waldorf—Mike, Peggy or Jordan—was in their rooms. I left urgent messages all over the place, giving my office number, and walked back to Paddy's.

Just inside the door, I got Joe's eye. He gave me a harried look over the heads of ten or twelve thirsty patrons. Did a double-take when he saw my expression. I tilted my head to the far end of the bar and he nodded. Thirty seconds later he joined me there. It was still noisy but at least we weren't in danger of being overheard.

"Jake's dead," I told him. It took a second for that to sink in. Then his eyes widened.

"Wha—! What happened?"

I held his eye. "He either fell or was pushed off the Forty-Second Street subway platform. Right down the street here."

"God, I don't believe it."

"Believe it, Joe. I'm sorry. He was a good guy." Joe's eyes filled and he turned away. "Look," I said. "I've got to ask you something. Anything about that second call you can tell me? Between you and me, I think Jake was murdered. And the caller's probably the guy that did it."

Joe studied me. "You a cop?"

"Private." I showed him the license. He studied it.

"Geez, I don't know. It was a guy. Kind of—"

"You're sure? Couldn't have been a woman? Maybe disguising her voice?"

Joe frowned. "Let's see . . . no. Just sort of a normal-sounding guy. Said something like, 'Jake Steiner, please.' I said—I always say—'Who's calling, please?' Some of the guys don't like people to know they're here. And he said, 'Tell him it's the guy with the dough.'"

I thought about it. "'The guy with the dough'? Those exact words?"

Joe nodded. "Yeah, I think so."

I thought a little more, especially about voices. "How would you compare the guy's voice to, say, mine? I mean, mine the way I sounded on the phone."

Joe scratched his head. "I don't know. Maybe a different accent. Not a lot different. Maybe a little fancier-sounding, know what I mean?"

"Better educated?"

Joe flashed a grin. "Hey, you said it, not me." He sobered. "But yeah, I guess. Maybe better educated."

On the cab ride home, amid the jumble of ideas, suspicions and questions, I had a new question: how had the killer known where Jake was? In the brief time Rozanski had had him on the air, neither he nor Jake had so much as mentioned Paddy's Pub.

51

REGAN was at least as startled as Joe had been to learn of Jake's death.

"Oh, dear God!" he muttered. He closed his eyes and crossed himself—the only time I've ever seen him do that without prayerbook in hand.

"He might have been murdered," I said, trying to shake him out of it.

His eyes popped open. "Of course he was murdered," he snapped. I'd definitely jolted him out of any thoughts of God. "I should have anticipated this, David. I was criminally negligent."

I gawked. "What're you talking about? How in the hell could you—?"

"We should have phoned Mr. Steiner from the airport. His offer to name the murderer was an open invitation to murder. But I never thought—" He stopped and took a deep breath, followed by an even deeper one. "I'd like to be alone for a while, David. If you don't mind." I nodded at him and went to my office.

I sat for five minutes, doing nothing. I was trying to think about the case, about Jake's murder, but I was all thought out. I wondered what Regan was up to. Praying? Thinking? Doping out who the murderer was? Or beating up on himself that he hadn't anticipated this?

I was just about to call Rozanski again to see if he'd got my message when Regan buzzed. I stuck my head into his office. He'd rolled over to his favorite spot near the south window. His back was to me, so I cleared my throat.

"Come in, David." He sounded tired.

I closed the door behind me. Regan didn't move, so I didn't either. He spoke musingly, staring out the window. "All right. Tell me everything you know." I went to my chair, sat and told him everything that had happened in the previous hour. It's one of the most complete reports I've ever given without working from notes. Fifty minutes later he had everything. That was thirty-five minutes of briefing and fifteen of interruptions, those being two phone calls: Mike Kearney and then Chet, both returning my calls.

The one with Mike was short but didn't produce what I wanted: a definite suspect. I started out by asking him when they'd landed in New York.

"I don't know, Dave. Why?"

"Look, Mike, just answer my questions, would you? I promise you, it's got everything to do with Jim and getting him out of jail."

Mike's voice was glum. "If you say so. Okay, what do you want to know?"

"When did you land and when did you get to the hotel?"

"Umm, let's see. We touched down a few minutes before five. Took the helicopter to the Pam Am building. We were in our rooms at the hotel by five-forty-five."

I thought for a minute. "Then what did you do?"

"Me?"

"All of you."

Kearney's tone was exasperated. "Shit, how do I know? Jerry went to his room and I haven't seen him since. I just called his room a few minutes ago and got no answer. Have no idea where he is. Every time we come to New York, the guy just disappears."

He sighed. "Well. You want to know about Peggy and me. We ordered up some drinks from room service and started to unpack. Then Peggy had to go somewhere, and I had a few phone calls to make. She's not back yet."

"Peggy went out? When?"

"I don't know." Mike sounded more exasperated than ever. "I didn't have a stopwatch on her." I waited him out. "About six-thirty, I guess. We'd been watching the news and she got a phone call."

"What channel?"

"What?"

"What channel were you watching?"

"How the hell do I know? What do I know about TV channels?" He sighed. When he resumed, it was with exaggerated patience. "Look. Dave. Peggy had the TV on, okay? She seemed to be interested in it. At least some of it."

"What part of it?"

"I don't know! Let me spell it out, Dave. I wasn't watching. Peggy was. Ask her."

"I'd love to," I said. "But you say she's gone out."

"Right." Sarcastic.

"So," I summarized, unfazed, "Peggy's been gone since six-thirty and you haven't seen Jordan since five-forty-five."

"Something like that, I guess."

"And you've been on the phone all this time?"

"Right. I went down and used the pay phone in the lobby. Damn hotel charges you a buck a call, even when you do it on your own credit card. I won't pay it."

"Can't blame you," I said, wondering why a guy who takes his own jet to New York, pays a bundle for a helicopter ride to save maybe fifteen minutes in a cab and orders up drinks from room service at a four hundred percent markup won't pay an extra buck a call to have the convenience of using his own hotel-room phone. People are strange.

I'd gotten back with the Bishop and resumed the briefing when Rozanski called. The Bishop was too depressed to even make a face when I excused myself for the second time.

And I guess I was, too. I answered the phone with "Yeah, Chet, what do you want?"

"What do I want? Well, let's see, Davey. First of all I want to know why you called me. After you answer that, we can get into all the other things I want."

I shook my head. "Sorry, man. I'm a little out of it." I took a breath. "I'm afraid I've got some bad news."

"Yeah?" Chet's tone was guarded. He knows my voice. He knew I wasn't about to crack a joke.

"Yeah. Your guy, Jake Steiner?" Chet grunted. "The man's dead."

"What?"

"Yeah, sorry. He fell, or in my opinion, was shoved into the path of a subway train, not a hundred yards from the sidewalk where you interviewed him three hours ago."

Rozanski breathed, audibly for a while. "Christ!" he finally said. "He *wasn't* lying. He *had* seen the damn murderer. Hadn't he?"

"Looks like it, yeah. He saw him, tried to extort money from him and then got killed instead of paid."

"Christ! I can't believe it! I thought the guy was the biggest four-flusher I ever met!"

I smiled without humor. "That's funny. He used exactly the same words to describe you."

Chet thought about that for a minute. Then, softly, "I guess he had a point. I *did* promise him a hundred bucks. But the longer we talked, the less believable he became. I finally told him to either tell his story on-camera or take a hike, and if he told it, I'd pay him what I thought it was worth. Did you see the spot?"

"Yeah. And I can't really blame you, Chet. I'd have done the exact same thing. But I do have a question: did he say anything to you before—or after—the show that'll help me figure out who did him?"

"No, nothing. Not for lack of wanting to, I assure you." Chet sounded shaken. "Damn! I let myself get mad, the way he showed me up on camera. When he walked back into that damn bar, I thought about following him in there, see if I could get anything out of him, but—I didn't. I just headed back to the studio. God! I wish to hell I'd gone after him!"

I offered to tell the Bishop about both phone calls but, aside from wanting to know who it was, he wasn't interested. He just wanted to hear what I knew about Jake's death. He sat back when I finished, eyes closed, and starting shaking his head. He finally quit that, opened his eyes and gave me a steady look.

"I wanted to talk to him. I'd hoped he could tell me something to confirm my conjecture. Instead, his death will have to serve. Ironically, it's even stronger confirmation than anything he could have said." He spun around and pushed off for the south window with less vigor than usual. But he had enough vigor to give orders.

"Your notebook, David. We need another meeting. Here, if at all possible. And as soon as possible. I need four questions answered." He reached the south window and spun the chair ninety degrees to the right. "If the answers are the ones I expect, I know who the murderer is."

"You do." I studied his weary, handsome face in profile. "You want to tell me?"

He glanced out the window. "I'm not yet certain myself. We'll have certainty soon enough."

I know better than to argue with him when he's in that mood. I opened the notebook. "Okay. Who do we invite?"

Regan turned and rolled back in the direction of his desk. I was surprised to see a twinkle in his eye. "First of all, your friend Lieutenant Blake."

I smirked. "Yeah, that'll be the day. Shall I see if Pat Buchanan is also free?"

The twinkle left his eye. "I'm serious, David. Mr. Blake's attendance is essential. He's the one person who both can and will answer my single most important question."

I shrugged. "I guess this proves that "Never say never" applies to Bishops as much as it does to us regular folks." Regan gave me a sharp look, then nodded and gave a brief twitch of one shoulder: his version of a shrug.

I reluctantly wrote "Blake" in my notebook, shaking my head. Regan despises Blake at least as much as I do. They first met back on the Lombardi case. On that one, I (well, okay, the Bishop) had made a monkey out of Blake by first identifying, then locating the evidence to convict the kidnapper/murderer of the little Lombardi boy. This, while Blake, with a task force of twenty cops, was running around in every direction but the right one. When I turned over all my (okay, dammit: Regan's) findings directly to the D.A. instead of going through Homicide, Blake had actually barged into the mansion and chewed Regan out. That's the closest I ever saw the Bishop get to absolute rage. He endured the tongue-lashing, but gave me orders afterwards that Blake was never again to be permitted within the walls of the mansion. In fact, I seem to recall the word *never* being used five or six times.

"Okay," I sighed. "Got it. Who else? Richard Nixon?"

Regan didn't have even the ghost of a smile for that. "Mr. Rosen."

"Lenny? Didn't I ask the right questions the other night?"

"*Question.* Singular. No, you didn't, David, not the one I need answered. But don't take umbrage. It wasn't your fault. The question I need answered only occurred to *me* ten minutes ago." I jotted down "Rosen."

"Mr. Kearney."

I stared. "You just talked to him this morning."

"*Not* Michael Kearney. For him I have only accusations, no questions." I lowered the notebook and stared but he ignored me and continued, "No, *James* Kearney. Will he be permitted to come? If not, you could have Mr. Baker question him in jail. But it would be preferable to have him here. In addition to the question, I have something to say to him."

I nodded. "With the help of Baker and our buddy Kessler, we might be able to get him. Of course, as an about-to-be indicted murderer, he'd have to be in cuffs and accompanied by at least two armed guards."

Regan grimaced. "I'd prefer—but my preferences are not at issue. If I can put up with Mr. Blake, I can put up with two armed guards. Get him if you can, with whatever strictures Mr. Kessler insists upon imposing, but get him." He frowned. "The final question is for Dr. Castle."

I stared again. "What are we doing here, 'This is your life, Davey Goldman'? You're talking about *Sally* Castle?"

"The same. And ask her to bring with her, if she would be so kind, a copy of the *DSM-Three*."

"The—?"

Regan glanced significantly at my notebook. "Take it down, David. DSM-Three. Roman numeral three, if you want to follow the convention." I put "*DSM III*" in the notebook and Regan, watching, nodded approval. "More secrets?" I sneered. "Or are you going to tell me what it is?"

Regan shrugged. "*Diagnostic and Statistical Manual of Mental Disorders, Third Edition.*" I put it down. I looked twice at *Statistical*, hoping I'd spelled it right but doubting it. Regan waited for me to finish writing. "A standard reference book of the American Psychiatric Association, David. In fact, I should own a copy. Please inquire of Dr. Castle at your leisure how I might obtain one. A copy to consult during the Penniston case, in fact, would have been highly useful. Though not as urgently needed as now."

Regan closed his eyes in thought, giving me a minute for some thoughts of my own. A manual of mental disorders. One of our suspects was nuts? Could be. Images of Mike, Peggy, Jordan flashed through my mind. None of them struck me as crazy. On the other hand, neither had Diamond Jack, the serial murderer I'd trapped, arrested, interrogated and testified against back when I was on the force. And all he'd done was tie his victims to the wall in his basement and listen to them scream while the rats had at them. And recorded it all on tape. Said it was his way of getting inspiration to compose an opera.

I had to ask. "You think someone's crazy?"

That *did* draw a smile. "No, David, I don't. But on reflection, I believe I have detected symptoms of a certain personality disorder." He frowned. "In fact, ask Dr. Castle if she could come a half-hour before the other guests. I'd like the opportunity to discuss my theory with her outside their hearing."

I made two notes, one in the notebook, the other one mental. The one in the book said "Call Sally—come 30 min. before others." The one in my head said "What the hell is going on?"

52

WE wound up with eleven guests at our little party—one more than originally invited. It kicked off at eleven o'clock Saturday morning. I know: you think Regan set it up that way to fit his six-to-eleven morning session in the chapel. Wrong. Eleven just happened to be the earliest Jim Kearney could be temporarily sprung from jail. In fact, Regan had to settle for only four hours of praying that day. I hope God didn't feel short-changed.

He came down from the chapel at ten (the Bishop, not God) and summoned me into his office to find out how I'd complied with his orders. I gave him a full report. I hadn't seen him Friday night. By the time I'd got everything set up, he'd long since gone to bed. Now he looked refreshed.

"First thing I did," I told the boss, "was call Mike back. He wasn't real happy to hear about another meeting, but when I told him Jim was coming, he changed his tune fast. Once he found that out, I don't think Saddam Hussein backed by the whole Iraqi army could have kept him away."

Regan winced at the analogy but didn't comment. He wasn't one of Bush's most stout-hearted fans during the forty-two-day war.

"Lenny Rosen," I went on, enjoying Regan's scowl, "was a little harder to get hold of." Actually, that was putting it mildly. If the phone-answerer at the Lettuce Inn had had her way, I'd have *never* talked to him.

"Mr. Rosen has just finished a performance," she'd said in a snippy voice. "He doesn't take calls at the theater."

I wasn't having any of that. "Ma'am, you're going to have to trust me on this one. The man's going to kill you if he doesn't get this message." I immediately regretted the metaphor but the words were already out.

She didn't appreciate my tone. "Well, I have my instructions and—"

"Well, you'd better think again. This is Detective Goldman and I need to talk to Mr. Rosen about a matter of urgent concern. If he's not on this line in thirty seconds, the theater may not open tomorrow night."

That stopped the argument dead in its tracks. Lenny was on the line in a hurry. When he discovered it was me and not the cops, he had very mixed emotions. It's hard to feel relieved at the same time you feel made a fool of and vice versa. I told him the girl had misunderstood me, I hadn't meant to threaten, was terribly sorry, blah, blah.

He cut me off. "So why are you calling, Davey?"

"Okay, let's get to it. As you know, Lenny, the Bishop and I are convinced that Jim didn't kill Nick. The Bishop is almost ready to name the killer—and don't ask me who he thinks it is, he won't tell me—but he needs the answers to a few questions before he can make up his mind. And you're the guy with one of the answers he needs; at least he hopes you are. Could you join a group we're having over to discuss it?"

"What question?" Lenny sounded nervous.

"Sorry. I don't know that either. Can you come?"

He tried a few more questions, but when he found I couldn't give what I didn't have, he finally gave in and said he'd come.

Regan's frown was lengthening as I described the conversation. "What's the matter?" I asked. "Did I mispronounce one of your favorite words?"

"I was wondering why you didn't speak first with Inspector Kessler. I thought you said extensive arrangements would have to be made to obtain Mr. Kearney's temporary release from jail."

"Well, yeah, sure, but I had to catch Lenny before he left the theater. And, as for the Kearney-Jordan crew, I knew Mike was at the Waldorf because I'd just talked to him. I wanted to get him before he left for the evening."

"All right," he grumbled. "But I trust Inspector Kessler was the *next* person you phoned."

"Nope. Davis L. Baker, Attorney at Law." Regan scowled. "Hey! He's the guy's attorney of record. I'm not going around making deals with cops to take a prisoner someplace without the lawyer's okay. In fact, had I called Kessler without having talked to Dave, the first thing he'd have said would have been, 'Does Baker know about this?' "

Regan raised his hands in surrender. "I should have known better than to quibble with you on matters of police procedure. I'll interrupt no more. I take it you were able to reach Mr. Baker?"

"Yeah. Caught him at home. Of course he wasn't happy about it. Wanted to know what we had, what you knew, what questions you wanted answered, and on and on and on. He finally grumped around and said maybe it was okay, but, by God, he was going to be here with his client, come hell or high water. Of course that's fine by us. Uh, isn't it?"

The Bishop nodded wearily. "I trust you also invited the complete cast of *Les Miserables*?"

I laughed. "Hey, that's very good. My kind of humor! I think my personality's rubbing off on you."

"God forbid," he shuddered. "Go on."

"You'll be happy to know Kessler *was* the next name on my list. But while talking to Baker, I got an idea. A conference call!"

Baker had liked it. He even offered to get hold of Cheryl at home and have her set it up, but I stopped that nonsense.

"Hey, what are you talking?" I said. "I don't know how to arrange a conference call? Just sit tight and don't go anywhere. If Kessler's at home, I'll get it done."

Less than ten minutes later, Baker, Kessler and I were chatting away like three magpies. Well, maybe more like two magpies and one pissed-off crow.

". . . and you two jerks want me to break all the rules and bring a probable murderer so the good Bishop can ask him a few questions. You guys are certifiable, you know that?" There were a few expletives too, but those I've deleted.

"Hey! Whoa, Inspector," I said. I decided to stretch the truth a bit. "Look. It's not just that he wants to ask him—or you—a question. He *knows* who did it. He really does. But if you don't bring Jim, I'm afraid the Bishop'll make a few deductions, name the murderer and turn it all over to Harrington. Like we did in the Lombardi thing. I mean, I try to control the guy, but you know how he is. So if you—"

"This is blackmail!" Kessler sputtered. "And you can't get away with it! So help me, Davey, if the Bishop has some information he's holding back, I'll—"

"I know, I know. But trust me, he doesn't know anything you don't. In fact, you know a lot *more* than he does. Which brings up the next request: he not only wants Jim here, he wants you. Or, rather, your favorite lieutenant. Your friend and ours, Lieutenant Blake."

Silence. Finally Kessler answered. "What the hell *is* this, Davey? You and I both know, Regan'll become a Buddhist before he'll ever let Charlie inside his house again."

"That's what I thought, Inspector. But this time Regan needs him." Kessler muttered something about what happened the last time. I chuckled.

"I know, Inspector, I know. I kicked him out the last time you brought him. But that time he wasn't invited. This time he is. In fact, it's a command performance. The Bishop's got a certain question he needs answered and Charlie's the only guy in the world who can answer it."

"And what might that be?" I heard a grunt from Baker. He didn't seem to buy Regan wanting Blake any more than Kessler did.

"I'm sorry. I honestly don't know, Inspector." Kessler let out an expletive. "Hey, no need for that. I wouldn't lie to you. I really *don't* know. In fact, I can't think of a single solitary thing Charlie could *ever* say that the Bishop would have even the remotest interest in hearing. That's another reason I'm looking forward to this meeting."

Kessler's been around long enough to know when he's beating a dead horse. So he gave it up.

"Okay, guys," said the Inspector. "I'll be there. And I'll bring the prisoner. What time's the meeting?"

"Whenever Jim can make it," I said. "Whenever you can get him here."

Kessler thought a minute. "Eleven o'clock tomorrow morning good?"

"Perfect," I said. "You'll be here, Dave?"

"Try to keep me away," the lawyer said grimly.

Regan listened to my recital of the three-way conversation without interrupting. "So," he said. "All those I requested will be here?"

"Right. And then—"

"And Dr. Castle? When will she be here?"

"I was just going to tell you."

Sally had been icily polite. "To what do I owe the honor of this phone call?"

"To the good Bishop. He requests the pleasure of your company. But may I add that, for me personally, it would be a very great pleasure to see you."

"What about?" Her tone implied *As if I cared.*

"The Most Reverend Bishop is holding a seance tomorrow morning at eleven. He says he has four key questions to get answered, where-upon he may unmask the true killer of one Nick Carney. You're being subpoenaed as an expert witness. In fact, he would like you to come earlier—at ten-thirty—and to bring along the, uh, *DSM-Three.*"

My stumbling over the name of the book turned out to be a good move. It brought a little humor, if not warmth, into her voice. "And I suppose you know what that stands for?"

She'd stepped right into my trap. "Well, of course. Doesn't every-one?" I squinted at the page of the notebook where I'd written it. *"Diagnostic and Statistical Manual of Mental Disorders, Third Edition,* of course. What do I look like, a bumbling idiot?"

Sally actually let out a chuckle. I allowed myself to relax. Maybe I was actually going to come out of this thing alive. Even better, without losing a girlfriend.

"All right, Davey..." *Davey!* All right! "... tell the good Bishop I'll be there no later than ten-thirty. Book in hand. Ready for my quiz."

I gave the Bishop only the gist of that conversation. He looked up at the clock. "It's nearly ten-thirty, David. Perhaps we should see if..." The doorbell chimed.

I never got to learn, thank God, what Regan and I should see if.

Sally was at the door, book in hand. Fat in bulk, bilious chartreuse in color. I mean the book, not Sally. She was as slender and non-bilious as ever. No ponytail this time, the honey-blond hair combed straight back, tucked behind the ears. She was very businesslike in a prim, dark suit and horn-rimmed glasses I'd seen on her only about twice in my life. But her eyes came through the corrective lenses just as blue and beautiful as ever.

The way to a woman's heart is through her funny bone. I took the book from her: *DSM III*, as advertised. I riffled quickly through the pages and handed it back to her. "Okay, got it. We won't need you now."

She grinned at me. "You forgot to check the index. Better let me stay and take you through it."

I kept my own grin off my face. "You may have a point. Come on in."

53

SALLY, the Bishop and I settled in for a half-hour seminar on the ever-popular *DSM III*. My big chance to learn all about psychiatry. Or at least all about why the Bishop wanted a psychiatrist and a psychiatric manual in attendance at today's meeting. I was looking forward to the education. Never got it.

I'd fetched coffee from the kitchen, Ernie being away on one of her once-a-month visits to her Staten Island convent. The Bishop, paging through the *DSM III*, didn't want coffee. He waited for Sally to take her first sip before he cleared his throat and started. "I'm interested, Doctor, in borderline personality disorders. I'd like you to—"

I couldn't resist a little humor. *"Borderline* disorder? Maybe I should have invited someone from Immigration and Naturalization."

Both Regan and Sally shot me irritated looks. It obviously hadn't been quite as funny as I'd thought. I was fumbling for some way to recoup when the doorbell chimed.

Regan looked relieved. "If you'd get that, David?" he murmured and turned back to Sally. "As I was saying, Doctor . . ."

Hurrying down the hall, I was exasperated. I'd told everyone to be here by 11:00 and no earlier than 10:50. It was now 10:36. Some people never get the message. Despite my sad attempt at humor, I was dying to know why Regan wanted to learn about borderline disorders. Whatever the hell they were.

But when I saw who was at the door, my feelings changed quickly from irritation to a combination of joy and dread. Standing on the stoop was a non-invitee. Dinker.

I took a second to think. And made a snap decision. I pulled my hand back from the knob, ducked into my office, grabbed the phone and hit the intercom button.

"Yes, David!" Regan's voice told me he'd about had it with my interruptions. Since I didn't feel like explaining that I was in a lot of trouble (being trapped between two girlfriends is no joke), I equivocated. Or temporized. Or something.

"It's Dinker Galloway," I told him. "I didn't invite her. Did you?"

"No." A pause. "This may be fortunate, David. I had thought of inviting her but decided against doing so, since I have no questions for her which can't be answered by others. Nonetheless, she has a legitimate interest. Ask her in and take her to your office. See if she knows of our meeting and, if so, from whom she learned it." The doorbell chimed again. "When Dr. Castle and I have completed our discussion, I will signal you on the intercom. If anyone else arrives before I signal, ask him or her to wait." My education in borderline personalities was on indefinite hold.

I hurried and threw open the door. "Sorry, sorry, sorry! We're all at sixes and sevens around here. Know the source of that saying, by the way?"

"Not now, Davey." Dinker brushed past me into the house, giving me another scent of the perfume I'd smelled the first time we met. I spun, ready to give chase if her plan was to repeat that mad dash into Regan's office she'd pulled Wednesday. But no. She turned to face me, dark eyes furious. Over her head I could see the door to Regan's office standing open. No voices were coming from it, but they soon would. I needed to get her out of earshot.

She opened her mouth but I cut her off. "The Bishop's holding a meeting," I murmured. "Come into my office. Then you can tell me off at your leisure." She gave an abrupt, unsmiling nod and marched straight in. I followed her, ready to offer her a chair, but she was already perched on the leather couch she'd napped on Monday night. Hard to believe that had only been five days before. Then, she'd been an attractive woman I'd barely met. Now . . .

I started to offer coffee, took one look at her face and changed my mind. I sat behind my desk. "Okay, Dinker. Out with it. What'd I do this time?"

"Lenny came over last night," she said quietly, and waited. I nodded sympathetically. Seeing I wasn't going to say anything, she rushed on. "Davey, what you've done is despicable. I think—"

"*Me*? What'd *I* do?"

"Oh, don't act so damn innocent. You and the Bishop are trying to pin Nick's murder on Lenny and you know it. He said you called last night right after the show and told him he had to come over here this morning at eleven o'clock or go to jail. He said you—"

"Hold it, Dinker." She stopped, breathing hard, face pink. "First of all, I don't have the power to throw Lenny, or anyone else, in jail. Secondly, that's nothing *like* what I told him. All I told him was that the Bishop has a question for him."

"What question?"

"I don't know." She opened her mouth, eyes angrier than ever, but I cut her off. "I really don't, Dinker. But why not stick around and find out?"

She was still suspicious. "Do you suspect him? Of killing Nick?"

I shrugged. "Hey, I don't suspect *anyone*! All I know is, *Jim* didn't do it."

She brightened momentarily. "You *are* on Jim's side, aren't you?" Then her eyes narrowed again and bored into me. "Then who do you think did?"

"I told you before, Dinker, I don't have a clue. But I think the Bishop does. Why not stay and see what he says?"

She was sullen. "Lenny said a whole group was coming. And I'm not invited."

"Yes, you are." How temperamental can a woman get? "I just invited you. The Bishop wants you. Really. Stick around."

She managed a small smile. For the first time since she'd entered the house, she sat back and relaxed. She toyed with her luxuriant hair.

I had a thought. "Hey, should I call Lenny? I wonder now if he's even coming. Do you know?"

"Sure he is. He's afraid what'll happen if he doesn't."

The doorbell chimed. I excused myself, looked in on the Bishop and Sally before answering it. The book was still open on Regan's desk and the discussion seemed to be continuing. Regan, flushed and intense, looked up over his reading glasses. "Yes, David?"

"They're starting to arrive. How you coming?"

Sally, looking wan and unhappy, shrugged. The Bishop glanced at her and back to me. "Have them come in, David. Bring them in here straightaway. Including Miss Galloway." He turned to Sally. "I believe you and Miss Galloway are friends, are you not, Doctor?"

Sally's face took on a little more color. I didn't stick around to hear her answer. Through the glass of the front door I could see Inspector Kessler and Charlie Blake. And as I opened the door, Jim came up the steps, walking beside and handcuffed to, Sergeant Mike Burke. I know: you're thinking I blew it when I told Regan it had to be *two* armed guards. Wrong. Burke, alone and unarmed, is the equivalent of two armed guards any day.

Kessler looked grim, Blake cocky, Burke his usual impassive self, Jim scared. And me, I was mostly curious. What the hell did Regan have up his sleeve? I opened the door. The party had begun.

54

THE Kearneys, Mike and Peggy, and Jerry Jordan were the last to arrive, just before eleven. They'd finished a brief chat with Jim and had just sat down when the minute hand on the wall clock went vertical.

People had more or less introduced themselves as they arrived. Most of them already knew each other. Lenny was the only one who had to be introduced to the cops. Blake, normally a pushover for a pretty face, made no effort to talk to Dinker. It didn't occur to me to wonder about that. I was more concerned by his gloating attitude.

He threw a lot of smirks my way, exultant over the way he'd made a monkey out of me. I ignored him, wishing I knew how he'd used me to find Jim. I was expecting a few taunting words as well, but they weren't forthcoming. I decided Kessler must've told him to lay off: no salt in my wounds. If so, that was cruel of Kessler. Rubbing salt in my wounds is one of Charlie's favorite pastimes and he doesn't get the chance that often.

Sally and Dinker seemed to have resolved their differences. I'd shown Dinker in, right after Jim and his police escort got settled, and she'd gone straight to Sally. Within two minutes they were chattering away like nothing had ever happened. Though Dinker was doing most of the talking. Sally seemed friendly but strained. She kept glancing at the *DSM III* open on Regan's desk.

I used the moment to quietly brief Regan on Dinker. His eyebrows went up a notch when I told him she'd heard about the meeting from Lenny, and another notch at learning that Lenny was afraid we were trying to set him up.

Davis Baker came alone. He fancies himself a good-looking guy (he isn't, really), and went straight to Dinker with a "Nice to see you again, Miss Galloway." She flushed and seemed to enjoy his inspection. (Well, I didn't say he was *bad*-looking.)

After a few more words with Dinker and Sally, Davis headed for the couch to sit with Burke and Jim. They moved over so he could be by Jim, ready to advise his client as, if and when needed. Jim's wrist, naturally, stayed cuffed to Burke's. Baker grumbled about it, but subsided when he saw Kessler wasn't about to budge.

Between arrivals of guests, I'd wheeled the thirty-cup urn from the kitchen to the office on the rolling table. I plugged it in and suggested that people serve themselves, which was a waste of breath. Baker and Blake were already helping themselves before the table came to a complete stop. Baker toted coffee to Sally and Dinker and got what he was after: smiles from both.

So everyone was relatively comfortable and in place at eleven, when Regan's voice cut through the hubbub. "Ladies and gentlemen. If you please." He waited for quiet, which took about a second. It's got something to do with the quality of his voice.

"Thank you. I assume you all now know each other and that whatever introductions are necessary have already been made. We are here for a very serious—indeed, a tragic—purpose. And I am not in the mood for small talk. Or even politeness. Let us begin."

I was getting ready to take notes, and glanced around the room. Mike, square jaw set, looked truculent. Peggy, beside him, looked and acted nervous, shifting in her chair. Their greeting of Jim had seemed stilted, due partly, I'm sure, to his attachment—literal—to Burke. Peggy had kissed Jim on the cheek, Mike had squeezed his uncuffed hand. But they hadn't said much and no tears flowed.

Jordan was in his usual posture: slumped in a chair. The coffee cup rattled on its saucer whenever he picked it up. But his shrewd eyes, fixed on Regan, were steady.

Kessler was stroking his beard, probably wishing he could light his pipe. There are no ashtrays in Regan's office, which will give you an idea of how the boss feels about smoking. Though when Kessler comes alone with information Regan wants, Regan's not above sending me into my office to bring an ashtray. He thinks Kessler's vocal cords work better when the pipe is going, and he may be right.

Blake, next to Kessler, was in the catbird seat, metaphorically speaking. I'd never seen him more smug. His smugness was about to be shattered, though I had no inkling of that at the time.

Regan continued. "The tragedy that was the murder of Nick Carney is emblematic, and a direct result, of a family tragedy. A tragedy constructed of years of deceit, dishonor and malign neglect.

"Then, last evening, came a second tragedy: another murder." Regan glanced around. "At least I have good reason to believe it was murder. A man named Jake Steiner was hit by a subway train. I am convinced he was pushed into its path. Pushed by Nick Carney's murderer, who believed—rightly, I think—that Mr. Steiner had penetrated the killer's disguise."

"Just a minute, Bishop," Kessler interrupted, without looking up from what he was doing: polishing his glasses with a handkerchief. He's almost as good as Regan at commanding the attention of a roomful of people without raising his voice. Maybe it goes with being a high school debating champ—which they both were, thirty-five or forty years ago.

Kessler, satisfied he could now see everything, placed the glasses carefully back on his nose and adjusted them at the proper angle. He looked at Regan. "I know your theory about the death of Jake Steiner, Bishop. And okay, it's got to make you wonder. I mean, to get hit by a subway train less than two hours after he told Rozanski on TV that he could identify Nick Carney's murderer! But I also have good reason to believe the murderer was safely behind bars at the time. So I want to voice my disagreement with your theory."

He looked around the room and raised the volume. "I want to make it clear to everyone, right from the start, that my presence here in no way confers any status or approbation whatsoever on anything that Bishop Regan might say. I don't want there to be any doubt about that in anyone's mind."

He took a breath. "And I trust that no one was coerced to come. Mr. Goldman has been known to stretch a point and give people the idea—" he glared at me "—that I'm involved, or the police are involved, in something that's strictly his own idea. Or the Bishop's." He looked around, nervously stroking his beard. "If anyone is here because they're under the impression that I ordered, or even authorized, this meeting, I want to know about it right now."

I waited for him to look my way again. When he did, I gave him my brightest grin. His expression didn't change an iota. I don't think he really expected anyone to 'fess up, but hope springs eternal. No one, of course, did.

Kessler turned to Regan. "Excuse me, Bishop. I just thought I should clarify the situation. Please continue."

The Bishop gave him a tiny nod and resumed. "Ironically, what the murderer was trying to avoid—identification as such by Mr. Steiner—was precisely brought about by his murder. Nothing Mr. Steiner could have told me would have identified the murderer any more effectively than did his death."

Regan glared around the room, examining every face. He homed in on Mike Kearney. The boss's green eyes turned cold.

"But before I approach that issue, I have something to say to you, Mr. Kearney. I have pondered the death of Nick Carney, I have meditated on its significance, and I tell you, sir, I hold you in large part responsible." Peggy gasped. Kearney, eyes intent on Regan, didn't move or make a sound.

"I doubt that you ever will acknowledge your immense culpability in everything that's happened, sir. I must say, I have yet to detect any anguish whatsoever."

Mike flicked his eyes to Peggy, back to Regan. He was about to respond and Regan waited, but he changed his mind. The Bishop took a deep breath and resumed.

"Am I being overly harsh? I don't think so. Look at the facts, sir. First you married a woman you barely knew, with whom you had virtually nothing in common, the late, unfortunate Mona Smith Kearney. I'll grant that you—oh, spare us the pained look, sir, or the sidelong schoolboy glances at Mrs. Kearney. I am not telling tales out of school. Your wife has known for some years about your first marriage—and you have *known* that she knew. As to that first marriage, I'll grant that—"

"That's a damn lie!" Mike was outraged. "Peggy didn't know till just now, when you spilled it! This is outrageous!"

Regan was contemptuous. Eyes fixed on Mike, he spoke to his wife. "Tell him, Mrs. Kearney, tell him. Isn't it time that someone—anyone—in the Kearney family faces the truth about *something*?"

Peggy looked sadly at her husband. "You're right, Bishop," she said softly. "He *did* know I knew, didn't he? We've been keeping secrets from each other for so many years, we don't know how to live without them. Only they're not really secrets. They're just ways to close ourselves off from each other."

Her voice got stronger. "Mike. I forgave you for that a long, long time ago. My God, you were just a kid then."

Regan cut in, his eyes still boring into Mike's. "But you never told him that, did you, madame? Well," Regan shrugged, "he's not a kid any longer, albeit he continues to handle his relationships like one. What an image you cultivate, Mr. Kearney! A brave, hearty man of affairs! The truth is that you are a cowering, timorous mouse, unable to confront anyone honestly, least of all those in your own family, in any way other than that which will result in the least amount of suffering for you.

"Unable to confront your wife about your first marriage. Unable to confront your older son—ever. From the moment of his birth! Unable to confront your second son to tell him he had a brother. Blood of his blood. And yours.

"No, I won't give you that much credit. Not unable, but *unwilling*. I tell you frankly, sir, the twisted family life you have fostered over the years has been an accident waiting to happen. All that was needed was the presence of an outside party—a party with particular personality traits. And tragedy became murder."

Regan's eyes returned to Kearney. "My advice to you, sir, is to repair your relationship with the Almighty. You seem to have interrupted it many years ago."

Kearney's eyes, meeting Regan's, glittered with hatred. The Bishop met him glare for glare. Mike finally spoke, his voice choked with rage. "Damn you, you damn—cleric! How dare you humiliate me in front of my family! And in front of these strangers! My God, you're totally irresponsible! Is that why you got us over here, to humiliate us! I thought you were trying to *help* us! But this!"

Regan wasn't fazed. "Mr. Kearney. My own preference would have been to confront you privately. Or not at all. But that would have been to shirk my own duty as badly as you have shirked yours." He raised a hand as Kearney started to answer. "Please, sir, just let me finish. This is important.

"You and I, sir, are both Irish males of similar age, and we suffer from similar maladies. I am *not* contemptuous of you—at least no more contemptuous than I am of myself. I suffer from the very same failings that you do.

"As I said, my preference would have been to tell you privately— or not at all. I did it this way for two reasons. First, the damage your behavior has caused is public. Public misdeeds cry out for public disclosure and acknowledgement.

"Second and more important, talking to you privately would have done no good. Be honest, sir. What's the likelihood that this same speech, made privately, would have moved you in the slightest? Would have changed your behavior an iota?" Kearney looked away, brow furrowed. He was either considering what the Bishop had said or pondering ways to kill him. I still hadn't taken a single note.

Regan looked around the room. He had everyone's attention, even Davis Baker's, which isn't easy. Baker's got the lowest threshold of boredom of anyone I know. "I wanted to begin with that," Regan said, "because I prefer to assign ultimate causes. Furthermore, understanding the Kearney family dynamic is a necessary prolegomenon for what is to follow.

"Now. Let's get at the reason we are all here, which is, of course, to explore the question: Who shot Nick Carney? I now think I know, but I need answers to four questions to confirm it." A murmur arose around the room, including a couple of snorts from what I was beginning to think of as Cops' Corner. Regan sent his eyes that way.

"I realize this sounds overweening and, in view of my present unwillingness to name the person, perhaps even melodramatic. But I prefer not to name names till I am certain, and I need answers to achieve certainty. Dr. Castle has already answered my first question; rather, confirmed my supposition." His eyes homed in on Lenny. "Mr. Rosen." The actor looked sharply at the Bishop.

"Yes, sir."

"My question for you relates to your theater's physical layout. Who has access to the properties and costumes and makeup?"

Lenny shrugged. "Theoretically, only me. Realistically, anyone who knows where the keys are kept—in my dressing table. We're pretty loose. And, believe it or not, we don't lose much sh—uh, stuff."

"Are people permitted to take items from the theater?"

The director shrugged. "Not supposed to, but we all do it all the time. Costume parties, you name it. Like I say, we're pretty loose down there."

"Are you aware of any missing items in the last week or so? Or has anyone in the cast been taking anything out of the building—with or without permission?" Another shrug.

Regan nodded. He swiveled in the direction of the couch and Jim Kearney. "Mr. Kearney. Your attorney is here and may not want you answering questions in front of so many witnesses, especially with the authorities present."

The Bishop glanced at Baker. "I will leave it to your discretion, Mr. Baker, how to advise your client. But I believe you'll find the questions innocuous. At least for your client." Baker, looking a little confused, nodded gamely.

"Good. Mr. Kearney." Jim's eyes met the Bishop's. "Your brother called you last Friday or Saturday to give you the combination to the outer door of his office building, did he not?" Jim nodded. "At what time did he call?"

Jim glanced at Baker beside him, getting a slight nod from the lawyer. Jim frowned. "Uh, it was, oh, just before three in the morning. Saturday morning. Like I told you, he'd been worried about the blow-up at the party and wanted to apologize."

"And once you learned it, you told no one else the combination?"

Same legal consultation. "Nope. No one."

"And you were sleeping at the time? In your apartment?"

Jim didn't even bother to check with Baker. "Right."

Regan waited for total silence before asking the next question. He asked it softly. "Were you alone?"

I'll never forget the first time I got knocked down by an ocean wave. I was six or seven and we were on Point Pleasant Beach for the Fourth of July weekend. One minute I was in a gentle surf, fascinated by the water sucking the sand from under my feet. The next minute I was upside down in hell, the massive power of the sea trying to screw my head into the sand, my back twisted like a pretzel, salt water in my nose, my eyes, my lungs. It was two more summers before Pop was able to get me back in the surf.

That three-word question—"Were you alone?"—hit the same way. One second I was casually jotting the words in the notepad. The next, their meaning crashed over me like that long-ago wave.

I looked at Regan, feeling something akin to terror. I guess I wanted him to tell me the question didn't mean what I knew it meant. He was waiting for my look, facing me, eyes sympathetic.

And I knew with the certainty of the damned where he was heading; and, oddly enough, I knew that he was right. It didn't make sense yet—the pieces hadn't fallen into place for me the way they had for

Regan—but somehow I knew. And I was suddenly, incredibly sad.

At that point I went on autopilot. Today, reading the notes I took that day is like reading something someone else wrote. It's my own shorthand, so I know I did it. But it was the work of an automaton.

I looked around at faces. Dinker's first, of course, and it looked like mine felt: suddenly pale. Jim's next. He still didn't get it. He was whispering something to Baker, neither of their faces showing any emotion.

And the cops. *Everything* was going over Burke's head, as usual. Blake was starting to look a little puzzled. Kessler was the only one besides me and Dinker who seemed to understand where the Bishop was going. He got Regan's eye and pointed an acknowledging finger at him. Regan didn't acknowledge.

Jim and Dave had finished their consultation. "No," Jim said. "Dinker was with me. But she was asleep."

"So you went into the living room to talk to Nick?"

Jim nodded. Regan nodded back. He still hadn't looked at Dinker. He turned to Blake. "Mr. Blake. I have just one more piece to fit into the puzzle, and for that I'll need you. I suspect you know why you're here, sir. That is, you know why I invited you. Well. Here is my question: how were you able to find Mr. Kearney in his Newark hideaway?"

Blake's eyes widened. "I'm not answering that! And you don't have the right to—"

"I have every right, sir. And your bluster won't deter me. You have boasted to Mr. Goldman that you were able to follow him to Mr. Kearney's place of concealment. Haven't you, sir?" Blake glared, mouth shut tight. "I ask you: how were you able to do it?"

Blake looked away, his face stubborn.

Regan nodded and glanced at Kessler. "All right, sir. Rather than insist that Inspector Kessler order you to tell me, let me advance my own hypothesis. I suspect you will let me know if I'm right.

"My hypothesis is this: you planted a radio device in James Kearney's suitcase. Thus, when Mr. Goldman took Mr. Kearney his change of clothes, you could follow him without the need to keep him in sight. So that any evasive maneuvers would be foiled."

Blake's eyes flicked my way and I felt my face getting red. I'd been carrying a radio sender? But how—?

Blake chuckled, pleased at my embarrassment. "Okay, you guessed it, Bishop. And Davey led me straight to Kearney. I still—"

"And how were you able to accomplish that, sir?" The Bishop's voice cracked like a whip. "How did you *know* Mr. Goldman would go? Or that he would take that particular suitcase? Or that he wouldn't check it first?"

I was staring at Regan, asking myself the same questions. Why *hadn't* I? But before I could answer my own question, Regan bored in on Blake, who was beginning to turn red. "You had a confederate, didn't you, Lieutenant? The person with whom you were in cahoots *ensured* that Mr. Goldman would take the suitcase without suspecting a thing. You had the perfect confederate—you thought. But in your desire to entrap Mr. Goldman, you elected to trust as your confederate the very murderer you should have apprehended."

His eyes moved slowly to the beautiful brunette to his left. "Isn't that true, Miss Galloway? Didn't you murder Nick Carney?"

Dinker's eyes, unblinking, met his. I don't think she knew she was doing it, but she gave him a small nod.

55

THAT little nod buried my last hope that Dinker might be innocent. Blake went on blustering about Regan not having a leg to stand on, he was crazy to think Dinker was the murderer, and on and on. I was too sad to listen.

It *was* Dinker. Little things began to fall into place. Like the night I came back from St. Cloud, Tuesday. (God! It felt like years ago.) Dinker'd been waiting for me, wondering where Jim was. She'd "napped" in my office while I briefed Regan, even promised not to eavesdrop! But she had. She was a good enough actress to make me think I'd caught her in the act of waking up, not eavesdropping.

And later that night, at Jim's, getting his suitcase—his *bugged* suitcase. The sudden physical attraction: all a ploy. I looked at her, but her attention was all on Regan. Only Sally, beside her, was looking at me, her eyes sympathetic.

Regan had had enough of Blake's blathering. "Please, Lieutenant Blake. You've said quite enough. Your failure to deny my assumption has provided the final confirmation of my hypothesis."

Regan looked at Kessler. "It was, in fact, your uncanny ability to follow Mr. Goldman to James Kearney that first pointed me toward Miss Galloway. As Mr. Goldman told me of his extreme measures to avoid being followed that morning—eschewing my car because it might have been bugged, hailing a taxicab at random, the elaborately evasive maneuvers by the driver—it seemed impossible that you could have done it." Regan raised a finger. "Unless! Unless he himself, or something he was carrying, was bugged. But for that you'd have needed a confederate. And the confederate had to have been Miss Galloway.

"She it was who suggested that Mr. Goldman go see Mr. Kearney, she who suggested he take him the change of clothing, she who let them into Mr. Kearney's apartment, she who selected the suitcase, she who packed it.

"Of course, that Miss Galloway chose to assist the police in locating her lover was no proof that she was the murderer. But it *did* start a chain of thought. If she was your confederate, her anguish over his capture was feigned. If her anguish was feigned, she was willing to lie—convincingly and in great detail—to disguise her role in the capture. And if she was willing to go to such lengths to deceive Mr. Goldman and me, of what else, I began to wonder, might she not be capable? I began to assemble a mental dossier on Miss Galloway: an ever-expanding dossier.

"Item: *As You Like It.* The role of Rosalind requires the actress to spend more than half the play in the guise of a male. Was Miss Galloway capable of disguising herself as a male offstage as well? For instance, on the sidewalks of New York—or of St. Cloud, Minnesota?

"This gave rise to a whole new line of thought. Could Miss Galloway, in some disguise, have been the pistol thief? Far-fetched? So it seemed. Any number of factors militated against it, not least the great distance between New York and Minnesota and her required attendance at dress rehearsals each evening. But, upon consideration, the difficulties were not so insuperable." He glanced at Dinker, who smiled at him. She was listening as calmly as if he was lecturing on dramatic theory.

"Using what facts I had," Regan continued, "I began to construct a scenario. Suppose she had flown to Minnesota that crucial Wednesday. Flights leave as early as six A.M., arriving in Minneapolis around nine.

"She made dress rehearsal that evening—but just barely. She had a story to excuse her lateness, but it sounds lame for an actress as dedicated as she. Furthermore, why come in a cab, when one's apartment is only a block away? And what were the contents of the two heavy bags?"

Regan looked at Kessler. "So I deemed it quite possible that she had gone to Minnesota and returned that day. But getting to Minnesota and back was the easiest aspect of her self-imposed assignment. How was she to travel the seventy-three miles from the airport to that house, get in, take the gun and return to the airport, all unnoticed? Seemingly impossible. Yet, here again, the pieces began to fall into place. Consider the following:

"Item: she knew from Mr. Kearney about the work going on at his parents' home—meaning there would be strangers in the house.

"Item: her visit there last spring had given her the layout of the house and indicated the existence of the gun cabinet. Also, there would have been numerous opportunities to learn the combination.

"Item: sufficient costumes and makeup were doubtless available to her at the Lettuce Inn to transform her into a male workman.

"Oddly enough, I suspect her most serious problem was getting from Minneapolis to the Kearneys' home in St. Cloud. In the limited time she had, only a car would do. But a rental car was out; unlike the airlines, rental agencies have to be shown a valid driver's license— something not obtainable from the properties room at the theater. And she couldn't afford to leave a trace of her presence in Minnesota that day.

"But she was fortunate in having an extremely absentminded lover. And she took full advantage of that fact. I suspect she is the promulgator of the story that he left the keys in the car. Oh, it's true, he had forgotten to leave the car keys at the ticket counter in Minneapolis. But I don't think he left them in the car. I think he absentmindedly brought them with him back to New York."

Mike broke in contemptuously. "Of course he left them in the car. I sent a guy over there on Thursday to pick it up. The keys were in it."

Regan raised a hand. "Yes! But were they in the car Tuesday night? I think not, sir. I think James Kearney brought them back with him to New York. And Miss Galloway managed to spirit them from him, no matter how. Just as she spirited his apartment keys from him Wednesday night in jest before they left the bar with Mr. Goldman and Dr. Castle. I know that because, you see, Mr. Goodman is, for me, a very valuable contact with the world." He smiled at me and I glowed all the way to my gut.

"Those car keys were the final piece of the puzzle. With them she had accomplished the most difficult part of her operation: round-trip transportation from the airport to your house. When she returned to the airport, she left the keys in the car, thus backing up her desired version of the story."

Mike stared at him, taking it in. "So that's where those extra miles on the car came from! She—!"

Regan nodded. "That's right, Mr. Kearney. As you surmised, the car had made *two* round-trips, not one." He looked at Jim.

"Yes, Mr. Kearney? You have something to add?"

Jim was even paler than he'd been in my office on Monday. "I *thought* I had those keys! I'd have sworn I didn't leave them in the car! But what I don't understand is—why?" He looked at Dinker, who was still smiling that strange smile. "Why, Dinker?"

Everyone's eyes moved to her. She was smiling at the Bishop. It was almost the look an adoring student might give her teacher.

"I think," Regan growled, "Miss Galloway will answer in a moment, Mr. Kearney. This was, frankly, an aspect of the case that had puzzled me early on: the obvious attempt of the murderer to cast suspicion on you. In fact, I'm sympathetic to Mr. Kessler's rejection of my reasoning and his selection of you as the primary—indeed, the sole— suspect. Because one thing was clear: either you were guilty, or someone had gone to a great deal of trouble to make it appear that you were. The question was: who hated you sufficiently to go to such pains? And the apparent answer was: no one."

The Bishop looked at Sally. "I think a psychiatrist should speak to this. Dr. Castle?"

Sally, very pale, turned to Dinker. "I won't do this if you don't want me to, Dinker."

Dinker turned the same smile on Sally she'd been giving Regan. "No, no. Go ahead, Sally."

Sally looked around the room and ran her fingers through her blond hair. She'd ditched the horn-rims but she still looked very professional. "What I believe Miss Galloway suffers from," she said, circling the room with her eyes, "is what is called in psychiatry a borderline personality disorder. Actually I'm giving you the Bishop's analysis, not mine, but we've discussed it and I concur. Our judgment is based on certain elements of her comportment both of us have observed: wide emotional swings, obsessive and manipulative behavior patterns, seductive activity toward men.

"Now, Dinker is a very dear . . ." Sally's voice broke. She stopped, rubbed her eyes, swallowed hard and continued, her voice strained. "Miss Galloway has been a very dear friend of mine. I'm not in the habit of analyzing my friends. And especially not with non-professionals. But when Bishop Regan—whose knowledge of psychiatry, frankly, borders on that of a professional in the field—made me walk him through the article on borderline personalities in the *DSM-Three* this morning, he convinced me. I believe his analysis is correct. The types of behavior patterns that he has observed in Miss Galloway—I have also seen. But I never adverted to it because she and I were friends."

Sally looked at Jim. "You want to know why she did it, Jim?" She glanced at Dinker. "It's the way she relates to the world. She probably felt you let her down somehow and that you needed punishing. That would fit the pattern. Borderline-disorder personalities often turn love into hatred just that way. They try to punish their former lovers, sometimes well beyond societal limits." She shrugged. "That's as clear as I can make it here."

"Thank you, Doctor," Regan said. He turned his full attention on Dinker. "Obviously, Miss Galloway, you also carried an animus toward *Nick* Carney. Whatever the source of it, you had determined that he must die and that James Kearney be accused of his murder. Yes? Much of what I'm saying here is guess and hypothesis, Miss Galloway. Would *you* care to enlighten us?"

Dinker cleared her throat. "No, I don't mind. I want to—"

Kessler interrupted. "Whoa! Hold it right there, Bishop!" The Inspector was on his feet. "Miss Galloway, it is my duty to warn you that I'm getting very close to preferring charges against you in the matter of Nick Carney. This isn't my meeting but I am here; and I have to warn you, especially in a roomful of witnesses, that anything you—"

"Anything I say," Dinker interrupted, still smiling, "can and will be used against me. Yes, Inspector, I know all about that. And I can see Davey jotting furiously over there." She smiled at me. "I'm really sorry to have played you like that, Davey. You're a nice guy." She shrugged and shook her head.

She turned back to Kessler. "Don't worry, Inspector. I know what I'm doing."

Kessler ran his hand through his hair and glanced at Regan. "You're not represented by counsel, Miss Galloway," he said. "Are you sure you want to do this? I have to tell you, you stand a very good chance of being arrested before you leave this room."

Dinker shook her head. "I know what I'm doing, Inspector, believe me." She smiled at Regan. "Yes, Bishop, you're right. I'd already decided Jim had to be punished." She looked over at Jim on the couch. He was staring at her, pale as ever. Kessler sat down, pulled out a notebook and started jotting in it. He told me later he gave me a high-sign to take complete notes and that I gave him a thumbs-up. I have absolutely no recollection of that.

"Trouble was," Dinker went on, to Regan, "I didn't know how to punish him. Maybe you know he walked out on me, Bishop. He wanted to be free, he said. Free—to see other women! He broke my heart, Bishop. He said I was too possessive. You want to know the trouble with Jim? He wants things all his own way." She turned and looked at Jim. "You do, Jim, you know. You really do." Jim started to answer but she had turned back to the Bishop.

"I decided Nick Carney would be my way to punish Jim. Nick had it coming. He was always coming on to me. Sometimes after rehearsals he'd come to my dressing room and want to talk. Talk! What he wanted was to screw me."

Dinker's face was grim. "Finally he did it. He touched me—and then laughed about it. So when Jim told me that Sunday night that they were brothers, I knew what to do. Nick would pay for touching me and Jim would be safe in prison. And I'd go see him every day. He'd finally realize how faithful, how loving I really am." She turned to Jim, her eyes bright. "I am, Jim. I really am."

She went back to Regan. "So I started the plan. When Jim got back from Minnesota Tuesday afternoon, he came to my apartment. I found out his parents had two crews of workmen coming in the next day. That was my chance. I took his car keys when he was in the bathroom—he didn't even know he had them. I worked him around to thinking he'd left them in the car at the airport. He's done that before, you know."

She smiled at the Bishop. "It worked. I went to the airport next morning and caught the six A.M. flight. Paid cash and used a false name. The hard part was finding the car in that parking garage. It took me half an hour but I found it. I hadn't dared ask Jim where it was or what it looked like." She smiled. "He'd have probably forgotten anyway.

"I'd been to the house before, so I knew the way. On the way I got in character—as a workman. I put on a turtleneck under the coveralls—it was hot but I couldn't afford to let my neck show. Women's necks are too skinny. Mine would have given me away.

"It turned out to be easier than I ever expected. I had no key, so I had to decide whether to ring the bell or wait outside for someone else to come. I decided it'd be safer to wait. I'd brought an apple. I've learned to eat an apple like a man: helps the illusion.

"So when the plumbers came, I just chomped away on the apple and they let me right in. I asked them who they were, and when they said they were plumbers, I told them I was a dry-waller.

"Once inside, it was even easier. I just made each crew think I was with one of the others, and waited for a chance to get in the den when no one else was there. It only took me half a minute once I did. Then, soon as I could, I got out of there and back to the airport. And that's where things went bad." She made a noise of disgust.

"The flight back almost ruined everything. I'd planned to go home first and dump my bags. There should have been plenty of time. But we got delayed in Minneapolis, sitting out on the runway; and then had to wait half an hour for a gate in New York. It was a nightmare! And of course I'd checked a bag—I couldn't carry the gun onto the plane—and the damn *baggage* got delayed. Then I was twenty-fifth in line for a cab!

"So I had to go straight to the theater. When I saw you and Davey, Sally—" She turned and smiled at Sally, who looked away "—I *really* panicked! I thought, my God, they'll know I didn't catch a cab here from home, just two blocks away! But . . ." She looked from Sally to me . . . "you bought my story about trying on the new makeup." She smiled at me. I didn't smile back.

"Let's see, what next? Oh—last Friday night. When Nick called Jim, we were asleep. Jim grabbed the phone right away and I pretended to go on sleeping. When Jim told him to hang on, he'd go into the living room to talk, it was perfect: I didn't even have to be careful how I picked up the phone because it was already off the hook. I just lay there and listened to Nick give Jim the time of their meeting, the combination to the door and Milt Manning's phone number." Dinker's smile disappeared. "As soon as I had all that, Nick was a dead man. He never should have touched me.

"Next day I used the same wig and mustache I'd used in St. Cloud. I'd paid attention to Nick's limp and I'd practiced it.

"So I got rid of Manning with a phone call, using Nick's voice. I wasn't sure how well Manning knew him, so I was deliberately hoarse, just in case. That's why I told him I was sick—because I needed to sound that way. And I wrote Jim a note using Nick's signature, telling him Manning wasn't coming and he should come on up.

"Then I did myself up as Nick and went out. I got to the building about one-thirty, let myself in and stuck the note on the door. Then I buzzed Nick. I told him I'd been thinking about him a lot. That I liked him and wanted to see him. He buzzed me right up. I changed roles in the elevator: from Nick Carney to a slut. Nick was glad to see me. I gave him a passionate kiss—he loved that. I told him I was through with Jim, and he had to help me tell him. He loved that even more.

"When Jim buzzed, Nick told him to come up, he had a surprise for him. That was my moment—while Jim was in the elevator. So I went over and pretended to look out the window behind the desk. Nick turned around in his chair to watch me, which wasn't part of the plan. The plan was to shoot him in the back of the head. So I looked past him and said, 'Hi, Jim!' When he turned around, I shot him quick. Three times, right in the back of the head, just like the plan. I think the first one did it. By the third one I was shooting straight down—his head was already on the desk. It only got a couple of spots of blood on my clothes.

"Then I just waited. It was hard with Jim pounding on the door. I didn't know who else might be in the building, who might have called the cops. But I had to do it. I just kept still, the way Daddy used to have me do in the duck blind.

"Then the worst thing happened! Made me almost jump out of my skin! Jim was pounding at the door and Nick actually *moved*! And made a kind of bubbling sound—like he was trying to whisper something. I just about fainted! But he only did it once, thank heavens.

"When Jim went away and I heard the elevator going down, I looked for a place to hide the gun. I *had* to leave it—that was what was going to send Jim to prison. I finally found some tape in Nick's desk, pulled the bookcase out from the wall a little and taped the gun to the back of the bookcase. I knew the police would find it sooner or later. Then they'd have to think that Jim put it there.

"I put both wigs in the bag, put on the coveralls again, wearing my own hair..." Dinker suddenly reached up and pulled the luxuriant brunette mop off her head, revealing her own hair in a short, pixie cut. She was as pretty, but in a different way. Her face just looked a little rounder.

"What else? Oh. When I got down to the lobby, there was that old guy there. Jake. He got a good look at me; I hadn't put the mustache back on, though I was dressed like a janitor. I pretended to be picking up trash, to hide my face. But I was too late. He'd seen me.

"So I was shocked to find him here the other day. I just about fainted when he said he'd seen me before! I tried to be as feminine as I could with him, but he was thinking about it, I could see it in his eyes.

"Then, when he came on TV last night and said he knew who the murderer was, I was scared again. But what did it was those last words—'My love to the little lady!' I knew he meant me! That's what he'd called me here in your office. So he had to go." She looked up at Regan with annoyance.

"Why'd you say Jake's death told you who the murderer was? You were just trying to spook me, weren't you? Why would my killing him tell you anything?"

Regan shook his head. "I wasn't trying to spook you, Miss Galloway. You were the only suspect who knew how to reach Mr. Steiner; the only one who knew he was an habitué of Paddy's Pub. The television show failed to mention the name of the bar—or even that there was a bar."

Dinker stared at him a minute. "You're pretty smart, you know it? I called him at Paddy's and told him I'd give him five hundred dollars for exclusive rights to his story. I was using a different voice, and told him I was with the New York *Times*. I told him to take the first train up to Columbus Circle and I'd have the money for him.

"I was across the street when he came out of the bar. It was easy to follow him down the steps to the platform. I didn't expect my chance to come so soon. I knew I'd have plenty of chances. But he came down on the platform and got right out on the edge, past the warning line. It was just a question of timing. I pressed right in behind him in the crowd, put my hand gently on his back and watched the train approach. When it was ten feet away, I gave a hard push and walked away fast.

"Someone yelled! That scared me. But I didn't turn around, kept right on going. Nobody chased me."

She cocked her head at Regan. "How'd you do it, Bishop? I had it all worked out perfectly. I can't believe you unraveled the whole thing."

He nodded to her, spun his chair and headed for the door, drawing stares from everyone, including me. As he passed me, he murmured, "I'm going to the chapel, David. Please see to our guests." And he was gone. Without a wave, a goodbye or even so much as a sneer. Pretty damn rude. About par for the course, though.

"Well, I guess that's my answer!" Dinker said brightly. "And I guess that's the end of our meeting."

Kessler looked my way and I nodded. We were apparently in charge. I cleared my throat. "Ladies and gentlemen. The Bishop is going upstairs to pray. I'm turning the floor over to Inspector Kessler."

Kessler nodded. "Did you get all that, Davey?"

I glanced down, surprised to see that I'd automatically been scribbling shorthand the whole time. It seemed to make sense, so I nodded. "Good," said the Inspector. "Type it up for me as soon as you can, would you? I'll want everyone here's signature on it."

Kessler got to his feet. "Miss Galloway," he said quietly but in a voice that penetrated to all the corners of the office. "Will you come